1/18

NAPPANEE PUBLIC LIBRARY
Nappanee, IN 46550

W9-AMI-741

WHERE TREASURE HIDES

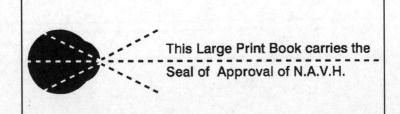

This Large Print Book carries the
Seal of Approval of N.A.V.H.

WHERE TREASURE HIDES

JOHNNIE ALEXANDER

THORNDIKE PRESS
A part of Gale, a Cengage Company

Farmington Hills, Mich • San Francisco • New York • Waterville, Maine
Meriden, Conn • Mason, Ohio • Chicago

Copyright © 2013 by Johnnie Alexander.
Scripture quotations are taken from the Holy Bible, King James Version.
Thorndike Press, a part of Gale, a Cengage Company.

ALL RIGHTS RESERVED
Where Treasure Hides is a work of fiction. Where real people, events, establishments, organizations, or locales appear, they are used fictitiously. All other elements of the novel are drawn from the author's imagination.

Thorndike Press® Large Print Christian Historical Fiction.
The text of this Large Print edition is unabridged.
Other aspects of the book may vary from the original edition.
Set in 16 pt. Plantin.

LIBRARY OF CONGRESS CIP DATA ON FILE.
CATALOGUING IN PUBLICATION FOR THIS BOOK
IS AVAILABLE FROM THE LIBRARY OF CONGRESS

ISBN-13: 978-1-4328-4595-7 (hardcover)
ISBN-10: 1-4328-4595-0 (hardcover)

Published in 2017 by arrangement with Tyndale House Publishers, Inc.

Printed in the United States of America
1 2 3 4 5 6 7 22 21 20 19 18

To my mom, Audry Alexander,
for all the books she's given me.
And to my own treasures,
Bethany, Jill, and Nathaniel.

ACKNOWLEDGMENTS

Writing is a solitary profession. But God has blessed me with loving family, encouraging friends, and supportive publishing professionals who walk beside me on this journey.

Special thanks to:

Kindred Heart Writers — Clella Camp, Karen Evans, Laura Groves, and Jeanie Wise. We've grown from writing partners to true kindred hearts. Praise God that you all were the answer to my prayer for "someone to eat meals with" as I drove to my first major writers' conference.

Imagine That! Writers — Chandra Smith and Rob McClain, and especially Renee Osborne and Pat Trainum. Your critiquing talents are invaluable, and I thank God for each of you.

Justin Jett, my son-in-law, played along when I said, "Pretend you're a British soldier. What would you do if . . . ?"

Carol Anne Giaquinto and Mandy Zema loved an earlier story I wrote so much they insisted on a sequel. Ian and Alison's love story would never have been imagined if not for the two of you.

Joy Van Tassel, one of my trusted first readers, realized an important detail I missed.

My brother Adam Alexander, my sister Hebe Alexander, and my niece Payton Alexander know things I don't. Thanks for your advice and suggestions.

David and Linda Jett, Simone Reitzema–van der Burg, Karl Reitzema, and Dick van der Most answered a variety of questions and shared photos of Rotterdam.

God answered my prayer for the right agent when Tamela Hancock Murray offered to represent me. Thanks, Tamela, for believing in me and for your insightful advice.

God answered my prayer for the right publisher when Jan Stob acquired this story. Thanks, also, to Sarah Mason for her excellent editorial expertise. It's great working with you both and the rest of the Tyndale team.

Most of all, thank you to my family. My parents, John and Audry Alexander, encouraged me to read and imagine. Bethany &

Justin and Jillyanne & Jacob have blessed me with the greatest grandkids (more family treasures). And Nate is this mom's favorite son. I love you all.

CHAPTER ONE

AUGUST 1939

The stringed notes of "Rule, Britannia!" grew louder as the crowd quieted, eyes and ears straining in their search for the violin soloist. The patriotic anthem echoed through Waterloo Station's concourse, and as the second chorus began, sporadic voices sang the lyrics. Travel-weary Brits stood a little straighter, chins lifted, as the violinist completed the impromptu performance, the last note sounding long after the strings were silenced.

Alison Schuyler gripped her leather bag and threaded her way through the crowd toward the source of the music. As the final note faded inside the hushed terminal, she squeezed between a sailor and his girl, murmuring an apology at forcing them to part, and stepped onto a bench to see over the crowd. A dark-haired boy, no more than seven or eight, held the violin close to his anemic frame. His jacket, made of a finely woven cloth, hung loosely on his thin shoulders. The matching trousers would have slipped down his hips if not for his hand-tooled leather belt.

Either the boy had lost weight or his parents had purposely provided him clothes to grow into. Alison hoped for the latter, though from the rumors she'd heard, her first assumption was all too likely. She stared at the cardboard square, secured by a thick length of twine, that the boy wore as a cheap necklace. The penciled writing on the square numbered the boy as *127*.

Other children crowded near the young musician, each one dressed in their fine traveling clothes, each one labeled with cardboard and twine. Germany's castaways, transported to England for their own safety while their desperate parents paced the floors at home and vainly wished for an end to these troublesome days.

"Now will you allow him to keep his violin?" A man's voice, pleasant but firm, broke the spell cast over the station. The children fidgeted and a low murmur rumbled through the crowd. The speaker, dressed in the khaki uniform of a British Army officer, ignored them, his gaze intent on the railroad official overseeing the children.

"He better," said a woman standing near Alison. "Never heard anything so lovely. And the lad not even one of the king's subjects. I'd take him home myself — yes, I would — if I'd a bed to spare."

Alison mentally sketched the tableau before her, pinning the details into her memory. The officer's hand resting on the boy's shoulder; the official, a whistle around his neck, restlessly tapping his clipboard with his pencil; the dread and hope in the boy's eyes as he clutched his prized instrument. The jagged square that tagged his identity.

The travelers at the edge of the children's irregular circle collectively held their breaths, waiting for the official's reply. He shifted his glance from the nervous boy to the expectant passengers, reminding Alison of a gopher she had once seen trapped between two growling mongrels. The memory caused her to shudder.

"He might as well. Don't know what to do with it if he left it behind." The official waved a plump hand in a dismissive gesture. He certainly hadn't missed many meals. He blew his whistle, longer than necessary, and Alison flinched at its shriek.

"Get organized now. Numbers one through fifty right here. Fifty-one through a hundred there. The rest of you . . ."

The show over and the hero having won, the onlookers dispersed, their chatter drowning out the official's instructions to his refugees.

Alison remained standing on the bench, studying the man and the boy. They knelt next to each other, and the boy carefully laid the violin into the dark-blue velvet interior of its case. His slender fingers caressed the polished wood before he shut the lid. The man said something too softly for her to hear, and the boy laughed.

The spark flickered inside her, tingling her fingers, and she *knew*. This glimpse of a paused moment would haunt her dreams. It rarely occurred so strongly, her overwhelming desire to capture time, to freeze others within movement. She quickly pulled a sketch pad and pencil from her bag. Her fingers flowed lightly over the paper, moving to a rhythm that even she didn't understand. Tilting her head, she imagined the notes of the violin soaring near the high ceiling, swooping among the arches.

Her pencil danced as she added determination to the man's jawline and copied the two diamond-shaped stars on his collar. She

14

highlighted the trace of anxiety in the boy's eyes, so at odds with his endearing smile. What had he left behind? Where he was going? She drew the cardboard square and printed the last detail: *127.*

The man clicked shut the brass hinges on the violin case and, taking the boy's hand, approached the station official. Alison hopped down from the bench and followed behind them, awkwardly balancing the pad, pencil, and her bag.

The brown hair beneath the officer's military cap had been recently trimmed. A pale sliver, like a chalk line, bordered the inch or so of recently sunburned neck above his crisp collar. Alison guessed he was in his midtwenties, a little older than she. Identifying him, from his bearing and speech, as gentry, she positioned herself near enough to discreetly eavesdrop.

"Where is young Josef here going?" asked the soldier. "Has he been assigned a home?"

The official gave an exaggerated sigh at the interruption. He lifted the cardboard square with his pencil. "Let me see . . . number 127." He flipped the pages on his clipboard.

"His name is Josef Talbert."

"Yes, of course, they all have names. I have a name, you have a name, she has a name."

He pointed the eraser end of his pencil, in turn, to himself, to the soldier, and to Alison.

The soldier looked at her, puzzled, and she flushed as their eyes met. Flecks of gold beckoned her into a calm presence, sending a strange shiver along her spine. She turned to leave, but her stylish black pumps seemed to stick to the pavement. She willed her feet to move, to no avail.

When the soldier turned back to the official, Alison thought the spell would break. She needed to go, to forget she had ever felt the pull of his calm determination, to erase those mesmerizing eyes from her memory. But it was too late. The Van Schuyler fate had descended upon her, and she was lost in its clutches. Her heart turned to mush when the soldier spoke.

"My *name* is Ian Devlin of Kenniston Hall, Somerset. This lad's *name,* as I said, is Josef Talbert, recently come from Dresden. That's in Germany." He stressed each syllable of the country. "And your *name,* sir, is . . . ?"

The official scowled and pointed to his badge. "Mr. Randall Hargrove. Just like it says right here."

Ian nodded in a curt bow and Josef, copying him, did the same. Alison giggled, once more drawing Ian's attention.

"Miss?"

She flushed again and almost choked as she suppressed the nervous laughter that bubbled within her. "So sorry. My *name* is Alison Schuyler."

"You're an American," said Ian, more as a statement than a question.

"Born in Chicago." She bobbed a quick curtsey. "But now living in Rotterdam, as I descend from a long and distinguished line of Dutch Van Schuylers." Her fake haughtiness elicited an amused smile from Ian.

Mr. Hargrove was not impressed. "Now that we're all acquainted, I need to get back to sorting out these children."

Ian's smile faded. "Mr. Hargrove, please be so kind as to tell me: where are you sending Josef?"

"Says here he's going to York." Mr. Hargrove pointed at a line on his sheaf of papers. "He's got an uncle there who has agreed to take him in."

Ian knelt beside Josef. "Is that right? You're going to family?"

"*Ja,*" Josef said, then switched to English, though he struggled to pronounce the words. "My father's brother."

"All right, then." Ian patted the boy's

shoulder. "Keep tight hold of that violin, okay?"

Josef nodded and threw his arms around Ian's neck, almost knocking him off balance. *"Danke. Tausend dank."*

"You're welcome," Ian whispered back.

Alison signed and dated her sketch, then held it out to Josef. "This is for you. If you'd like to have it."

Josef studied the drawing. "Is this really me?"

"Ja," Alison said, smiling.

Josef offered the sketch to Ian. "Please. Write your name?"

Ian glanced at Alison, then put his hand on Josef's shoulder. "I don't think I should —"

"I don't mind," she said.

"You're sure?"

"For him." She whispered the words and tilted her head toward Josef.

Borrowing Alison's pencil, Ian printed his name beside his likeness. He returned the sketch to Josef and tousled the boy's dark hair. Ian opened his mouth to say something else just as another long blast from the official's whistle assaulted their ears. They turned toward the sound and the official motioned to Josef.

"Time to board," he shouted. "Numbers

119 to 133, follow me." He blew the whistle again as several children separated from the larger group and joined him.

"Go now, Josef," Ian urged. "May God keep you."

Josef quickly opened his violin case and laid the sketch on top. He hugged Ian again, hesitated, then hugged Alison. They both watched as he lugged the violin case toward the platform and got in the queue to board the train. He turned around once and waved, then disappeared, one small refugee among too many.

At just over six feet in height, Ian was used to seeing over most people's heads. But he couldn't keep track of little Josef once the boy boarded the train. *Watch over him, Father. May his family be good to him.*

"I hope he'll be all right," said Alison.

"I hope so too."

"So many of them." She gestured toward the remaining children who waited their turn to board.

Ian scanned the young faces, wishing he could do something to take away the fear in their anxious eyes. "Their families are doing what they think best."

"Sending them away from their homes?"

"Removing them from Hitler's reach." Ian

19

turned his attention to the American artist. He could detect her Dutch heritage in her features. Neither tall nor slender enough to be called statuesque, she wore her impeccably tailored crimson suit with a quiet and attractive poise.

"It's called the *Kindertransport.*"

"I've heard of it. Are they all from Germany?"

"A few come from Austria. Or what used to be Austria before the *Anschluss.* The lucky ones have relatives here. The rest are placed in foster homes."

"Jewish children."

"Most of them."

While he spoke, he held Alison's gaze. She reminded him of a summer day at the seashore. Her blonde hair, crowned with a black, narrow-brimmed hat, fell in golden waves below her shoulders. Her pale complexion possessed the translucent quality of a seashell's pearl interior. The gray-blue of her eyes sparkled like the glint of the sun on the deep waves.

"Josef played beautifully." Even her voice felt warm and bright. "He's very talented."

"So are you. Your sketch was skillfully done."

"That's kind of you to say." A charming smile lit up her face. "At least I'm good enough to know how good I'm not."

Ian took a moment to puzzle that out and chuckled. "You made me better-looking than I am, and I appreciate that. For Josef's sake, of course."

"I assure you, Mr. Devlin, there was no flattery."

Ian smiled at her American accent and tapped his insignia. "Lieutenant. But please, call me Ian."

"Ian." Alison tucked away her pad and pencil. "I suppose I should go now."

Her words burrowed into Ian's gut. He couldn't let her leave, not yet. "To Rotterdam? Or Chicago?"

She glanced at her watch. "Apparently neither. I found myself so inspired by a young boy and his violin that I missed my train."

Ian felt as if he'd been handed a gift. Or had he? Suddenly aware of an absence, he looked around expectantly. "Are you traveling alone?"

A twinge of her apparent impropriety tensed Alison's mouth and chin but didn't dim the sparkle of her clear eyes. "Quite modern of me, don't you think?"

"Rather foolish," Ian began, but stopped himself. "Though it's not for me to say."

"You're perfectly right, of course. My

great-aunt accompanied me to Paris, but she became ill and I couldn't stay away any longer. So I left her to recuperate within walking distance of all the best dress shops on the Champs-Élysées, and *voilà!* Here I am. Alone and unchaperoned."

Ian drew back in surprise and raised a quizzical eyebrow. "Wait a minute. You're traveling from Paris to Rotterdam via London? Most people take the shortcut through Belgium."

"Yes, I suppose it is a bit of a roundabout way." She avoided his gaze, and the awkward moment pressed between them.

"It's really none of my business."

"Perhaps not. But there's a simple explanation." Her voice sounded too bright, and Ian sensed the nervousness she failed to hide. "I had a . . . a commission. A portrait."

Her expressive eyes begged him to believe the lie they both knew she had just told. With the slightest nod, Ian agreed, though he was curious to know her secrets. He suddenly pictured the two of them wandering the fields and woods on his family estate, talking about everything and nothing, Ian capturing her every word and safeguarding it deep within himself. But he doubted a woman who traveled alone across northern Europe, especially in these unsettled times, would enjoy the quiet boredom of country life.

He had tired of the unchanging rhythms of village traditions himself in his teen years. But after several months of combat drills and facing an uncertain future, he had been looking forward to a few days of idleness and local gossip.

Until now.

"I feel somewhat responsible," he said.

"That I missed my train?" She shrugged. "A small inconvenience. I'll leave early in the morning and be home in time for supper."

"What about supper tonight?"

Alison chuckled. "It's too early for supper."

Ian glanced at his watch. "Though not too early for tea. A British tradition, you know."

Conflict flitted across her features. She wanted to say yes, but something held her back.

"I'm not exactly a damsel in distress."

"It's only tea."

"May I ask you something?"

"Please do."

"Would you have taken Josef to, what was it? Kenniston Hall? If he hadn't had an uncle waiting for him?"

Ian hesitated, not wanting to tell this

beautiful woman how his father would have reacted if he had arrived home with the young Jewish boy. True, he could have made up some story to explain the boy's need for a place to stay. Even if his father suspected the truth, he'd have the story to tell those neighbors whose thinly veiled anti-Semitism skewed their view of what was happening in Germany. As he so often did, Ian wondered how long the blindness would last. What would Hitler have to do before his insatiable thirst for power was clear for all to see? "I don't know."

"He played that piece so magnificently. No one who heard it will ever forget this day."

"I don't think Mr. Randall Hargrove was too happy about it. But at least Josef got to keep his violin."

"Why wouldn't he?"

"Hargrove wanted to confiscate it. He insinuated Josef had stolen it, that it was 'too fine an instrument' for a child like him to have in his possession."

"So you stood up for him."

Ian flushed with sudden embarrassment, but smiled at the memory. "I asked the lad if he could play. And he did."

"You are a chivalrous knight, Lieutenant Devlin. I will never forget you."

"That sounds too much like a good-bye."

"Just because I missed my train doesn't mean you should miss yours."

"My train doesn't leave till late this evening."

"But I thought —"

"I only arrived in time to see Hargrove making a ninny of himself."

"Surely there's a train you could take without waiting till this evening."

Ian glanced around as if to be sure no one was paying attention to them and leaned forward. "True," he said in a conspiratorial whisper. "But my commanding officer entrusted me with a secret commission. I'm to deliver an important message to a lovely young woman who lives in the West End." With a flourish, he pulled a pale-blue envelope from his jacket pocket and handed it to Alison.

The thick envelope, made from high-quality paper, had been sealed with gold wax and embossed with two *M*s entwined in a scripted design. Alison guessed that the stationery inside would be of similar color and quality. The commanding officer was evidently a man of good breeding and taste. She turned the envelope over and read the broad black strokes written on its face: *To*

My Darling Trish.

"His girlfriend?"

"His wife," Ian whispered with a furtive glance around them.

Alison played along. "Your commanding officer must think quite highly of you to trust you with such an important mission."

He slipped the envelope back into his pocket with a slight shrug of his shoulders. "He knows I wouldn't pass through London without seeing Trish."

"Oh?" A slight tremor in the simple syllable betrayed her interest.

"I loved her first, you see."

A thousand questions raced through her mind. But it didn't matter. After today, she would never see him again. His past didn't matter. Whom he loved didn't matter.

Except that it did.

Aware that the man who had unwittingly, almost negligently, captured her heart couldn't seem to take his eyes off her, Alison found one safe response. "But she chose him instead."

Realizing her failure to achieve just the right amount of nonchalance and pity, she tried again and found herself asking the very question she wanted to avoid. "Did she break your heart?"

Again, Ian leaned forward as if divulging a

great secret, and Alison bent her head toward his so as not to miss a word. "Something so personal shouldn't be discussed in the midst of Waterloo Station. But there's a little place near the Westminster Bridge that serves the most delicious cherry scones you'll ever eat."

"You mean Minivers?"

"You know it?"

"My father took me there for my sixteenth birthday. He ordered a cherry scone for each of us and stuck a pink candle in mine. Then he sang 'Happy Birthday' to me." She remembered closing her eyes before she blew out the candle and wishing that every birthday, every holiday, could be spent with her father. That he and her grandfather would make up their quarrels so that she no longer had to choose between them. But she had hugged the futile wish to herself, telling it to no one, and laughed at her father's clumsiness with the dainty teacups and miniature pastries. The cheerful memory felt as perfect, yet fragile, as the pristine white linens and delicate china that graced Minivers' cozy tables.

"He felt awkward there, I think. It's not exactly a gentleman's place of choice, is it?"

"The scones are worth a bit of discomfort."

"What about your secret mission?"

His eyes twinkled. "Trish isn't expecting me, so she won't know if I'm late."

The corners of Alison's mouth twitched and she turned from Ian's hopeful smile toward the entrance of the station. She couldn't see the telegram office from where she stood, but it was there, looming before her like a scolding parent. Missing the train had been foolish, but spending the rest of the afternoon with Ian was sheer stupidity. He was a soldier on the eve of war. That was reason enough to guard against any romantic entanglements.

But worse, she was a Schuyler. He couldn't know how his warm hazel eyes affected her, how drawn she was to his confident demeanor and gallant charm. Or the sting of jealous curiosity she endured when he spoke of this other woman. Though she felt his mutual attraction, it was better that he never know that he already held her heart in his hands. The Van Schuyler fate may have destined him to linger forever within her, but she could still make her own decisions.

She squared her shoulders and faced him.

His smile charmed her as he offered his arm in a boyish gesture. "Shall we?"

Alison hesitated, then tucked her hand

within the crook of his elbow. "I should exchange my ticket first."

CHAPTER TWO

The hostess at Minivers seated Alison and Ian near a wall decorated with a huge tapestry depicting a scenic garden and a distant woods. "I believe this is the same table where I sat with my father," Alison said as she looked around the room to get her bearings. "I remember being intrigued by the needlework on this tapestry. Papa said it was Flemish. Seventeenth century."

Ian glanced at the wall covering as he held Alison's chair for her. "I'll take his word for it."

"You're not an art connoisseur?"

"I know the difference between a Rembrandt and a Van Gogh. And I know enough to be more than impressed by the sketch you did for our young violinist."

Alison twisted toward the tapestry and absentmindedly scanned the intricate stitching that gave vibrancy and life to the static scene, memorializing an artist's vision of a

NAPPANEE PUBLIC LIBRARY
Nappanee, IN 46550

single instant. She felt a kinship with the embroiderer, the mysterious need to preserve a slice of time before it flowed into the mists of memory.

"I had to capture the moment."

"It's a moment I'll never forget."

"Neither will I." Alison faced Ian's steady gaze, knowing that this was another moment that would exist with photographic clarity for the rest of her days. Though he wasn't movie-star handsome, his straight nose and strong chin revealed his Anglo-Saxon heritage. She ached with the sudden desire to see his face in a myriad of moods, to be near him as age added its own idiosyncratic lines. His would always be an interesting face, touched with contradictions for those who had the eyes to see. A face to challenge her artistic skill, should she ever have the opportunity to attempt more than a quick sketch. His expression, so open and direct, invited trust. She felt she could tell him anything without fear of betrayal. Yet she had already lied to him.

The approaching waitress shattered the spell with a teapot and menus. After Ian ordered sandwiches and the famous scones, Alison poured hot tea into the delicate cups and felt an odd jolt, as if she were sixteen again and pouring tea for Papa. How strange

NAPPANEE PUBLIC LIBRARY
NAPPANEE, IN 46550

to sit in the same chair, to go through the same motions, all these years later for another man. A man she barely knew.

She carefully set the teapot on its matching tray and rested her hands in her lap. "How did we get here?"

"We took a taxi across Westminster Bridge." Ian plopped two sugar cubes into his tea and stirred it with a tiny silver spoon. She feigned annoyance, and he chuckled. "Okay, how about this? We're here because neither of us wanted to say good-bye."

"I meant to."

"I'm glad you didn't."

She was glad too, but frightened at the same time. The feeling of déjà vu struck again. A similar nervousness clutched at her stomach, and her heightened emotions felt as taut as the strings on young Josef's violin. Perhaps the strange jolt intended to warn her of her folly. Even when all was right with the world, anything more than a casual friendship with a foreigner could be difficult. These days were anything but normal. And she knew with deep assurance that Ian, foreigner or no, could never be just a casual friend.

"It's not the best of times, is it?" Ian asked.

Alison narrowed her eyes without shying from the warmth of his gaze. Were her thoughts, usually inscrutable to others, so transparent to him?

"The time for good-byes will come soon enough," he continued. "But until it does, we shouldn't think about it." He raised his teacup as if delivering a toast. "Agreed?"

He was right, of course. The brief time they spent together should be filled with cheer, not regret, so that the memory could be bright. It had been the same on her birthday. Her father couldn't — or wouldn't — stay in London more than the one day. Alison had purposefully ignored his imminent departure rather than allow it to dull their precious time together. She needed that same intention now, to enjoy Ian's company for as long as possible.

Shaking away the lingering memories of her last visit to this place, she exhaled softly and relaxed her shoulders. "Agreed."

They tapped their cups together and sipped the steaming tea to seal their toast.

"Of course," Alison said with a mischievous smile, "we're also here so you can tell me about your commanding officer's wife. What was her name? Trish?" She gazed at Ian as innocently as possible, though her stomach churned with the hope that he no longer pined for the woman.

His sheepish grin and twinkling eyes

calmed her nerves, and she instinctively expected him to deliver a punch line.

"I've loved Trish for as long as I can remember. Though I was only three when she was born."

"Your families are close?"

"Family. One family." Ian leaned back in his chair and held Alison's gaze. It took less than a second for her to understand his meaning.

"Trish is your sister." She pressed her lips together and shook her head. "You are such a . . . a . . ."

He chuckled. "A cad?"

"Worse." Alison sniffed. "I was worried she had broken your heart."

"Worried? Then my ploy worked."

"Are you always such a tease?"

"Only when I don't want to say good-bye to a lovely and talented woman."

The warmth of his words settled within Alison, and she dropped her eyes in unexpected shyness, unsure what to say. She enjoyed his teasing, but her own feelings frightened her.

Enjoy this moment. Chances are you'll never see him after today.

Ian shifted in his seat. "You aren't angry, are you?"

Alison nodded toward their approaching

waitress and leaned forward conspiratori-
ally. "Miniver scones atone for a multitude
of sins."

Ian let out a short chuckle, and Alison
responded to his relaxed smile with one of
her own as the waitress placed their selec-
tions on the table. The finger sandwiches,
tiny slivers of dark bread layered with slices
of cucumber and watercress, were delicately
arranged on a silver tray. The warm scones
nestled in a cloth-covered basket.

As Ian devoured one of the dainty sandwiches in two bites, Alison stifled a giggle.

"Papa said he could leave here hungrier
than when he came in. If not for the scones."

Ian nodded in agreement as another petite
sandwich disappeared. "Is your father an
artist too?"

"He is. Was." Alison twirled her finger
around the rim of her teacup. "The Van
Schuyler Fine Arts Gallery has been a
renowned Rotterdam institution for almost
three hundred years."

"What happened to your 'Van'?"

"Papa emigrated to America and dropped
it somewhere in the Atlantic Ocean. At
least, that's the story he used to tell me
when I was young. I was born in Chicago."

"But now you live in Rotterdam."

"With my grandfather, yes. He owns the

family gallery."

"And your parents? Are they still in Chicago?"

"Papa . . . travels."

"For the gallery?"

"Mostly for himself." Alison felt Ian's gaze upon her as she added more tea to her cup. "You're wondering about my mother."

"You haven't mentioned her."

Alison stared at her cup for a moment. The words were never easy, but she had learned over the years to keep them few and simple. "She died shortly after my fifth birthday."

Not unexpectedly, sympathy appeared in Ian's eyes. That was how most people responded when hearing her forlorn explanation. But unlike most people, Ian didn't look embarrassed or awkward. "That's a difficult wound to heal," he said gently.

"Papa never painted again." The words slipped out without warning, and Alison coughed with surprise. She had buried that truth deep inside, had felt churning anger when her grandfather condemned his son for throwing away his talent. But she used them as an excuse for him, her personal consolation to explain Pieter Schuyler's paternal lapses. Unfortunately, the excuse, a double-edged sword, only compounded her loneliness. Eventually she had lost her father, too.

"We were fine for a while." Alison held her cup with both hands, staring into its depths as if to find some explanation for the odd willingness to share her family history with a stranger. But she wanted Ian to know. Somehow it felt right to tell him. "Our gallery was small but reputable. The clientele was growing and Papa seemed to be coping with his grief. Then the stock market plummeted. Taking our gallery with it."

The Great Crash. October 1929. It hadn't meant much to Alison, caught up in her little-girl world of school lessons and china dolls. But only a few short months later, that innocent childhood had grown frighteningly dark.

"Our clients couldn't pay their accounts; no one could afford our paintings." She shrugged, trying to lessen her embarrassment at the family's financial failure. Of course, men with more savvy than Papa had suffered just as much, perhaps even more. A few had killed themselves rather than face the shame of bankruptcy.

She shuddered, remembering the grown-up whispers she had overheard, Papa's crying moans when he thought she was asleep. "There was an auction. We lost everything."

Ian reached across the table and covered her fingers. His hand felt cool and strong against her skin, giving her the courage to face the long-buried memories. She didn't pull away.

"Everything but *The Girl in the Garden.*" Her voice softened almost to a whisper as she imagined the painting. "My mother's portrait."

"She was his muse?"

"And his life. He painted it shortly after they met at Wrigley Field."

"They were baseball fans?"

"No, that's what was so strange. Neither of them particularly cared for sports. But it was love at first sight."

Love at first sight. Like us? The unbidden thought caught Ian off guard. Before today, he would have scoffed at such nonsense, dismissing it as the romantic fancy of schoolgirls and spinsters. But sitting across from Alison, he wasn't so sure. There was something different about her, and something different about him when he stood next to her, walked beside her. Looked into her unusual gray-blue eyes.

He realized he was staring when she blushed and withdrew her hand to pour more tea in his cup. Lifting back the linen cloth from the pastry basket, he gestured for Alison to take one of the scones. The fragrance of warm cherries and walnuts drifted between them. She broke hers in half and bit into the flaky tartness.

"As good as you remembered?"

"Mmm. Better."

He grinned as she dabbed cherry icing from the corners of her mouth. "What happened to the painting?"

She swallowed and returned her napkin to her lap. "Papa couldn't bear to see it on the auction block. He shipped it to my grandfather before turning over the gallery to the creditors. He shipped me there too."

"Alone?"

"He accompanied me as far as Brussels. I met my grandfather there for the first time and I've lived with him ever since. *The Girl in the Garden* is the centerpiece of our gallery, but my father has never seen it hanging there. He won't step foot in Holland. We meet here in London or in Paris. Anywhere but home."

"I take it he and his father don't get along."

Alison shook her head. "That's why Papa left the gallery."

"And dropped the 'Van'?"

"Yes." She finished her scone and brushed the crumbs from her fingers. "Now it's your turn to expose a family skeleton."

She sounded a little sheepish, and Ian guessed she didn't often tell strangers about her family's misfortune. He shifted his weight in the petite chair and placed his napkin beside his plate. "It's possible — though not proven, mind you — that the Devlin fortune came from piracy and a fair amount of smuggling."

Alison's eyes widened in mock horror. "That's scandalous."

"To our credit, we eventually turned from our thieving ways and became fine, upstanding citizens, loyal to king and country. Raising sheep may not be as exciting as thievery, but it's much more reputable."

"So you're the son of a country squire."

"My father is the seventh lord of Kenniston."

"Making you a lord-to-be?"

"I'm a lieutenant in His Majesty's Army."

"But someday?"

Ian shifted uncomfortably and stared at his plate.

"I didn't mean to pry."

He heard the faint hurt in her voice. No wonder. He had seen the pain in her eyes as she shared her childhood tragedy with him.

40

She deserved to hear about his. "Let's take a walk, shall we? There's a small park at the end of this square."

After Ian paid the bill, they stepped outside and followed the sidewalk to an open wrought-iron gate that led into a well-tended park. Elms, birches, and maples shaded wide paths bordered by late-summer flowers. Fat gray squirrels scampered among the trees, chattering and scolding. Ian gestured toward a weathered bench facing a sun-dappled granite fountain, and they sat beneath the thick branches of a sheltering sycamore.

In the tranquil seclusion of the park, Ian stared along the path to a short hedge bordering a bed of decaying roses, the fragile red and pink petals dotting the mulched ground. Reminders of floral arrangements surrounding a burnished coffin. Reminders of an exuberant life too soon spent.

He took a deep breath. "I was the second son. The title was never supposed to go to me."

As he watched her face, needing to know that she understood what he had left unsaid, her features softened in sympathy. He tried to clear his throat, but the lump of remembered sorrow didn't cooperate.

"You don't need to explain." Alison slipped her hand into his, and a warmth he'd never before known swept through him. Amid the chilling memory of the death of the older brother he'd worshiped, his father's rightful heir, a vivid certainty emerged. An ordinary trip to London had turned extraordinary by an immigrant boy with a violin and a young lady with a sketch pad.

And his heart would never be the same again.

Alison watched Ian's profile as he clenched and unclenched his jaw. She wished she could read his thoughts as he visibly relaxed and squeezed her hand. The small gesture jolted her with warmth.

"There was an accident." He faced her and one corner of his mouth lifted slightly. "We were just boys. Daring, foolish boys playing a foolish game."

She waited for him to continue, but he seemed lost in memory. "I'm so very sorry."

"Me too."

The chimes of Big Ben, the great bell of the clock tower at the Parliament building, broke through the silence. Alison braced against the tolling of the hour, each echoing clang a portent of the moment when circumstances would force them in different directions.

"It's getting late. Your sister will want her letter."

"Come with me. I'm sure she'd like to meet you."

Alison stared at the water shooting above the fountain before falling as a misty spray into the shallow basin below. Lit by the late-afternoon sun, the glistening droplets shimmered, miniature rainbows of red, green, and blue. Transitory rays of cheerful color destined to disappear as the sun settled beneath the London skyline.

"We should say good-bye now. Believe me, Ian. It's for the best."

"Best for whom?"

"Perhaps for both of us." She slowly withdrew her hand from his and her fingers turned cold.

"Do something for me first?"

"If I can."

"A drawing."

"Of course." Relief reverberated through the two short words. "Though I don't know if I can duplicate it exactly since one of my models is well on his way out of London."

"I want a sketch of you."

Alison's eyes widened. "Of me? Why?"

"Because it would be . . . you." The gold

flecks in his hazel eyes deepened as he struggled to explain. "More than just a likeness. Something you did. Of you."

"I'll try." She frowned as she pulled her drawing materials from her bag and opened the pad to a blank page. Closing her eyes, she visualized her features as if she were looking in a mirror. When that didn't quite work, she thought about the photograph taken of her last Christmas as a gift for her father. With that image clear in her mind, she opened her eyes and began to draw.

"May I watch?"

"No," she said in mock horror. Shifting so he couldn't see her work, she concentrated on the drawing. After adding a few final touches, she closed the pad and handed it to him. "You may be disappointed."

"Never." He began to flip through the pages, but Alison stopped him.

"Please wait. Until after I'm gone."

"But there are other sketches in here."

"Keep them. Or not." She stood. "Just promise me that you won't look at it until later."

Ian stood beside her as the quarter-hour notes chimed in the twilight skies above them. Alison took one last look at the gray shadows of the granite fountain, the dim colors of the surrounding blossoms, and imagined the scene as a watercolor painting. She'd create it when she got home and keep it always as a souvenir of the day she lost her heart.

CHAPTER THREE

They shared a taxi, saying little on the drive to the train station. When they arrived, Alison wrote a telegram to her grandfather: *All's well. Still in London. Will arrive tomorrow 4:45 p.m.* She retrieved her overnight bag from a locker, and Ian carried it for her to the nearby Wellington Hotel.

After registering and receiving her room key, she turned to face Ian, forcing a smile she didn't really feel.

He looked down at her. "The offer still stands. Meet my sister. Dig up more family skeletons."

Alison laughed softly and glanced around the lobby, filling her mind with images of dark wood, muted colors, and upholstered furnishings. How different it had appeared earlier in the day when she had left for the train station, eager to experience the freedom of traveling alone across the North Sea and into Holland. She couldn't have known that she would be coming back for another night's stay. All because of a young boy and his violin, and because of the soldier-hero who stood in front of her, willing her to change her mind.

It was a temptation she could not indulge. The indisputable family lore, grounded in factual dates, loomed before her. *"Strength and honour . . ."* She grasped at the familiar phrase from Proverbs 31, her mantra in difficult situations, and smiled brightly at Ian. "Thank you for everything. It was a lovely afternoon."

"For me, too."

The elevator door opened with a ding, startling Alison. She glanced at the uniformed operator, who responded with a polite nod.

"I must go." She took an awkward step toward Ian, then entered the elevator instead, unable to find any parting words, afraid to try.

As the heavy door began to close, Ian lifted a hand. "This isn't good-bye, Alison. Never good-bye."

They stared at each other until the door slid shut between them. The elevator car shook, causing Alison's stomach to lurch as it began its ascent. "I didn't tell him to be careful," she murmured.

"Should we return to the lobby, miss?"

She hesitated, then shook her head.

"He'll know you meant to, miss, if you don't mind my saying. He'll come back to you." The operator's cheeks reddened in a youthful blush.

Alison gave him a sad smile but shivered at what the future held for her, for Ian, if the elevator operator was right.

Ian pushed through the doors of the Wellington into the waning heat of the fading August day. The city, this close to Waterloo Station, pulsed with life as departing passengers maneuvered their way into the terminal against the tide of those just arriving in London. Traffic moved forward in orderly spurts with an occasional blare of a horn rising above the late-afternoon din.

The hotel doorman caught Ian's attention. "Taxi, sir?"

Ian considered for a fraction of a moment, then shook his head and walked in the opposite direction from the bustling station. The visit to Trish could wait a little longer. He wanted to look at Alison's sketches while the memory of their time together remained new and sharp. After a few blocks, he ducked into a familiar pub, the Black Fox. He settled at a corner table near the window and, while waiting for a pint of ale, relived the afternoon.

He hadn't planned to create a scene at Waterloo, but the sight of the sad and frightened Kindertransport children, clutching their meager belongings, had disturbed him. Then, when he heard the station official threaten the little refugee, saw the fear in the young boy's eyes, his blood had boiled. *Unto one of the least of these.* The phrase had resonated through his mind as he confronted Hargrove. Though he hadn't prayed, he knew the idea to have Josef play the violin had been divinely inspired.

When Hargrove pointed to Alison, Ian had seen only a brief vision of blonde hair and crimson clothing, sparkling eyes and a fine face. That first glance had shaken him, but he had pushed the feeling aside to do what needed to be done for Josef. Duty always took precedence over feelings in a good soldier. And Ian was a good soldier, even when he was on leave.

At least Hargrove had done him the favor of having the girl introduce herself. Alison Schuyler. Her name fit her loveliness, her spunk. And she had a kind heart, caring enough about Josef to give the boy the sketch.

He remembered her voice, whispering

above Josef's head, *"For him."*

They had been strangers, but the moment had brought them together into a tiny trinity.

The ale arrived, foaming in a thick glass mug, and he took a large swallow before settling back in the wooden chair. Flipping open the pad, he studied the sketch on the first page and recognized the looming towers, the gargoyles, the famous rose window of Notre Dame. But the Paris landmark served only as a backdrop for the focal point of the drawing.

In front of the cathedral, Alison had drawn an elderly couple sitting on a bench, heads bent close together in quiet conversation. They were dressed in clothes that may have been elegant at one time, but now showed the lament of shabbiness for people who had known more affluent days. It was there, in the telltale signs of dust on the man's hat, the shiny patches of the woman's black dress. The man appeared weary, ready to give in to life's downward pressing. But the sadness in the woman's eyes conflicted with her refusal to give up, as indicated by her clenched fist. Alison had captured an entire story in one focused moment.

The second sketch featured a portrait of the conductor on a ferry boat. Alison must have drawn him when she crossed the English Channel from France. The man's rounded cheeks and bright eyes seemed to hold the secret of happiness as he posed against the boat's railing.

Ian stared intently at the next sketch, leaning forward and tilting it beneath the pub's dismal lighting to get a better look. Smeaton's Tower. Ian and his family had stayed at Plymouth Sound every summer of his childhood. The story of John Smeaton and his innovative lighthouse had always fascinated him. Built in the mid-1700s, the lighthouse had withstood harsh winds and crashing waves, but not the weakness of its own foundation. In 1882, the old lighthouse had been moved to the shore and made into a memorial, replaced by the lighthouse that now stood on a neighboring rock out at sea.

He found it incredible that Alison had sketched one of his favorite places. This couldn't be the commission she used as an excuse for her roundabout trip from Paris to Rotterdam, or else she wouldn't have left it with him. It was a mystery, one he might never solve unless he figured out a way to see her again.

The next page showed the sketch he had requested. Unlike the other three, which had been oriented as landscapes, this one was oriented as a portrait. She had drawn a good likeness, but she had omitted the spark that drew him to her. Perhaps an artist's humility had kept her from capturing her own essence.

"Another pint?" The deep, scratchy voice broke through Ian's thoughts.

He shook his head and dropped a few coins on the table.

A gentleman never accepted a lady's gift without giving her something in return. He knew the perfect present for Alison, and he planned to give it to her tomorrow morning before she boarded her train.

CHAPTER FOUR

The morning sun hid behind heavy gray clouds that spit rain on the city's early risers. Alison heavily tipped a hotel employee to drive her the short distance from the Wellington to Waterloo Station. Once inside, she headed for the Dover platform, settling at a tiny table with a cup of hot coffee and checking her tickets against her itinerary. From Dover, a steamship carried passengers across the North Sea to The Hague, arriving about an hour before a commuter train departed for Rotterdam. Then the short drive to the tall canal house that had been her home for the past decade.

Perhaps by the time she unpacked her belongings, the few hours spent with Ian would be no more than a faded memory instead of an emotionally charged dream.

She dug out her drawing pencil and, almost absentmindedly, outlined Ian's face on a paper napkin. The noise of the station

53

receded as she concentrated on the shape of his eyes, the jut of his chin.

"Is that me?"

She looked up, startled, and felt her cheeks warm. Scrunching the napkin, she hurriedly stuffed it in her bag. "What are you doing here?" she asked with feigned indifference.

Ian chuckled and sat down across from her. "I don't suppose you'd believe I was in the neighborhood."

"You didn't go home?"

"I stayed with Trish. So I could see you again." He slid a thin, oblong box across the table to her. "And to give you this. A thank-you for the sketches."

"You didn't need to —"

"I wanted to. Please. Open it."

Alison lifted the lid and pulled back layers of tissue paper to reveal a miniature light-house. She held it in the palm of her hand, assessing the weight and the workmanship. "It's exquisite. Pewter?"

"Yes. Look at the base."

Alison peered at the recessed bottom and pressed the button she found there. The melodic tones of "Greensleeves" played and the beacon sparkled. Her mouth formed a delighted O.

"It's a replica of the original Smeaton's

Tower. At Plymouth Sound."

A slight smile crossed Alison's face. "The drawing."

"When were you there?"

"Two or three days ago," she said as offhandedly as possible. Not that the Sound had anything to do with her grandfather's secret mission. Her detour to Plymouth had been little more than a whim. But the less Ian knew about her time in England, the better. And she didn't want him to know anything about her side trip to Wales.

He looked at her curiously, but then leaned back in his chair with a contented smile. "I've been there countless times. The tower always fascinated me. It seems so symbolic."

"Of what?"

"Faith." He shrugged. "Knowing where one's strength comes from."

Alison set the lighthouse upright on the table and ran her finger along the miniature's length. "A foundation built on solid rock instead of a cave weakened by tides."

"Yes." Their eyes met and an understanding passed between them that both thrilled and unnerved her.

But decorum had its rules.

"I can't accept such a valuable gift."

"It's important to me that you do."

"Why?" She whispered the question and waited, eyes lowered, shoulders tense, for his answer.

Ian leaned forward and lifted her chin so he could see into her eyes. When he spoke, he appeared to choose his words with care, as if they were fragile things. "I look at you and see the girl I've spent my life dreaming about. And thought I'd never find. You probably think I'm crazy. But it's the truth." He reached for her hand. "And I think you feel the same about me."

Alison held his gaze and took a deep breath. "There are . . . circumstances."

His eyes darkened and his hand slid from hers. She watched, stunned, as conflicting emotions appeared and then disappeared beneath a forced smile. "Who's the lucky fellow?"

A spontaneous smile lifted her cheeks and she shook her head. "It's not that."

"Then what?"

"Some dreams just can't come true."

"Give me one reason why this one can't. Just one."

Alison leaned back in her chair, her gaze direct and unwavering. "Geography."

"I'll move."

"Leave the family estate? You couldn't."

"*You'll* move. You can open your own gallery. Geography problem solved." He playfully smacked the table.

Alison longed to get caught up in his pretense, but she understood the impossibility of their dream better than he did. Better than he ever would. "It's not solved. And it's not the only reason."

His smile faded. "The war."

"It hasn't even begun. Yet look what we witnessed in this very station. Children sent from their homes." Alison's voice caught on the words and she took a deep breath to compose herself. "Holland will no doubt stay neutral, as we did in the Great War, but what about England?"

"Neutrality is not an option."

"You'll be sent overseas."

He nodded.

"You could . . ." No. She dared not speak the ugly word, dared not allow it into her thoughts.

"Die." Ian finished the sentence. "All the more reason to grab happiness in the few days we may have."

The words ricocheted in her head and crashed to her feet, her thoughts suddenly consumed with her parents' whirlwind romance and its tragic ending. The same fate, she had no doubt, waited for the one she loved.

She opened her mouth, but choked by confusion, she couldn't speak. She stood abruptly and stared at him. "You don't know what you're saying."

Ian rose beside her, a chagrined look on his face. He touched her shoulder. "I don't want to upset you. But you can't leave without telling me what's bothering you."

The station loudspeaker crackled, and the static-filled announcement invited the Dover passengers to begin boarding. Alison reached for her overnight case and set it on the table beside her bag.

"That's my train."

"Wait a minute." He tentatively brushed a stray curl from her face. "I may have to go to war. I may have to fight. But I'll come back. And when I do, I'm going to find you."

Alison struggled to compose herself, to keep the tears that stung her eyes from falling. "You can't keep that promise."

"I will." He pulled her into an embrace, catching her off guard, but she found herself melting in his arms. She raised her face to his, lost in the moment, and relished the warm tenderness of his lips against hers. Another never-to-be-forgotten moment.

The loudspeaker crackled again with the last call for the Dover passengers. With a final hug, Alison stepped back from Ian and slid her bag's strap over her shoulder. She picked up her tickets and rested her hand on her overnight case.

He put the lighthouse back in its box and slipped it into her bag. "No matter what happens, keep this. Remember what it means. Remember me."

"I'll always remember you, Ian Devlin." Tears spilled onto her cheeks. "Always."

She turned and hurried away, pushing to the front of the passengers getting on the train. Sitting near the window of her compartment, she couldn't resist the urge to look for him among the crowd on the platform. When she caught his gaze, she waved. He waved back, mouthing a single word: *Remember.* She nodded.

As the train pulled out of the station, Alison leaned back in the seat, her heart pounding in rhythm with the clacking wheels. She found the scrunched-up napkin in her bag and smoothed it out on her lap.

"You're safe now, Ian Devlin," she whispered. *"I've left you, and now you're safe."*

CHAPTER FIVE

The dreary rain followed Alison to the seaside port of Dover, across the narrow width of the North Sea that separated England from continental Europe, and along the railway to Rotterdam. Her stylish crimson outfit, despite its overnight freshening by the hotel laundry service, felt limp and damp. She pulled a novel out of her bag, Daphne du Maurier's *Rebecca,* but the black letters lost their shape, fading to a gray mass against the white page until another image appeared. The image of a determined soldier hovering over a frightened boy. By the time she arrived in the city of her ancestors, the thrill of a solo journey had dissipated and a dull ache resided in her right temple.

As she expected, Jacobus Brant waited on the platform to welcome her home and gather her errant luggage. No mere chauffeur, Brant oversaw her grandfather's domestic affairs with the help of his wife, Gerta.

Alison leaned her head against the soft ivory leather of the Bentley while Brant finished stowing her luggage in the boot. Rain-heavy clouds darkened the afternoon skies, casting an early twilight across the centuries-old city.

Brant ducked into the driver's seat, closing the door quickly against the downpour, and caught Alison's eye in the rearview mirror. "Your grandfather asks you to come to the gallery."

"He's anxious to hear my report."

"Yes. But there will not be much time. Company is expected for dinner."

She inwardly groaned. "Who?"

"He didn't say. But someone of importance from all appearances. I've been instructed to open a bottle of the Château d'Yquem."

Alison raised an eyebrow at this extravagance. "It must indeed be someone important."

"We'll know soon enough. Dinner will be served at seven."

She glanced at her watch. The slender hands on the diamond-encrusted face marked the time as two minutes after five. Two hours to transform from dreary traveler to dazzling hostess for a mysterious guest important enough to interrupt her homecoming. She had expected a much different evening, an informal supper discussing what she had learned in Paris, in Wales. The reason she had taken such a roundabout way from France to Holland.

"To the gallery, then."

Brant nodded and maneuvered the heavy vehicle out of the parking area. Alison stared out the window as they drove past tall, thin buildings with narrow alleyways, along canals swollen with rainwater, and into the maze of slender streets that distinguished this historic district.

"Front or back?" asked Brant as he turned onto Oude Binnenstraat.

Alison looked down at her rain-splattered skirt and frowned. She definitely wasn't presentable enough to meet any potential customers who might be in the gallery's showroom. "Back, please."

While Brant expertly nosed the Bentley into the gap that led to the rear parking area, Alison stared up at the three-story brick building, its various shades of red and brown darkened by the early-evening shadows. *The Van Schuyler Fine Arts Gallery.* Established in 1662. At this location since 1803. A history she had known nothing about until ten years ago, when her father's business collapsed and she finally met her grandfather and his only sister.

Brant parked the car and opened the passenger door. Alison stepped out beneath the brick *porte cochere,* hurrying inside to escape the damp chill that settled between the tall buildings. A bell tinkled softly with the opening of the door — a familiar three-note chime she found strangely comforting as it welcomed her back to the world she knew and loved. Her heritage. Her legacy.

Still shivering, she entered the gallery's fully equipped kitchen. An impeccably dressed man, tall and slightly stooped, entered at the same time from the showroom corridor. His thin lips curled into a smile at odds with his sharp features and hooded eyes. "Welcome home, *mademoiselle.* I brewed a fresh pot of coffee in anticipation of your arrival. May I pour you a cup?"

"Thank you, Monsieur Duret. I'd love that." She removed her hat and tried, without much success, to tame her unruly waves. "Where's my grandfather?"

"He is in his office." Duret's nose wrinkled. "With a visitor."

"Tonight's mysterious dinner guest?"

"I believe so. Apparently someone who

wishes to renew his acquaintance with you." He took two cups from a shelf and carried them to the kitchen table.

Alison's heart lurched. Could Ian have somehow gotten here before she did? She dismissed the thought, feeling more disappointment than she liked. No doubt, Ian was relaxing with his parents at the estate that would someday be his. She envisioned a typical English manor, squat and U-shaped with an expansive courtyard and manicured lawns. In a couple of days, Ian would return to his military unit, and only God knew where he might go after that. She shook away the anxiety of that thought. "Does our mysterious guest have a name?"

Duret poured the coffee. "It's not my place to reveal a surprise."

"A surprise?" Alison added two cubes of sugar and a generous amount of cream to her mug. "A pleasant one, I hope."

She caught Duret's almost-imperceptible shrug. He and her grandfather, Hendrik Van Schuyler, had met at a symposium at the Sorbonne in the summer of 1897 and found they had much in common. Both were heirs to reputable art establishments, specialized in the Old Masters, and possessed shrewd business acumen.

They shared one other thing: both became

widowers at a tragically young age and never remarried.

When the Germans looted and burned the Duret family's Paris gallery during the Great War, Hendrik had offered his friend employment. Etienne Duret accepted and, twenty years later, knew as much about the Van Schuyler enterprise as Hendrik himself. The Duret family's looted inventory was never recovered.

"Should I join them," Alison said, "or wait till this evening?"

This time, Duret's shrug was slightly more pronounced. "Your grandfather is understandably anxious to know what kept you in London."

"Been wondering that myself," said Brant as he entered the room, a teasing glint in his eyes. "I was just buttoning up my driving jacket yesterday when I got the word of your delay."

"Did you find the London art scene that intriguing?" Duret sniffed. "I can't think how."

"Perhaps it was the British cuisine," suggested Brant. "I'm rather partial to a good shepherd's pie myself."

Duret actually shuddered and Alison rolled her eyes.

"If you must know, gentlemen, I was

65

detained by a young man."

The men exchanged glances. "Who, exactly, is this . . . young man?" asked Duret, his French accent more pronounced than usual.

Alison smiled to herself, knowing that both of them burned with curiosity. She blew gently on her coffee, cradling the mug in her chilled hands, her expression blank. "His name is Josef Talbert. A handsome fellow. Perhaps seven or eight years old; I'm not sure."

The sighs of relief were almost audible. Alison lifted her cup in a *so there* gesture and took a careful sip of the steaming coffee, savoring its heat. More than anything she wanted a hot bath and a change of clothes. But Duret's deliberate evasion had sparked her own curiosity. "If you'll excuse me, I think I'll have a peek upstairs."

She climbed the back staircase and stopped at the landing to the second floor. Muted voices came from her grandfather's office, but his closed door kept her from hearing what was being said. Quietly entering a tiny square of a room that had been renovated into a lavatory late in the last century, she frowned at her reflection in the opulent full-length mirror behind the door. There wasn't much she could do about her wrinkled outfit, but fortunately she kept a few toiletries here for just such emergencies. She brushed out her hair and pinned the length into a bun at the nape of her neck. A splash of cold water lessened the tired lines of her pale face.

As she stared in the mirror to apply vibrant pink lipstick, her thoughts strayed once more to Ian. Reliving the magic of his unexpected kiss sent a shiver through her body. His face replaced her reflection in the mirror, the longing look in his eyes piercing her heart. The dull pain in her head shifted, and she grabbed the vanity to stop herself from reeling.

The moment passed, and Ian disappeared.

Taking a deep breath, she forced a smile. But she couldn't completely diminish the forlorn ache in her weary eyes. She could only hope her grandfather wouldn't notice.

Outside his office door, she smoothed her skirt one last time before knocking and entering. Two men sat in the luxurious leather chairs within the bay window that overlooked the cobbled street below. Both stood as Alison entered, but she had eyes only for her grandfather, her *opa*. He came to her, enveloping her in a warm and welcoming hug. She buried her face in the soft cloth of his tailored suit and inhaled deeply of his pipe tobacco. Though he knew nothing of her heartache, his thick arms comforted her. The sting of loss lessened, and there was nothing forced in her smile when she looked into his face.

"Finally, you are home," he whispered, loosening his grip enough to search her face. "And tired from your travels."

"It's been a long day."

"Travel from Paris is always grueling." His emphasis when he said *Paris* was so slight, Alison wondered if she had imagined it. But his steady gaze also held a warning.

"But worth it." She injected a gaiety she didn't feel into her reply. "Though I may have spent all my wardrobe allowance for next year."

Hendrik laughed heartily, then gestured toward his visitor while keeping one arm around Alison's shoulders. "We have a guest."

The man came forward, even white teeth brightening his dimpled smile. Blond hair, several shades lighter than Alison's, contrasted with his tan except where a pale scar crossed his lower cheek and jawline. A well-tailored charcoal suit perfectly fit his tall, athletic frame.

Recognizing him, Alison gasped. "Theodor?" At her grandfather's nudge, she held out her hand. "What a surprise, after all this time."

"Alison." Theodor drew out each syllable of her name in his rich Prussian accent. He lifted her fingers to his lips while keeping his eyes on her face and switched to his native German. "You are even lovelier than I remembered."

"Danke," she murmured, tucking an errant strand of hair behind her ear. She continued in German, her accent nearly flawless. "What brings you to Rotterdam?"

"Art." His tone suggested there could be no other reason for his visit, but his eyes swept over Alison with a proprietary air.

"Count Scheidemann is restoring an old family chalet in Bavaria," said Hendrik. "He wishes something special for the main room."

" 'Count'?"

Theodor bent his head in a mournful pose. "My father died last winter."

"I'm so sorry."

"As am I. His shoes are not easy to fill, but I do my best."

Alison glanced at her grandfather, who smiled indulgently at her. "The count is joining us for dinner."

Again, a cautious undercurrent appeared in Hendrik's expression — a veiled warning

69

to stay on her guard. She favored Theodor with an engaging smile. "How lovely. I should go home and oversee the preparations."

Theodor made a deliberate show of checking the time on his substantial gold watch. "I also have a matter or two requiring my attention. I shall say my good-byes. Albeit temporarily."

"I'll see you out," said Hendrik.

"No need. I'm sure you are anxious to visit with your granddaughter after her absence."

"I insist." Hendrik turned to Alison. "Please ask Brant to wait for me and we'll go home together."

"Of course."

"Till this evening, then," said Theodor with a slight bow.

Alison squeezed her grandfather's arm and left the office. She descended the back stairs and tiptoed to the door leading to the gallery showroom. Hendrik and Theodor appeared from the front staircase and crossed the polished parquet floor to the foyer. Theodor walked with his hands clasped behind his ramrod-straight back, his confident stride that of a man used to getting what he wanted. And what he wanted was always expensive and fine.

Despite herself, Alison's pulse raced as the memory of the first time they met appeared before her. How flattered she had been at the attentions of this incredibly handsome man with money to burn and an impressive lineage. His knowledge of art was like an extra coat of varnish, making him even shinier in her eyes. The glisten had worn away, though for no reason she could remember. They had exchanged letters a few times; then he had faded away, no more than a schoolgirl's crush.

Theodor's sudden appearance may have been more welcome if not for Ian. But the handsome and charming count couldn't topple the mischievous British lieutenant from his pedestal. Not in her thoughts and not in her heart.

She came out of hiding as Hendrik locked the front doors after Theodor's departure. "Why did you invite him to dinner?"

"He gave me little choice."

"And the Château d'Yquem?"

"A minor sacrifice."

"He's buying something," she teased. "What?"

Hendrik veered toward a display wall and gestured to one of the paintings hanging on it. "He showed interest in *A Young Lady Reading.*"

71

Alison tilted her head, studying Jean Raoux's shadowed portrait of an auburn-haired woman, eyes downcast as she read a letter by the meager light of a window partially hidden by the folds of a luxurious rose drape. "I hate to see her go."

"She has been with us a long time. But if we do not sell —" Hendrik shrugged — "we do not eat. Or buy pretty dresses from Paris."

"I bought only one." Alison faced her grandfather. "And only because *Tante* Meg insisted."

Hendrik tapped her nose with his finger. "You are truly a Van Schuyler. More interested in Paris's museums then in her *haute couture.*"

"To Tante Meg's dismay. Have you heard from her?"

"A telegram, yes. My dear sister is well, but set no date for her return."

Alison gazed again at the portrait and wondered, not for the first time, who had written the letter that so captivated the attractive woman. When she spoke, she kept her voice as nonchalant as possible. "What about Papa? Any news from him?"

"Not even a postcard."

He failed to completely hide his anger, but she loved him for trying.

She brushed the ornate metallic frame with her fingertips, eager to change the subject. "It's the Rembrandt-like quality that appeals to Theodor. The mastery of the lighting."

Hendrik cleared his throat. "He's interested in a second portrait."

Something in his tone caused Alison to face him. She inhaled sharply at what she read in his eyes. "My mother's portrait? You told him it wasn't —"

"Of course, of course." Hendrik gestured impatiently, then tucked Alison's arm in his. "But we must tread carefully. Our future may depend on the goodwill of men like Count Theodor Scheidemann. You understand this?"

"What harm could he do us?"

"I only wish him to know we value his patronage." A flicker of unease appeared in Hendrik's eyes but disappeared so quickly, Alison wondered if she imagined it.

A curl of fear settled in her stomach. "What's bothering you, Opa?"

"Only the future, *mijn schatje,* only the future."

My little treasure. Hendrik had greeted Alison with his pet nickname for her the first time they met, enveloping the confused twelve-year-old in a comforting embrace. It was the only time she had seen tears fill his eyes.

He led Alison to the kitchen. As they entered, Brant stood and buttoned his jacket. "Shall I ready the car, sir?"

"We'll leave in a moment." Hendrik waved Brant back to his seat and poured himself a cup of coffee. "Tell us quickly what you learned, *schatje*. We don't have much time."

Alison perched on a stool, tucking her fears away till later. She focused her thoughts on her whirlwind trip, sparked by rumors of German aggression and fueled by Germany's destruction of Spanish landmarks in the recent Spanish Civil War.

"Arrangements are being made, but very secretively. The most important paintings and sculptures in the Louvre will be hidden in *chateaux* south of Paris. I met with Monsieur Bertrand. He showed me the crates and packing materials. He is also stockpiling gasoline."

"He fears war, then." A trace of despair sounded in Hendrik's voice.

"Definitely."

"Did he say which *chateaux*?" asked Duret.

Alison shook her head. "He only told me as much as he did because of your letter of introduction."

74

"What happened in Wales?" Hendrik joined them at the table.

"The museum officials took me to a slate quarry near Manod. You should have seen me, Opa. I wore coveralls and a hard hat with a lantern in it. We went deep into the cavern. I'll show you." She took an envelope from her bag, pulled out a sheaf of papers, and spread them out on the table. "This is a blueprint of how the cavern is divided into rooms. And here's the technical diagram for the machinery that controls the air quality."

Brant studied the schematics. "I know someone who can help us with this."

"Someone who won't ask questions?" asked Duret.

Brant glared, but didn't bother answering.

"All we need is a place," Alison said. "A deep and secret place where treasure can hide."

CHAPTER SIX

As Alison savored the final bite of her scrumptious chocolate fudge cake, Brant entered the dining room, whispered in Hendrik's ear, and departed. His discreet movements and silent footsteps gave the moment a surreal quality, as if a black-clothed apparition had suddenly appeared by Hendrik's side, delivered its message, and disappeared again.

"Please excuse me for a moment," said Hendrik. "Apparently my presence is needed elsewhere."

"Nothing too serious, I hope," said Theodor.

"No, no." Hendrik stood. "A simple matter. I'll join you soon."

As he left through one door, Alison led Theodor through another into the parlor. Two wingback chairs, richly upholstered in russet damask, faced a matching sofa across a rosewood coffee table. A wall of shelves held leather-bound books interspersed with a tasteful variety of pottery and sculptures. Slender glass vases scattered around the room held yellow and pink tulips, their buds fully open.

Rain spattered on the trio of lead-paned windows that rose above a cushioned built-in seat. Alison glanced toward the windows as a streak of lightning lit up the night sky. Settling into one of the wing-backs, she wondered if rain fell on Kenniston Hall.

"Do you remember when we met?" Theodor stood beside the parlor hearth, framed by the fireplace's stone and a mahogany pedestal displaying a bronze Arabian stallion, its front hooves pawing the air.

Despite Theodor's relaxed stance, or perhaps because of it, Alison suspected his pose was deliberately designed to catch her eye. She imagined him wearing breeches and stockings, a waistcoat and broad-brimmed hat, a subject worthy of Rembrandt. She smiled to herself at the thought of the great master painting this twentieth-century man of the world.

"So you do remember."

She blinked, realizing she had been staring at him. "Yes, of course. It was four years ago at the Boijmans *Vermeer: Origins and*

Influences." The museum, one of the oldest in the Netherlands, had showcased the influential seventeenth-century painter, famous for his domestic images of Dutch life and the rarity of his work, as the first exhibit in their new building. No more than three dozen Vermeers were known to exist.

"You were enchanted by *Girl Interrupted at Her Music.*"

"I was — I still am — intrigued by her expression."

"I was more intrigued by yours."

"I'm sure I looked very foolish." She remembered standing before the painting, her fingers aching to sketch the young girl from that long-ago world. As if in a trance, Alison had raised her hand and mimicked Vermeer's strokes. The museum faded away, leaving her in the master's studio, where she could almost smell the oils of the paints, the pungent candles. Theodor had broken the spell by offering to buy her invisible painting. They had laughed and wandered through the rest of the exhibit together, playfully arguing over their different interpretations.

"You looked beautifully preoccupied. An artist of great talent," Theodor said, bringing Alison back to the present just as he had on the day of the Vermeer exhibit.

"Not that great."

"Better than you believe." He sat on the sofa across from her, his voice weighting each word with meaning. "After all, you are a Van Schuyler. Sole heir to an artistic legacy. You only need to find your inspiration."

"Perhaps you're right." Images flashed before her. Young Josef and his violin. Ian at Minivers. The stone fountain in the park. Perhaps she already had.

Hendrik appeared in the doorway, waving his unlit pipe and spouting good-natured apologies for abandoning his guest. Another streak of lightning flashed outside the windows, and he closed the wooden shutters before settling into the other wingback.

"You concluded your business satisfactorily?" Theodor asked.

"Oh yes. As I said, a simple matter." Hendrik retrieved a match from a nearby silver holder, taking his time lighting his pipe. Soon the familiar aroma of his tobacco overcame the sweet and unassuming fragrance of the tulips.

"I was about to compliment Alison on your fine painting." Theodor nodded toward the immense gold-framed portrait above the fireplace. "A Frans Hals the Elder if I'm not mistaken."

"One of his later works, yes."

"And the gentleman in the portrait? A long-ago ancestor, I presume."

"The founder of our gallery."

"Three centuries." Theodor shook his head, as if amazed, yet Alison detected something false behind the sophisticated warmth in his brilliant blue eyes. She dismissed her uneasiness, blaming her suspicions on the weariness descending upon her. Stifling a yawn, she stared at the portrait as if she had never seen it before. Johann Van Schuyler, hailed as the founder of the family dynasty and blamed for each heart-wrenching tragedy endured by his direct descendants.

"I imagine many secrets hide in this house," Theodor said. "Old Masters tucked away in odd corners. Forgotten beneath the attic eaves."

"Our personal collection is a fine one, of course." Hendrik gripped the lapel of his jacket, a sure sign of his agitation. "However, I venture you would be more likely to find lost works among your own vast holdings."

"True, true." Theodor's superior smile grated on Alison's nerves. "Still, there must be dozens, if not hundreds, of valuable paintings in this country, their owners totally oblivious to their true value."

"Perhaps." Hendrik shrugged. "But I assure you that is not true in our home. Is it, my dear?"

Alison smiled as engagingly as she could. "We keep a detailed inventory."

"If only all stewards of art were as conscientious." Theodor returned Alison's smile and stood. "You must be tired after your long day of travel. And I fear I have overstayed my welcome."

"Not at all," Alison protested as both she and Hendrik rose from their seats. But an insistent yawn, only partially hidden behind her hand, gave the lie to her words. "Forgive me," she said with an embarrassed laugh. "But you are right. It has been a long day."

"I trust you'll be at the gallery tomorrow. Shall we say ten o'clock?"

Alison glanced at her grandfather, who gave a slight nod. "Yes. Ten o'clock will be fine."

Theodor bowed slightly from the waist and Brant appeared to escort him out amid another round of good-nights. Alison and Hendrik waited, still as the Grecian statues on either side of the window seat, until they heard Brant closing and locking the front door.

Alison collapsed in her chair. " 'Stewards

of art'? What in the world does that mean?"

"I don't know, but the prices just went up on anything he purchases tomorrow. Add at least ten percent. Twenty."

"He knows what he's doing. If the prices are too high, he'll go elsewhere."

"Let him."

"Are you no longer interested in eating?" she teased. Hendrik harrumphed and Alison plucked at the lacy overlay of her lavender evening gown. When she spoke, her voice felt small in the overstuffed room. "We could use the money."

Hendrik stopped pacing and reached for Alison's hand. "Yes, *mijn schatje,* it is true. But we are not desperate yet. Besides, I prefer Dutch *kroners* to anything belonging to that German. Even American dollars would be better."

Alison grinned at him. His prejudice against anything American had become something of a family joke. The seeds of distaste were sown when his son, Alison's father, had forsaken his native soil in favor of the seductive land of opportunity. Hendrik blamed that far-away country both for the brief success his son had found there and for the economic disaster now rippling throughout Europe.

"You are the only good thing to come

from that upstart of a place." Hendrik kissed her fingers with a loud smack. Alison squeezed his hand. It was what he always said after one of his rants.

He smiled at her, then took a deep breath, his mood becoming more somber. "Brant and I need to go out for a while."

"Where?"

"It's best you don't know."

"I want to help."

"You already have. The blueprints and schematics will help us hide our national treasures."

"I can do more."

"Perhaps later. After the arrangements are made." He held her gaze, his gray-blue eyes so like her father's, like her own. "But for now, no."

She frowned, too tired to argue and knowing his mind was made up.

"Off to bed with you," he said, his voice tender. "You have an important appointment tomorrow with our friend the count."

Alison kissed him good night and headed up the curved stairs to her bedroom at the back of the house. Pulling aside the chintz curtain, she peered out her rain-streaked window, but the well-tended garden that sloped to the turbulent canal was shrouded in shadows. Unseen stars hid behind ebony clouds, leaving the world wrapped in darkness.

Again her thoughts turned to the occupants of Kenniston Hall. How had Ian's parents welcomed home their only son? What special foods had graced their supper table? Did he stare up into the night sky and dream of her?

The igniting of a car engine broke through the splattering rain. A moment later, parallel streams of yellow light arced and disappeared as Hendrik and Brant headed to their secret meeting.

Letting the curtain fall into place, Alison retrieved her bag from where she'd dropped it earlier and sank into a powder-blue armchair. She unpacked the miniature lighthouse and pressed the recessed button. As the music box played its poignant notes, she smoothed out the crumpled napkin and studied the sketch she had made of Ian that morning. Only a few hours ago, but to her heart, an eternity. She traced Ian's features with her finger as the tinkling melody of "Greensleeves" brushed against the staccato notes of the drumming rain.

CHAPTER SEVEN

"She's not for sale." Alison crossed her arms. She and Theodor stood in front of *The Girl in the Garden,* prominently displayed as the gallery's centerpiece. The dark-haired young woman in the painting, Alison's mother, wore a simple dress in the blue favored by Vermeer. She stood beside a tall birch, one hand resting on the silvery bark, as if ready to slip behind the tree. Her deep-brown eyes, gazing from the canvas, extended a wordless invitation to a game of hide-and-seek. A riot of color surrounded her, a Monet-esque garden of light. Pieter Schuyler's masterpiece. A mystical homage to an Old Master and a modern Impressionist.

"You look very much like her," said Theodor. "Except for the color of your hair and eyes."

"I have my father's eyes, his coloring."

"It's just as well."

Alison turned to him, puzzled. "What does that mean?"

"It means you have nothing to worry about."

"What should I be worrying about?"

Theodor grasped her hands, his eyes softening as he held her gaze. "It has not been easy waiting for you to grow up."

"You've been waiting —"

"Four very long years." He smiled down at her, his fingers cool and strong against her skin. "Too young to know your heart. But now . . ."

Alison stepped back, but he held on to her hands and kept her close.

"I knew that first day," he said, "standing in front of the Vermeer, that we belonged together. Our fates are intertwined. Surely you see this too."

"Theodor," she began. "I don't . . . You must know that I can't —"

"I am not afraid of the Van Schuyler curse."

She pulled away, her eyes wide with surprise. "It's not a curse. It's . . . it's just the way it is with us."

"How does it go? *Love that burns bright and fast is the love that cannot last. 'Tis the Van Schuyler tragic fate, that Death steps in, a heart to break.*"

"How did you know that?" The cursed poem had been nibbling at her since she met Ian. Suddenly cold, she rubbed her arms. She had first heard her papa reciting it in a drunken singsong voice after her mother's funeral. Later she had found its lines scrawled along the borders surrounding an old family tree. One with dates that gave proof to the words.

"I make it my business to know things." Theodor laughed at her frozen expression. "I meant what I said, Alison. You're old enough now to decide what you want from life. Whether you're going to stay in this provincial country or participate in the renewal of an exciting future."

"Renewal?"

"A golden future, governed by the superior race." Theodor gave her a patronizing smile. "You and I, Alison. We are among the elite."

She stared at him, wondering if she had somehow misunderstood what he'd said. But no. His eyes gleamed with certitude. She was opening her mouth, still unsure what to say, when a commotion came from the entryway. A rotund man, squeezed into a Luftwaffe uniform, stood in the arched entrance as if he himself were on display.

"Ah." Theodor smiled and grasped Alison's arm. "I want you to meet someone.

Commander Hermann Göring."

Theodor tugged at his pristine white cuffs, adjusting the square gold links so that the embossed monogram could be easily seen beneath the sleeves of his pinstriped jacket.

"This is a tremendous honor," he said, leaning close to Alison. "Herr Göring's patronage may garner the attention of the Führer himself. No doubt Herr Hitler would have been one of the greatest painters of his generation — *the* greatest — if the needs of his country had not called him to public service."

"I didn't know."

"The Führer has many talents." Theodor inwardly smiled at the wonder shining in Alison's expressive eyes as he smoothed his silk tie and straightened the golden clasp. "His artistic vision will transform Europe. And the Van Schuyler Fine Arts Gallery can be a significant contributor to fulfilling his dreams."

Alison's eyes widened and Theodor clasped her elbow, pleased that his surprise had left her speechless. He wished to tell her more about the Führer's plans, the secret behind his own visit to Rotterdam's famous museums and galleries. But even his associates didn't know that the inventories they were creating, with the help of the foolish curators, would later be used by the Führer to reclaim Germany's cultural heritage. The lists would help identify every painting by a German artist, every sculpture stolen by that egomaniacal Napoleon Bonaparte, any art rightfully belonging to the German *Volk*. As well as any other remarkable works needing the protection of the Third Reich. Once the works were acquired, they would be properly displayed in the Führer's planned architectural wonder, his *Führermuseum.*

All in good time, of course. Timing mattered for any worthwhile endeavor. And reward invariably came to a man with patience.

Theodor squared his shoulders as Alison shifted beside him. He admired her tense profile and, gratified by her nervousness, followed her gaze. "No need to fear," he murmured. "Come. I will introduce you."

He steered Alison toward Göring and the adjutant who accompanied him, then snapped his heels together and extended his arm. "Heil Hitler."

The two officers returned the salute, their deep voices resonating through the quiet gallery. Out of the corner of his eye, Theodor saw Alison flinch, ever so slightly, and he placed his hand at the small of her back. His touch seemed to calm her, he noted with satisfaction.

"Commander Göring," he said. "I am honored that you accepted my invitation."

"Count Scheidemann." Göring gazed deliberately around the showroom, his eyes finally coming to rest on Alison. He stared at her with an appreciative leer. "The gallery is small, is it not?"

Theodor felt Alison bristle at the subtle insult in Göring's tone. He would explain to her later that this was the way of powerful men. Authority must be asserted in even the smallest matters. He chuckled politely. "I prefer to think of it as intimate. May I present Miss Alison Schuyler? The gallery has been in her family since its founding in the late 1600s."

Göring offered his hand and Alison hesitantly took it. He pulled, forcing her to take an awkward step toward him. "You will be my tour guide, yes? Of this —" he half-closed his eyes — "*intimate* gallery?"

Alison glanced at Theodor, her eyes betraying her discomfort, and he gave her an encouraging smile. With Göring as a favored patron, the gallery had the potential to become the premier establishment in Holland. Perhaps in Europe. An ambitious plan, but not improbable, given Theodor's own aristocratic connections. Alison's artistic genealogy, impeccable and lengthy, was an unusual dowry, but the perfect accompaniment to his own Prussian nobility. Their shared love of art would be a gift to their children, who would also inherit the artistic talent he coveted but did not possess.

"We specialize in Old Masters," Alison said, her voice cordial. "Though we also have a few modern works, including a Picasso and a Degas."

"Degenerate garbage," Göring practically spat. "Such trash does not belong in a reputable establishment."

"Our clientele might disagree with you."

"Only the uneducated."

"Herr Göring might like the Lievens landscape your grandfather showed me yesterday," Theodor said before Alison could reply. "This way, isn't it?"

"Yes," she said. "An oil on panel."

Theodor followed as Alison led Göring to the painting. It hung on a freestanding wall with several other seventeenth- and eighteenth-century landscapes.

Göring studied the display. "Who is this Lievens?"

Theodor exchanged a quick glance with Alison, who looked as stunned as he felt by the self-proclaimed art connoisseur's question. "A contemporary of Rembrandt. They shared a studio for a time."

"Of course, of course." Göring made a show of examining the painting. "Now this, my dear, is art."

He lumbered to the next display, giving the collection of medieval portraits scant attention before moving on. Theodor and Alison trailed behind until the commander stopped before a foot-high marble sculpture, *Diana the Huntress,* an alert hound at the goddess's feet. He picked it up, hefting it in his hand. Only Theodor's polished manners prevented him from gasping at the commander's audacity. He purposefully ignored Alison, knowing she must be horrified at Göring's cavalier handling of the antiquity.

Göring pointed Diana's head at Theodor. "What painting interests you?"

"Not a painting, Commander." He feigned embarrassed meekness as the lie flowed from his lips. "I am purchasing the *Huntress.* May I?" He held out his hand, his gaze unflinching before Göring's suspicious stare.

"You were examining a painting when I arrived, Count."

"True." Theodor shrugged and touched the figurine's base. "A painting of such value to the Van Schuylers, they refuse to part with it."

Göring gave the sculpture to Theodor with as little care as if it were cheap pottery. "You must learn, Count, that everything has a price. For those willing to pay."

"I assure you," said Alison, "the painting is not for sale. At any price."

"I have seen such a tactic before." Göring waved his hand in a dismissive gesture. "Always the painting was mediocre, the artist of no talent."

"The artist is my father." Alison bristled, her hands forming fists at her side. "And the painting is exquisite."

"I shall judge its worth."

Theodor stepped between them, blocking Alison's glare from Göring's view. "This way, Commander." He led them around the display walls to the gallery's center, cradling the sculpture and swallowing his distaste of the commander's boorish behavior. It was not what he expected from a member of the upper class. A long-ago memory stirred, a whispered rumor that Göring's mother hailed from Bavarian peasantry. Theodor unconsciously sniffed and positioned his tie clasp.

Someday, he was sure of it, he and Alison would laugh as they recalled this day. But right now, he regretted that he had asked Göring to come to the gallery. He doubted Alison would politely ignore any criticism of her father's painting, especially not by someone as ignorant of art as Göring was proving to be. Theodor refused to speculate on Alison's response if Göring tried to bully her into naming a price.

Since they first met, Theodor had been intrigued by Alison's forthright attitude. He found her refreshingly different from the polished sophistication of the young ladies in his social circle. But that independent spunk, sprung from her American roots, could endanger the relationship he hoped to foster with Göring.

Not that he held much regard for the Luftwaffe commander, especially not now. But he highly esteemed Göring's access to Hitler, a privilege he sought for himself before Europe capitulated to German superiority. Nothing must upset his plans.

He held the marble *Huntress* protectively, its solid weight resting heavily within his palm, and swore to guard Alison against her own naive impulses. Smiling to himself, he brushed his finger along the cool surface of the sculpture.

Alison struggled to suppress her rising anger

as she lagged behind Göring and Theodor, feeling uncomfortably like a tagalong child the grown-ups tolerated, but only if she obeyed their unspoken admonition to be seen and not heard. She grudgingly admitted that Theodor's calm demeanor had defused a potential confrontation. Her inclination had been to grab the *Huntress* and bash Göring's head with it.

She smiled to herself, knowing she wasn't capable of such a deed. Van Schuylers did not deliberately damage priceless antiquities, though bodily harm to an enemy could be justified. After all, an eighteenth-century ancestor once fought a duel over the disputed ownership of a Vermeer. The family chronicles proclaimed him a hero. She stared at Göring's broad back and wondered what had happened to that dueling pistol.

They stopped in front of *The Girl in the Garden,* Theodor standing so close to Alison that the masculine notes of his cologne teased her nose. She mentally stepped back and envisioned the tableau in front of the painting, how she and Theodor, shoulders practically touching, angled to its left. Göring stood to the right, but too close for a proper perspective of the artistic intricacies within the frame.

His massive bulk leaned forward, and Alison's throat constricted as she imagined her mother being smothered by the sheer weight of Göring's presence. Fighting to breathe, she unconsciously tucked her hand into the crook of Theodor's arm, trapping her fingers between the warmth of his jacket and the unyielding marble of the sculpture.

"It lacks a certain —" Göring paused, his hand twirling as if to pluck the proper word out of the air — "s*ophistication,* does it not? The woman is lovely, yes, but not a lady." He turned his head to stare at Alison, a dare shining in his piercing eyes. "Am I right?"

Though Alison had often charmed the most pompous and arrogant of the Dutch art world with her poise, Göring's sinister gaze rankled her stomach with loathing. Her frozen face refused to smile. She gripped Theodor's arm, digging her nails into the soft fabric, and drew resolve from his demeanor. He didn't exhibit any sign of discomposure. Neither would she.

"She is my mother." Alison met the gaze of the young woman in the painting, and pride thawed her lips into an upward curve. "An American."

"Ah. An American." Göring chuckled. "That explains so much, does it not?"

"You don't think much of Americans?"

"They think highly enough of themselves."

"They are worthy allies in a fight," Alison retorted, then inwardly cringed at the pronoun that had slipped from her mouth. She hadn't meant to separate herself from her mother's heritage. She jutted out her chin to hide her embarrassment. "*We* are worthy allies."

Göring's round face turned crimson and Theodor stiffened beside her. The veiled allusion to Germany's merciless defeat in the Great War, like a stone from a slingshot, had sunk deep into its mark. Emboldened by her victory, Alison slid her hand from Theodor's arm and stepped closer to the painting. She imagined the girl watched her, approval in her loving gaze.

"Allies." Göring spat out the word, his face turning an impossible shade of red. "I will show you what I think of Americans."

His arm jerked down and back up again, metallic black gleaming from his fingers. Alison spread her arms across her father's masterpiece and sensed Theodor grabbing for her. A blinding flash roared through the gallery and Alison felt herself falling, slowly, gently, toward the parquet floor as someone frantically called out her name.

She rested her cheek on the floor's polished surface and blinked. *Diana the Huntress* lay beside her, her vacant eyes paralyzed and cold. Alison slowly turned her head toward *The Girl in the Garden,* pushing her way through the wrenching pain that pressed against her skull. She clenched her teeth and raised her eyes toward the painting. A ragged wound ripped across the silver birch and slashed her mother's cheek.

"No," she groaned, her voice barely audible. She stretched her fingers to the injured *Girl,* scarcely able to lift her arm from the floor. A shadow fell across her and she stared into Theodor's eyes, brilliant with agony, before her eyelids fluttered and she descended into darkness.

CHAPTER EIGHT

Ian dove from the overhanging cliff into the deep waters of the Bristol Channel. He surfaced and swam with powerful strokes toward the rocky promontory that rose from the seabed like a giant's hand, palm facing the sky. Reaching the graveled cove formed by the space between the giant's thumb and index finger, Ian waded ashore and followed the steep, winding path across the palm to its northwestern side. A natural bench, carved from the stone by centuries of wind and waves, provided a sheltered lookout where a young boy could dream of do-or-die adventures in faraway lands. Or a man could dream of the future.

The heat of the August morning sun dried Ian's clipped hair as he settled onto the bench and searched the far horizon. Wales lay across the channel, but the Atlantic stretched to the west. And beyond those deep ocean waters, an immense land that he'd given little thought to before meeting Alison. Chicago — that's where she said she was born. He knew of the city, of course, but only as a name. He'd have trouble pointing it out on a map. Somewhere in the middle, he mused, stretching his bare foot into the foaming tide.

Alison. She may have left him at the station yesterday morning, but she hadn't left his thoughts. Or his heart. Somehow everything he did, everything he thought, led him back to her. He wondered what she was doing this morning, if her feelings were as tangled as his. Out here by himself, alone with the sky and the sea, he imagined strolling into her grandfather's gallery. In his daydream, she froze in surprise, then ran into his arms, tears of joy streaming down her lovely face.

"There you are!"

Startled, Ian turned and nearly slid off the wet ledge. He shaded his eyes against the sun that backlit a dark silhouette.

"Trish." He shook his head in exasperation "What are you doing here?"

His sister, clad in a turquoise swimsuit, clambered down the rock to sit beside him. She tugged the rubber bathing cap off her head, freeing a mass of auburn curls. "What do you think Mark would say if I told him I snuck up on you?"

"What would he say if I told him you were swimming in the channel by yourself? You broke the family rule."

"So did you."

"That's different."

She playfully smacked his leg with her cap.

"Ow!" He rubbed the reddening spot, felt the grit of sand against his skin. "I should have left you in London."

"I'm glad you didn't." Trish closed her eyes and took a deep breath of the sea air. "It's good to be home. Especially with you here."

"Why don't you move home? Until all this is over?"

She appeared thoughtful, then shook her head. "Thursday night it was you who showed up at my door unannounced. Someday it will be Mark. He'll only have a day, maybe two. Just enough time to get to London before returning to his command. And when he gets that day, I'll be there."

"I'm sorry it was me instead of him this time."

"Me too." She grinned at him and a spark of mischief shone in her eyes. "Except then you wouldn't have met the girl on the train."

Her words sunk into Ian's stomach like a stone. He thought of his earlier daydream and wondered how different the reality might be. He couldn't be sure that Alison would be overjoyed to see him if he showed up at her door. *"Some dreams just can't come true,"* she had said. But she wouldn't, or couldn't, give him a reason why not.

"You'll see her again, Ian." Trish hooked one arm through his and laid her head on his shoulder. "If it's God's will, you'll see her again."

He brushed his lips against her windblown hair and felt a chill as an ominous cloud dimmed the sky. "A storm is brewing. We better go."

They climbed to the top of the path and followed it back across the giant's palm. Before descending to the cove, Ian stopped and stared eastward. Alison lived beyond that horizon, as tied to her family's gallery as he was to the estate. And to that odd superstition. Thunder cracked overhead, and a strange foreboding gripped him. His legs shook, and he groaned as he clenched his chest. Trish turned, worry pinching her mouth, and rushed to him.

"Are you all right?" She grabbed him and he leaned against her. "What happened?"

The dark clouds parted and a slender beam of light slanted toward the giant's thumb. The wave of anxiety faded and Ian took a deep breath. "I'm not sure. Maybe a touch of vertigo or something."

Trish stared at him, her brow furrowed with worry. "I don't think you should swim."

"It's not that far." He faked a smile in an attempt to alleviate her concern. "I'll be fine. In fact, I'll be at the gazebo before you," he said, challenging her with their childhood race. Across this narrow width of the Channel to the white sandy beach, up the wooden steps to the lower garden of Kenniston Hall, a final sprint over the clipped lawn to where the arched gazebo offered its occupants a breathless view of the sea.

She frowned, her head tilted to one side as she studied his face. Then her expression shifted, and she tagged him before running pell-mell into the waves.

Ian ran after her but stopped at the water's edge and stared east again. "Protect her, Father," he breathed. "Whatever is happening, please protect her."

Theodor stared into the empty fireplace in the canal house, finding it difficult to believe that only two nights before he had stood in this exact spot, content in the afterglow of a simple but hearty meal and an extraordinarily fine wine. He glanced at Alison's chair, remembering how the lightning from the evening storm, streaking past the unshuttered window, had illuminated the golden highlights in her hair. Her translucent skin, glowing with vitality, tormented him. So inviting, but not yet his.

He sprawled on the couch and rubbed his forehead in a futile attempt to escape his last memory of Alison before that French lackey Duret had forced him from the gallery. Göring's harsh threat resounded between Theodor's ears. *"I will show you what I think of Americans."*

Unbelieving, stunned into stillness, Theodor had watched as Göring drew the revolver. He flushed again with shame that Alison had responded first, protectively — foolishly — rushing in front of the painting. Her movement broke his frozen spell and he grabbed her as she crumpled to his feet. The dropped *Huntress* smacked the gallery floor, the sound joining with the reverberating echo of the pistol shot, creating a cacophony of ear-splitting noise.

Kneeling beside Alison, Theodor had stared up at Göring, shock mingled with anger, only to be met with a withering gaze. Without a word, the Luftwaffe commander calmly walked away, his heavy footsteps pounding a regular beat in Theodor's head.

From the rear of the gallery had come the sound of softer footsteps, voices rushing toward him. He had turned back to Alison, whispered her name, pressed his linen handkerchief to the blood streaking her temple as her pale eyelids fluttered against bloodless cheeks.

Startled from his thoughts by the opening of the parlor door, Theodor stood as Hendrik entered, his face grave and still. He glared at Theodor, and when he spoke, his voice held no trace of its usual mild deference. "Why have you come?"

"I only want to see her." Hearing the quiver in his words, Theodor stood straighter. "To express my . . . my regret."

Hendrik emitted a harsh chuckle. "Your regret will not heal her."

Theodor glanced around the room, seeing nothing. Seldom did he need to ask permission of anyone to do as he wished. Only his father, with control of the purse strings, had insisted on that courtesy. He took a deep breath and faced Hendrik again. "Please, sir."

Hendrik moved to the window and pulled his pipe from his jacket. He stared at it a moment, then looked at Theodor. "Do you know where Commander Göring is now, Count?"

"No, sir."

"Neither do I." Hendrik paused, his breath labored. "But I will tell you where he is not." He waved his pipe stem at Theodor, punctuating his words. "He is not in a jail cell. This . . . this monster comes into my gallery, shoots my granddaughter, and he . . . he receives no punishment. Nothing is done to him while my Alison, *mijn schatje . . .*" His voice broke and he turned his back on Theodor.

"Please allow me to make some amends. For Alison's sake."

"Do you have the power to bring Göring to justice?" Hendrik threw the words over his shoulder, a challenge that Theodor didn't have the power to accept.

"The painting needs repair. Allow me to arrange it." He moved closer to Hendrik. "As my gift to Alison."

Hendrik turned, his bristling glare fixed on Theodor and his voice rising in anger. "That painting is a Van Schuyler. And only a Van Schuyler will restore it."

Theodor stepped backward as the swirling tension in his stomach hardened into a tight ball. He swallowed his own anger, vowing to remain polite despite Hendrik's stubborn insistence on blaming him for Göring's actions. "I meant no disrespect. If you will excuse me, I'll take my leave now."

Hesitating in front of the parlor door, Theodor glanced at Hendrik, who faced the window, his hands clasped behind his back. "She will recover?"

"Yes," Hendrik said, bowing his head as if in prayer.

Theodor nodded, though he didn't know to whom. Grabbing his hat from the foyer table, he quickly left the house. Once outside, he gazed up at the second floor and wondered if any of the front windows belonged to Alison's room. Somehow he had to find a way to see her, to let her know how much he loved her. Hendrik couldn't keep her away from him forever.

He climbed into the backseat of his Mercedes and instructed the chauffeur to drive to Amsterdam. As the car carried him past vegetable farms and emerald-green meadows, he leaned back and closed his eyes, suddenly tired of the intrigues and falsities thrust upon him by his position and his ambitions. If only he could persuade Alison to run away with him, perhaps to a secluded villa in Italy or a quiet Greek village. He shook his head slightly. Such daydreams were not for him. His birthright determined his destiny, and he would gain the power he craved, whatever the cost.

A week ago, he had admired a Rembrandt landscape at a gallery located in the historic heart of Amsterdam. A perfect gift for Göring, who — Theodor huffed — at least knew that artist. Such extravagance should smooth over any lingering doubts in Göring's mind as to Theodor's allegiance. If he could persuade Hendrik to sell him *Diana the Huntress,* then he would give it to Göring too. Let Göring think it came from the Van Schuylers as a gesture of peace and goodwill. Neither Hendrik nor Alison need ever know.

CHAPTER NINE

The tinkling music box notes filtered through the fading darkness of Alison's consciousness, inviting her to leisurely wakefulness. She lay still, eyes closed, till the tender melody ended. Blinking several times, she fought against the heaviness of her lids. As she struggled to keep her eyes open, the shadows of the dim room sharpened into her dresser, her cheval mirror. She glanced at the miniature lighthouse on her nightstand. *"Remember me."* The words flashed into her memory, followed closely by an onslaught of images. A soldier and a boy. Cherry scones. A fountain in a park. Her heart breaking as she waved good-bye. *Ian.*

"Play it again," she whispered.

"Hello, dear." Her great-aunt's soft voice cradled her in warmth. A cold compress settled on her forehead.

"Tante Meg," she said, sounding hoarse.

"When did you get here?"

"The day before yesterday." Margarite Van Schuyler sat on the edge of her niece's bed, clasping Alison's hand in her own. "We've nicknamed you Sleeping Beauty."

The corners of Alison's mouth turned up in a slight smile that stretched her chapped lips. "What day is it?"

"Tuesday." Meg dipped a cotton cloth into a tumbler of water and patted Alison's mouth. "Do you feel like sitting up? Just enough to sip some water?"

"I'm not sure." She pressed her fingers against her aching head and felt stiff bandages. Her eyes closed against a rush of disjointed impressions, and her body jerked as she relived the bursting glare and searing heat that had driven her into darkness. But not before she had seen a scarred birch tree, a slashed figure.

"Papa's painting?" With a deep sigh, she opened her eyes and searched Tante Meg's gently wrinkled face for an answer.

Meg shook her head, but her gaze stayed steady. "Time enough later to worry about that painting. Now's the time for you to get well."

"Theodor tried to stop me."

"A good thing, too." Meg's voice betrayed a rare flash of anger. "You must promise me

110

that you will never do anything so foolish again."

"Does Papa know?"

"Your grandfather is trying to locate him."

"The news will break his heart. All over again."

"You little darling." Meg smiled affectionately. "Your father will want to know about you, not his garden girl."

Alison nodded agreement, but in a secret place deep in her heart she wondered if that was true. Her father would die to protect his masterpiece; how could she do anything less? A century from now, their lives might be forgotten. But not *The Girl in the Garden*. She would live forever upon her canvas, smiling at her admirers, wordlessly inviting them into her world.

"Theodor comes almost every day. The flowers are from him." Tante Meg pulled back the drapes and the afternoon sun brightened the room. Alison's eyes widened at the colorful bouquets of lilies, tulips, and roses that adorned practically every surface. "Your grandfather didn't want you to have them. He's quite angry with the count. But I overruled him. Do you mind?"

"No." Alison shivered as the memory washed over her again. "He couldn't have known this would happen."

111

"Of course not." Meg gazed out the window, deep in thought, then seemed to make up her mind. "There's something else." She slid a yellow piece of paper from Alison's nightstand and handed it to her. "A telegram. It arrived Saturday afternoon."

Alison's heart raced as she quickly read the brief message.

Alison, must know whether all is well with you. Yours, Ian.

"Did you send a reply?"

Meg shook her head. "How could we, not knowing the circumstances? He's a stranger to us." She picked up another item from Alison's table, a smoothed-out napkin. "Though I'm guessing this is a good likeness."

Alison's cheeks warmed as she took the sketch from her aunt and traced the penciled outlines with her finger. "We met last Thursday in London. At the train station."

"What would you like me to tell him?"

"Nothing. I . . . I can't."

"Why ever not?"

"You know why not." Alison spoke as if each word were a delicate thing, easily broken. She stared at the miniature lighthouse, her eyes clouded with unshed tears.

Meg followed her gaze and picked it up. "He gave it to you?"

"Yes."

Meg pressed the recessed button and smiled slightly as the music played again. Handing the lighthouse to Alison, she softly exhaled. "He is the one."

It wasn't a question, but Alison nodded anyway, her eyes downcast.

Meg's cool fingers lifted Alison's chin so their eyes met. "You should sleep. I'll tell your grandfather you've awakened and ask Mrs. Brant to prepare a broth for you." She walked toward the door.

"I won't see him again."

Her aunt turned back. "Sleep now, Alison. We'll talk later."

After the door closed, Alison read the telegram again. Ian had sent it Saturday afternoon, just hours after the incident. *How could he have known?* She twisted the bedcovers, clenching her hands until her knuckles turned white. *How could he possibly have known?*

Mud splattered Ian's face as he bellycrawled under multiple strands of low-hung barbed wire. After a strenuous run across the Army base's rugged landscape, he almost enjoyed this part of the obstacle course. Except for the mud in his eyes. And the burn in his legs.

After clearing the last row of wire, he scrambled to his feet and sprinted toward the final hurdle, a trio of knotted ropes against a high wooden wall. He grabbed the middle rope and climbed hand over hand, his boots rhythmically hitting the boards. At the top, he pulled himself over and dropped to the ground. Pausing just long enough to take a deep breath, he raced toward the flagged pylons marking the finish line.

"Move it, Dev!" Captain Mark Manning held a stopwatch and paced next to the pylons. His khaki cap covered ginger hair and shaded serious green eyes. The instant Ian ran across the line, Mark clicked the watch.

Hands on his hips and breathing heavily, Ian headed back toward Manning, both his commanding officer and brother-in-law. "Well?"

Mark frowned. "Next time, I'll take the long weekend pass, and you can stay here and train."

"It couldn't have been that bad." Ian snatched the watch and read the time. Almost five minutes shy of his record. Without a word, he handed back the watch and began the long walk to the barracks.

"You can ride with me."

"I'm a muddy mess." Ian flung the words over his shoulder without breaking his stride. A motor revved, and a moment later Mark pulled alongside in his Scout, slowing to a crawl.

"Get in, Dev."

Ian ignored him, even though his limbs ached. Sweat dripped from his forehead, trickling streaks of mud into his burning eyes. The walk would be a self-imposed punishment for his poor performance. He kicked a stone and watched it skitter in front of him.

Tires squealed and Ian stopped short as Mark sharply turned the Scout and braked in front of him. "I gave you an order, Lieutenant."

For a long moment, the two men stared at each other.

Ian glanced away first, the glint in Mark's eyes suddenly reminding him of that long-ago day in the caves — the day his older brother had disappeared within an eddy and Ian dove headlong into the pool after him. Mark, recognizing the danger — and the futility — of attempting a rescue, dove in too, and pulled Ian out. "Go get help," Mark had shouted above Ian's thrashing sobs, pinning him to the cave floor. "You go. I'll search for Steven."

Back then, the fierce glint in Mark's eyes had compelled Ian to obey. Ever since that tragedy, Ian had claimed his brother's best friend as his own. But he hadn't told Mark about Alison. Not yet. With each day that passed, their time in London felt more like something he had dreamed. If only she would answer his telegram.

Without looking at Mark, he climbed into the Scout.

Mark shifted and punched the accelerator. "What's bothering you, Dev?"

"I've had better days, that's all."

"Agreed."

They rode the rest of the way in silence, with Ian chastising himself for allowing his concern about Alison to interfere with his duty. Losing a few minutes on a military obstacle course was inexcusable, but wouldn't get him killed. A lack of concentration in the heat of battle, though — that could be deadly. His men deserved his best, and he'd let them down by not giving his full attention to the task at hand. It wouldn't happen again.

Mark parked the Scout and Ian opened the latch, then hesitated. "I'll run it again tomorrow," he said. "Ahead of my squad."

"The squad is scheduled for 0700."

"Then I'll be there at 0600."

"Find yourself another timekeeper."

"You'll be there." Ian gave him a sidelong glance. "You always are."

Mark let out an exaggerated sigh. "Then 0600 it is. Now go clean yourself up and get this mud out of my Scout." His slight smile undercut his stern expression. "That's an order, Dev."

"Yes, sir." Ian performed a quick salute and headed for his quarters.

He was almost to the door when someone shouted his name. He turned to see Browning, the unit's pale, gangly clerk, waving at him from the administration hut.

"Special delivery package for you, sir. You need to sign for it."

Ian's heart quickened, but he quickly squelched the hope that the package was from Alison. At least, he tried. Hope bubbled up despite his best efforts. He jogged to the hut, his legs miraculously healed from their earlier agony.

After he scrawled his name on the mail log, Browning handed him a square parcel wrapped in brown paper and tied with string. Ian eagerly scanned the return address and his heart sank, then lifted again with curiosity. *Abraham Talbert, Esquire.* It could only be Josef's uncle. Ian smiled to himself, remembering the young violinist and his impromptu concert. Which carried his thoughts once more to Alison. If not for Josef, Ian wouldn't have met her. "I owe you one, little man," he murmured.

"Excuse me, sir?" said Browning.

"Nothing, nothing," Ian said sheepishly. "Just talking to myself." He was almost to the door when he remembered something and turned back. "Captain Manning's Scout needs cleaned. Especially the passenger seat. Take care of it, will you?"

"Me, sir?" Browning practically squeaked.

"I don't see anyone else in here." Ian gave a jaunty salute. "That's an order, Browning."

After a hot shower, mostly spent scrubbing the mud out of his hair and ears, Ian put on a pressed uniform and sat on his bunk with the package. It had been sent to Kenniston Hall, then forwarded to him here. He cut the parcel's string with his pocketknife and removed the thick brown paper. Inside the box, he found a collection of homemade biscuits, assorted Swiss chocolates, and an ivory envelope affixed to a smaller package. He popped a chocolate in his mouth and slit open the envelope.

The letter, typed on matching stationery

and bearing the letterhead of the Talbert law firm, thanked Ian for his "kind service" on Josef's behalf and asked him to accept the package as a small token of the Talbert family's gratitude.

The sketch of you and Josef at the train station is now framed and hangs beside his bed. He prays for you and the "lady artist" every night. Please do us the favor of expressing our gratitude to her as we lack the means to do so ourselves.

We trust you will do us the kindness of accepting our services on your behalf should an opportunity arise in the future.

May God keep you and protect you.

With warmest regards,

A distinctive hand had signed the letter in broad strokes. It seemed that Josef had found a safe and loving refuge away from his home. Ian opened the second sheet of paper and chuckled. Josef's drawing showed a boy waving good-bye from a train window. On the platform, two figures waved at the boy. His signature and the date filled the lower right-hand corner.

The package contained two slender boxes. Ian's name was inscribed on the one wrapped in gold, and Alison's name adorned the silver-wrapped box. Unwrapping his present, he found a gold Montblanc fountain pen, monogrammed with his initials. He twisted the barrel to reveal the nib and wrote his name on a scrap of paper. The ink flowed across the page as he wrote Alison's name beside his own.

Without knowing it, Abraham Talbert had performed a great service for Ian by sending Alison's gift to him. Now he had another excuse — no, not an excuse, a *reason* — to get in touch with her. Not that it did much good if she didn't reply.

Ian spent the next several minutes writing letters to Josef and Abraham Talbert. With those ready to post, he dated a clean sheet of stationery.

Twenty minutes later, Mark appeared at his door. "Ready for supper?"

"I suppose so." Ian glanced at his letter. *Dear Alison* was as far as he had gotten. He put the writing materials away and straightened his bunk. Grabbing his hat, he and Mark headed for the mess hall.

"The Scout looks great," Mark said. "Better than I expected. Thanks."

Ian grinned broadly. "Anything for you, Captain."

CHAPTER TEN

Alison's mouth watered as she inhaled the soothing aroma of the hot beef broth. Bits of celery and carrots floated in the delft-blue soup bowl. She blew on a spoonful, then let its flavor warm her throat. "It's delicious."

"Mrs. Brant will be pleased." Meg drew the armchair closer to the bed and settled into its cushions. "All our menus for the next several days revolve around 'Miss Alison's' favorites."

"Good. I'm hungry." And tired, but she didn't want Meg to know that. Hendrik and the doctor had awakened her about an hour earlier. The doctor had left after examining Alison's wound and applying a fresh dressing, but eventually Meg had to shoo the pacing Hendrik out the door. Then both Mr. and Mrs. Brant had popped in to fuss over their "little miss."

Meg entertained with idle chatter while

Alison ate her broth. She scooped the last bit of carrot and swallowed the final spoonful, then leaned back into her pillows with a satisfied sigh. The sharp ache in her head had lessened, and the new bandage felt lighter against her skull. The bullet had grazed her temple, the doctor had explained, leaving unsaid how fortunate she was to have lost only a narrow swath of hair.

"How did you meet him?" Meg's quiet voice floated in the space between them.

Alison concentrated on the soup bowl's pattern, utterly fascinated by the scene depicted within.

"Please tell me."

"There was a boy. At the train station." Alison exhaled, then related the whole story, growing more animated as she told her aunt about how Ian had stood up to the railroad official and how she had missed her train, about tea at Minivers and the secluded park.

"He sounds like a fine young man."

"The finest." Alison blushed and glanced at her aunt with a sheepish smile.

"I'm sure he is." Meg picked up the sketched napkin. "He's obviously concerned about you. Won't you answer his telegram?"

"I can't take the chance." Alison focused her attention on the twilight sky outside her window. The sun had already passed below her vision, but it colored the early-evening sky in pinks and yellows.

"You're worried about the fate."

Alison nodded, unable to speak past the growing lump in her throat.

"You can't let it control your life. Don't you see? It's nothing but a superstition."

Alison stiffened. "A superstition? How can you dismiss it like that?"

"Because I trust in God. He's in control of our lives."

"I trust in God too."

"But?"

Alison bowed her head and picked at a loose thread on her blanket. "I have no mother, no grandmother. And it was the same for you."

"Sometimes tragic things happen," Meg insisted. "But we have long marriages in our genealogy too. Our family is not cursed."

"No." Alison spat the word. "Not cursed. Only fated to live with broken hearts."

Meg sat ramrod straight in the chair, as if summoning resolve from a deep, internal well. "Even if the fate is true, you have already broken it. For the first time in three hundred years, the firstborn child in our line has not been a son. Unless your father marries again, the Van Schuyler line ends with him." She looked down at her hands, as if unwilling to see Alison's reaction to her next words. "In a way, it already ended with Hendrik, since your father changed his name."

Alison wished she could accept Meg's rationale. What she said was true. For generations, the not-very-prolific Van Schuyler men had loved their women with a fervent passion that somehow cost many of those women their lives. But not until they had given birth to an heir, a blond-haired, gray-and-blue-eyed boy to carry on the family name.

Her own grandmother, Hendrik's wife, had died in childbirth. Adding to the tragedy, Hendrik had inexplicably placed the blame for his loss on the tiny shoulders of his newborn son, Pieter.

Pieter crossed an ocean to escape the fate, and thought he had when his young wife surprised him with a daughter instead of a son. But even then, God had allowed the fate to snare him, leaving him a widower at too young an age.

"She shall rejoice in time to come." The ending of her Proverbs 31 verse slid into her mind, but she dismissed it. Weighed down with the tragic knowledge of her family tree, Alison couldn't take the chance that she might be a rare exception. Not with Ian.

For reasons beyond her understanding, he had entered her heart, and he'd always be there. But a life with him would only bring sorrow. She brushed an errant tear from her cheek.

"I have something to show you," said Meg, leaning forward. "If you'd like to see it."

Alison faced her aunt, intrigued by an unusual tone in her voice. "Of course."

Meg unclasped her gold necklace and fingered the delicately painted ivory pendant framed in gold filigree. She wore it often, though Alison had noticed that frequently only the chain remained visible against the back of Meg's neck.

"You've seen this before, I know," said Meg. "But there's something special about it. A secret."

"Tell me."

Meg slid the ivory sideways from its golden frame to reveal a miniature portrait and handed it to Alison. A dark-haired man with chiseled features stared back at her, his dark eyes shining with intelligence and charm.

"Who is he?"

"Someone I once knew. And loved."

Alison stared at her aunt, understanding flowing between them. "You gave him up."

"Yes." Meg reached for the pendant. Her still-elegant features softened as she studied the portrait. "Because I was afraid for him."

"What happened?"

Meg laughed strangely and looked toward the ceiling, then turned her attention to Alison. "He died. Sick and alone." Tears glistened in her pale-blue eyes. "I didn't save him from anything."

A giant knot pressed against Alison's throat. She clasped her aunt's frail hands. "I'm so sorry. So very sorry."

Meg dabbed her eyes with a lacy handkerchief and smiled weakly. "I advise you not to dismiss your lieutenant too quickly, Alison. Your heart will not allow it. Don't you see this may have nothing to do with the fate? This could be God's will for you."

Pained by her aunt's question, Alison looked away and found her attention caught by a sepia-tone snapshot of her father as a young boy that she kept on her dresser. It showed him in a small rowboat on the canal behind the house, smiling brightly as he pushed forward on the oars. She'd found it in a neglected family album shortly after her arrival in Rotterdam. It comforted her to know he had once been happy.

She glanced from the photo to her aunt and back again, sorting out her thoughts.

Two paths lay before her. If she followed her heart, she risked enduring the heartbreak that had crippled her father, turning him into a grief-stricken widower who had pretended all was well for her sake until the sorrow grew too great and he fled. Or she could hide from her heart's desire, as Tante Meg had done, and endure the sting of regret in her old age.

She closed her eyes against a future fraught with loneliness. "I'm afraid," she murmured.

"I know," Meg said gently. "But you mustn't let fear rule your life." She squeezed Alison's hand. "Won't you write to your young man? Let him know you're all right?"

Sorrow and exhaustion pressed against Alison's chest, and the ache in her head spread across her temples.

Not knowing what to do, it was best to do nothing. Alison shook her head. "I'm tired," she said, easing beneath the covers.

"I'll leave you, then." Meg kissed Alison's forehead and gathered the tray. "Sleep well, my darling."

Her eyes barely open, Alison watched her aunt leave the room, closing the door behind her with a soft click.

She glanced at her father's boyhood photo, then shifted her focus to the bouquet beside it. More roses from Theodor, she supposed.

A third path suddenly opened in front of her. A safe path. *Theodor.*

CHAPTER ELEVEN

SEPTEMBER 1939

A couple of days later, Alison rested in the garden behind the house, a new sketch pad in her lap. A thick hedge bordered both sides of the narrow lawn, which sloped down to one of the wide canals that protected the city from flooding. The morning rays cast sunpennies upon the clear water. Her father's boyhood rowboat, weathered gray by time and neglect, bobbed gently beside its narrow dock. She drew two jagged parallel lines, the banks of the canal, before dropping her hand to the paper, too lethargic to do any more.

She had settled into a dull routine, finding respite from her troubled thoughts in long hours of restless sleep. When Theodor called, asking to see her before his return to Germany, she almost said yes. Though half-convinced that only he could provide her with a safe future, her heart held on to other hopes. She'd told Tante Meg that she was embarrassed for him to see her bandaged head. But the truth was much more complicated.

At her insistence, Hendrik had placed the damaged *Girl in the Garden* on an easel in the parlor. Reclining on the couch the day before, she had stared at the injured painting. Its wound festered deep within her, tearing the scabs off long-ago pain of Mama's death, Papa's abandonment.

Pushing aside her heartaches, she gripped the pencil, moving it first hesitantly, then feverishly across the page, shading a strong jaw and giving life to pale eyes.

A sob caught in her throat as she stared at the finished sketch, and she scribbled heavy lines across the drawing.

"Oh, Papa," she murmured. "Where are you?"

Meg crossed the lawn to the wicker seating arranged near a trio of slender poplars. The sun glinted off the diamonds in her bracelet as she perched in a chair next to Alison. "Dr. Meijer is here to see you. He's waiting with your grandfather in the parlor."

With a nod, Alison laid her drawing materials on the table between the chairs and started to rise, then fell back into her seat. Meg reached toward her. "Are you all right? I'll get Dr. Meijer to come out here."

"No!"

Stunned, Meg pulled back. Her hands fluttered, smoothing nonexistent wrinkles from her dove-gray skirt.

"I'm sorry." Alison met Meg's shocked gaze before quickly glancing away. But not fast enough to hide a dark edginess in her eyes that Meg had never seen before.

"I just felt a little dizzy; that's all," Alison said, clipping her words. "I'm all right now."

As if to prove her words true, she stood and smiled without warmth. "I don't need any help."

Meg watched Alison until she disappeared into the house, then eased into the cushioned chair. Dr. Meijer, who came every day to examine Alison's wound — and to sample Mrs. Brant's freshly baked pastry over coffee with Hendrik — had reassured them that the gash was healing nicely.

If only he could pull a cure for an injured heart out of that black bag of his. Meg sighed and picked up Alison's sketch pad. She lifted the cover, expecting to see a new rendering of the handsome lieutenant. Instead, heavy black scratches marred Pieter's likeness. Meg covered her mouth in shocked sorrow.

In the past ten years, she had seen hundreds of Alison's sketchings. But nothing like the raw outrage unleashed on this page.

A wisp of anger curled within her. If she could get her hands on her nephew, she'd give him a tongue-lashing he'd never forget. How dare Pieter treasure his heartaches more than his own daughter?

Hendrik had sent messages attempting to find his son. One to Geneva, where Pieter's last postcard had come from, others to places he was known to frequent. But no one had any news of his whereabouts. The ungrateful scoundrel.

They might not be able to find Pieter, but he wasn't the only one who could lift Alison's spirits. Meg turned to a clean page and, after a moment's thought, wrote a message in her flowery hand. She found Brant in the garage, working over some kind of diagram, and hurried him to the telegraph office.

With a self-satisfied smile, Meg made her way to the parlor. She opened the door and had the strange feeling of intruding upon a tableau. Alison sat in a corner of the couch, her feet tucked beneath her, while Hendrik and Dr. Meijer occupied the chairs. Both men resembled stone statues as they listened to the console radio.

"What is it?" Meg demanded.

Hendrik turned toward his sister, his expression grave. "Germany has invaded Poland."

Mark slid the latest edition of the *Daily Telegraph* across his desk to Ian. "It's begun."

Ian scanned the story, though it didn't tell him anything he didn't already know. The base commander had announced the grim news at morning roll call. Last night, according to German officials, Polish saboteurs had attacked a German radio station near the two countries' shared border and broadcast a threatening message. Citing other border incidents, the German government claimed it was duty-bound to protect its citizens who lived in Poland by taking defensive measures.

"Do you think Hitler was behind this?"

"We may never know." His brother-in-law shook his head. "I'm not sure it matters."

"Of course it matters."

"Only to the historians." Mark leaned back in his swivel chair, hands clasped behind his head. He appeared relaxed, but deep lines puckered the corners of his eyes. "The consequences for this battalion won't change. If Chamberlain keeps his promise

133

to Poland, we'll join the British Expeditionary Force. My guess is that our days here at the base are numbered."

Both the British and French governments had pledged support to the Polish Second Republic several months ago, after Hitler defied the Munich Agreement and invaded Czechoslovakia. Neville Chamberlain, the British prime minister, had signed the Polish-British Common Defense Pact only the week before, just two days after Hitler and Stalin formed their Nazi-Soviet Pact.

Ian wandered to the window and spotted Browning leaving the administration hut. He faced Mark again. "Any guesses where we'll be going?"

"I imagine we'll know in a day or two."

"You should send for Trish."

"I'd like to." Mark took a deep breath and exhaled heavily. "But I'm not the only soldier here with a sweetheart he's left behind."

"No special privileges for the brass?"

Before Mark could answer, Browning appeared at the open door and held a slip of paper toward Ian. "A telegram for you, Lieutenant."

"Thanks." Ian's facial muscles tensed as he scanned the message, then read it a second time.

Alison recovering from injury. Please visit us soon.

Margarite Van Schuyler

"From Trish?" Mark asked, his voice overcome with worry.

"No, not Trish," Ian said absentmindedly, studying the telegram again. His mind raced as he puzzled over the cryptic message. Margarite Van Schuyler, he reasoned, must be Alison's great-aunt, the one she left behind in Paris. If her aunt was now in Rotterdam, then Alison . . . He refused to finish the thought. Whatever had happened to Alison, she was recovering.

"What is it, Dev?"

Ian stared at Mark for a moment, then blurted, "I need a pass."

"You just had a pass."

"It's important," Ian pleaded. "You know I wouldn't ask if it wasn't."

"We're on the eve of war, Dev. Nobody gets a pass." Mark rose from his chair and leaned against the front of his desk. "It's the girl, isn't it? The one on the train."

"Trish told you?"

Mark gave a slight nod. "In that letter she sent back with you. I'm supposed to find out everything I can about her and send Trish a report."

The corners of Ian's mouth lifted in a slight smile. That sounded just like his nosy little sister. He wasn't sure why he hadn't told her more about Alison when they were together at the estate. It was the not knowing, he decided. Not knowing if he would ever see Alison again, and wanting to keep her to himself for as long as possible.

"Excuse me, Lieutenant." Browning interrupted Ian's thoughts. "The messenger is waiting in my office in case you want to send a reply."

Ian looked hopefully at Mark, who shook his head. "I'm sorry. There's nothing I can do."

"Something's happened to her." He handed over the message. "It's from her aunt. Great-aunt, actually."

Mark examined the telegram. "Maybe you could call her. Browning, you can set up a call to Rotterdam, can't you?"

"Twenty-four hours," Ian cut in. "That's all I'm asking."

"You're asking the impossible."

"Maybe not, sir," Browning said nervously.

Mark glared at him. "Excuse me?"

"Lieutenant Devlin could volunteer for diplomatic courier duty. A packet for our embassy in The Hague is on its way here

136

now from London."

"How far is it from The Hague to Rotterdam?" asked Ian.

Browning tilted his head in thought. "Twenty-five to thirty kilometers."

Ian snapped to attention. "Permission to volunteer, Captain."

Mark feigned irritation. "Who's in charge of this mission, Browning?"

"Major Ashcroft, sir."

"Permission granted," Mark said, "on one condition."

"What's that?" Ian asked, ready to agree to anything.

"You tell me about this girl."

Ian grinned. "She's beautiful."

"I assumed that." Mark playfully punched Ian's shoulder. "You realize that just because you make it to The Hague doesn't mean you'll get to Rotterdam."

"I'll take that chance."

Mark reached for his hat. "Let's go see the major, then." He headed out the door, leaving the others to follow him.

"Thanks, Browning," Ian said, as they exited the office. "I owe you one."

"I just hope the major agrees, sir." Browning's face turned a slight shade of green. "Otherwise I'll have to go. And I really don't like to fly. Sir."

Ian chuckled and clapped the clerk on his back. He almost felt guilty that he had ordered Browning to clean Mark's Scout. Almost.

Meg pushed the slender embroidery needle through the stiff tapestry, forming crimson petals from the silk thread. She had taken up needlework only a few years ago, to keep her fingers nimble, and found she had a talent for combining the colored threads to create subtle depth and texture in her completed pieces. Not that she was surprised. She was a Van Schuyler, after all, though more interested in fashion and textiles than in musty Old Masters.

Afraid of missing any news updates, particularly on the British response to Germany's aggression, she had the console radio tuned to London's BBC station. The current program played a selection of classical music that she found soothing on this long and difficult day. Dr. Meijer had left hours ago and Hendrik had disappeared with Brant after a quick lunch, leaving the gallery in Monsieur Duret's capable hands. Alison, her anger seemingly softened by worry, either napped on the couch or stared out the window. She slept now, but fitfully, as if disturbed by her dreams.

The telegram, addressed to Miss Margarite Van Schuyler, arrived shortly before dinner. Meg feared Ian couldn't come see Alison, not after the morning's disastrous news. But she hoped that his telegram would somehow ease her niece's troubled spirit. Her hands shook as she removed the thin, folded paper from its envelope.

Reading the short message, Meg gasped with surprised delight. Unless his superiors ordered him otherwise, Ian hoped to be in Rotterdam late tomorrow afternoon. Meg arranged to send a welcoming reply before settling once more with her needlework, the telegram carefully folded and tucked in her embroidery bag. A secret from Alison, in case Ian's plans changed and he couldn't come.

On the couch, Alison stirred and her eyelids twitched, but she didn't awaken. Meg glanced from her niece to the painting on the easel. Pieter's masterpiece. A fine painting to be sure, but Meg had never liked *The Girl in the Garden.* To her, it symbolized Pieter's wanderlust, first to America and now to wherever his feet took him. And her own role in his heart's tragedy.

Gazing at the portrait with its gaping wound, Meg understood why the damage affected Alison so deeply. The bullet had killed her beautiful mother all over again.

With a start, Meg stared at the girl's expressive brown eyes. They seemed to be staring back at her, soft with gratitude. She blinked, giving a slight shake of her head, and looked at the girl again. But the sensation was gone. A trick of lighting, Meg decided, stabbing her needle into the cloth while casting sidelong glances at the portrait.

CHAPTER TWELVE

A week had passed since the "Göring outrage," Hendrik's favored term for the shooting, but Pieter's whereabouts were still unknown. The only letter addressed to Alison in Saturday's mail delivery was from Theodor, written shortly after he returned to his Prussian estate. He told her how much he regretted the "incident at the gallery" and promised to return to Holland as soon as his duties permitted.

Tossing the letter on her desk, she paced from her bed to the window and back again, unable to shed the restlessness that gripped her. She owed Theodor the courtesy of a reply, she supposed, if for no other reason than to thank him for the bouquets of flowers that still freshened her room with their late-summer fragrance.

Plucking a drooping daisy from her favorite arrangement of purple and yellow wildflowers, she brushed the fragile petals with her fingertip. The idea of a third path into her future, at first so unsettlingly frail, refused to be ignored. It didn't lead to heart-pounding love, but neither did it lead to lonely regret.

She wanted to trust God for her future. But how could she when the days ahead held no joy? Not for her. Perhaps contentment was the most life could offer her without crushing her spirit. Perhaps Theodor could give her that.

She dropped the limp daisy on top of Theodor's letter and sat at her desk to write to him. A sharp ache jabbed her head wound and she glanced at her watch — 4:23 p.m. Too soon to take more aspirin. Closing her eyes, she willed the pain to subside.

Once the throbbing lessened, she took her pen from its holder and felt her fingers tingle. Her father's face, obliterated by black lines, flashed through her mind. If she redid the sketch, perhaps he'd return home.

Alison admonished herself for the silly thought, but couldn't shake it. Grabbing her drawing materials, she headed outside to the poplar tree.

Alison barely noticed the slight breeze that troubled the canal's water as she sketched the abandoned rowboat with broad, confident lines, reclaiming it from years of neglect. Drawing her father wasn't as easy. She closed her eyes, recalling another boat that Papa had rowed off the shores of Lake Michigan during a long-ago Fourth of July celebration. He handled the oars with ease, pretending it was an accident when he occasionally splashed her.

The glorious day ended with colorful fireworks shooting high into the night sky, the reflection glowing upon the water. "You're a lucky girl, Alison," he had said. "The first American Schuyler." His laughter, a rare but glorious sound, bounced across the waves. Across the years.

Holding on to that image, Alison tentatively penciled his silhouette and filled in the details. As she drew, the restless tension that had hounded her the past few days eased. She felt its absence in her fingers, in her shoulders. Even the constant dull ache in her head dissipated while she concentrated on her work.

With a frown, she erased the mouth and tried again, rounding the bottom lip to smiling fullness. Pleased with her progress, she tapped the end of the pencil against her chin. The sketch resembled the photograph in her room, except the boy was now a man. And someone she missed very much.

Soft footsteps, rustling through the grass, came from the house and she felt a twinge of guilt over her brattish behavior to Tante Meg over the past few days. Mentally preparing an apology, she added a few touches to the sketch while she waited for her aunt to sit beside her.

"I hoped you were drawing me."

Alison's head snapped toward the masculine voice, and her sketch pad slid from her lap.

Ian chuckled as he stooped to pick up the pad. "Who is he?"

"My father."

He nodded; then Alison registered the swift flash of anger in his eyes when he spotted her bandage. He gently touched it, his fingers lingering in her hair. An icy stone, a coldness she didn't know existed within her until this moment, melted at his touch.

"Your grandfather told me what happened. Are you sure you're all right?"

"I'm fine." She laughed at his skeptical look. "Truly, I am."

"Your friend, that count or whatever he is, should have done something."

"I think he tried. It's all a bit of a blur, but I know he dropped the *Huntress*."

"The *Huntress*?"

"A statue he was holding. Fortunately, it

144

wasn't damaged." Unlike Papa's painting. Still, Theodor should have been more careful.

"Fortunate indeed," Ian said sarcastically, his face grim.

"Oh, Ian." She smiled at him, amused by his jealousy and touched by his concern. "What are you doing here?"

"Your aunt invited me." Settling his long frame into the chair beside her, Ian explained about the telegram and his diplomatic assignment to The Hague. "I couldn't pass up the chance to see you again. You're not mad, are you?"

"I'm too surprised to be mad." She gazed into his eyes, afraid that if she looked away he might disappear. "When do you have to go back?"

"My flight returns to the base tomorrow afternoon."

"Will you stay with us?" Her cheeks flushed at how eager she sounded. She shook her head to cover her embarrassment. "I mean, we have a guest room. If you'd like to stay."

"Sure you don't mind?"

Alison's eyes dropped to her sketch, seeking an answer in her father's laughing eyes. Perhaps she was fated to follow in Papa's footsteps, her path into the future no longer hers to choose. A bird squawked and Alison looked up to see a snowy egret circling above the canal. It swooped, then landed with a nonchalant air on the edge of the rowboat. She envied the bird its freedom to bask in the dying rays of the setting sun with no thought for tomorrow.

Determined to embrace that same freedom, if only for a few hours, she faced Ian with a shy smile. "I want you to stay."

He grinned and a mischievous gleam lit his eyes. "Good," he said, taking her hand. "Because 'Tante Meg' stowed my gear in the guest room and Mrs. Brant set another place at the table. I'm to tell you it's time for dinner."

"And I suppose Opa offered you his pipe and slippers?"

Ian chuckled. "Nope. Only his Bentley, in case we wanted to take a drive in the morning."

"You seem to have cast a spell on my entire household."

"It's the Devlin charm." He gave an innocent shrug, then pulled her to her feet. "Come on. I'm starving."

In the dining room, lit by a crystal chandelier and ivory candles, Gerta Brant served roasted lamb with port wine sauce, potato medallions, brussels sprouts, and a ragout of mushroom and peppers. By unspoken agreement, and much to Alison's relief, the dinner conversation avoided the tumultuous events in Europe. She didn't want to think about what would happen to Ian if the British government honored its commitment to Poland. This evening, she only wished to enjoy the company of the handsome young lieutenant who had captured her heart when he befriended a young German refugee.

When Ian first arrived at the house, Hendrik had viewed him with suspicion. But Meg had explained about the telegrams and Ian had filled in the details of how he and Alison had met. Throughout the meal, the elder Van Schuylers peppered Ian with questions about his family and life in Somerset. They discussed art and history, the museums of Paris, and the medieval ruins of Scotland.

Amid much congenial gaiety, Hendrik and Ian outdid each other recounting the outrageous deeds of their ancestors. By the time Mrs. Brant served a selection of cheeses and fruit, Alison had learned that Ian was almost as well-traveled as she and could speak passable French and German.

"Come to the library, my boy," Hendrik said, rising from the table. "I challenge you to a backgammon match. You do play, don't you?"

"I'm afraid not," said Ian.

"Good. Odds are in my favor, then."

"Hendrik!" Meg gave her brother a meaningful stare. "Ask Brant to play that silly game with you. Alison and her young man want to spend some time together. Without you."

Alison blushed, then glanced at Ian. His expression told her that he hadn't minded Meg's referring to him as Alison's young man. Or being the subject of a family spat. Her cheeks plumped as she stifled a giggle.

"It's only one match," Hendrik retorted. "Alison can watch us if she'd like."

"I don't mind if they play." Alison patted Meg's arm and caught her gaze. "Let's go upstairs for a few minutes."

Meg nodded her understanding, just as Alison expected she would, before turning back to Hendrik. "Enjoy your game, gentlemen," Meg said. "We'll join you soon."

Alison flashed a smile at Ian before Hendrik herded him toward the library. "One of the oldest board games in the world, backgammon."

"Is that so?"

The dining room door closed behind them and Alison cradled her head in her hands.

Meg pressed a cool hand against her forehead. "Do you need to lie down?"

"No. It only hurts a little."

"Where's your pain medication?"

"I don't want to take it. Not tonight. It makes me so drowsy."

"What can I do for you?"

"I thought if I could freshen up. Put on a different dress." Alison flicked her skirt, a yellow dotted swiss that was fine for everyday, but not for entertaining guests. Especially not a guest as special as Ian.

The corners of Meg's mouth turned up in a sweet smile. "A new dress always makes me feel better."

Alison gently clasped Meg's hand. "I'm sorry for . . . how I've been the last few days."

"There's no need —"

"Yes, there is. I've behaved abominably." She sighed and bit her lip. "I feel so . . . lost. And afraid."

"We live in fearful times." Meg brushed Alison's bandage with her fingertips. "I'm only thankful we didn't lose you. Even if it means putting up with your moodiness."

"You've always been so good to me."

"We Van Schuyler ladies have to look out for one another." The teasing lilt in Meg's voice lessened the bittersweet poignancy of her next words. "There are only the two of us."

Alison nodded sad agreement and slowly rose from her chair, sighing from the effort. Linking arms with her aunt, they headed upstairs. When they reached the top landing, Alison spontaneously kissed her aunt's cheek. "Thank you."

"For what?"

"For Ian."

CHAPTER THIRTEEN

After losing the backgammon match, two games to one, Ian followed Hendrik into the parlor. His heart did a backflip at the sight of Alison perched on the window seat, wearing a sapphire-colored dress that deepened the blue sparkle of her eyes. A narrow silk scarf, arranged as a headband, hid most of the bandage.

Before Hendrik could relax in his favorite chair, Meg intercepted him. "I must speak with you. In private."

"Now? But what about our guest?"

Meg gave him an unladylike jab. "Hendrik, you promised."

"So I did." He waved his pipe stem at Ian. "If you get bored with Alison's company, come to the kitchen and we'll raid Mrs. Brant's pantry."

"I'll do that." Ian chuckled as Meg rolled her eyes. Without Alison, the last hour had been torture. Not that he hadn't enjoyed playing backgammon with her grandfather. After the convivial dinner and quiet game, Ian believed he had passed a test devised by the older gentleman. "I can't thank you enough for allowing me to stay the night."

"We're very glad to have you with us." Meg smiled at him. "We'll say good night now."

"Thank you," said Ian. "Good night."

Hendrik crossed to Alison and kissed her forehead. "You look lovely, *mijn schatje.*"

"Good night, Opa."

"Hendrik!"

"Coming, coming." He winked at Ian before taking his sister's arm and escorting her from the room. As they disappeared into the hall, Hendrik's booming voice rang out. "Better a Brit than a Prussian," followed by a loud *shhh* from Meg.

Ian glanced at Alison and couldn't help laughing at the mortified look on her face.

"They aren't very subtle," she said apologetically.

"Wait until you meet my family. I'm sure they'll find ways to embarrass me."

A shadow crossed Alison's face. "Shall I meet your family?"

"I hope so. Someday."

"Someday." She stared out the window a moment before turning to him. "Let's not talk of the future. Not tonight."

The pleading look in her eyes pressed against Ian's heart. Squatting in front of her, he took her hands in his and gained courage when she didn't pull away. "I know why you're afraid."

"I don't think you do."

"You mean the Van Schuyler fate?" At her surprised expression, he hurried on. "Your aunt told me when I asked about the painting." He nodded toward the damaged *Girl in the Garden,* still propped on the easel in a corner.

She stared at the painting and Ian watched her closely as a confusing array of emotions settled into sad resignation. "We don't usually talk about it."

Ian searched for the right words to free Alison from this strange superstition that held her so strongly in its grip. He had tried, ever since she waved good-bye to him in London, to come up with a logical explanation for her misgivings. But Tante Meg's revelation had defied anything he could have imagined. He wished Alison could dismiss it all as nonsense, though he understood why she could not. After all, she had endured the sting of losing her mother and being abandoned by her father.

Still holding her hands, he squeezed

beside her on the narrow seat and followed her gaze to the painting. "Your parents must have loved each other very much. You can see it in her eyes."

"They did."

"What happened to her?"

"Appendicitis. The doctors operated, but it was too late." She clutched his fingers. "I had just turned five. I remember she made this beautiful cake for my party. It had pink icing with strawberries and chocolate curls. And five pink candles. We were all so happy."

Silence filled the room for a moment as Ian chose his words with care.

"I don't think she would have traded a few years with you and your father for a long life without that kind of happiness." He tried to see her face, to gauge her reaction, but her head was bent. "Neither would I."

She looked at him then, and as he gazed into her eyes, he descended into a frightening depth of longing for this woman, feeling the same exhilaration as when he dove off a high seaside cliff into a tumbling surf. He inhaled and cupped her chin between his fingers. "We belong together, Alison. No matter what."

"Another piece of pie?" Alison offered. They

had migrated to the kitchen when Ian's stomach unromantically grumbled.

"No." Ian patted his stomach. "Two were plenty."

Alison started to gather up their used plates, but he stopped her. "Let me do that."

"No, I'll do it."

His eyes narrowed and she laughed at his attempt to look stern. "I insist," he said. "You look tired."

"I guess I am." She hated admitting it, but her eyelids felt heavy and the pain in her head had grown from a dull throb into a sharp, persistent ache.

"How's your head?"

"Fine."

"Liar."

She shrugged and gave him a grim smile. "Guilty."

"Are you taking anything for the pain?"

"Dr. Meijer left something. But it makes me sleepy so I didn't take it." She smiled up at him as he stacked the dishes and gathered the silver. "I don't want to miss a minute with you."

"Nor I with you." He glanced at his watch. "It's almost midnight."

"When do you have to leave?"

"The time zones work in my favor. The flight leaves at 15:20 Holland time and arrives at the base at 15:05 British time." Ian carried the dishes to the sink and Alison yawned while his back was turned.

"I almost forgot." Ian returned to the table and touched her shoulder. "I have something for you. Wait here."

Alison watched him disappear through the swinging door. While she waited for him to return, she pinched her cheeks, willing herself to stay awake awhile longer.

Ian returned and handed her a slender package.

"A present?" She looked at him questioningly as he sat diagonally from her.

"I got a letter from Abraham Talbert, Josef's uncle. He asked me to give this to you."

Alison unwrapped the package. "How is Josef?"

"Seems to be doing fine. He framed your sketch and hung it on his wall." Ian pulled a folded envelope from his shirt pocket and laid it on the table. "Here's the letter if you'd like to read it."

She opened the box and found a silver Montblanc fountain pen inside. Her initials were engraved near the base in an elegant script. "What a generous gift."

"I have one too." Ian held up his own gold monogrammed pen. "We can use them to write to each other."

A shiver raced up Alison's spine, a fear or foreboding that made her voice quiver. "Will you write me?"

"You know I will, Alison." A promise shone in his eyes. "Every chance I get."

Without a word, Alison slipped her pen in his shirt pocket and placed his pen in her box. "Someday we'll trade back again."

The corners of Ian's mouth lifted in the mischievous grin that never failed to tilt her heart. "Wanna bet?"

The next morning, Alison awoke with Ian's departure time looming before her like a dark beast. She longed to give him a tour of Rotterdam's historic center and her family's gallery. Not only the displayed paintings, but also her studio with its bright watercolors. To share her private world with him. But that would have to wait till later, after church and Sunday dinner with Opa and Tante Meg.

During the service, she joined Ian in quietly singing the familiar hymns in English, an intimate time of worship, as all around them Dutch voices sang praises to their Heavenly Father.

Alison had spent countless Sundays in the medieval Grote of Sint-Laurenskerk. But with Ian beside her, near enough for her sleeve to brush his, to smell the clean aroma of his soap, the sanctuary seemed strangely unfamiliar and new. Perhaps God was giving her His blessing. Maybe a life with Ian, worshiping each Sunday in this church, was what God planned for her future.

But how could it be? Not when Ian had an estate to inherit. And no doubt a church of his own near Kenniston Hall. Perhaps one even older than this fifteenth-century Gothic tower. The Van Schuyler fate didn't need to separate them. Their long family legacies already did.

As the minister preached, Alison prayed for answers, lifting her heart to God when the right words were impossible to find. A prayer for freedom from the family fate. A plea for Ian's safety whatever the future held for him.

Returning home, they found Etienne Duret waiting for them in the parlor, hands clasped behind his back.

"Good, you're home," he said. "The British prime minister is about to speak."

Brant fiddled with the knob on the radio console as his wife hovered nearby. Alison crossed her arms, bracing herself against bad news. Stepping close, Ian put his arm around her waist, his body tense against hers. The radio crackled, then cleared as Brant adjusted the volume. A BBC announcer introduced Neville Chamberlain.

"I am speaking to you from the Cabinet Room at 10 Downing Street," said the prime minister. "This morning the British ambassador in Berlin handed the German government a final note stating that, unless we hear from them by eleven o'clock that they are prepared at once to withdraw their troops from Poland, a state of war would exist between us. I have to tell you now that no such undertaking has been received, and that consequently this country is at war with Germany. . . ."

The dreaded words sliced into Alison's heart. She blindly reached for Ian's hand and gripped it until her knuckles turned white. The prime minister's next words were lost to her as her thoughts turned inward. What she feared most was happening. Ian was going to war, and she might never see him again. The barrier she had broken through only the night before began to rise again, building a shield wall around her fragile heart.

She looked up and met her aunt's tender gaze, silently telling her to be strong for Ian. While the radio droned on, Alison fought her own inner battle. By protecting her heart, she also protected Ian. It wasn't too late to save him from the family fate. But bruising his heart on the eve of battle to protect her own was selfishly cruel.

Ian shifted beside her and Chamberlain's voice intruded on her thoughts: "There is no chance of expecting that this man will ever give up his practice of using force to gain his will. He can only be stopped by force. We and France are today, in fulfillment of our obligations, going to the aid of Poland, who is so bravely resisting this wicked and unprovoked attack upon her people. . . ."

"Our countrymen once again join together," said Duret, looking pointedly at Ian, "to defeat evil."

Ian straightened, as if accepting a call to a tremendous task. "This time, may we put an end to it. Once and for all."

"That is my prayer also."

Alison peered at Ian beneath her lashes, memorizing his resolute jaw, the intensity in his eyes, as the broadcast continued: "Now may God bless you all. May He defend the right. For it is evil things that we shall be fighting against — brute force, bad faith, injustice, oppression, and persecution — and against them I am certain that right will prevail."

Brant turned down the volume, but no one seemed willing to break the somber mood.

A long minute passed; then Ian leaned forward. "I need to return to the embassy. This announcement may have changed my flight time."

"Not before dinner?" protested Meg.

Hendrik reached out a hand toward his sister. "No, Meg. He's right to go."

"I'll drive you if you'd like," said Brant.

"Just to the station if you don't mind." Ian glanced at his watch. "The express line to The Hague runs in about twenty minutes, doesn't it?"

It seemed to Alison that each man in the room checked the time and nodded agreement while she sat still as a statue.

"If you'll excuse me, I'll pack up my gear."

Mrs. Brant offered to prepare a lunch for Ian and headed for the kitchen. Her husband followed her on his way to the garage. Hendrik excused himself and Duret went with him.

Meg joined Alison on the couch. "Your lieutenant is a good man."

Alison nodded. "The best."

"Will you go with him to the station?"

"Yes." Alison bit her lip. "I may never see him again."

"That's true," Meg said thoughtfully. "But your love may protect him. Keep him from reckless deeds."

Alison laid her head on her aunt's thin shoulder. It seemed Meg had read her conflicted thoughts. "I do care about him," she whispered.

"Be brave, my darling," said Meg. "You'll have the rest of the day to cry your tears."

Alison pasted on a smile and stood as Ian entered the parlor, followed by Hendrik and Monsieur Duret.

"Take it and practice," Hendrik said. "And next time we play, maybe you will be the victor."

"Thank you, sir. This means a great deal to me." Ian faced Alison and held up a rectangular leather case with brass hinges. "Look what your grandfather gave me."

"His traveling backgammon set?" Alison's eyes widened. Opa frequently took the portable case with him when he traveled. She remembered how he had taught her to play on the long train ride from Brussels when they first met.

For the next few minutes, Alison was in the midst of a whirlwind as gratitude was expressed and farewells were said. Mrs. Brant scurried in from the kitchen with sandwiches and a slice of apple pie for Ian to take with him.

"Godspeed, my boy," Hendrik said, clasping Ian's hand and gripping his shoulder. "Be safe."

All too soon, Alison and Ian were on their way to the train station. As Brant maneuvered out of the drive into the narrow street, Ian clasped Alison's hand. His gentle grip made her feel cared about and cherished. She tucked the sensation into her heart and refused to dwell on whether he'd ever hold her hand again.

Dread twisted her stomach when Brant parked at the station. After they all got out of the car, Brant and Ian shook hands. "Take care of yourself, Lieutenant."

"I will. Thank you."

"I'll wait here for you, Miss Alison." She nodded, and Brant climbed back into the driver's seat.

"We should say good-bye here," Ian said.

"No. I'll wait in the station with you till the train comes."

"Alison —" he laid his palm against her cheek — "you need to go home. To get better."

"I feel fine."

He leaned forward till his face was barely inches from hers. "Liar," he whispered.

Before she could deny it, he pulled her

close and kissed her. The gentle warmth of his lips sparked a yearning that left her breathless.

"Pray for me."

She wrapped her arms around his neck and pressed her cheek against his. "Every minute."

He drew back and the intensity in his eyes seemed to penetrate into the depths of her spirit. His smile seared into her heart. "I love you, Alison Schuyler."

She tried to tell him that she loved him too, but the three little words caught in her throat. Disappointment flickered in his eyes at her silence and tears moistened her lashes.

"Ian, we can't —"

He put his finger to her lips. "I do, with all my heart. You need to know that." Picking up his bag, he turned to walk away.

She grabbed his arm and stood on tiptoe, kissing the corner of his mouth, pressing her lips against his, desperate to memorize this moment. Only the last boarding call for his train pulled him from her.

"Be safe, Ian. Please be safe."

"As safe as I can be." His grin flipped her heart, and she blinked away tears as she watched him go, his purposeful stride taking him into a frightening future. He turned once, giving her a playful salute, and she waved, smiling bravely until he disappeared from sight.

"Good-bye, Ian," she whispered, certain that the Van Schuyler fate had claimed another victim.

CHAPTER FOURTEEN

APRIL 1940

Alison tapped the bottom edge of the frame, moving it slightly to the left. She steadied the corner and peered over her shoulder at her grandfather. "How's that?"

Hendrik scrutinized the placement of the painting, a geometric assortment of warm colors, while Alison and Monsieur Duret waited for his verdict. "Perfect," he said, without enthusiasm.

Duret climbed down from the short stepladder. "I never thought to see the day when such 'art' graced these walls."

"It's a sacrilege," Hendrik agreed, shaking his white head.

Alison smothered a smile. The painting wasn't to her taste either, but she could appreciate its vibrant energy, the competing hues caught within heavily defined borders. It was what she wished she could find within herself in these days of cold uncertainty.

More than seven months had passed since Ian's visit. In that time, Brant had scrounged the needed materials to retrofit an abandoned air raid shelter with equipment designed to control air quality. The first shipment of twelve Old Masters was securely packed and crated, waiting for night to fall upon the city so they could be hidden from covetous hands.

One at a time, so as not to cause suspicion in their more perceptive clients, each highly valued painting had been replaced by a more contemporary work. The newer pieces exuded a gaiety in their corner of the gallery, but Alison missed the somber portraits and dark landscapes.

She had always felt a twinge of sadness when a sold painting was taken away. It left a vacancy on the wall and in her spirit until another antiquated piece took its place. With so many of the gallery's paintings destined for the shelter, she expected that vacant feeling to persist until each one was returned to its rightful place. Including the damaged *Girl in the Garden* who, all these months later, still rested on the easel in the parlor. Alison steadfastly refused to allow anyone to touch the painting, trusting that

167

only her father could heal his injured masterpiece.

If only Papa would come home. A Christmas package had arrived in January, postmarked from Dosel Azul, Bolivia. Alison searched Hendrik's giant atlas for the town, but apparently it was too small to merit a dot on the Bolivian map. Pieter's letter had asked Alison to join him before more troubles befell Europe. Her reply, that she couldn't leave her opa and tante, came back long weeks later marked *Recipient Unknown*. Hendrik sent out inquiries to various Bolivian officials, but to no avail. Apparently, Papa had once again given in to wanderlust.

Hendrik pulled his pocket watch from his vest and checked the time. "Dine with us this evening, Etienne. Afterward, Brant will drive the truck to the shelter."

"You should stay home, Hendrik." Duret folded the ladder and hefted it onto his shoulder. "Brant and I will secure the paintings."

"I must see to them myself." Hendrik patted his friend's shoulder. "You understand?"

"*Oui.* We are entrusted with a great task."

"May we be worthy of it."

A forlorn look appeared in Duret's brown eyes before he headed toward the utility room. His back seemed burdened by a

168

weight heavier than that of the ladder he carried. The harder he worked to protect the Van Schuyler paintings, the more the long-ago memories of his family's lost gallery seemed to haunt him. Both he and Alison's grandfather had visibly aged during the frozen winter, the coldest in more than a century, as they worked to find a safe haven for the treasured artwork.

"I want to go with you tonight," Alison said, squeezing her grandfather's arm.

"Not this time, *schatje*. Stay home and keep Tante Meg company."

"She can come too."

Hendrik gave a short laugh. "This is not a Sunday afternoon drive into the countryside."

"But it is an adventure."

"One fraught with danger."

"From whom?" Alison made a pouty face, one her grandfather found hard to resist. "The Germans aren't here. They may never come."

"Perhaps you are right." He looked around the gallery, a wistful expression on his face that Alison found endearing, but sad. "All our precautions may prove unnecessary. I will be glad if this is so."

"Holland will stay neutral, won't it? As it did in the last war?"

"I believe so. But Etienne does not. Neither does Brant." He sighed heavily. "I do this more for them than for myself. And I do it for you, of course. I would not risk losing your inheritance."

Alison rested her head on Hendrik's arm. She had heard the discussions, the arguments, on numerous days as the northern wind swept across the frigid countryside. Here, at the gallery's kitchen table over steaming mugs of coffee, and at home, in front of the fireplace in Hendrik's library, the men tried to forecast the future, to plan for the probabilities. They emptied the coffee pot, watched the fiery logs burn to ash, but still they had no answers. Nothing was certain.

Slipping her hand into her skirt pocket, she folded her fingers around her latest letter from Ian. Since mid-September, he had been stationed somewhere along the border between France and Belgium where the biggest danger, to Alison's great relief, appeared to be boredom. With nothing much happening from a military standpoint, pundits had begun referring to the perceived standoff as the Phony War.

His frequent letters gave Alison hope that peace would come soon. She longed for Ian's return, even as she feared it. As long as he stayed away, she could daydream about a future with him. In her pretend world, they laughed, they danced, and the sun always shone. But she shuddered to think how easily that dream could become a nightmare. Or what Ian would feel if he knew that Theodor also wrote her letters. And that she wrote him back. Guilt knotted her stomach.

Hendrik's affectionate pat on her arm jolted her from her thoughts. "Our gallery has survived troubles before. We will survive this, too."

"How long do you think it will be? Until the Masters can be hung again?"

"Only God knows. And He hasn't told me." He pinched her cheek. "Come now. We must behave as if this were any ordinary day and not the day the Van Schuylers tucked their tails."

"Is that what we're doing?"

Hendrik gave her an enigmatic smile. "Have you ever considered the *Mona Lisa* question?"

"You mean her identity? She was a noblewoman, a friend of Leonardo's. At least, that's the prevailing wisdom, though there are other theories."

"No, that isn't it." Hendrik chuckled, then became somber. "This is a philosophical question. The Louvre is on fire and only the *Mona Lisa* or the child standing beside it can be saved. Which do you choose?"

"The other students discussed this sometimes, the year I was at the Académie des Beaux-Arte."

"And you did not?"

"No. It's a meaningless hypothetical."

"But what if it wasn't? What if you, in a split second, had to choose?"

"Naturally, I'd choose the child."

"And yet you stepped between a gun and a painting. A painting of much less value than the *Mona Lisa.*"

"Not to me."

"So, the answer depends on the painting?" Hendrik's expression turned grim as he glanced at the narrow scar that creased Alison's temple and disappeared beneath her hair. She touched the ridge in a fluttering, self-conscious gesture.

"Perhaps it also depends on the child," he said gently, then sighed. "Since the days of Rembrandt and Vermeer, we have devoted our lives to the art of our people. Tonight we hide a few of them away. It's in our blood, *schatje,* yours and mine.

He paused, pulling his empty pipe from a pocket. "So if we were at the Louvre, without a moment to think, what would we protect?"

Alison felt a chill as she thought of a world devoid of the *Mona Lisa*. Could she let it burn? The question repulsed her, and she couldn't voice an answer.

CHAPTER FIFTEEN

Despite all her pleading wiles, Alison couldn't persuade her grandfather to change his mind. She stayed home that evening, driving Tante Meg to distraction with her restless pacing. Hendrik and Brant returned near midnight, joking about their unnecessary precautions.

"The paintings belong to us. Why can't we drive them around in the back of a truck if we want to?" Hendrik chuckled.

"But keeping it a secret makes it more fun, eh?" Brant winked at Alison.

"Next time we go in daylight." Hendrik puffed on his pipe. "I didn't think we were ever going to find that turnoff to the shelter."

"Just as long as I can go too," Alison said, crossing her arms and sticking out her lower lip in a pretend pout.

Two weeks later, on a rainy Sunday afternoon, Hendrik handed her a small black spiral notebook and told her to change into work clothes. "Wear boots. And bring your camera."

In less than thirty minutes, Alison found herself wedged between Hendrik and Brant on the bench seat of a beat-up produce truck. Brant had bought it earlier that spring and covered the bed with wooden framing and heavy canvas. Several crates, packed with paintings, sculptures, and objets d'art, were secured in the back. Three of the crates belonged to the Van Schuyler gallery. The rest were from two other galleries whose owners, longtime colleagues and sometime rivals, had contributed to the retrofitting of the air raid shelter.

Brant drove along side streets until they were out of the city, then headed northwest along narrow country lanes. Alison bounced between the two men as Brant maneuvered the truck around the worst of the muddied ruts. After about half an hour of driving past colorful tulip fields and low-lying vegetable farms, Brant turned into a grass-covered path practically hidden behind thick hedges. He drove a few more kilometers, then parked alongside the shelter, a relic dating back to before the War to End All Wars.

Leaving Brant to unload the crates, Hendrik led Alison to the newly hung door, custom-fit and made of thick oak. After unlocking it, he stepped inside the dim interior and pulled the chain dangling from a single bulb in the low ceiling. Alison followed him, her camera bag slung on her shoulder, and blinked as her eyes adjusted to the poor lighting.

"We created a room over there." Hendrik pointed toward the rear of the shelter, where a second oak door was set in a wall of concrete blocks. He unlocked it and reached inside to turn on the lights. A string of bulbs, stretching from one corner of the room to the other, lit up the space.

Machinery similar to that she had seen in the Welsh quarry purred in a corner. Metal rods with outstretched extensions, resembling sculpted trees, were braced to the floor. One of them held a few of the paintings that Hendrik had previously brought from the gallery. The rest of the paintings hung on the concrete wall.

As Brant brought in the crates, Hendrik unpacked them. Alison photographed each item and assigned it an alphanumeric code that indicated the owner's gallery. On a separate piece of paper in her black notebook, she wrote the name, artist, and a detailed description of each piece. On a master sheet, she listed the assigned codes and individual pieces for the three galleries. The work was tedious but rewarding. Her contribution to the preservation of Holland's art might be small, but it was worthwhile. And the intrigue added its own aura of excitement.

After Alison checked the items against the lists provided by the other owners, Hendrik and Brant carefully packed them in labeled crates. Some items were either attached to one of the metal rods or hung on the wall.

Alison inventoried the last item, a porcelain pitcher dating to the seventeenth century, and handed it to her grandfather. He wrapped it carefully in packing materials and laid it beside other fragile items in one of the crates. Brant nailed it shut and stenciled the lid with the date — May 5, 1940 — and the code referring to its contents. Before he finished the last number of the code, Alison snapped his picture.

"What did you do that for, Miss Alison?"

"It's for your grandchildren."

Brant rubbed his sleeve across his forehead. "What grandchildren?" His only son seemed to prefer life on a fishing vessel in the North Sea to a home on the mainland with a wife and children.

"Will is going to change his mind someday. When the right girl comes along."

"I hope you're right." Brant packed up his tools.

"I'm sure I am." Alison glanced around the room, at the paintings once proudly displayed on gallery walls now attached to concrete. At the stacks of stenciled crates and the gleaming steel machinery. "Do you mind if I take photos of the room, Opa?"

"Quickly. It's getting late and I don't want to be gone much longer. Meg will worry."

Standing in each corner of the room, Alison focused her lens on the opposite corner and snapped the shutter. "There's enough film for one more shot." She smiled her sweetest smile. "I want a picture of my two favorite men."

"Do you hear that, Brant? Today we are her two favorite men," Hendrik said teasingly. "But when her British soldier returns, what will she say then?"

"She will forget all about us."

"Never!" Alison laughed, but only because they expected it. Their teasing, though well-intentioned, probed the tender, confused places in her heart. She hid her discomfort by giving them orders, posing them beside one of the metal trees. They stood, stiff and ill at ease, while she adjusted the lens.

Even in the clothes of a laborer, Opa

somehow managed to look dapper and prosperous. His mere presence dominated the shot. Alison shifted the focus to place Brant slightly in the forefront of the frame. "Smile," she said, then snapped the shutter.

Brant parked the truck behind the garage, and they entered the house through the back porch. Gerta Brant opened the door from the kitchen as they took off their muddied boots. "About time you got back," she scolded. She appeared relieved to see them, but a slight tremor sounded in her voice and tension showed in her usually warm eyes.

"How long before supper?" Hendrik patted his stomach, apparently oblivious to Mrs. Brant's mood. "It won't take us long to change, will it, Alison?"

"Sir." Mrs. Brant's hands twisted her white apron as she faced Hendrik. "Miss Meg asks that you and Miss Alison come directly to the parlor."

Alison touched Mrs. Brant's arm. "Is something wrong?"

"Please, miss." Her eyes darted from Alison to Hendrik. "Miss Meg is waiting."

Hendrik slid his feet into a pair of cloth slippers. "Come, Alison," he said, taking her by the arm. "Let's see what has your tante in such a dither."

Alison preceded Hendrik into the parlor, and her aunt, a grim look on her face, rose from her chair.

"Alison?" A man stepped forward from the shadows near the fireplace.

She stared at him, taking in his gaunt frame and weary gray-blue eyes, then practically fell into his outstretched arms. "Papa," she murmured. His blond hair, in need of a trim and slightly damp, tickled her nose. He wore one of Brant's shirts and smelled of chamomile soap. His shoulders, once strong and broad, felt thin beneath her embrace.

Behind her, Hendrik gasped.

Pieter stiffened, but he smiled at Alison. "Look at you. So grown up."

"Where have you been, Papa? We've been so worried."

A shadow crossed his face. He turned from her and extended a hand toward Hendrik. "Father."

Hendrik hesitated, then clasped his son's hand. "The prodigal finally returns home."

"If you will allow me."

Alison held her breath as the two men stared at each other. A strange sense of déjà vu swept over her at how closely they resembled each other. In that moment, she could see the man her grandfather used to be and the man her father would someday become.

"This is your home," said Hendrik, his voice husky. "You have always been welcome here."

Pieter's eyes darkened and he opened his mouth, then closed it again, shaking his head. "I don't plan to stay long," he said too brightly.

"Why not?" protested Alison.

Before Pieter could answer, Mrs. Brant appeared in the doorway. "I've laid out a bit of supper on the buffet, ma'am," she said to Meg, casting a curious glance at Pieter. "For whenever you're ready."

"Thank you, Mrs. Brant. A bit of supper is just what we need." Meg turned to the family and gestured toward the dining room. "Shall we?"

Alison clasped her father's frail arm and smiled up at him. He returned her gaze with tender affection, then frowned and touched the pink ridge on her temple. "What's this?"

Momentarily confused, Alison flinched. Apparently Tante Meg hadn't told Pieter about the shooting. But surely he would have asked about the damage to his masterpiece. He had to have seen it. She glanced at *The Girl in the Garden* and knew Pieter did the same.

From the corner of her eye, she saw him clench and unclench his jaw, the way he always did when he concentrated, seeking a solution to a dilemma, the perfect balance of a composition. And she knew from the thrust of his chin when the pieces clicked into an answer.

He lifted her face to his and stared deep into her eye, his own flashing with temper. "Were you there? When that Nazi monster shot my painting?" He touched the ridge again and tears glistened in his eyes. "He shot you, too?"

Alison's throat constricted, and she couldn't speak.

Pieter rounded on Meg. "I can't believe this. We were here all afternoon and you didn't tell me that my daughter had been shot?"

"I'm sorry, Pieter." Meg took a composing breath. "You were so distraught over the painting, I hadn't the heart to tell you about Alison."

Alison wrapped her arm around Pieter's thin chest, and he squeezed her shoulder. "I'm fine, Papa. Honest I am."

"We tried to find you, Son." A hint of accusation tainted Hendrik's words.

"But I had disappeared." The remorse in

Pieter's voice burrowed deep into Alison's heart.

"You're here now," she said. "Nothing else matters."

"Come," Meg urged. "Let's go in to supper." She gave Hendrik a little push and motioned for Alison and Pieter to follow.

"You tried to protect the painting, didn't you?"

"It just . . . happened. I didn't think about it."

Pieter shook his head. "I've neglected you too long, Alison. But things will be different now. I've made plans."

A tense knot, part curiosity and part dread, settled in Alison's stomach. "What kind of plans?"

"Plans for your future." Pieter gave her an encouraging smile. "To keep you safe."

They entered the dining room, and Meg motioned them toward the buffet. Hendrik had already helped himself to a heaping bowl of beef stew from the silver chafing dish. Alison mulled over her father's words as she ladled stew into a bowl for him. Whatever could he mean, plans for her safety? A thread of resentment attached itself to the tightening knot. He had planned for her safety once before and dumped her with a grandfather she'd never met. In fairness, that had turned out all right, but it had been a lousy thing to do.

She placed the stew before him and accepted his thanks with a gracious smile. She'd listen to his plans, but she would decide for herself whether or not to go along with them. Pieter had given up his right to tell her what to do ten years ago when, fighting back tears, she had watched him walk out of that Brussels hotel lobby.

CHAPTER SIXTEEN

During supper, Alison listened spellbound as her father talked about his life in South America. Her imagination overflowed as he described his labors at emerald mines and ancient archaeological ruins. While living in Bolivia, he joined a friend on a ten-day expedition along the Amazon River. But he became deathly ill, and after being diagnosed with malaria, he had spent several weeks in a Brazilian hospital.

By the time he returned to Dosel Azul, his two-room apartment was occupied by a couple of brothers who had no intention of leaving. Homeless and concerned about the news coming from Europe, he worked odd jobs to earn the passage for his return across the Atlantic. Hendrik huffed when he heard this and Alison knew what he was thinking. If only Pieter had asked, Hendrik would have arranged first-class accommodations for his son.

Long after Hendrik and Meg retired, Alison and Pieter stayed up, sometimes talking, sometimes in contented silence. When he asked about a beau, she told him only that she corresponded with a British lieutenant she had met in London. She had no idea what her father would think of Ian, or what advice he would give her. She didn't really know what he thought about anything of importance. The weight of that knowledge depressed her, and when she kissed him good night, it tempered the warmth of her peck on his sun-aged cheek.

The next morning, Alison stifled a yawn as she and Pieter wandered through the gallery. He stopped in front of the display of modern paintings. "So the pretentious Van Schuyler Fine Arts Gallery has finally entered the twentieth century," he said. "Did you bring about this miracle?"

"No, these are only here temporarily."

"What does that mean?"

Alison hesitated, aware that Hendrik had avoided talking about their afternoon trek to the secret shelter during last night's conversation.

"Don't tell me the Masters got shot up too."

Alison folded her arms across her chest. Surely Papa had a right to know about the paintings. They were part of his heritage too. "We've hidden them."

Pieter's eyes widened. "Where?"

"An old air raid shelter between here and Amsterdam."

"It was a wise thing to do." He nodded approval. "Especially after what happened in Poland."

"Opa heard that the Veit Stoss altarpiece has disappeared."

"I heard that too. Along with paintings by Leonardo da Vinci and others. What those brown-shirted brutes didn't steal, they destroyed. All that history and culture . . . demolished." His voice deepened in anger. "Hitler acts as if the whole world is his for the taking."

"The British will stop him. And the French."

"While Holland clings to her historic role as spectator," Pieter said bitterly.

"What else would you have us do?" Hendrik suddenly appeared from behind one of the movable display walls. "Attack the Germans? With what? We have no tanks, no skilled military men."

"That complacency will cost us our lives."

"Only if the Germans invade us."

"Which they've threatened to do."

"Only to frighten the Brit—"

"Stop it!" Alison pressed her fist into her palm. "Please. Neither of you know what the Germans will or will not do."

The men eyed each other; then Hendrik turned to Alison. "You are right, *schatje*. Our zeal has overcome our manners."

Pieter shook his head. "If you don't believe the Germans will attack, then why are you doing this?" He waved his hands toward the wall of modern art.

"I have my opinions, but I don't claim to be infallible," Hendrik said pointedly. "Hiding the paintings is merely a precaution."

"It's not enough."

"You know something more we can do?" Hendrik spread out his hands. "Tell me."

Pieter took a deep breath and glanced at Alison before facing his father. "We can leave."

"Leave?" Hendrik grunted in disbelief. "This gallery? Our home?"

"We can go to New York. Or Australia. Anywhere you'd prefer." Pieter's voice rose in pitch as he paced within the tiny area between the display walls. "You can move the entire gallery. Or sell it and start over. Or retire."

The color drained from Hendrik's face at Pieter's proposal. Alison gently took her opa's arm, offering her support to him against an idea that was akin to heresy.

"Please, Father." Pieter stopped pacing and spoke in a calmer voice. "Think of it as a vacation. When the war is over, you can return."

"Papa, you can't expect him to —"

"No." Hendrik held out his hand, as if he were warding off evil. "It is not to be thought of."

"They're already rationing in England. How long do you think it will be before rationing starts here?"

"We've survived hard times before."

"Stay, then." Pieter pressed his lips together and his expression darkened. "But Alison is coming with me. Tante Meg, too, if she wishes."

Alison started. "I'm not going anywhere."

"You aren't staying here," Pieter said in a tone of voice that reminded Alison of when she was eight and he refused to let her walk to the corner grocery by herself.

She involuntarily stepped backward as her thoughts became a kaleidoscope of confusion. Love for her father collided with love for her opa and all he had taught her. She missed Papa when he was gone, missed him desperately, but it was Hendrik who had given her pride in her ancestry, confidence in her abilities to manage the gallery. She had learned from him that being a Van Schuyler was more than being held hostage to an old family fate, a lesson she had almost forgotten since that day she heard a little boy play his violin at Waterloo Station.

"You don't know what it's like during war, Alison." Pieter's voice took on an urgent note. "I was here the last time Germany tried to take over Europe. Even if the Germans stay out of Holland, I, for one, don't want you living through the shortages, the terror of not knowing if you'll survive."

"You were here?" Hendrik's face reddened. "You abandoned us. On Sunday, July 18, 1915, *you* abandoned us. Your family. Your country."

Pieter's shoulders drooped, as if in surrender. "I had to go. You know why I had to go."

"Yes." Hendrik started to reach for Pieter, then dropped his hand back to his side. He raised his eyes to the ceiling and said in a voice so low Alison barely made out the words: "I know."

Another secret. She glared at both men. Their eyes, already so similar, mirrored the same faraway look. Her anger faded as she sensed the truth. She had seen the look before, not only in their eyes, but reflected in her own mirror. "Mama. You left because of Mama."

Pieter nodded once.

"But I thought you met in Chicago. At a baseball game."

"It was our story." His eyes met hers. "Because that's where our new lives began."

"I don't understand."

"Excuse me, sir." Monsieur Duret hurried toward them. "There is news. The Germans say their occupation will begin on May 8."

"Two days." Pieter gripped Alison's elbow. "We have to leave. This afternoon."

She stared into her father's eyes, so very like her own, then glanced around the gallery. "No," she said firmly. "We have to save the paintings."

By the end of the day, the remaining paintings and sculptures that Hendrik had designated for the shelter had been photographed, inventoried, and crated. Pristine rectangles shone on the walls where the paintings had hung, the spots left bare until more substitutes could be found. Additional art pieces were packed up at the house, including the Frans Hals the Elder portrait of Johann Van Schuyler that had hung above the fireplace.

On Tuesday morning, Pieter and Brant

loaded the crates in the back of the produce truck, then stopped at the other two galleries before driving out to the air raid shelter. Alison had begged to go too, but Pieter wouldn't hear of it. When Hendrik sided with Pieter, Alison reluctantly gave her father the camera bag so he could take photographs of the items from the other galleries. Then she busied herself baking bread with Mrs. Brant until the men returned.

Wednesday dawned bright and clear, the promise of a beautiful day if not for the dread that snaked throughout the land. The hours passed slowly, but the Germans did not appear. As the sunlight dimmed in the west, Hendrik's mood brightened. Alison could see that he felt vindicated in his belief that Germany's threats were meaningless, that the Nazis had too much respect for their northern cousins to invade the Low Countries.

But Pieter remained restless, seemingly unable to accept that they were safe. He had spent a couple of hours that afternoon developing the film in the gallery darkroom so that Alison could create an album of the hidden treasures. Now he paced from the parlor to the library to the kitchen and back again, not settling anywhere for long.

When he wandered back into the parlor

and stood staring out the window, his hands tucked deep in his pockets, Alison joined him. "Sit with me," she said, gently tugging his arm as she lowered herself onto the window seat. "I have something to show you."

"What is it?" Pieter said with little curiosity as he shifted beside her.

Flipping open her sketchbook to the drawing of Pieter in his rowboat, she handed it to him and waited anxiously for his response. His impassive face hid his reaction as he studied the sketch, and her stomach did a flip when finally the corners of his mouth lifted, revealing a tiny dimple in his left cheek.

"It reminds me of a photo," he said.

"I have it in my room."

"Do you really?"

She nodded. "I keep it on my dresser."

"The days I spent in that boat . . ." His voice sounded wistful, as if remembering happier times. "We'd race sometimes, the other lads and me. I almost always won."

Alison smiled, encouraged by the slight change in her father's demeanor. The tension that kept him wound so tightly seemed to have eased as he reminisced about his childhood.

"The drawing has a forlorn quality." He

smiled at her, but sadness shadowed his eyes. He blinked and nudged her with his elbow. "This is very good, Alison. You've got the Van Schuyler touch."

He turned the page and Alison reached for the pad. "You don't want to see the others."

Pieter clutched the pad as he twisted from her. He peered back at her over his shoulder. "Of course I do."

"Papa, please."

"Who's this?" Pieter's eyes twinkled as he held up a portrait of a young man with strong features and a mischievous grin. "Tell me again about this British officer you met."

Alison stared down at her clasped hands. She had dreamed of intimate moments like this with her father. But a rare shyness made it difficult for her to speak.

"I used to make sketches like this of your mother." Pieter cleared his throat. "Seems I couldn't keep her out of my mind."

Alison raised her eyes to *The Girl in the Garden* and felt the warmth of her mother's smile. "How did you meet her?"

"At the gallery." Pieter gave a small chuckle. "I was changing the display in the front window and there she was, standing on the sidewalk watching me. She motioned me to move the painting to the left — a Botticelli — so I did. Then she motioned me to move it to the right."

"And you did?"

"To the exact spot I had it to begin with." He hesitated a moment. "Then she laughed, and I looked into her eyes." He gazed at the portrait on the easel and shrugged. "And I knew."

Alison laid her head on Pieter's shoulder. He'd known, just as she had. No matter how she tried to deny her feelings, they were there . . . in her sketches of Ian, deep within her heart.

"Why did you leave?"

"Her parents were dead. She lived with an uncle, a cruel man." His voice trembled with anger. "He forbade her to see me. He hit her."

An involuntary shiver ran down Alison's spine. She shut her eyes against the brutal image evoked by her father's words and suddenly remembered running toward her mother's outstretched arms, tears streaming down her face because of some long-forgotten hurt. Mama had kissed her cheeks and enveloped her in musical laughter. Alison hugged the memory to herself, a shield against the monster who had inflicted cruelty on her kind, gentle mother.

"I sent her to America. Later I joined her.

It was the only thing we could do."

"And started a new life."

"Yes," he said softly.

Alison fidgeted and took a deep breath. "Would you do it again?"

Pieter stiffened beside her and Alison wished she could disappear into the window seat, dragging the question with her. She opened her mouth to apologize, but her father tapped the drawing. "Where is he?"

"Somewhere in France."

"At least now I know why."

She raised her head and searched his face. The pain in his eyes mingled with resignation. "Why what?"

"Why you won't go home."

"This is my home, Papa. It has been for ten years."

He slipped his arm around her shoulders and pulled her close. Enveloped in his comforting warmth, she breathed in the lingering odors of the photographic chemicals he had used earlier in the day.

"Then it's my home too."

CHAPTER SEVENTEEN

On Friday, May 10, Alison and her family stood outside their home and stared upward as countless Germans descended from the clouds. Their white parachutes appeared angelic against the gloriously blue sky. Planes soared across the heavens and rumbling explosions echoed in the distance.

"They're bombing The Hague," said Hendrik. The stricken look on his face gripped at Alison's stomach.

"Probably the airfields," said Pieter.

Meg nervously fingered the pendant at her neck. "I pray the queen and her family will be safe." Like the vast majority of Dutch families, the Van Schuylers prominently displayed a royal portrait in their home. The long-reigning, strong-willed Queen Wilhelmina had led her people through decades of political and economic difficulties.

"Pray for our safety too." Pieter smiled gently as he put his arm around his aunt's waist and led her toward the house. "We need to get inside."

"The gallery." Hendrik's eyes lacked focus. "I must go to the gallery."

Pieter caught Alison's attention and tilted his head toward Hendrik. She nodded and took her grandfather's arm. "Monsieur Duret is at the gallery, Opa. He'll take care of it until we can get there."

Except for their meals, which Meg insisted they eat in the dining room, the family spent most of the day near the console radio, eager for even the tiniest scrap of news. Hendrik fussed about going to the gallery, but as the German planes buzzed above their industrial city and tanks rumbled on nearby streets, even he had to admit that it was too dangerous to leave the house.

As darkness fell, the city settled into an uneasy quiet. Pieter and Brant, dressed in dark clothes and wearing knit caps, slipped out of the house and across the lawn to the canal. Alison watched from a back window, barely able to discern the men from the shadows of the night, as they paddled away in the rowboat.

"To be young and spry," Hendrik said wistfully.

"To be a man," Alison countered.

"Touché."

They joined Meg and Mrs. Brant, whose hands were busy with needlework, in the parlor. Settling in his chair, Hendrik filled his pipe bowl with tobacco. Alison curled up at one end of the couch and studied the clock. If all went well, her father and Brant would be at the gallery in twenty or thirty minutes. A quick report from Monsieur Duret and they'd be on their way home again. An hour, two at the most.

Exactly ninety-three minutes later, Pieter and Brant came in through the kitchen door. "Duret is fine," Pieter announced. "And the gallery is still standing."

"As it has for three hundred years," said Hendrik.

"And will until the end of time," said Papa.

Over the next couple of days, Alison and her family listened to the scanty radio broadcasts that reported Nazi victory over Holland's ill-prepared military. Numb to the noise of planes, tanks, and gunfire, Alison couldn't concentrate on her watercolors or sketches, so she spent more time than usual helping Mrs. Brant in the kitchen.

Early Sunday morning, Pieter drove his father to the gallery so Hendrik could see for himself that all was well there. Hendrik brought Monsieur Duret back to the house with him so the Frenchman could enjoy a hearty, home-cooked meal. Pieter stayed behind to guard the gallery. He had taken *The Girl in the Garden* with him, promising Alison he would try his best to restore the painting.

A sliver of hope lightened their spirits later that afternoon when they learned that Dutch forces were preventing the Germans from crossing the north bank of the Nieuwe Maas, the broad river that ran through Rotterdam. They listened as the queen, safe in England, broadcast a message of courage and resolve to her people. After the broadcast, Monsieur Duret returned to the gallery and Pieter came home.

Alison sat with her father as he ate a late supper. "What was it like, being in the gallery by yourself all day?"

"Strange." Pieter dipped a thick slice of bread into his potato soup. "Quiet."

"I don't know how Monsieur does it. Night after night." Duret had lived in two adjoining rooms on the second floor of the gallery building since before Alison had come to Holland.

"I think he likes to be alone. Solitude is a salve for some men."

Men of sorrow. Like you. Alison mentally

200

shrugged away the thought and shifted in her seat. Another matter pressed between them, one that had occupied her thoughts throughout the long day.

"Well?" she asked.

Pieter took a sip of the hot tea she had prepared, gazing over the rim of the cup at her. "Well, what?"

"Mama's portrait."

He returned the cup to its saucer, seemingly mesmerized by the tea's dark translucence. "I'm not sure I have the skill. Or the patience."

"But you will try?"

"Does it matter so much?" He leaned back in his chair and looked upward, as if gathering his thoughts. "Isn't it more important that the job is done right than that I do the job?"

Alison stood, rubbing her palms along the sides of her skirt before stirring the soup that remained in the pot. She didn't know the words to express what she felt about the painting. She only knew that it made her ill to think of someone other than a Van Schuyler performing the restoration.

Living in Chicago, her mother had remained an outsider, a name on the branch of the tall family tree, but never truly a part of its heritage, its traditions. Pieter had been her only connection to the Van Schuyler legacy. But even he had turned his back on the family when he went to America. For her sake.

"We owe it to her," Alison said softly.

Pieter carried his cup and saucer to the sink, his back to his daughter. "Then you may have to do it."

"Me?"

"I tried, Alison." His voice quivered. "I really tried. But it's gone."

"What is?"

He spread his fingers, palms up, and examined his hands. When he faced her, his eyes were rimmed in red. Stubble darkened his jaw. "Our gift. I cursed it." He jammed his hands in his pockets and gave a harsh laugh as he turned from her. "And now it curses me."

"I don't believe that. I won't."

He spun back toward her, eyes flashing. "A word of advice to you. Love your art or love that soldier. But don't think you can have them both. It's our greed that destroys us."

Alison stepped back from her father's anger and tried to fit his words into a composition that made sense. But they clashed and jarred, a surreal collage of sharp edges.

"That's the truth behind the cursed 'family fate.' Thinking that because we're Van Schuylers, we can have it all." He rubbed the back of his neck, his anger seemingly spent, then walked past her. At the kitchen door, he hesitated. "Take it all, and you'll wind up with nothing."

Alison's throat constricted as the door closed behind him. Her legs wobbled and she grabbed for a chair, sliding into its solid reality as she labored to breathe. His final words reverberated through her heart, and she fought against them until something else he had said snapped within her.

He couldn't paint? She shook her head. That couldn't be possible. She loosened her grip on the chair's seat and spread her hands before her, fingers stretched, palms up. To lose that tingle when her fingers ached to create what her mind envisioned — nothing could be worse.

Oh, Papa. She moaned. *No wonder you are so lost.*

CHAPTER EIGHTEEN

Alison reclined on the parlor window seat, her back against the side wall so that she could easily see out the panes. Not that there was much to see. Their neighbors no longer gathered on the sidewalk to chat about the weather or each other. Even the squirrels and the birds seemed to be in hiding.

She held a half-finished letter to Ian propped against her knees. According to the radio broadcasts, the Germans had finally attacked the British Expeditionary Force gathered along the French-Belgian border. The Allied battalions were slowly retreating toward France's northern coastline along the channel. Leaning her head against the windowpane, Alison wondered how near Ian was to the front lines of the battle. In the thick of it, she supposed, as she stared toward the sky and dreamed of an end to war.

Two polished black Mercedes drove slowly along the street, and Alison watched with apprehension as they pulled in front of the house. Dropping the stationery on the window seat, she headed for the foyer. Someone pounded on the door, shaking it in its frame. Alison hesitated, then turned as Tante Meg entered the hallway.

"Who is it?" Meg mouthed.

Alison shrugged as the pounding started again. She peered between the shutters covering the foyer window. "It's Theodor." He wore a sharply pressed German uniform, his impatience evident in his stance.

She opened the door. "What are you doing here?"

"Alison." He looked her over, as if ensuring himself she was unharmed, and exhaled in relief. "I must speak with you."

"Please, come in." She stood aside and gestured in welcome.

"Good morning, Count Scheidemann," Meg said, with cold politeness.

"Fräulein Van Schuyler." Theodor acknowledged her with a brief nod, then faced Alison. "Is your grandfather home?"

"He and Papa are at the gallery."

"Papa? Your father has returned?"

"He was concerned for my safety."

"I see." Theodor smiled brightly at Meg.

"Fräulein, would you excuse us? I wish to speak to your niece in private. With your permission, of course."

Alison nodded in response to Meg's questioning glance.

"I'll be in the library," said Meg, "should you need me."

Alison ushered Theodor into the parlor and invited him to sit down.

"I'd rather not. We don't have much time."

"Time for what?"

A shadow crossed Theodor's face as he stared at Alison's temple. She lowered her head and self-consciously touched the ridged scar. He lifted her chin with the tips of his long fingers and genuine concern shone in his eyes. "Your grandfather made a dangerous enemy."

"My grandfather did nothing."

"He tried to have Commander Göring arrested."

Her eyes flashed. "As he should have been."

"Göring will pay for what he did to you." Theodor gently traced the ridge into her hairline. "I promise he will not go unpunished."

She flinched and stepped away.

"You have to leave here, Alison. Immediately. My chauffeur has instructions to escort you to Geneva. I have an apartment there for you."

"I'm not . . . I can't just leave."

"Alison, you don't understand. I can protect you."

"Protect me from what?"

Theodor stepped closer and took her hands in his. "Göring and his men are at the gallery. He is taking everything."

Alison felt the blood drain from her face. "I have to go there."

"No." Theodor kept hold of her hands. "It's too late."

"But what about Opa? And my father?"

"They won't be harmed. As long as they cooperate."

Fear gripped her stomach as she fought to hold back tears. Monsieur Duret and Brant were at the gallery too. She couldn't imagine any of them standing by while Göring looted their collection. *Protect them, Father,* she silently prayed. *Please protect them.*

"Don't despair, Alison." Theodor tenderly touched her cheek. "You have been chosen for a great privilege."

She bit her lip, striving to control her emotions. "What privilege would that be?"

"The perfection of the human race."

She stared at him, trying to reconcile the cultured young man she had met at the Vermeer exhibit with the man who stood before her.

"I know it sounds grandiose," he said sheepishly. "But *der Führer* has a grand vision. You are exactly the type of woman to fulfill this great destiny. Together, we can transform history."

"I'm not a type, Theodor." She pulled away from him and returned to the window. Staring out at the street and hugging her arms to her chest, her thoughts were consumed with the gallery and what was happening there. Foreboding haunted her, and she feared that whatever evil the day held, it was only the beginning of their sorrows.

"True." Theodor stood behind her and placed his hands on her shoulders. "You are singularly talented and lovely. Say you'll come with me."

She shrugged away, unable to bear his touch, and turned to sit on the window seat. Theodor picked up the stationery she had left there and sat beside her. Realizing he held her letter to Ian, she tried grabbing it from him. "Give me that."

He held it out of her reach and his facial muscles twitched, skin reddening, as he read the letter.

"You have no right to —"

"I have every right." He stood, his expression controlled. "Ian? He fights against us?"

"Against those intent on destroying all of Europe."

"Not destroy, Alison. Rebuild."

"All I know is that you've invaded my country. For no good reason."

"I see." He crumpled the letter and Alison watched, mesmerized, as it dropped to the floor.

"As my wife, Göring would not have dared to harm you," Theodor said coldly. "Or your family." He glanced at the fireplace and his eyes narrowed as he focused on the blank wall above the mantel. He faced Alison, and she read the question in his eyes.

But the location of her long-ago ancestor's portrait was none of Theodor's business. And neither was her letter to Ian. Gathering her courage, she stood, posture straight and tall. "Please go."

He clicked his heels and walked smartly to the parlor door, then hesitated and turned inside the frame. The chill in his brilliant blue eyes softened. "I can save you, Alison. All you have to do is come with me." He sounded more like the man she had once been infatuated with than an ambitious Nazi officer. She wished he'd become that man again.

"I belong here," she said, her voice shaking. "This is my home."

He barely nodded and his eyes hardened. "Do what you can to save it. Our bombers will be here at noon."

CHAPTER NINETEEN

Acrid fumes from burning oil stung Ian's eyes as he crouched beside an abandoned supply truck near the French coastline of the English Channel. Beneath the black smoke, pounding waves crashed against the shore, relentless in their arrhythmic pounding. Survivors of the British Expeditionary Force staggered across the exposed ground as German cannon fire exploded around them. Weighed down with combat gear and their boots filling with water, the soldiers waded awkwardly through the surf toward a small flotilla of fishing boats. Farther out from the shore, larger ships waited to take the evacuees home to England.

Somehow he needed to get Mark into one of those boats.

He wiped the sweat from his stinging eyes and crept to the rear of the truck where Mark sat propped against the wheel. Blood seeped from the makeshift bandage, a cotton handkerchief that Ian had stuffed into the bullet wound only a hand's width from his brother-in-law's heart.

"Go, Dev." Mark coughed, and a trickle of blood appeared at the corner of his mouth. "Before it's too late."

"Are you trying to get me in trouble with Trish?" Ian joked. But the same helplessness that had suffocated him when he failed to save his brother clutched at him now. Closing his eyes, he breathed a silent plea for courage.

"Tell her . . ." Mark struggled to speak. "Tell her I love her."

"Tell her yourself." Ian stared skyward as a German Messerschmitt roared overhead and fired at the fleeing soldiers on the beach. A moment later, the late-afternoon sun glancing off their metallic fins, four British Spitfires appeared from the northwest.

The Messerschmitt did a wide U-turn but couldn't outrun the Spitfires. The German fighter exploded in a steel cloudburst that flashed outward in a metal arc. The cannon fire on the ground ceased as the Spitfires zoomed above the German artillerymen.

"It's now or never." Ian grunted as he hoisted Mark across his shoulders, slipping his arm between the captain's legs. He staggered beneath the weight, then caught his balance. Peering over the hood of the truck, he assessed the chaotic retreat and marked the path he planned to take to the coast.

"Stay with me, Mark," he said, taking a precarious step forward. He shifted his brother-in-law's weight and cautiously paced through the scrub. In the shrouded sky, the Spitfires flew in and out of the black smoke as they circled above the rescue vessels.

A few other soldiers emerged from behind abandoned military vehicles and zigzagged across the beach. Ian guessed he wasn't the only one counting on the Royal Air Force to keep the Germans from firing at them.

"Lieutenant!"

Ian faltered and fell to one knee. Browning, the corporal from the base, his babyish face streaked with dirt and sweat, ran toward him. Ian struggled to rise and fell again. Bullets whizzed above his head and he rolled Mark to the ground and stretched across him.

An anguished scream tore the air as Browning grabbed his leg and pitched forward, writhing in the sand. Ian bellycrawled to him, scarcely aware of the thorns and pebbles clawing his chest and thighs.

"My knee," Browning moaned, eyes

squeezed shut.

Ian quickly opened his pocketknife and cut Browning's uniform around his shattered kneecap. The bits of bloody bone and torn muscle caused Ian's stomach to roil, but he swallowed the bile.

"You're going to be all right, chap," Ian lied. How could he possibly get both Mark and Browning to the shore? He glanced back at his brother-in-law, lying still in a patch of scrub, and hurriedly cut a ragged length of fabric from Browning's pant leg. The corporal moaned through gritted teeth as Ian wrapped the material around the destroyed knee.

"That's the best I can do for now. Just hold on, okay?"

Browning grabbed Ian's sleeve, twisting the material in a surprisingly powerful grip, and raised his head. "Don't leave me. Don't leave me here to die."

"The captain will die if I don't get him to the boats." His eyes pleaded with Browning to understand, but the corporal dropped his head to the ground and wailed. "I'll come back for you. I promise."

He clasped Browning's shoulder before running, stooped over, the few yards back to Mark. The captain's shallow breathing barely raised his chest. With a last glance at

Browning, Ian draped Mark over his shoulders again and awkwardly raced toward the boats, his mind focused on nothing more than reaching the shore and his heart fervently praying for a shield from the bullets and the mines.

He waded into the surf, searching the sea for an approaching boat. Two soldiers from his unit, both breathing heavily, caught up to him.

"There," shouted one, pointing to the right. A red-and-white motorboat bounced across the waves toward the shore. "We need to get to that one."

"Take the captain," Ian ordered, lowering Mark into their arms. He took a deep breath and coughed as the smoke-filled air entered his lungs. Scooping up a double handful of the channel water, he splashed it over his face. "See to it he gets on that boat."

"We will, Lieutenant," said the second soldier, Private Gregg. Dirt streaked his freckled complexion and sunburnt nose. Earlier that summer, encamped along the Belgian border, the unit had dunked the boy in a nearby creek to celebrate his twentieth birthday.

Ian turned away and Gregg called after him, "Where are you going, sir?"

"Browning." Ian gestured toward the

scrub. The gunfire, though less frequent, sounded closer. "He can't walk."

"I'll find Browning, sir," said Gregg. "You go with the captain."

Ian shook his head and waded out of the surf. "I made a promise," he shouted over his shoulder. A promise made the day they buried his brother. A promise to protect the people he loved, the people he cared about, no matter the cost.

Head bowed, he ran past several retreating soldiers toward Browning, ignoring the burn in his calves and the ache in his side. He found the clerk half-hidden beneath a thin covering of brush, an indistinct trail showing where Browning had dragged himself. His eyes partially opened, appearing glazed, and his lips moved as if he were reciting an inaudible prayer.

"I'm here, chap," Ian said softly. "Time to go home."

Browning's eyes opened wider and he focused on Ian. "Home?"

"That's right. Are you ready?"

Before Browning could answer, a mine exploded somewhere on the beach. Ian flattened himself on the ground and covered his head as he was pelted with debris. For a brief pause, all was eerily quiet. He raised his head, peering at the line of German soldiers between him and the beach. He glanced backward and his heart dropped to his stomach. More Germans advanced toward them.

They were trapped.

Staying low, he studied the beach again through a gap in the brush, trying to find an escape route through the German line. The men in the channel looked like toy soldiers, the kind he played with as a child, bobbing up and down among the boats sent to rescue as many as possible from their brutal enemy. He couldn't find the two privates who carried Mark, or the red-and-white motorboat.

Brush rustled behind him. As he wheeled around, a bullet ripped across his shoulder. Yelping in anguish, he grabbed at the searing pain. Blood oozed between his fingers, sticky and hot. The stench of seared flesh mingled with blood, the burning oil tanks, the diesel fumes of the boats, the fishiness of the channel. And the smell of death.

Ian heaved, swallowed, and heaved again. Vomit filled his mouth and he spewed it into the dirt. He rolled onto his back with a dull thud and forced his eyes to stay open. Above him, the quarter moon appeared as an ivory crescent against the sunlit sky. If only the God who had halted the sun in Joshua's day would quicken its descent beneath the horizon now. Maybe then, in the fading dusk, he and Browning could slip through the German line and into the surf.

But this twilight hour was not destined for cosmic-size miracles. Perhaps not for small ones, either.

Except for the flotilla of boats, both military and civilian, ferrying Allied soldiers to safety. Except for Mark, heading home on one of those boats. Except for . . . Alison. He shut his eyes, tried to shake her away. To think of Alison during a battle was to break a cardinal rule. But she refused to leave him, her gray-blue eyes willing him to stay strong. To come back to her.

Holland had been invaded, Rotterdam relentlessly bombed. Any letters she had sent to him since then were stuck in a mail bag somewhere, far behind the units fighting for their lives at Dunkirk. But she had survived the city's destruction; of that he was certain. God was not deaf to their prayers. Surely not. Ian groaned, biting the inside of his cheek. *Surely not.*

"Lieutenant?" Browning's voice, though weak, sounded too loud, and Ian realized the gunfire had ceased again.

"I'm here." Ian turned his head toward Browning and their eyes met.

"You shouldn't . . . shouldn't have come back."

"I owed you one."

"Owed me?"

"For getting me on that diplomatic plane to Holland last September. Remember?"

Browning nodded, face scrunched in pain.

"Besides —" Ian grinned — "the captain likes the way you clean his car."

"Wasn't me, Lieutenant." A puckish smile creased Browning's face. "Gave that job to Private Gregg."

Ian snickered. "He's a good man." He raised himself, groaning with pain, so he could see the channel. *Hope he made it onto that boat.*

"Sir." The edge in Browning's voice sounded a warning. Ian glanced at him, then followed his gaze to three Germans coming their way, weapons pointed at them. He reached for his pistol but hesitated when one of the Germans aimed his Karabiner rifle at Ian's belly.

"Do not move," ordered one of them in German-accented English. "You are now prisoners of the Third Reich."

Ian blew out air and dropped his chin to his chest. *A POW.* He turned toward the channel, barely visible between the brush, and a wave of longing washed over him. The boats would return home, leaving him and Browning behind. No more fighting. No more options.

One of the Germans stepped closer and Ian stared at the dirty black boots. He moved his eyes upward, taking in the gray-green uniform, the barrel of the Karabiner.

"Stand up."

Gritting his teeth against the pain in his shoulder, Ian managed to stand, hands half-raised in surrender. The German slung his rifle over his shoulder and took Ian's revolver from its holster. Grinning at his spoil of war, he examined the Enfield, hefting it in his hand and showing it off to his pals. Then he pointed it at Browning. "You. On your feet."

Ian reached toward Browning, but the German pressed the Enfield against his stomach. Ian glared at him. "His knee is shattered. He needs help."

"It is a long march to the transport trucks." The German arched his brow. "Will you help him each step?"

Ian subtly straightened and his eyes never wavered from the German's malicious smile. "Each and every one."

The German tilted his head, as if considering. "I think not," he said and in one smooth motion fired the revolver twice into

Browning's chest. Ian lunged for the shooter, but another German slammed him with a rifle butt. Ian staggered but did not fall. He refused to fall in front of these murderers.

"If you do not wish to join your friend," said the German, "you will march. That way." He gestured away from the beach.

Ian stared at Browning's lifeless body, then bent down and closed the corporal's eyes. "I'm sorry, chap," he whispered. "Sorry I didn't get you home."

CHAPTER TWENTY

Theodor flipped through the stacks of framed paintings that leaned against a wall in the Berlin warehouse. "These are all the paintings from the Van Schuyler Gallery?"

"From the showroom, yes," said Herr Wilhelm Gerrits. His career as an assistant curator at the Rijksmuseum in Amsterdam had been cut short when a prized Egyptian scarab had mysteriously disappeared. But the art connoisseurs of the Third Reich valued his expertise in establishing provenance and valuations. "The paintings taken from the upper rooms are in those crates." He pointed to a half-wall of crates that formed an alcove for the loose paintings.

"Is there a catalog?"

"No, sir. Only an inventory list."

Theodor held out his hand.

"The list is in the office, Count Scheidemann." Herr Gerrits bowed. "If you'll excuse me . . ."

With a wave of his hand, Theodor dismissed the overfed minion and focused again on the line of paintings. Several of these, he would swear an oath on it, had not been hanging in the gallery showroom last August. And several of the paintings he had seen, even admired, that day, were not in the stacks.

That day. Again he saw Alison, her blue eyes flashing with anger, throwing herself between Göring and her mother's portrait. As if he were an indifferent spectator, he also saw himself dropping the sculpture and grabbing for Alison. But the bullet sped faster, and all he could do was kneel beside her, to cradle her bleeding head in his lap.

He dismissed the memory, vanquishing it with Prussian resolve, and focused on his duty. The missing paintings. Perhaps Hendrik had sold them, but Theodor's intuition told him otherwise. What he'd refused to acknowledge when he saw the blank space above the fireplace in Alison's parlor could no longer be ignored.

Herr Gerrits appeared with a thick folder. "The Van Schuyler inventory, sir."

Theodor scanned the first page. With typical German efficiency, the typed list described each piece of art, the artist when known, and any other pertinent information. The items taken from the showroom were listed first, then the items taken from the other rooms in the gallery. He flipped through the pages, scanning each one, till he came to the document titled "Third Floor Studio."

The first entry caught his attention. Though untitled, the description could only be of *The Girl in the Garden,* its damage duly noted. The following entries described watercolors, each painted by the same artist: Alison Schuyler.

Theodore slipped the studio document from the file and skimmed through the rest of the folder. The final document recorded the Van Schuyler sales and purchases over the past year as indicated by receipts taken from the gallery. Frowning, Theodor examined the list more carefully. The most recent purchases described the contemporary paintings he had just seen in the stacks. But he could only find a sales record for three of the paintings he remembered seeing at the gallery. One of those was for *A Young Lady Reading,* the painting he himself had purchased.

"They hid the paintings," he muttered.

"Excuse me, sir?"

"Nothing." He half-smiled, pleased to have deduced a secret that Göring and his sycophants didn't even know existed. He also found himself intrigued by Alison's cunning. The lady had depths beyond the Aryan ideal of beauty and talent he had envisioned. He would play her hide-and-seek game. And he would be the victor.

"Is there anything else, sir?" The insincerity of Herr Gerrits's groveling tone irked Theodor.

"Do you have more urgent business needing your attention?"

"Not at all, sir."

"I thought not." Theodor handed him the studio document. "Where are these items?"

Herr Gerrits examined the list, comparing its code to markings on the crates until he found the right ones. "These three."

"Are you certain? Only those three?"

"Do you wish them opened, sir?"

Theodor thought quickly. He wanted those crates. But he couldn't let Göring know or the Luftwaffe commander would certainly take them for himself. It was better to cut Göring out completely.

"Do you have a truck I can borrow, Herr Gerrits?"

The round little man blinked his myopic eyes. "Yes, of course we have trucks, but —"

"Good." Theodor took the studio list,

folded and pocketed it. He motioned toward his adjutant, waiting unobtrusively several yards away. "My lieutenant will oversee the loading of the truck and then you will give him the keys."

"Count Scheidemann, I must protest. This is highly irregular."

"Do not fear, Herr Gerrits. The truck will be returned."

"It is not the truck that concerns me."

Theodor sighed heavily. "Tell me. What does concern you?"

Gerrits wheezed. "The paintings."

"What paintings?"

"Count Scheidemann, please. Herr Göring has a special interest in this collection. He will be quite displeased if the inventory does not agree with the listings."

"This is the complete Van Schuyler file, is it not?" Theodor handed Gerrits the folder.

"Except for . . ." Gerrits gulped. "The document you . . ."

"Herr Gerrits," Theodor said with great patience. "Does the Van Schuyler folder not include all the lists for the crates you have stored here? If not, perhaps Commander Göring should be advised of your carelessness."

"There is no carelessness, Count," said Gerrits, in a defeated tone of voice.

"I didn't think so." Theodor smiled broadly and turned to his adjutant. "My business here is finished. Do not let my crates out of your sight, Lieutenant."

"No, sir."

Theodor strode away, then turned as if something had just occurred to him. "Herr Gerrits, I own two or three paintings that no longer interest me. I will gladly pay a generous commission to someone who could arrange their private sale. Are you interested?"

"I would be honored, sir."

"Excellent. I will send an advance with the lieutenant when he returns the truck. A gesture of my goodwill."

"Thank you, Count Scheidemann. You can be sure I will do my best."

"And I can count on your discretion?"

Herr Gerrits nodded. "To the fullest."

Theodor gave him a sharp salute and whistled as he left the warehouse. Alison's watercolors now belonged to him. More importantly, so did *The Girl in the Garden*. Alison had risked her life trying to protect the painting. What would she do to get it back?

CHAPTER TWENTY-ONE

Alison wandered to the rim of the canal where the rowboat, still in one piece, floated serenely on the calm water. She was tempted to climb inside, untie the knot, and let the boat drift along the city's canal system to wherever the flow carried her. To never look back.

Instead, she sat on the embankment and slipped off her shoes. Rippling the surface of the sun-warmed water with her toes, she stared, transfixed, at the expanding circles, the droplets that slipped from her ankles when she lifted her feet.

Staring into the canal, she could pretend the stately old brick house still stood behind her. Could pretend that her home, like so much of Rotterdam, had not been demolished by German bombs. She could pretend that Gerta Brant still baked her delicate pastries in the kitchen, that Tante Meg still embroidered in the parlor.

Her fingers caressed the old-fashioned locket she now wore, knowing she couldn't spend all day staring into the canal. She avoided looking at the rubble on the opposite bank as she gazed upward to the tranquil sky. Innocent clouds scampered across a crystalline-blue field.

Alison mentally traced the bright vision, ignoring for a moment its stark opposition with dark earthly reality. Then she prayed for God to repeat His ancient miracle and stop the sun in its path. Because if He didn't, the sky would darken into night. Before dusk came, she had to ride her bike through the city's treacherous streets back to the gallery. Past piles of brick and stone, the jagged walls and bombed interiors of her home and those of her neighbors. Past German patrols.

She sighed an apology for her foolish whim. Miracles neither large nor small had fallen on Rotterdam the last couple of weeks. Only bombs.

"Mind if I join you?" Without waiting for an answer, Willem Brant settled beside her, half-reclining and propped up on one elbow. He'd arrived at the gallery a few days ago, too late for his mother's funeral, but not too late to sift through the skeletal remains of his childhood home. Three years older than Alison, he'd paid scant attention to "the little miss who came all the way from America," as his mother called her when she first arrived at the canal house. But by the time he had left home, drawn to a fisherman's life beside the freezing waters of the North Sea, he and Alison had become the siblings neither had.

"You shouldn't come here by yourself." Will plucked a blade of grass and positioned it lengthwise between his thumbs. "The streets aren't safe anymore. Not with those Nazi goons on every corner." He placed his thumbs to his lips and blew against the grass, creating a piercing whistle. "Can you still do that?"

Accepting his challenge, Alison selected a broad blade. She held the whistle for several seconds, then dropped the blade as she remembered the shrill whistle of the pompous official at Waterloo Station.

Will tapped her elbow to get her attention and raised his eyebrows.

Tucking her knees against her chest, Alison wrapped her arms around her shins. "There was this boy, Josef. At the train station the last time I was in London." She explained about the Kindertransport, the cardboard number, and the violin solo. "I didn't understand how parents could send their children so far away. But now, after all this . . ." She gestured toward the broken houses across the canal.

" 'How doth the city sit solitary,' " quoted Will, " 'that was full of people! how is she become as a widow!' "

"Did you write that?"

"You're a silly goose." Will lay back in the grass, arms folded beneath his head. "It's from Lamentations. Jeremiah was referring to Jerusalem. But I think it describes Rotterdam, too."

The poignancy of the verse caught in Alison's throat as she silently repeated the prophet's words. *"How doth the city sit solitary that was full of people!"*

Her home was gone. Her five-hundred-year-old church heavily damaged. Exploding bombs and raging fires had destroyed more than twenty-five thousand homes, churches, schools, and stores. Even a hospital had been hit, the bomber ignoring the giant red cross painted on its flat roof. The death count grew daily as missing loved ones were found beneath bricks and timber.

"Tante Meg begged me to stay home," Alison said softly as she clasped the locket in her palm. "We argued."

The grass rustled as Will sat up and scooted next to her.

"But I had to go to the gallery. I had to see it for myself."

Will rested his arm across her shoulders and pulled her close. "It's a good thing you did. Otherwise you'd have . . ." His voice broke and he cleared his throat. "God protected you, Alison. It was a miracle you weren't killed too."

A miracle? No. She refused to see her survival as anything except a monstrous mistake born of her own wayward selfishness. She deserved her punishment.

"I never got to tell Tante Meg I was sorry," she confessed, pressing her tear-streaked face into Will's shoulder. "And now it's too late."

The days after Ian's capture slipped by in a monotonous blur. The Germans forced him and their other prisoners to march along the battle-scarred roads southeast toward Germany. At night, he shivered on the cold ground until he fell into a restless sleep. A couple of times, he and the others were herded into nearby barns, where the sweet-smelling hay provided as welcome a comfort to his weary body as a down-filled mattress.

His meager rations scarcely eased the hunger that gnawed at his belly, but those who didn't march were mercilessly shot.

So Ian marched.

He journeyed through Belgium, barely aware of changes in the landscape or the days of the calendar. He experienced only the heat of the day, the chill of the night, and the emptiness of his stomach. His shoulder, medically treated at the first gathering post, constantly ached. But so did the rest of his fatigued body.

At a collecting point near a broad river, the Germans divided the prisoners by nationality. Barges and lorries carried away several of the soldiers. Ian and his fellow Brits climbed into cattle trucks covered with heavy canvas. Despite the jostling, he managed to doze, finding respite in sleep.

On the afternoon of the fourth day, the convoy stopped in the courtyard of a medieval castle. Ian hopped down from the truck bed and quickly scanned his surroundings, memorizing as many details as he could. The square castle overlooked a wide river. A town, with the settled look of age, spread across both banks.

"Any idea where we are?" he asked no one in particular.

"Laufen. In Bavaria." Captain Mitch Harris, his right arm in a sling, gestured toward the castle. "This used to be the country estate of the archbishop of Salzburg. Fifteenth century."

Ian stared across the river, gauging its width and current. "Austria?"

Captain Harris nodded. "Until about a century ago, boats transported salt along the Salzach River. Laufen thrived on the salt trade until the railroads came along."

"You've been here before?"

"Years ago. My grandmother was Austrian."

German guards emerged from the gated archway to take custody of the Allied prisoners. Four of them held the leashes of large, snarling shepherds. Others sauntered in front of the POWs, chanting, *"Für Sie der Krieg ist vorbei."*

For you, the war is over.

A pimple-faced private brandished his Karabiner and sneered in Ian's face. *"Für Sie der Krieg ist vorbei,"* he taunted.

Ian calmly held the adolescent's gaze. "You're a brave one, aren't you?"

The private's eyes flickered and Ian hardened his own. The kid involuntarily stepped back and his face reddened. He puffed out his chest and his Adam's apple bobbed in his scrawny throat as he shouted the phrase again. On the *Krieg,* his voice cracked. Ian's mouth twitched, while the prisoners on either side of him chuckled.

Anger replaced humiliation on the kid's face. When he swung his rifle butt forward, Ian was ready. He sidestepped the blow and the kid stumbled. Before he landed on his face, Ian caught him. The prisoners laughed and the guards shouted as the kid awkwardly steadied himself. He backed up and pointed the Karabiner at Ian.

"Achtung!" a firm voice commanded, rising above the melee.

Both the German guards and the British prisoners immediately snapped to attention. The private nervously shouldered his rifle, and Ian showed no emotion.

A German major, tapping a baton against his leg, walked the line between the prisoners and the guards. He halted in front of Ian.

"Your name."

"Ian Devlin. Lieutenant. British Army."

"Where is your home, Lieutenant Devlin?"

Before Ian could answer, Captain Harris spoke up. "He doesn't have to answer that question."

"I meant no harm," said the major. "I once visited your Lake District. You are familiar with it, no?"

"It's a popular holiday spot," said Ian.

"Yes. The fishing was excellent." The

major's impassive expression gave away nothing. But as they sized each other up, Ian could find no enmity in the German's intelligent eyes. When he spoke, his voice was firm but congenial.

"Where did this war end for you, Lieutenant Devlin?"

Ian sensed the major wished a peaceful end to the confrontation, and he also needed to restore the pimpled adolescent's authority over the POWs. Glancing at the kid, whose armpits were damp with sweat, Ian decided to play model prisoner. Besides, he didn't really want to spend his first night at the historic castle in solitary confinement.

"At Dunkirk."

"There is no shame in that, Lieutenant." The major sounded sincere. "Your countrymen exhibited great courage in that evacuation."

"Agreed."

The major nodded, then continued down the line. Finishing his inspection, he centered himself in front of the British officers. "Prisoners of the Third Reich, I am Major Sebastian Krueger. Welcome to *Oflag* VII-C, your home until Germany achieves victory. Forget that it is your duty to escape, and you will live to see that glorious day. Attempt to escape and you will be punished according to the rules set forth by the Geneva Convention."

He paused, letting the threat linger, then smiled cordially. "The International Red Cross will be informed of your presence here. They will advise your superiors and your families. You are dismissed."

One of the guards immediately shouted orders and the prisoners filed between the gates into the castle grounds. Glancing back, Ian saw the major watching him.

"I'm not sure whether you've made an enemy or a friend," said Captain Harris.

"Time will tell," Ian said, scrutinizing the grounds as he walked beneath the archway. If there was a way to escape this Oflag, he was determined to find it.

CHAPTER TWENTY-TWO

The Scheidemann chalet, nestled high in the fir forests of the Bavarian Alps, had served as the private retreat of each reigning count for over three hundred years. For Theodor, being allowed use of the chalet was almost a rite of passage. Amid the chiseled mountain peaks, he felt a deep kinship with the long-ago ancestors who hunted among the trees, fished in the glacial lakes, and fought for honor and glory. Neither the immense Prussian estate nor the sophisticated Munich apartment could provide him with the serene contentment he experienced in this place.

His grief over his father's death had been genuine, and he still missed the older gentleman's presence. But along with the title, he had inherited welcome responsibility and privilege. All his life, he had prepared for this role — attending the finest schools, participating in the estate's management, serving in the German military. His wealth and prestige gave him entry to the finest households throughout Europe, and he was destined for greatness, a rising Aryan star among the shining lights of the Third Reich.

Theodor climbed the front steps to the chalet's veranda and leaned against a corner post. He had driven here straight from a strategy council headed by Hitler himself to finalize Operation Barbarossa, the impending invasion of Russia. With intention, Theodor contributed little to the planning sessions. He preferred to cultivate a persona of thoughtful deliberation and quiet wisdom, qualities the Führer needed in those closest to him. And certainly not seen in that windbag Göring.

The grim-faced Heinrich Himmler, *Reichsführer* of the overzealous *Schutzstaffel,* known more colloquially as the SS or Protection Squadron, had been there too. With eyes bulging behind rimless spectacles, he had systematically spat out numbers. Numbers in the concentration camps, numbers in the ghettos, numbers forced to labor.

Numbers of the dead.

Theodor loathed the man and his cold calculations, even as he accepted the necessity of his work. The future of the Third

Reich required a sacrificial cleansing. In a few years, though, victorious Germany would rebuild Europe. Hitler would no longer require the destructive services of Göring and Himmler. All in good time, Theodor planned to replace first one, then the other.

Gazing at the variegated greens of the mountain firs, he inhaled deeply, breathing in the fragrances of late spring. Here was the simplicity he longed for, without all the trappings that usually accompanied him. A private retreat belonging totally, wholly to him.

Renovating the chalet was his special project, his escape from the more unsavory aspects of the war. *A Young Lady Reading,* the painting he purchased last September from the Van Schuyler Gallery, hung in a sitting room redecorated in masculine browns and warm reds. A similar room, on the opposite side of the hall, was empty except for the crates containing Alison's watercolors and her mother's damaged portrait.

The crates had been delivered and pried open the week before. He had come to the chalet today to sort through the watercolors and choose the ones to display in the dining room. Someday, he hoped to surprise Alison with the exhibit. Surely she'd be glad that he, not Göring, possessed her works.

He emptied the first two crates, propping the frames against the bare wall. The streetscapes portrayed varying aspects of Rotterdam — the gallery exterior, the tall canal house, a corner café. Sunsets and sunrises. Fields of tulips dominated by a stereotypical windmill. Each with a promise of talent, but missing that indefinable spark of genius.

From the third crate, the largest, he unwrapped *The Girl in the Garden.* With somber tenderness, he touched the girl's torn cheek, and the distress he'd felt when Alison fell echoed in his heart. His jaw tightened at the wanton destruction, at the scar that now marred Alison's temple. At his own inability to stop Göring's careless spite.

Examining the painting's wound more closely, Theodor noticed the first tentative attempts at restoration. He realized, in a flash of insight, that Alison's emotional attachment to the painting required her to restore it. But her inexperience made her fearful.

"If she wants to restore you," he said to the girl, "then she shall." He carefully carried the painting into his library and propped it upon the sofa.

Returning to the crate, he knelt beside it and pulled out portraits in oil of Hendrik, Meg, the Brants, and the overbearing Monsieur Duret. Intrigued by the next painting he unwrapped, he held it at arm's length and studied it.

Sparkling sprays of water gushed from a stone fountain surrounded by beds of muted flowers. The setting sun cast its final rays across the scene, lighting prisms in the falling water and lengthening shadows across the park.

Theodor glanced from the watercolor to the first ones he had unpacked, then back again. There was something mysterious about this painting, with its aura of hope intermingled with sadness. Alison's technique hadn't changed, but she had. He turned it over and read the note written on the back: *A park near Minivers (London).*

Minivers. London. As he puzzled over the cryptic note, jealousy slithered into his veins. An interrupted letter. *Dear Ian.*

He stared at the painting of the park and knew, as if he had witnessed it himself, that this Ian had been there too. With Alison. And because of that pretentious Brit, she had found her spark.

■ ■ ■ ■

Alison checked on a pan of cloverleaf rolls in the oven, releasing their yeasty smell into the gallery's kitchen. Just a few more minutes, and they'd be perfect. Will sampled then seasoned a pot of chowder simmering on the stove. They were alone in the gallery, their home since the destruction of the canal house.

Hendrik and Monsieur Duret had driven to Amsterdam that morning to meet with other art collectors, while Pieter and Brant checked on the hidden paintings at the air raid shelter. But all four men were expected to return later in the evening. When they did, Alison planned to heat up the chowder and pop more rolls in the oven.

"Try this." Will thrust a wooden spoon, its bowl filled with soup, toward Alison's mouth.

She sipped the hot chowder while he held the spoon and waited for her verdict. "Mmm. It's delicious."

With a pleased smile, he stirred the pot and sampled it for himself. "Not as good as Mother's," he said wistfully.

"No one made chowder like she did. But yours is much better than mine." She shaped the last of the dough into a miniature roll and wiped her hands on her apron. "I'm glad you're so willing to help with the cooking, Will. We'd be starving otherwise."

"I guess being a bachelor all these years has had its benefits."

"I'm amazed no one has snapped you up."

"They try," he laughed. "But I'm too slippery for them."

"There's truly no one?"

"Aren't you the curious cat?"

"Don't tell me, then."

"There's nothing to tell," he protested, taking bowls out of the cupboard. "I'm still waiting to meet the girl that turns my heart upside down. I won't settle for less."

"Be careful what you wish for, Will. Sometimes an upside-down heart hurts."

"You still haven't heard from him?"

She pressed her lips together and shook her head, intent on counting out two napkins and placing them just so beside their plates. She still prayed that Ian was among the many Dunkirk evacuees, safe and sound in England. But as the days passed with no word from him, her hope was slipping away.

"Perhaps you could write his parents."

"They may not know anything about me."

"You said he had a sister."

"In London."

"Write to her."

Alison met his gaze. "Do you really think I should? That it's proper?"

Will chuckled as he wiped flour from her chin. "Etiquette may be one of the first casualties of war. You write the letter, and I'll figure out a way to mail it."

"You can do that?" She pulled the rolls from the oven and, burning her fingers, arranged them in a wicker basket.

"I may be able to do more than that."

Put on her guard by a curious tone in his voice, Alison looked up from the bread basket. His back was to her as he ladled the chowder into bowls.

"What can you do?"

He carried the bowls to the table. "Sit down and I'll tell you."

She took her seat, and Will folded his hands to say grace. Following his *amen,* he buttered a roll. "Remember when you told me about the Kindertransport?"

"Yes."

"Your father wants me to start our own version."

"Is that necessary?" Alison thought about the children she knew, the sons and daughters of neighbors and customers. She couldn't imagine their parents agreeing to such a plan.

Will shrugged. "He seems to think so. Mostly he wants you out of Holland. He's asked me to take you to America."

"You're to go with me?" She could hardly believe that's what Papa planned. "I thought he wanted to leave too."

"Obviously he's changed his mind."

"I'm not going."

"Perhaps you should consider it. I think we'd all feel better knowing you were safe."

"I wouldn't feel better. If I have to go, we should all go."

Will added homemade raspberry jam to his roll with such care that Alison knew he was gathering his thoughts. "There is work to do here. Necessary work, but dangerous. I won't take you all the way to America, but I can get you to England. You can arrange passage from there."

"What is this work?"

"It takes different forms."

"I want to help."

"This isn't a game, Alison." He stared into her eyes. "And there's much more at stake than hiding a bunch of old paintings."

"They're not just a bunch of old paintings." She frowned, irritated at how easily he dismissed the importance of protecting the Masters.

Will glanced at her scar, and she self-consciously bent her head, hiding it with her hair. He touched her arm and she lifted her eyes to his. "Do you have the courage to risk your life for the children as quickly as you did for that painting?"

Alison wanted to say yes — of course, yes. But how could she know? She pressed her fingers against her scar. It was there because she had acted without thinking. Courage had nothing to do with it. Courage was deliberate, like when Ian stood up for little Josef. The image of the boy's sweet smile as he talked to his hero nestled in her memory.

"Truth be told," Will said, interrupting her thoughts, "we need you. The Nazis are less suspicious of women." He looked at her appraisingly, as if he'd never seen her before. "You're pretty enough to be a distraction."

Then he smiled sheepishly. "Please don't tell your father I said that."

"You'll let me join your work?"

"I'd like to. But your father will never agree."

"It's not his decision. It's mine," she said firmly. "Let me help the children." Somehow she'd find the courage she needed. For Josef's sake. And for Ian's, wherever he might be.

CHAPTER TWENTY-THREE

APRIL 1941

Freed from solitary confinement, Ian walked ahead of the guard into Major Krueger's office located on the second floor of the German wing of the castle. At one time, the room had been a library with shelves against three walls. On the fourth wall, tall windows provided a view of the inner courtyard formed by the four wings of the square castle.

A fireplace, situated between the windows, confined a short stack of burning logs. Standing just inside the door, Ian could barely feel the fire's meager heat. After twelve days locked in a stone cellar, with only a tattered blanket for warmth, he longed to stretch his chilled limbs before those flames.

The major sat behind a plain pine table more suited to the kitchens than the archbishop's fifteenth-century library. He gestured for the guard to leave and shut the door behind him. Leaning back in his wooden chair, the major gave Ian the once-over and waved toward the fireplace. "Warm yourself, Lieutenant. As best you can in this dismal place."

Ian crouched before the fireplace, grimacing as his knees creaked. Extending his chapped hands to the heat, he closed his eyes and put his unshaven face as close to the flames as he dared.

"Why?" asked Krueger.

"It's my duty." Ian tilted his head toward the major and grinned. "And the war isn't over yet."

"For you, it is."

"Not if I get home."

With an exasperated look, Krueger rose from his chair and straightened the hem of his belted tunic. "Always the same. You disappear. My guards find you and bring you back." He poured brandy into two glasses and offered one to Ian. "Do you enjoy solitary confinement?"

"I enjoy freedom." Ian stood, unconsciously rubbing his shoulder as he turned his back to the fireplace and eyed the brandy snifter.

"None of us are free." Krueger pressed the snifter into Ian's hand. "Drink it,

Lieutenant. We won't be seeing each other again."

Ian looked puzzled. "Are you being transferred?"

"You are."

"Why?"

"Three escape attempts last summer. As soon as spring arrives, you try again. Since you are not content with my hospitality, the Third Reich is sending you to a place from which there is no escape."

A cold shiver raced up Ian's spine, followed immediately by an incomprehensible peace. "Do you mean to kill me?" he asked calmly.

"Those are not my orders." Krueger stiffened and thrust out his chin. "Besides, I would not condone such senseless carnage."

Since the day Ian arrived at the archbishop's castle, Krueger had been an enigma. He required precise military discipline from his guards and punished the prisoners in strict accordance with the Geneva Convention. But he didn't lord his position over his men or let them mistreat the POWs. Food rations were shared equally among the captors and the captives.

Ian swirled the brandy, mesmerized for a moment by its amber translucence. He swallowed a mouthful, relishing its warmth in his throat. "How did you end up here, Major?"

"It's where I prefer to be." Krueger clasped his hands behind his back and stared out one of the windows. "There's no killing here."

"There'd be no killing at all if not for your Führer," Ian said boldly, then tensed as he waited for Krueger's reaction.

But the major only stared out the window. After a long moment, he poured more brandy into his glass and glanced at the door. Facing Ian, he spoke in a low, deliberate voice. "I love Germany. I love her art, her music, her literature. But I hate what she has become. Here I do what I can to alleviate the imprisonment of the Führer's enemies. But they are not my enemies. You are not my enemy."

He clinked his snifter against Ian's. "To your freedom, Lieutenant Devlin. And to mine."

"To freedom."

Both men emptied their glasses.

"So." Ian exhaled. "Where am I going?"

"An inescapable fortress. Colditz Castle."

"A new challenge."

"Be careful, Lieutenant. The commander there may have sharper eyes than mine."

"Are you saying — ?"

Krueger held up a warning hand. "I could not allow you to get far. You understand?"

"The next time you take your holiday in England," Ian said with a grin, "come to Somerset. Kenniston Hall. We'll go fishing."

The corners of Krueger's lips turned up into a slight smile, but his eyes appeared plaintive. "God go with you, Ian."

"And with you, Sebastian."

Krueger gave a slight nod, then brusquely returned to his desk. "Enter," he said loudly. The guard waiting outside opened the door. "Return the prisoner to his quarters. He is to take the transport to Colditz tomorrow at 0700."

Colditz Castle, sharp-edged and solid except for the rounded clock tower, sprawled atop a stone promontory high above the surrounding town. A dry moat encircled the gray walls and a large sign, *Oflag* IV-C, hung across the stone arch leading into the ancient fortress. When Ian and the other transferred prisoners passed under the arch into the central courtyard, they were greeted by shouts from other POWs leaning out of the windows high above their heads. Colorful banners fluttered in the slight breeze. The British Union Jack. The French *drapeau tricolore*. The Dutch red, white, and blue, and the Belgian black, yellow, and red.

Ian, Captain Mitch Harris, and two other British POWs were processed into Oflag IV-C with impeccable German efficiency. They returned to the courtyard, where the senior officer of the British contingent introduced himself.

"Everybody around here calls me Dodge," he said.

"Is this place as escape-proof as they say?" Ian asked, staring up at the high walls and the watchtowers.

"Several have tried, but most get caught within a day." Dodge chomped on the stump of an unlit cigar. "Though two of the Poles made it all the way to Krakow before the goons caught up to them. They returned to our happy little league of nations the day before yesterday."

"So it's not impossible," said one of the newcomers, a lieutenant who bounced on the balls of his feet like a skittish colt.

"One of the Frenchies took off last week. We'll throw him a bash just for trying as soon as he gets back."

"Sounds like you want him to get caught," said the lieutenant.

"You bet I do." Dodge spoke around the cigar stump. "We can't have a Frenchy scoring the first home run, now can we? It's a matter of honor."

The British officers laughed in agreement. To score a home run out of Colditz, to make it all the way back to Britain — that kind of bragging rights would get an escapee a free drink in any pub in England.

"I volunteer," Ian said. "The sooner the better."

"All in good time, my boy." Dodge pointed toward a wall extending from the clock tower. "Those are the punishment cells. The prodigal Poles are in there now. Will be for another two or three weeks. Above them —" he pointed — "the French quarters. Near the top, right below the attics, that's where you boys will be lodging."

Gazing upward, Ian inwardly sighed and rubbed his shoulder. He had hoped to escape during the trip, but the guards had been especially vigilant. No wonder, since each of their prisoners had a reputation for disappearing. Now here he was, inside the so-called inescapable fortress. He glanced around the irregular courtyard and the massive walls that met at odd angles. Inside those walls, he guessed, must be more than a hundred rooms, joined together by a maze of hallways, stairs, and alcoves.

"How mean are the guards?" asked Harris.

Dodge shrugged. "They're mostly veterans from the Great War. Or babies too young to fight. Not a bad lot, really. You'll learn quick enough who's who and what's what."

Shouts came from across the courtyard, drawing their attention. Two prisoners, dressed in gray, were brushing dirt onto a third while two German guards argued with each other.

"What's going on?" Ian asked.

"A Polish ritual," answered Dodge. "If a guard even barely touches one of them, his buddies dust him down. None of them will even speak to a German except through a translator."

"I can't say I blame them."

"Me either, the way they're treated." Dodge removed the cigar stump and stared at it a moment. "The Nazis say that the Geneva Convention only applies to recognized states. Since Poland no longer exists, the Polish officers aren't protected."

Ian shook his head in disgust. "They get away with that?"

"One of the reasons we're fighting this war, Lieutenant."

Ian and Mitch settled into a square room with two wood-framed beds, a wardrobe, and a small desk. From the lone window,

Ian could see the thick wall enclosing the dry moat.

"Found a way out of here yet?" Mitch tested the thin mattress.

"Sure. All we need are wings."

Mitch grinned. "When the time is right, Dev, God will see us home."

"You aren't making plans to leave us already, are you?" Dodge said from the doorway, chomping the cigar stump.

"Only thinking about it," said Ian.

"When you start doing more than just thinking, I'll want to know about it."

"You're the escape officer?"

Dodge nodded. "Each nation here has one. We meet together, keep each other apprised of what our boys are doing."

Mitch ran his fingers through his hair. "Isn't that risky?"

"Not as risky as unintentionally working against each other. Despite what I said in the courtyard, I don't want to be responsible for messing up anyone's attempt to get home." He smiled around the cigar. "Not even a Frenchy's."

CHAPTER TWENTY-FOUR

MAY 1942

Alison didn't relax until the train pulled out of the rural station for the three-hour trip to Rotterdam. She untied the paisley scarf and slid it from her hair, twisting it between her fingers to relieve her tension. Two more Jewish children, a twelve-year-old girl and her nine-year-old sister, were now safely hidden from Nazi eyes thanks to the hospitality of a dairy farmer and his wife.

Besides delivering the sisters to their new home, she had found two additional families willing to open their hearts and homes. God knew the need was dire. In the two years since Germany first invaded Holland, the laws imposed on the Jewish people had become increasingly heinous. Hundreds of German Jews who had fled to Holland before the invasion were already imprisoned in the camp at Westerbork.

Now Dutch Jews were being systematically rounded up and transported to the northeastern camp. Alison had heard rumors that trains routinely transported prisoners from Westerbork to unknown destinations.

Prisoners! Since when was being Jewish a crime?

Closing her eyes, she breathed a short prayer for the safety of the children she had left behind. Finding appropriate homes was becoming more difficult, and a few of the farmers volunteered because they wanted free labor. But Alison had to accept that even those farms were safer for the children than Westerbork.

Even she, with her vivid imagination, could not envision how horrid that overcrowded camp must be. No more than she could envision the fortress that imprisoned Ian.

She opened her purse and slipped out the letter from him that had arrived yesterday, just before she had left Rotterdam with the children. The form, printed on glossy paper, had the German word *Kriegsgefangenenlager* printed on the top left margin. To the right was the word *Datum,* followed by a line. Ian had written the note, on the seven printed lines, on March 27, almost six weeks before. He was only allowed to write one letter a week, and he also wrote to his parents and sister.

Her fingers traced his blocky handwriting, taking what comfort she could in touching the graphite from his pencil. He thanked her for the package she had sent and told her about his role in the prisoners' production of *The Importance of Being Earnest*. His last line wished her a happy birthday with the hope that they'd be together on her next one. She could tell he hated it there, but she thanked God for his imprisonment. As long as he was at Colditz, he wasn't in the fighting.

Resting her head against the train window, she stared at the passing countryside and longed for an end to the war. As the train chugged its way toward home, her eyelids grew heavy and eventually closed. She startled awake when the conductor touched her shoulder.

"Isn't this your stop, miss?"

Alison looked around her warily. "Yes, thank you, it is." She gathered her bag and waited for the aisle to clear. The conductor's attention was now on another passenger, but he appeared to be intentionally blocking her way. Her heart pounded as she tried to remember if she had seen him before. Was it possible he recognized her? That he had seen her leave Rotterdam with various children and return without them?

The other passenger moved on, and the conductor turned to her with a gentle smile. "My schedule, miss," he said, quickly pressing a piece of paper in her hand and walking away.

Alison shoved the paper in her pocket and hurried off the train. Inside the station, she sank onto an out-of-the-way bench. Once she could breathe normally, she pulled out the paper and smoothed it on her lap. Small printed letters provided dates, times, and train routes. Beneath the schedule was an outline of a fish. She smiled, thanking God for this blessing.

Outside the station, she found Will with two bicycles. "Look what the conductor gave me," she said, handing him the schedule. "We have a friend."

Will read the paper. "Do you trust him?"

"Didn't you see the Christian symbol? Besides, he had a kind face."

"I have a kind face and I blow things up. Your father has a kind face and he's a forger."

Pieter's artistic imagination may have left him, but his eyes and fingers worked perfectly to create the documents needed by the Dutch Underground.

Alison tilted her head in thought as she settled her bag into the bike basket. "Papa doesn't have a kind face. His eyes are too intense."

"Kind face or not, I'll see what I can find out about our new friend before we trust him." Will pocketed the paper. "How were our packages received?"

"With buttermilk and cake." Alison pedaled away, but Will quickly caught up. They cycled along the city streets toward the gallery in silence, ignoring the German soldiers who frequented the rebuilt restaurants and shops.

When they turned on Oude Binnenstraat, Alison stopped. Will slowed, did a U-turn, and maneuvered his bike alongside hers.

"Do you know what today is?" she asked.

He sighed deeply and jammed his hands in his pockets. "I know."

"Two years." But neither the memories nor the grief had eased. Too much had been lost on that single day.

"Let's go."

They left the business district behind and a few minutes later turned onto the cratered cobblestone street leading to the canal house. Because of the rough pavement, they walked their bicycles past the remains of a once affluent neighborhood, now a cemetery of bricks and stones.

The exterior walls of a few houses stood precariously upright, resembling dollhouses with their open interiors. Others had totally collapsed into rubble.

Alison and Will walked their bikes toward the mound of broken bricks and splintered lumber that had been their home. Despite their grief, both had reluctantly helped in the search for anything that could be salvaged from the debris. Papa had found one of the Grecian statues lying unbroken on top of a crushed ottoman. Many of the books in Opa's library had remained shelved, though the shelves rested horizontal on the ground.

Alison wandered around the perimeter of the rubble, kicking at the loose bricks that littered the ground. At the rear of the house, she climbed over a pile of debris to the area where her desk had been found, its legs sheared off the top. She had found a few of her belongings there, but not the keepsake she wanted most.

Once winter released the ground from its frozen grip, she had ridden her bike here once a week or so and dug in the debris. But the pewter lighthouse stayed hidden within the rubble. She didn't even try looking for it today. At least she still had Ian's gold pen safely tucked in her purse.

Instead she circled to where Will stood, near the remains of the kitchen hearth. Its pockmarked chimney stood about seven feet high, a silent sentinel guarding the tear-stained ground where Tante Meg and Gerta Brant had taken their last breaths.

CHAPTER TWENTY-FIVE

Immediately after the evening roll call, Ian slipped into the third-floor theater. He paused inside the door to let his eyes adjust to the darkness, then crept beneath the stage. Rustling among the odds and ends stored there, he found a bundle of clothing and escape aids that Dodge had hidden there earlier. Slinging it on his back, he shoved against a heavy trunk, sliding it away from the wall and revealing the square opening into a forgotten passage.

He and Mitch Harris had found the corridor while working on the scenery for a POW vaudeville production last winter. Throughout the cold winter months, they had secretly explored the passage and made their plans. In letters written to a fictitious aunt, Dodge, the British escape officer, sent coded messages to MI9, the London War Office. The equally fictitious Prisoners Welfare Fund smuggled escape kits to the prisoners in charitable packages of food, games, and cigarettes. The melting of the snow heralded the opening of escape season.

Ian took the pen-sized torch from the bundle and switched it on. The thin beam barely cut through the dark passage. Taking a deep breath, he raced through the corridor to narrow stone steps that spiraled against one of the round watchtowers. The stairs opened into an unused pantry, empty except for the cobwebs that laced the shelves together and a square window that overlooked the grassy moat.

Through the paneless window, he peered up at the quarter moon, his beacon to freedom. He wished Mitch was with him instead of in the prisoner cells. The captain had picked the wrong time to get caught in the parcels office. The goons thought he was pilfering items from the prisoner packages, stored there to be searched and x-rayed before being distributed to the POWs. He was pilfering all right — the contraband from the Prisoners Welfare Fund's most recent package. Fortunately, he had managed to hide the parcel, so another prisoner smuggled it out before the goons found it.

Ian wanted to postpone the escape attempt until Mitch was released, but Dodge wouldn't let him. "You're our guinea pig,

Dev," Dodge had said, chomping on his unlit cigar. "If you get out, Mitch can use the same route. So can others." Ian's protests had been ignored.

In a way, he was glad Dodge had outranked him. He'd already been at Colditz a year too long. And he surely didn't want to tell his grandchildren that he spent the entire war in a POW camp. He quickly changed into the laborer's clothes that Dodge had hustled for him. It was time to get back in the game.

He stuck the silk map and compass from the escape kit in his sock and pulled a navy-blue knit cap over his hair. A worn leather wallet, with the forged identification papers and money from the Prisoners Welfare Fund, went in his pocket along with a switchblade. There was nothing left to do but breathe a prayer and climb out the window.

Hanging off the window ledge, Ian dropped to the outer courtyard. He hugged the tower wall, on the lookout for the guards. Seeing no one, he edged his way to the gate that joined the watch tower with an outer wall. He knelt in the shadows and held his breath as a sentry strolled past the gate. Pressing his back against the tower wall, he counted to ten before peering out again.

The sentry had disappeared. Taking a deep breath, he dashed past the gate toward the outer wall and across the drawbridge. Sliding down the bank feet-first, he dislodged a rock and tensed as it bounced toward the bottom. He lay still, waiting for the sirens and rifle shots. But only the orchestra of the crickets and frogs from the nearby fish pond filled the night air.

After another calming breath, he slipped through the wicket gate that led into the dry moat, the gate he had seen so often from his upper-story window. He jogged along the broad moat as it circled the fortress, staying close to its wall, until he reached the park gate. Again, he dropped to his stomach while he listened carefully for any sounds of alarm.

When a long minute had passed, he slipped through the gate and scurried to the opposite side of the park wall. And kept on walking until early the next morning when he reached the train station at Leisnig and bought a ticket to Dresden.

"Why don't you go to bed, *schatje*." Hendrik closed his book. "They'll be home soon."

Alison looked up from her mending and glanced at the clock. It was almost two o'clock in the morning, and neither Will nor his father had returned. "I wouldn't be able to sleep."

"Something must have gone wrong." Pieter paced by the second-story window. Every minute or two, he peeked through the heavy blackout curtains. "I should have gone with them."

"Do you know where they are?" Hendrik asked his son.

"They didn't tell me."

"All we can do is pray they haven't been arrested."

Alison stared at her grandfather. "Arrested? Do you think — ?"

"No," Hendrik soothed, but worry deepened the wrinkles in his ruddy cheeks. "We cannot give up hope."

"They're here." Pieter rushed from the room.

Alison wanted to race after him, but she took her grandfather's arm and let him set the pace, knowing he was as eager as she to get downstairs.

They entered the kitchen and found Will sitting at the table, his head buried in his hands. Pieter appeared in the doorway from the back room, his face pale and a chill in

268

his gray-blue eyes. "Brant's been wounded," he said as he filled a pan with water and put it on the stove to boil.

"What happened?" asked Alison.

Pieter glanced at Will, but he didn't answer.

"An explosion," Pieter said, gathering towels from a drawer. "Brant has shrapnel in his legs. Alison, keep an eye on the pot. When the water gets hot, bring it back here."

"Will he be all right?" she asked.

"He won't be going on any more midnight missions. But if he stays off his feet for a few days, he should be fine." Pieter returned to his patient, and Hendrik followed him.

Alison drew a chair next to Will and put her arm around his shoulders. "Did you hear Papa? He said your dad will be fine."

Will raised his head and rubbed his hands over his face. His eyes were rimmed in red and blood caked his shirt.

Alison gasped. "Are you hurt too?"

He barely shook his head, as if the slightest movement pained him. "It's not my blood," he muttered.

"Your dad . . ."

"No." He gripped Alison's hand. "There was someone else. He . . . he died."

"Who was it?"

"I can't tell you."

"Please, Will. I want to know."

He studied her, as if making up his mind, and the sorrow in his soft brown eyes tore at her heart. "His name was Danny de Graaf."

"I know him." Stunned, she shook her head in disbelief. "He married a classmate of mine."

"Hannah."

"That's right." Tears sprang to her eyes. "They have children."

"Two-year-old twins — Aaron and Anna."

"Oh, Will. Does she know?"

"I brought Dad straight here and . . . How can I tell her, Alison? She didn't want Danny to work with the Underground. But then we found out his name was on the list for Westerbork. We had to hide him." He abruptly stood, knocking his chair to the floor and squeezing his head with his hands.

The water bubbled on the stove, and Alison turned off the burner. She poured the boiling water into an enamel basin. "I need to take this to Papa."

"Let me." Will rested his hands on either side of the basin. "Hannah isn't expecting to see Danny till later in the week. I'll go to her after the sun comes up."

"I'll go with you."

He shook his head. "It's my fault Danny died. I need to do this myself."

CHAPTER TWENTY-SIX

Alison had given little thought to Hannah de Graaf the past few years. But since Danny's death, she couldn't get the young widow out of her thoughts. Her heart ached for Hannah's tragic loss, but the senselessness of it made her angry. No matter how many acts of sabotage Will and the others committed, no matter how many documents her father forged, it wasn't enough. The needs only became more dire as the Nazis ground their heels deeper into the soul of the Dutch populace.

Danny was no more than a martyr to a lost cause. And now his wife and children were left to fend for themselves.

At least Papa and Will were spending more time at the gallery instead of sneaking out after curfew to attend their secret meetings. Brant, too, though he had little choice, as the pain in his legs prevented him from moving much beyond his bedroom.

Three or four days had passed before Alison realized the men, including Opa, were occupying themselves in different areas of the gallery. When they came together for meals, they barely spoke to one another. She found herself avoiding Papa after they had another argument about smuggling her out of the country. When she turned to Will for support, he had stared at her and left the room, wearing his guilt like an impenetrable suit of armor.

Only Opa provided quiet companionship as they relaxed together in Alison's sitting room in the hour before bedtime, he with a book, she with her mending or her paints. Her fingers busy with a needle or brush, she thought about Hannah and the fatherless babies, her mind wrestling with one persistent question: If on the eve of her wedding Hannah had been given a glimpse into the future, would she still have married Danny?

If Alison could return to the moment when she last saw Ian, would she tell him how much she loved him before she let him go?

Tired of being cooped up with Papa's angry sneer and Will's vacant eyes, Alison spent a busy morning in the kitchen. She wrapped her freshly baked strudel in an embroidered cloth and placed it in a basket along with a few ripe pears and four jars of green beans. With no one around to stop her, she left a note for Papa, tied a scarf around her hair, and headed out on the bike ride to the de Graaf home.

Hannah answered her knock, caution in her deep-brown eyes. Her dark, unruly curls were pinned away from her face, accentuating her high cheekbones. A yellow Star of David adorned her pale-green housedress.

Standing awkwardly on the stoop with her basket in both hands, Alison smiled brightly. "Hello, Hannah. I'm Alison Schuyler. Do you remember me? From school?"

"Of course I do." Hannah ventured a smile. "You're the American girl."

"That's right." Alison grinned. No matter how long she lived in Rotterdam, her earliest classmates always thought of her as the American girl. Strange to know now that the only thing American about her was her birth certificate and her passport. She was as much a Dutch girl as any of them.

"Please come in." Hannah opened the door and Alison entered a small, well-kept parlor furnished with an upholstered sofa and matching armchairs. A multibranched candlestick — a menorah — and a wedding photo in a silver frame were displayed on an antique hutch. A family heirloom, Alison guessed, perhaps fashioned by a de Graaf ancestor.

"I brought you a strudel." Alison offered Hannah the basket. "And a few other things."

"This is very kind of you," Hannah said as if the phrase had worn a groove in her mind, a record she was tired of playing. She set the basket on a nearby table and gestured toward the sofa. "Please. Have a seat."

"Will Brant told me about Danny. I'm very sorry." Alison smoothed her skirt as she sat down. "Is there anything you need, Hannah? Anything I can do for you?"

Hannah laughed a strange, humorless laugh. "Turn back time, perhaps?"

"I would." *"I love you, Alison Schuyler."* Her chin quivered and she shushed Ian's whisper. "If I had the power."

Hannah's reflective dark eyes studied Alison. "Not only for my own sake, I think," she said gently. "But also for your own."

Alison gave a sheepish nod.

"Come." Hannah suddenly stood, her voice firm. "We will taste your strudel."

"Before lunch?"

"And why not if we want to?" She grabbed the basket and led the way to a shining kitchen. Red geraniums bloomed on the windowsill over the sink, and a portrait of Queen Wilhelmina, the exiled monarch, adorned the wall over the oilcloth-covered table.

"Danny's mother has taken the children for a stroll." Hannah heated the coffeepot and gathered plates. "We will have time for a quiet visit before their return."

"I interrupted you," Alison said apologetically, "when you wanted to be alone."

"The interruption was welcome. Please, will you slice the strudel, and I will pour this black mixture. I refuse to call it coffee."

Alison chuckled and served the strudel while Hannah placed two steaming cups on the table. They sat across from each other, smiling as if they were naughty children sneaking dessert before dinner.

Hannah's dark eyes twinkled. "My Danny, he loved his whims. Sometimes I'd have to scold him not to behave like such a boy. But he never could resist a bit of fun. Even something as simple as this treat." Her cheeks flushed. "I can't be serious all the time, not if I'm to honor his memory."

"No, of course not."

Hannah looked across the table at Alison. "You know of my sorrow. Will you tell me yours?"

"Mine?"

"Why do you wish to turn back time?"

Alison laid down her fork, momentarily unsure how to respond to such directness. But Hannah's compassionate expression inspired confidence.

"His name is Ian. Lieutenant Ian Devlin."

"A soldier." Hannah's sigh was filled with sympathy.

"A prisoner, actually. At a place called Colditz in Germany."

Hannah stretched her hand across the table and clasped Alison's fingers. "I will pray that Adonai will bring him safely back to you."

"Thank you." Alison wondered why she and Hannah hadn't been closer friends in school. But the answer was painfully obvious. They had moved in vastly different circles, separated by class and by religion.

"If you ever need anything," Alison blurted, "you must let me know. If there's anything I can do for you . . ."

A shadow crossed Hannah's face and she stiffened slightly. "Did Will send you?"

"No." Alison narrowed her eyes and frowned, confused by Hannah's assumption. "Why?"

"It's nothing." Hannah forced a smile. "I am frightened of the future. Especially for the children."

"I can find them a home. Away from the city."

"Why would you do this for us, Alison?"

"Because your children are more important than the *Mona Lisa*."

Hannah's expression was puzzled. "I do not understand."

"Perhaps not." Alison gave an enigmatic smile. "But I do."

CHAPTER TWENTY-SEVEN

Ian slept in fits and starts, his body pressed between the protruding roots of a kingly maple. From Dresden, he had taken the train southwest to Nuremberg without incident. But the number of Gestapo officers patrolling that station had spooked him. Leery of risking another trip in a moving passenger car that offered nowhere to hide, and needing to conserve his meager funds, he set off cross-country toward the Swiss border. While near the city, he "boy-scouted," walking by night and sleeping by day. But the farther he got from civilization, the more he relaxed.

A playful shout jarred him fully awake, and he crouched behind the tree, alert to the sounds of rustling footsteps and boyish laughter. Whoever was out there was headed his way.

He darted as quietly as possible from one tree to another, receding farther into the sprawling woods. Still they followed, closing the gap. Looking up into the canopy of a full-leafed oak, he swung himself into the branches, climbing as high as he dared.

Peering through the limbs, he saw a group of teenagers dressed in tan uniforms. *Hitler-Jugend.* Hitler Youth. Each uniform bore a red-and-white diamond patch, the swastika in its center symbolizing their motto: *Blut und Ehre.* Blood and Honor.

Ian leaned back into the trunk and inwardly groaned. One of the Dutch prisoners who had escaped the summer before had been found by three Hitler Youth. Eager to show their devotion to Nazi doctrine and to receive the bounty placed on an escapee's head, they had viciously beaten the Dutchman before tossing his broken body in a cart and delivering him to the Colditz guardhouse. Not even the *Kommandant,* a German colonel who fought in the Great War, could hide his repulsion at the boys' brutality.

The teens, preoccupied with gathering plants and insects, wandered near Ian's tree. For a long hour, Ian pressed against the rough bark, his legs tucked against his chest. He ignored his cramping muscles as best he could by reminding himself that being stuck in a tree was a thousand times better than stretching out on a bunk in a dank prison.

As the boys' voices faded away, Ian stretched his stiff legs and rubbed his aching muscles. He shifted his back, finding a position only slightly more comfortable, and stayed in the tree another hour. Nibbling on a raw turnip he had pulled out of a garden the night before, he dreamed of roast beef, cubed potatoes, and pearl onions. Of Miniver scones and Mrs. Brant's apple pie. Of Alison.

With no more sign of the Hitler boys and a prayer that they were no longer a threat, Ian climbed down from the tree and checked his course with his button-sized compass.

For another three days he walked through the countryside, avoiding towns, wading across streams, climbing fences, and pilfering gardens. He came to a packed-dirt road and, discouraged by his slow progress through fields and woods, decided to follow it for a while. On the morning of the fourth day, he reached the top of a knoll. Pulling out his map and compass, he estimated he was still several days from Switzerland.

Somehow, he needed to find transportation besides his own legs. Exasperated, he looked out over the valley that spread before him. A small house and a barn were tucked into a corner formed by a wide stream. He shaded his eyes but didn't see any people. Or any vehicles. Houses were scarce along this isolated road that seemed to have been forgotten by civilization. Hungry and tired, he decided to take a chance on this one.

Leaving the road, he crossed a field and approached the house from the back, stopping frequently to listen for any sign of danger. But a desolate pall hung over the entire homestead.

He reached the barn first and cautiously opened the back door. Stepping inside the musty interior, he smiled.

"Hello, ladies," he said. Three red-and-white cows swung their heads toward him and batted their large brown eyes. One, in a pen by herself, mooed pitifully. He patted her swollen side and felt the movement of life beneath her hide. Odd that a farmer would leave a cow alone when she was so close to her time.

"How soon? Hmm?" Ian had often assisted the family's estate manager when the sheep were birthing. He guessed a newborn calf would be joining the herd before morning.

Finding an open bag of grain, he poured some in the mangers of the two stalls. The water troughs were nearly empty so he picked up two metal buckets and, blocked from view of the house by the barn, carried water from the stream.

While the cows drank greedily, their pink tongues slurping the cool water, Ian cracked open the front barn door. It faced the eastern side of the one-story house, where a trio of windows stared blankly back at him. A wide wooden porch faced the road and, at the other end, a back door opened onto a rock slab. At the end of a trodden path stood a stone well in the shelter of a stand of firs. He watched for shadows to cross the windows, for any sign of movement. Nothing.

Bent over in a running slouch, he darted for the back door and looked in its window. But a heavy curtain prevented his seeing inside the house. He jiggled the handle; it was locked. Cautiously circling the house, he peered through windows into a dim interior, seeing only the shapes of furniture. The front door, as he expected, was also locked.

From the vantage point of the porch, he scanned the road and the fields beyond it. No cars, no trucks. Not even a horse-drawn wagon.

Circling the house again, he found a cellar window with a broken latch. He forced it open, muttering an apology when the glass broke. Squeezing through the square opening, he dropped to the dirt floor and immediately flattened himself against a wall. He held his breath, listening for footsteps and squeaky floorboards. But the only sound was a buzzing fly.

The morning sun barely seeped through the cellar windows. While his eyes adjusted to the poor lighting, he took a deep breath. The smell of dirt and root vegetables permeated the room. Nosing around, he found burlap bags of potatoes and onions. Jars of preserved vegetables and fruits lined wooden shelves. His stomach growled and he selected an apple from a barrel in the corner, biting into its juicy tartness as he climbed rickety wooden steps to an upper door. Saliva filled his mouth in hopes of finding something more appetizing upstairs.

Slowly turning the knob, he eased open the door into a small kitchen dominated by a stove apparently used for both heating and cooking. A variety of purple, yellow, and white wildflowers drooped in a vase on a table covered with a blue cloth that matched the curtains.

He explored the rest of the house, a living room and two bedrooms. The furniture was worn but well cared for, the rooms immaculate. A quilt, in various shades of blue and trimmed in ivory, covered the double bed in the front bedroom.

On the plain wooden dresser, Ian found a leather-bound copy of the Hebrew Scriptures, the Tanak, beside a photograph in a cheap metal frame. He picked up the picture, realizing it had been taken in front of this very house. A young couple stared back at him. The man had one arm around the woman's waist and cradled an infant in the other. Though their faces were solemn, joy shone in their eyes. When the picture was taken, they were still young enough to believe a golden future awaited them.

But where were they now?

He set the photograph down and idly opened the Tanak's cracked black cover. Inside he found a marriage license, formalizing the union of Hans and Gretchen Steinberg on May 8, 1935. Beneath it were birth certificates, including one for a baby girl, Leiba, born on June 25, 1937.

The Tanak. Steinberg. That might explain their absence.

Except that the house didn't feel deserted. Someone lived here. Someone had picked the wildflowers from the stream bank. Perhaps little Leiba.

But why had her parents left the cows

unfed and unwatered?

He closed the Tanak and peered inside the sparsely furnished second bedroom. A child-size bed, covered in a pink-and-white quilt, took up one corner. A wooden chair and table sat beneath the window.

Perhaps the couple had taken their daughter someplace special for her birthday. Though he had lost track of the date, June 25 couldn't be that far away. Maybe a week or so.

He wiped his forehead on his sleeve and caught a whiff of his rank odor. A wave of nausea passed over him as the adrenaline that had heightened his senses when he broke into the house disappeared.

His filth disgusted him, hunger gnawed at his stomach, and his eyes burned with exhaustion. First things first. Returning to the kitchen, he found half a loaf of bread and a triangle of cheese. He ate slowly, savoring each bite and stopping before he was full. After cleaning up his crumbs, he went through the house again and rummaged through Hans's clothes. "Hope you don't mind, chap."

Grabbing a sliver of soap and a rough towel, he followed the stream past the barn to a bend shaded by a weeping willow. Praying that the Steinbergs stayed away awhile longer, he undressed and slipped into the sun-warmed water, ducking his head beneath the surface. In the shadow of the willow, he scrubbed the dirt of Colditz, its stench and its power, from his body.

After his swim, he dried himself and dressed in Hans's pants, an undershirt, and a hand-sewn shirt. The pants were a little too short for him, but they felt good against his skin. He hid the laborer's clothes he had worn for the past week beneath a rock in the stream.

Back inside the house, he shoved food into a canvas bag and found spare blankets in a closet. He carried his plunder to the barn.

"Shh." He placed a warning finger to his lips. "Don't let anyone know I'm here."

The cows blinked at him.

Climbing into the loft, he spread one of the blankets over the loose hay and stretched out. Feeling more secure than he had since leaving Colditz, he soon fell into a deep and restful sleep.

When he awoke, the slanting rays of the afternoon sun were shining in an upper window across his face. He groaned and covered his eyes with his forearm, then shot up and peered out the window. A black sedan pulled into the drive leading to the house, its motor intruding on the farm's tranquility.

A man, dressed in a military uniform, emerged from the driver's side and seemed to take in the quietness of the place with an appraising look. The passenger door opened and a woman stepped out. The woman from the photograph. Gretchen.

But Ian would have bet his last *reichsmark* that the officer wasn't Hans.

The German said something and gestured to the house. The woman hesitated and a little girl emerged from the car. Taking her by the hand, the woman walked toward the house. When she passed the officer, he grabbed her arm. She yanked away, then knelt by the girl.

Their foreheads almost touching, the woman spoke quietly to her daughter, who shook her head. Gretchen spoke again, gave her a quick embrace, and gestured toward the barn. The girl nodded, then walked toward the barn, her head down and dragging a cloth doll behind her.

"Run," the woman called in German. She watched the child, even as the officer grabbed her again and pulled her toward the house, his impatience evident while he waited for her to unlock the door.

The child ran, short legs pumping. Her hat flew off her head and she stopped to pick it up, then ran again.

Ian sat back on his heels and breathed a prayer for guidance. But he didn't need to wait for God's voice to know what he had to do. Hans wasn't here to protect his wife and child. So Ian had to do it for him. He slid down the ladder and hid in the shadows behind a wagon as the little girl slipped inside the barn and into an empty stall. He crept toward her, then paused as she sang the words to what he guessed was a lullaby.

Peering over the fencing of the stall, he saw her scrunched up in a corner, her doll hugged close to her chest. Not wanting to frighten her any more than he had to, he crouched in front of the stall. "*Guten tag,* Leiba."

The girl stared at him with deep brown eyes too large for her pixie face. As she stood up, bits of hay and straw clung to her dress and socks.

"Papi." Her face brightened and, dropping the doll, she flung herself into Ian's arms, almost knocking him off balance.

"Whoa, there." He braced himself with one hand and patted her thin back with the other.

Her arms tightened around his neck. "Papi," she said in German. "You've come home."

"Leiba." He picked her up as he stood. "Who is that man with your mommy?"

"He's bad." Her voice sounded muffled against Ian's shirt. "Make him go away."

Ian took a deep breath. "Look at me, honey."

Leiba raised her head from his shoulder and placed her hands on his unshaven cheeks. She stared into his eyes with such trust that Ian almost melted into the floor.

"Listen to me. You must do what I tell you. Okay?"

She nodded solemnly. "Yes, Papi."

He winced but decided not to correct her. There'd be time for that later. Hopefully.

"I want you to go into the loft and stay there. Don't come out until Mommy or I come for you. You can do that, can't you?"

"Yes."

"That's my girl." He picked up the doll and handed it to her, then stood her on the ladder and watched her disappear into the loft. Her head popped over the edge, and he motioned her back. "Hide, Leiba. And be very quiet. I'll come for you soon."

He took a couple of deep breaths, then grabbed a nearby hoe and laid the handle across his shoulders, his wrists hooked over each end. Whistling loudly, he headed for the back of the house.

The curtain covering the kitchen window moved, but Ian pretended he didn't see the German's angry face staring at him.

The officer stepped outside the back door. He no longer wore his jacket. Or his holster. "Who are you?"

With squinted eyes and a lopsided grin, Ian let the hoe slip into his hand and held it out to the officer. "I work," he said in German, keeping his words short and guttural. "Chop wood. Clear field."

The woman appeared in the doorway, her eyes shimmering with tears. A fresh bruise glowed on her cheek.

Ian nodded to her. "The cow. It's time."

"What are you talking about?" asked the officer.

Gretchen, appearing to summon all her courage, lifted her chin. "My cow is calving." She stepped in front of the officer and looked squarely at Ian. "This is her first time. Will you help her?"

"You should look." Ian tilted his head toward the barn. "Come."

"Yes, I should." Without looking at the German, the woman headed toward the barn. Ian smiled dumbly and followed her.

"Gretchen, come back here," ordered the German. "The cow doesn't need you."

The woman trembled, though she didn't

slow her pace. Ian couldn't help but admire her courage. He turned back to the German and shrugged.

"What is your name?" the German demanded.

Ian said the first name that came to his mind. "Hans."

"Where do you live?"

"Here and there. Here and there." He glanced toward Gretchen as she disappeared into the barn.

She was safe, but for how long?

CHAPTER TWENTY-EIGHT

"Art collecting is the new Nazi sport," Etienne Duret proclaimed as he dropped a bulging leather pouch on Hendrik's desk.

Amused by the Frenchman's uncharacteristic exuberance, Alison held out her hand. "Anything for me?"

"The prices they pay!" Caught up in the moment, Monsieur Duret absentmindedly pulled a peppermint out of his pocket and placed it in Alison's palm.

She frowned at it, then popped it in her mouth.

"Outrageous," he continued, shaking his head. "But do they know what they are buying? They do not even care."

"That is good for us." Hendrik opened the clasp on the pouch and pulled out a sheaf of paper and a stack of checks and cash. "We don't want them looking too closely at some of our Masters."

"Operation Rembrandt is a success."

"A tremendous success," said Hendrik, sorting through the receipts and the money. He had come up with the name for their clandestine scheme against the Nazi invaders. "Though most of these proceeds appear to be from legitimate commissions."

"Our sellers have made a good profit. And so have we."

"I wish Papa would let me paint a forgery." Alison propped her elbows on top of the typewriting table. She had been assisting her grandfather with correspondence when Monsieur Duret rushed into the alcove that was now the gallery's office.

Duret's eyes widened in horror. "You mustn't say this, *cherie*. Your father is right to protect you in this way."

"I might not be able to paint a Rembrandt, but I'm sure I could forge someone."

"No, no, no." Duret groaned. "Explain it to her, Hendrik."

"We don't doubt your talent, *schatje*. Or your skill."

"Then why can't I help?"

"Because to forge a painting," said Pieter as he and Will joined the others in the alcove, "is to diminish your own light."

"But you forge paintings," Alison said softly.

Pieter's eyes darkened, and he worked his

jaw. "My light was extinguished a long time ago."

"Our clients don't think so," Hendrik said gruffly, waving the stack of money. "Though they naturally believe they are purchasing a de Hooch or a van Heemskerk."

"A what?" asked Will.

"Contemporaries of Vermeer," Alison said, feigning irritation at his ignorance of his Dutch heritage. "You know who Vermeer is, don't you?"

"Him, I know. Who wouldn't, growing up with this family?"

Alison threw an eraser at him, but Will caught it and tossed it back. She ducked and squealed.

"Children!" Hendrik rose from his chair. "Behave yourselves. I'm taking this upstairs to the safe." Leaving the alcove, he waved the metal box that now held the contents of the pouch.

Pieter leaned against his father's desk. "Any news from Amsterdam?" he asked Duret.

"Our friend Göring will be there the day after tomorrow. On another of his shopping sprees."

At the mention of the beast's name, Alison unconsciously touched her scar. Over the past couple of years, it had faded from pink to white. Her father noticed, and she dropped her hand into her lap. "Why else would he come?" she blurted, trying to hide her embarrassment.

"I thought it wise to close our little enterprise." His earlier enthusiasm spent, Duret sank into one of the leather chairs facing the desk. "The unsold paintings are in the car."

"I'll bring them in," Will volunteered.

"I'll go with you," Pieter said. But before leaving the alcove, he bent over Alison. Resting his hand against her cheek, he kissed her temple. "Guard your light, *dochter*. In the end, it's all you have." Before she could respond, he left, jogging to catch up with Will.

Alison stared at the stationery rolled into the typewriter, a letter from Opa to a potential client who claimed to have recently discovered several "worthwhile paintings" in his attic. Similar letters came on a weekly basis.

After confiscating their inventory, Göring had blacklisted the gallery, essentially forcing it to close. But he couldn't stop them from wheeling and dealing behind closed doors. Ironically, the black market was driven by Nazi officers with ill-gotten money to launder and reputations as art connoisseurs to cultivate if they wished to impress their Führer. Suddenly the neglected landscapes and portraits that littered Holland's attics were fetching enormous prices. By acting as brokers for these works through a rented storefront in Amsterdam, the Van Schuylers were getting a commission on several of the sales.

The officers, including Göring, even bought the despised art that Hitler labeled as degenerate and fit only for burning. These paintings were often bartered for more coveted works.

Alison received respectable sums for her delicate watercolors, and Pieter's infrequent forgeries provided additional income. Opa no longer worried that the Van Schuyler Fine Arts Gallery would totally collapse under his watch.

Now that the Americans had joined the fight, he often said to Alison, the war would soon end. Tucking their tails between their legs, the German foxes would scamper back to their dens, whimpering in humiliated defeat.

When that happened, the gallery would be hers to rebuild in the reputable Van Schuyler tradition. Something she might not be able to do if she got caught painting forgeries now.

"What troubles you, *cherie*?"

Monsieur Duret's soft voice startled Alison from her reverie. She had forgotten he was still in the alcove. Getting up from behind the typewriter, she dragged a chair next to his and sat beside him.

"Do you think Papa is right? That my talent is all I have?"

"That is not true for you, *cherie.* Nor is it true for your papa." Duret sighed heavily. "But it is easier for him to bear his guilt if he believes his 'light is extinguished,' as he says it."

"Guilt for what?" Alison bit the inside of her lip as memory carried her to their Chicago home. To the moment when she had crawled under her bed, dragging her pillow and blankets with her, to shut out her papa's ferocious grief. "There was nothing he could have done to save Mama. Why can't he understand that?"

"Because he believes God took your mother's life. To punish him. So he traveled from one place to another, seeking forgiveness. But never seeking it in the right place."

"Forgiveness for what?"

Duret sighed again; then he reached for Alison's hand. "A secret can be a terrible burden. Have you the strength to carry it?"

Dread curled in Alison's stomach, and her

palms turned clammy. Yet another secret had been kept from her. "Is it about Mama?"

"It is not my place to tell you this. But it presses on me that you should know. Perhaps the truth will free you from the superstitious fear that you and your young man can't have a future together."

"You don't believe in the family fate."

"Not for you."

Hope flickered in Alison's heart, but she pushed it aside to think about when she was alone. Now she needed to find out this new secret. "Tell me about Mama."

"Her parents were ostracized from their families." Duret paused, seemingly lost for a moment in a faraway memory. "You see, her father was Jewish, but her mother was not. When they both died of scarlet fever within weeks of each other, there was no one to take her in except her uncle. But her very existence was a reminder of what he considered his brother's faithlessness. He treated your mother cruelly."

"Papa told me that. He said that's why they ran away to America."

"That's true, as far as it goes." Duret took her hand, and Alison braced herself, sensing that he was preparing her to hear something difficult. Something Papa didn't want her to know.

"The uncle wanted your mother to marry in the faith, not a Dutch Gentile. When Pieter asked for Amy's hand, her uncle beat him terribly. It was several days before Pieter saw Amy again. Her uncle had beaten her, too."

Alison closed her eyes against this horror, but the image pressed into her mind, vivid and grim. She squeezed Monsieur Duret's fingers.

"There is more, *cherie*. But if you wish, I will not tell it."

"Tell me," Alison said, her voice jagged.

"Pieter disappeared, and Madame Meg traveled with Amy to New York. It was all very sudden. But only two days after they left, Amy's uncle was found in a shed behind his house."

"He was dead."

"Yes."

"Papa killed him?"

"Only Pieter knows that answer." He gave a gallant shrug. "Perhaps your aunt also knew. But if so, she kept his secret."

"Tante Meg never told me she'd been to New York. Not even when I talked about being there with Papa. Before he . . ." The pain of Duret's revelation overshadowed Papa's abandonment and knotted her throat. She pressed her fingers against the ache and raised her eyes to Duret's.

His dear, familiar face appeared splotchy, his stooped shoulders even more bowed. "Forgive me for telling you these things, *cherie.* But you must believe — you must know — that your fate is not at all like your father's. Trust in God for your future, not in superstition."

"Even God can bring me sorrow."

"But only He can bring you peace."

CHAPTER TWENTY-NINE

With a steady grip on the hoe, Ian straightened to his full height and lost the sloppy grin. He narrowed his eyes, daring the officer to follow Gretchen into the barn.

Thrusting out his chest, the German sneered. "Who are you?"

"Nobody important." Ian shrugged, no longer hiding his British accent. "Who are you?"

The German swaggered closer, stopping a meter or two away from Ian. His eyes held a menacing challenge. "You first."

Better to let the Kraut think he had the upper hand. "Ian Devlin."

"Are you a soldier, Ian Devlin? In civilian clothes?"

The threat was clear. A soldier wearing civilian clothes in enemy territory was treated as a spy. And spies weren't granted the protection of the Geneva Convention. Not that it mattered. Only one of them would be leaving peaceably. If the German didn't drive away, preferably without his sidearm, then Ian would force him to go. Or die trying.

Ian switched to English. "Lieutenant. British Army."

"Hauptmann Walter Huber," replied the German in his native tongue. Then he, too, spoke in English. "Equivalent to your 'captain.' I outrank you, Lieutenant. And now I am placing you under arrest."

"I don't think so."

"Then I suggest you go on your way. Perhaps you will make it to England alive. If you stay out of affairs that do not concern you."

Ian glanced at the hoe, and Huber gave a short laugh and stretched out his hands. "Will you attack me? When I am unarmed? That wouldn't be very sporting."

Not very sporting at all. Which was why cruelty reigned over decency throughout Europe. But sometimes a man had to stand up to a bully. "I don't have to kill you," Ian said softly. "Only maim you."

Fear flickered in Huber's eyes, then changed to disdain. Ian realized the German was looking beyond him, and he glanced over his shoulder.

Gretchen stumbled toward them, wielding

a pitchfork in front of her. Determination shone on her bruised face, and her eyes were filled with hatred. She stopped when she reached Ian's side and pointed the tines at Huber. "Leave. Or I will kill you."

Despite the gravity of the situation, Ian almost wished his brother-in-law were here to see the absurdity of the two of them facing the Nazi with farm implements. He hoped he had the chance to tell Mark about it someday.

Huber swaggered another step closer. "My dear Gretchen. I thought you desired my company."

Gretchen plunged the pitchfork forward. It glanced off Huber's chest and fell to the ground. She stepped back, covering her eyes in horror as droplets of blood darkened his shirt. Cursing at her, Huber lunged for the pitchfork. As he picked up the handle, Ian tripped him with the hoe.

Huber fell to one knee but waved the tines at Ian, who jumped back. Huber stood, and the warriors faced each other with their medieval weapons. Out of the corner of his eye, Ian watched as Gretchen picked up a rock and drew back her arm. Huber must have sensed her movement. Before Ian could stop him, the German wheeled and thrust the pitchfork into Gretchen's abdo-

men with a victorious grunt. She grabbe
for the tines as he pulled it back, the rock
slipping from her hands. Blood spurted in
hot streams, ragged parallel lines that
stained her yellow dress. Her eyes pleaded
with Ian as she lurched forward and fell.

The haunting memory of Alison, the
bandage across her temple, flashed through
Ian's mind. With a primal yell, he swung
the hoe in a wide arc that landed the blade
squarely on Huber's neck. Dazed by the
blow, Huber collapsed, and Ian pounced on
him. Grabbing a fistful of the German's
hair, Ian slammed his head on Gretchen's
rock. Again and again, until the spasms of
raw anger that fueled his arm weakened. He
rolled Huber onto his back, and the German's cold blue eyes stared vacantly at the
heavens.

Ian sat back, forearm across his knee, head
bowed. His chest ached, as if a giant hand
had squeezed his ribs until there was no
breath in his lungs. *All Huber had to do was
drive away. Get in his car and drive away.* He
inhaled, a massive intake of air to start his
heart beating again.

A low murmur sounded behind him, and
he twisted around to Gretchen. Her eyes
flickered, and he brushed the hair from her
forehead before examining her wounds. The

eep punctures spewed forth rich pools of blood. Ian hurried to remove his shirt and pressed the wadded material against her torn flesh. She covered his hand with hers and attempted a grateful smile.

"I'm sorry," he said in German. "I'm so sorry. If I hadn't been here, maybe this wouldn't have happened."

"*Nein.*" She barely exhaled the word. Laboring to breathe, she struggled to speak. "My daughter — Leiba. She believes you . . . her papi."

"I know."

"He called her Libby. And now he's gone." The words came out in a sudden rush, as if she were late and anxious to be on her way. "Take her to your home."

"I can't . . . I . . ."

"Please." Her soft brown eyes glimmered, and she squeezed his hand. "Promise me."

Ian worked his jaw, nodded as her eyelids flickered shut.

"Promise?" she whispered. Her hand, pressing against his, relaxed.

"*Ja.*" He bent over her limp body. "I promise."

The creak of the barn door, eerily loud in the dead stillness of midafternoon, brought Ian to his feet. Libby's pixie face peeked

306

out at him, and he hurried to scoop her up and carry her back into the barn before she saw her mother's body. Too late.

"Is Mami sleeping?"

Ian sat on a bale of hay and settled the little girl on his knee. "Mami's tired."

"Is the mean man sleeping too?"

"He's sleeping too."

Apparently satisfied, Libby leaned contentedly into Ian's chest and yawned.

Ian tried to relax for the sake of the little girl, but his mind swirled with questions. What was he going to do with the bodies outside the barn? Where had Libby's papi gone? And most important, how much time did he have before someone started looking for the German?

The swollen cow blinked at him and gave a long bellow. Ian frowned as her sides heaved in and out. Just what he needed — something else to worry about.

"Betsy is going to be a mami," Libby piped up.

"Is that the cow's name? Betsy?"

"*Ja.* Mami said I can name the baby when it comes."

"The baby will be here pretty soon." Ian eyed the heaving cow again. Maybe this was the distraction he needed. "Libby, I need to take Mami to the house, okay? Will you stay

307

ere with Betsy? We don't want her to be
lonely."

"Will you come back?"

"Yes, I promise I'll be back very soon."
He picked up the little girl and placed her
in the bed of the wagon. Bits of straw and
dust littered the floor, but at least it would
keep her contained. As long as she didn't
try to climb out. "Stay here and I'll bring
you a snack. We'll have a . . ." His German
failed him, so he switched to English. "A
picnic."

Libby giggled. "Pic-nic."

"That's right. Just stay here. Why don't
you sing Betsy a song?"

Holding on to her cloth doll, Libby stood
in the corner of the wagon nearest the cow's
stall and sang the same lullaby Ian had
heard her singing earlier. He waved to her
and headed for the barn door.

Once outside, he hesitated, gripped by
indecision. But he didn't have the luxury of
time, so he shook away the fogginess and
considered his options. There was only one,
as much as he hated it.

Gretchen might not be missed, but Huber
would be. No one searching the farm could
find either one of them. Slinging Huber's
body over his shoulder, Ian staggered to the
well and slid the German into its dark

depths. *"Für Sie der Krieg ist vorbei,"* he said after hearing the distant splash.

He returned to Gretchen, easily lifting her in his arms. "I'd give you a decent burial if I could," he said apologetically, "but I don't have that luxury. Not if I'm going to save Libby." He breathed a wordless prayer, slipping her into the well as gently as possible. His lunch rose in his throat as she fell.

Before returning to the barn, Ian raided the house, hurriedly changing into another of Hans's shirts. Finding Huber's holstered sidearm on the bedroom dresser, he belted it around his waist. He tucked the Steinberg family photograph and the leather-bound Tanak into a bag. Getting safely across the Swiss border and all the way to Gibraltar with a child — he was foolish to even try. But the photograph and Tanak were the only things Libby would have to connect her with her family. He'd do his best to get them to England too.

Once he had the sedan packed with food and clothing, he returned to the barn with a tin of apple cake. Retrieving the blankets he had stashed in the loft, he folded one for Libby to sit on while she ate the cake. Delighted to have the entire tin to herself, she sat cross-legged on the floor of the wagon while Ian tended to the cows.

"You'll have to do this on your own, girl," Ian said, patting Betsy's neck. "I can't wait on you." He opened the stalls so the cows could leave the barn, then lifted Libby from the wagon and carried her to the sedan.

"Where's Mami?" Libby asked, clutching her doll.

"Mami can't come with us right now." Ian shot her an uneasy smile. He was going to have to tell her the truth sometime. But not yet. "She wants us to go on a trip."

"Where to?"

"To my house." *God willing.*

"Will Mami find us?"

He opened the car door and scooted her onto the bench seat before sliding in after her. "Please, Libby. You must trust me. Can you do that?"

"Yes, Papi." She sat close beside him, her doll tightly clasped on her lap.

He drove the car away from the farm, his heart pounding as he prayed for wisdom. The sedan could take them over greater distances in less time, but it was also conspicuous. He only hoped that God still listened to his prayers after what he'd done.

Killing on the battlefield — he lived with that as a necessary evil. But murder driven by rage? The sour feeling gnawed at him that if he hadn't been there, or if he'd stayed in the loft, Huber would have eventually driven away. Gretchen would still be alive. Libby wouldn't be an orphan.

And he wouldn't be a murderer.

"Vengeance is mine; I will repay, saith the Lord."

The familiar verse slipped into his heart, searing his chest with its convicting truth. Vengeance had strengthened his arms and clouded his mind. Huber had paid with his life for his brutality to Gretchen. But he had also died because of what that pig Göring had done to Alison.

Ian braked as he neared a bend in the road, fingers tapping the steering wheel. As he rounded the curve, he saw a truck parked at the side of the road, and he slowed to a crawl.

Libby tucked her doll under her arm and clapped her hands in delight. "You found our truck."

"That's your truck? Mami's truck?"

"It broke when Mami was driving. The tire went splat." She pressed her hands firmly together. "Then the mean man came, but he didn't want to help Mami. He wanted to come to our house."

"Where were you and Mami? Before the tire went splat?"

"At the store. I got candy."

The pieces of Gretchen's puzzle fell into place. She and Libby must have been on their way home, with only a few kilometers to go, when the truck's tire gave out.

Ian scrutinized the landscape as he parked behind the truck. Leaving Libby in the car, he pulled the Walther from its holster and approached the truck. The front tire on the passenger side was flat. Through the window, he saw a few parcels on the floor.

Glancing from the truck to the sedan and back again, Ian made his decision. He had yet to meet anyone on this road, but that could change at any moment. He and Libby would be less conspicuous in the truck. He checked the keys he had taken from Gretchen's house and inserted the one for the truck into the ignition. After a few tries, the engine kicked over.

Keeping a tight control on his nerves, he quickly replaced the truck's flat tire. Libby helped him move their belongings to the truck, proudly carrying a small bag of apples that Ian had taken from the cellar.

He lifted Libby into the truck, then looked back at the sedan. There was nowhere to hide it. The best he could hope for was to get as far away from the farm as possible before it was found. Drawing back his arm, he threw the sedan's keys into the nearby field. The metal glinted in the bright spotlight of the sun's horizontal rays as they arced and fell. A glint that momentarily blinded him with a strange vision of a guiding beacon. Somehow, he no longer felt quite as forsaken.

Chapter Thirty

My grandfather was Jewish.

That thought hadn't occurred to Alison when Monsieur Duret divulged her parents' secret history earlier that afternoon. At the time, she had been too preoccupied with the horror of the beatings and the mystery of the uncle's death. But later, reflecting on the tragic story as she wandered through the sparse gallery, the words resounded in her mind as loudly as if she had spoken them.

Her life had been rooted in a hodgepodge of New World patriotism and Old World tradition, a double dose of innate superiority. She found this revelation, that she belonged to an ancient heritage rooted in the pages of Scripture, both humbling and disturbing. What would it feel like to wear the yellow star, to be identified only by what it symbolized? To have the giant *J* stamped on her identity card? To be singled out for persecution?

She hoped to never find out, even as she longed to accept her mother's ancestral legacy.

Lost in her thoughts, her steps took her to the gallery's center wall, where *The Girl in the Garden* had hung and impishly invited her viewers into her Monet-esque world. Alison mourned the loss of the painting, stolen two years ago along with everything else during Göring's raid on the gallery. She imagined that fiend using the portrait for target practice, gleefully destroying the American.

If only he had known the truth.

Another painting hung on the center wall now, an oil on canvas of a middle-aged man in a weathered rowboat. His downcast eyes and wry smile spoke of heartache and pride. His lean muscles, beneath the rolled-up sleeves of a faded cotton shirt, halfheartedly pushed against the oars. A man of contradictions, no longer sure where he belonged or where he should go.

Alison's signature graced the bottom right corner. The project had taken weeks to complete, each stroke demanding the full attention of both her mind and her heart. By the time she finished, the sharp edges of grief — for Tante Meg and Gerta Brant, for her mother's portrait and the canal house, for the way things were before the Nazis came — no longer cut quite so deeply. She had learned to laugh again, to embrace the beauty of a sunrise, without the press of guilt against her chest.

"That's not the man I meant to be." Pieter came up behind Alison and put his arm around her shoulders. "You deserved a much better father."

"I have the only father I want." A half truth. They both knew it. Pieter had been home for a little over two years now. But she still turned to Hendrik for advice and comfort. And it was Brant whose teasing made her giggle uncontrollably. Not Pieter. "I should have painted you in a different mood. But this one —" she hesitated — "fit."

"Always paint what you see, Alison. Whether you're looking with your mind or your heart. That's the secret to genius."

"But you don't like it."

"It's an honest portrayal." He made a huffing noise. "I'm just sorry that's who I am."

"You did your best."

He brushed her hair from her forehead. "I wasn't here. When you needed me."

"You're here now."

"I want you to know something." His eyes darted away, then back again. "Sending you to your grandfather was the hardest thing I ever did. But it's where you belonged."

"I missed you, Papa." Alison bit her lip, choosing her words with care. She wanted him to know that Duret had told her about Mama's uncle. More than that, she wanted him to tell her himself. That seemed unlikely even now, when he was in a rare sentimental mood. "But you were right. I needed to grow up here. The only thing I wish were different is that you had been with us too."

He drew her close in a fatherly embrace. "No matter what happens, Alison, know that I love you very much."

Something in his voice caught her attention, and she searched his eyes for any secrets his words were hiding. But his gray-blue eyes, so like her own, shone with affection, and his smile charmed her.

"I know that, Papa." She leaned up and kissed his cheek. "I love you too."

Later that evening, Alison relaxed in her sitting room. Hendrik had left her alone only a few moments before, wishing her a good night and padding along the corridor to his own room. His slow footsteps tugged at her heart. During the day, he managed a facade of cheerfulness. But as the sun disappeared below the horizon, his spirits waned and his shoulders sagged, bowed by the pressures of war.

She bent over her stationery, writing a letter to Ian's sister, Trish, with the gold pen bearing his initials. At Will's suggestion, she had written Trish shortly after the Dunkirk evacuation and asked for any news about Ian. Trish had immediately answered, telling Alison that her husband, Mark, had made it home, though he was seriously wounded. All Mark could tell the family was that Ian had left him with two other soldiers in the surf, then returned to the battlefield. No one seemed to know what had happened to him.

A long week later, Trish had written again with the news that the Red Cross had notified Ian's family of his imprisonment. Since then, Ian wrote the weekly letter he was allowed to Alison, Trish, and his parents on a rotating basis, but the letters sometimes took weeks or months to arrive. Alison and Trish quickly fell into the habit of sharing any news they received from him and, in the process, became friends themselves.

Tonight's letter to Trish didn't include any news from Ian. Here it was, getting close to the end of June, and her last letter from him had been dated in April. She finished writing her letter and turned to a fresh page in her sketch pad. She was shading the contours of Ian's jaw when Will knocked on the frame of the open door.

"Busy?"

"Just doodling."

He sat beside her on the sofa and took the sketch pad out of her hands. "Him again? Why don't you ever sketch me?"

She grabbed the pad away from him. "Because you won't sit still for more than five minutes."

"Too many other things to do." He looked away, his hand beating a restless rhythm on the arm of the sofa.

"Something wrong?"

"Not really." He faced her, his mouth set in a firm line with the corners slightly turned up. "I lied to you."

"About what?"

"Do you remember . . . ? It's been a couple of years. Remember asking me if I ever loved anyone?"

"You said you were waiting for the girl who could turn your heart upside down."

"The truth is, I'd already met that girl. But she loved someone else. Married him. You know her."

Alison furrowed her brow, but it took only

319

a moment for her to bring up the right image. "Hannah?"

Will nodded. "I never stood a chance. Her parents wouldn't have approved. I'm not sure *my* parents would have approved." He frowned and gave a slight shrug. "Not that it mattered. She and Danny had known each other all their lives. I think they fell in love when they were still in diapers."

Alison touched his arm. "Oh, Will. I'm so sorry."

"I'm worried about her. I told her we could find a hiding place for her and the twins. But she won't go."

"Why not?"

"Because Danny's mother won't leave." He shook his head in frustration. "She's convinced Hannah that as long as they cooperate, everything will be fine. They can't see that it's only going to get worse."

"It's so bad now. How much worse can it get?"

He stared into her eyes, wordlessly giving her his answer. She looked away first, head bending over her sketch pad, seeing Ian's smiling face gazing back at her.

Will shifted and took her hand between his. "You must leave here, Alison. Soon."

She opened her mouth to protest, but he didn't let her speak.

"Do you have any idea what is happening in Poland? In Germany?"

"I've heard the rumors."

"They're not just rumors. Trains are leaving Westerbork more frequently than ever, crowded with Jews. Where do you think they're going?"

"I don't know," she said, hesitantly.

"You can bet nowhere good."

"That has nothing to do with me. No one is going to put my name on the lists." *Because no one knows, no one in any official capacity knows about Mama.* "Besides, you need me here. To find safe houses for the children. To take them to the farms."

"You won't be doing that anymore."

"Why not?"

"Because it's time for you to go," he said vehemently. "And you have to persuade Hannah to go with you."

Anger built in Alison's stomach. Why couldn't he understand that she had as much right to stay in Rotterdam as he did? Papa was even worse. At least once a month, they had the same argument, and she was sick of it. But she pushed all that aside, determined not to argue with Will when he already seemed so distraught. Instead, she took a different tack.

"Why would Hannah listen to me?"

"She likes you. She told me so."

Alison looked into Will's eyes and knew she was looking into his heart. Love, fear, uncertainty — a palette of clashing emotions. A palette she understood all too well. Poor Will. His heart was more hopeless than her own. Empathy overcame her anger and she leaned back into the sofa cushion, throwing her arm over her head. "I thought you were on my side about this. That you wanted me to stay."

"Things have changed."

"What things?"

"Nothing I can tell you." He stood and crossed to the window. Barely moving the heavy blackout curtain, he peered out into the night. When he turned back to her, his brown eyes held a strange resignation. "No matter what happens, take care of Hannah," he pleaded. "For me."

"This isn't fair, Will."

His jaw twitched, but he didn't say anything. He only looked at her, desperate for her promise. "If there's anything I can do to help Hannah, I will," she said. "That's the only promise I can make."

"I guess that will have to do, then. Good night, Alison." He kissed her on top of her head before hurrying from the room and down the stairs.

∎ ∎ ∎

A few hours later, she suddenly awoke, trembling, and tried to remember what had awakened her.

"No matter what happens." Papa and Will had both said the same thing. Both had given her an affectionate kiss. It was as if . . . She scrambled out of bed and pulled on her robe and slippers. The bedside clock showed the time as about twenty after seven.

In the hallway, she glanced through the open door of the room that Pieter shared with Hendrik. Finding it empty, she headed downstairs to the kitchen. The warm smells of ersatz coffee and fresh bacon teased her senses, causing her mouth to water. But the men weren't in the kitchen. She was about to go into the main room of the gallery when raised voices came from Brant's room.

"Why didn't you stop them?"

Stunned by the anger in Brant's voice, Alison stood just outside the door where she couldn't be seen. She had never heard him talk to her grandfather in that tone of voice before.

"What did you expect me to do? Tie them up?" Defeat lent a plaintive tone to Hendrik's soft voice. "They were determined to go."

"I'm going after them." Hearing groans and the squeak of bedsprings, Alison realized Brant was trying to get out of bed. His painful injuries, which had become infected despite their care, had kept him incapacitated longer than any of them had expected.

"No," Hendrik said firmly. "It's too late. The best we can do now is wait. And hope they change their minds."

Fear settled in Alison's stomach as she realized they were talking about Pieter and Will. She entered the room, facing both men. Brant tottered on the side of his bed, trying to get his bandaged legs into a pair of pants. Hendrik sat in an upholstered chair that had been salvaged from the wreckage of the canal house.

"Where are they?" Alison's voice held a note of hysteria.

Hendrik waved his pipe and stared out the window.

"Where did they go?" she said, more insistently.

"To Amsterdam."

"Amsterdam?" As soon as the name of the city left her lips, she understood. She leaned against the doorjamb to keep from falling.

"Göring? They're going to kill Göring?"

Hendrik nodded, his arm slack, the pipe bowl barely caught between his fingers.

"I'm going after them."

"You can't." Hendrik's voice was sharp, a tone he rarely used and never with her.

"If I'm there, they won't go through with it."

"You can't be sure of that." Hendrik tried to stand, but he fell back into the chair. Placing both hands on the chair arms, he pushed himself to his feet. "You could be caught up in whatever trouble they find themselves in."

"Our sons," Brant moaned. "They will be martyrs to a lost cause. What will happen to them?"

"Nothing." Alison summoned all her courage and straightened her shoulders. "I will find them, and I will stop them." She was almost out of the kitchen when Brant called her name.

"Miss Alison, come quick. Your grandfather."

Rushing back to the room, she found Hendrik slumped on the floor, Brant beside him, shaking his shoulders. She dropped beside Hendrik and laid her hand on his chest. "Opa? Opa, can you hear me?"

CHAPTER THIRTY-ONE

Alison stood next to Hendrik's hospital bed, her eyes glued to his pale face. His watery eyes focused on her, and he tried to smile. The effort seemed too difficult for him, and he grimaced.

"Are you in pain?" she asked softly. A heart attack, the doctor had told her earlier. One that had caused extensive damage.

"I feel fine." Hendrik's voice was barely above a whisper. His eyes roamed the cubicle, formed by movable screens that provided little privacy from the other patients in the ward. "How did I get here?"

"Monsieur Duret brought us."

"I imagine Brant had something to say about that." Hendrik's brief laughter turned to a gagging cough. Alison quickly offered him a drink of water, helping to hold up his head.

"He wasn't happy about being left behind at the gallery, that's for sure."

"Where is Etienne?"

"He went to Amsterdam," she whispered, not wanting anyone who might be listening on the other side of the screens to hear.

Hendrik slowly closed his eyes. "You've not heard from your papa."

"No."

"Foolish boy. My foolish, foolish boy." He took a deep breath and heavily exhaled as he nodded off. Alison watched him closely, breathing her own sigh of relief when his chest rose and fell, rose and fell, in medicated sleep.

The long hours since their arrival at the hospital had been spent in agony, pacing and praying in the waiting room, anxious for the doctor to bring her some news. Praying for Pieter and Will to come home. Praying Monsieur Duret found them before they attempted to exact their revenge.

Heavy footsteps sounded in the ward, coming closer. Shadows appeared against the screen.

"I must protest," the doctor said firmly. "This simply cannot be allowed."

"This is not your concern, Doctor."

Theodor.

Alison quickly scanned the room and just as quickly recognized her folly. Obviously there was nowhere to hide. Her muscles tensed, and her knuckles turned white as she grasped the bed railing.

Theodor appeared in the gap between two of the screens, the doctor close behind him.

"Alison," he said, his face awash in relief. "I must talk to you."

She glanced at her grandfather, whose eyes flickered open.

"Herr Van Schuyler," said the doctor, "I offer my apologies. But the count insisted on speaking with your granddaughter."

Theodor had not taken his eyes from Alison. The intensity of his gaze frightened her. "We must speak."

"It's fine, Doctor." Alison forced a smile. "Count Scheidemann is a . . . friend."

"Five minutes," the doctor said, vainly reasserting his authority. "No more."

"No more is needed." Theodor dismissed him with a nod, and the doctor reluctantly left them alone.

"How did you know I was here?" she asked as casually as she could.

"A man at the bakery told me. He said he helped carry your grandfather to the car."

"Yes, he did." She and Monsieur Duret couldn't manage on their own, and poor Brant was unable to help at all. The baker was known for being a gossip, so she expected the neighboring merchants to know about her grandfather's collapse. But not a Nazi.

Theodor interrupted her thoughts. "Where is your father?"

"I . . . I don't know." She tried to stay composed, but she couldn't keep the fear from her eyes. "Why?"

Theodor walked around the bed to stand beside her and lowered his head. When he spoke, he kept his voice low so only Alison and Hendrik could hear him. "There was an attempt on Reichsmarschall Göring's life outside the Rijksmuseum a few hours ago."

"What does that have to do with us?" Hendrik asked weakly.

"I hope, for your sake, nothing at all." Theodor held Alison's gaze. "Tell me the truth, Alison. Do you know anything about this attempt?"

"Why would I?" she said with a nervous laugh. Heat brightened her cheeks.

"Your father has reason to wish for the Reichsmarschall's death."

"I'm sure he's not the only one in Holland with that wish."

Doubt showed in Theodor's eyes, and something else. Fear. For her. He switched his gaze to Hendrik. "Your chauffeur, sir. What is his name?"

"Why do you ask?" asked Hendrik stonily.

"His name," Theodor said impatiently.

Hendrik only stared. Alison spoke up. "His name is Jacobus Brant. But he had nothing to do with the attempt. He is at the gallery, recovering from —" She glanced at Hendrik, then finished lamely, "An injury."

"He has a son," Theodor said. It was not a question.

"Yes," said Alison.

"Willem Brant."

"Yes."

"He has been arrested."

Alison gasped, and her knees buckled. Theodor caught her and helped her to a metal chair beside the bed. Her fingers trembled, and she clasped them together into tight fists.

Theodor knelt beside her, his voice soft and compassionate. "He did it for you, didn't he?"

She couldn't answer. Her tongue felt swollen, her lips frozen. Will's final words echoed in her mind. *"No matter what happens, take care of Hannah."*

"Is he in love with you?"

She looked in his eyes, surprised by the lack of jealousy, by his tenderness. "No," she stammered. "We grew up together. He is like a brother to me."

"I see."

"Where is he?"

"At Gestapo headquarters in Amsterdam. I doubt he'll be there for long."

"May I see him?"

"That will not be possible." Theodor shifted his weight but stayed kneeling. "Alison, you must listen to me. Göring will execute young Brant. He may also arrest his father. You, your grandfather, and your father will all come under suspicion. I offered to help you before. Please let me help you now."

"How can you help?"

"I have influence."

"You still wish to marry me."

"I have wished that for a long time."

"You can save Will?"

He shook his head. "Göring will insist on a public execution. But I will do everything I can to protect the rest of you from his wrath."

Alison bit her lip, thinking of her family, thinking of Ian. Perhaps this was her fate, to sacrifice her love for one man to save her father. *Where are you, Papa?* She wished she knew.

"If you truly love her," said Hendrik, his voice weak and halting, "arrange for her to go to London."

"Why London?" For the first time, a harsh

edge crept into Theodor's voice.

"She will be safe there." Hendrik struggled with his breathing. "The safest place."

"The British will yet bow to German superiority, Herr Van Schuyler. When they do, London will be only a memory."

"From London, she can go to America. Her home. Until the war is over."

"Perhaps that would be best." Theodor glanced at his watch. "I've delayed too long. The Reichsmarschall is certain to look for your father at the gallery. He will welcome the excuse to once again strip it bare. I'll meet him there and try to dissuade him from too much damage." He stood and pulled Alison to her feet with him. "You must not return there. Not for any reason. Do you understand?"

Her thoughts frozen, Alison nodded. She had no choice but to trust her life to this man, who in his own strange way loved her. Only he seemed to have the power to extricate them from their troubles.

All of them except for Will.

She cringed, recalling stories she'd heard about Gestapo interrogation techniques. A fancy name for torture. There had to be something she could do.

"Take care of Hannah. For me."

"Alison, are you listening to me?"

She snapped out of her thoughts, tried to remember what Theodor had said. "I won't go to the gallery. I promise."

"I may have to entertain the Reichsmarschall this evening." He practically shivered with distaste. "I'll return for you as soon as I can, either tonight or in the morning. If you must stay here for the night, ask the doctor to accommodate you. In secret."

"Yes, I will."

"Good." He paused, then spontaneously kissed her cheek. "Wish me well, my love."

"Thank you, Theodor," Alison said with more appreciation than she felt. Her mind had too many strands to follow; too many lives were at stake: Will, Papa, even Brant. What would happen to him when Göring arrived at the gallery? She pasted on a brave smile, and with a final nod, Theodor disappeared through the gap in the screens.

Hendrik clutched her hand. "Come, child."

"What are we going to do, Opa?"

"We're going to hide you, *mijn schatje.*"

CHAPTER THIRTY-TWO

Less than five minutes after Theodor's departure, Etienne Duret glided through the gap in the screens. "I thought he would never leave," the Frenchman sniffed.

Alison wrapped her arms around him. "Did you find Papa?"

"No, *cherie*. I was too late to stop their plans. Too late to stop the arrests."

"Was Papa arrested?"

"I do not believe so."

"Etienne," Hendrik interrupted, "Count Scheidemann is going to the gallery. We must warn Brant."

"It's too late for warnings. When I left him, he promised to lie low, as the Americans say." In quiet tones, Duret told them how he had followed the arrested saboteurs to the Gestapo station and waited outside the building until Count Scheidemann left.

"I followed him here all the way from Amsterdam. I thought he might go to the gallery, so I took a shortcut and arrived before he did." From inside the locked gallery, Duret had spied on the count through the upstairs windows as he talked to the baker.

"Does Brant know about Will?" Hendrik asked.

"He knows." Duret clasped his hands behind his back and bowed his head for a moment.

"We must hope that Pieter is in hiding. Perhaps he will find a way to save Will." Hendrik's voice sounded much stronger than it had during Theodor's visit. "The count has promised to use his influence with that thief Göring to protect us," he told Duret. "As long as Alison goes with him."

"He is a cad."

"Indeed," Hendrik said. "He may return at any time. How soon can you implement your plan?"

"What plan?" Alison asked.

"Your father dubbed it Operation Lighthouse," Duret said. "He said if anything happened to him, I should implement it immediately."

"Implement what?"

"The plan for your departure, naturally."

"You can't expect me to leave." Alison looked to her grandfather for support, but he turned his face away from her. She gripped Duret's arm. "Not when Papa may be in prison. When Opa needs me."

"*Schatje,* I have indulged your stubbornness for too long." Hendrik blinked and pulled at his beard. "My selfish desire to have you near me has endangered your life. Go with Etienne. He will send you to England. When the war is over, you and your young man can return to us."

"Will you still be here, Opa?"

"Van Schuylers will always be in Rotterdam. In spirit, if not in body." His speech became more labored, his breathing more ragged. "But you must live your own life, wherever the fate may take you."

"It only leads to heartache."

"And to great joy. You will see." He enveloped her hand and tucked it near his chin. "Now go. Quickly."

"Come, Alison." Duret stood in the gap between the screens and extended his hand to her.

"I'll go with Theodor. He'll keep his promise to protect all of us. I know he will."

"No. You will not sacrifice yourself." A spasm of coughing shook Hendrik's body. "Not for me. Not for your father. Now go."

"No more arguing, *cherie.* Do as your opa and your papa say. Allow them to fight their battles without fear for you."

Despite her protests, despite all the arguments with Papa, Alison had expected this day to come. Just not with her opa in the hospital and her papa facing arrest. Though she hated admitting it, Monsieur Duret was right. It was time for her to go.

She leaned over the bed rail and kissed Hendrik's cheek, as thin and delicate as parchment paper.

"God bless you and keep you, *mijn schatje.*"

"You, too, Opa." She almost choked on the words, and her eyes filled with tears.

"We must go." Duret took her gently by the arm and she let him lead her away. At the gap in the screens, she took one last look at her grandfather. His white fluffy hair surrounded his head like a snowy halo, and his whiskers fluffed above his chest. She imprinted the image in her mind: The crisp white linens, the brown blanket, the metal table and black-encased monitors, the cold overhead lighting that cast imperfect shadows in the corners.

With a sudden intake of breath, she realized that her dress, a rich amethyst with emerald and gold trim, provided the only color in the room. When she left, Opa would be alone with bland sterility and metallic coldness.

Alison hurried through the gap, peering through other screens till she found what she wanted. Smiling at the elderly woman who occupied the bed, Alison pointed to the nearby floral arrangement. "Please, may I have one of your flowers?"

The woman, confusion in her weary eyes, nodded.

"Thank you." Alison pulled a crimson rose from the bouquet and hurried back to her grandfather. Words failed her as she pressed the rose into Hendrik's hand.

She glanced at him before slipping through the gap for the last time. The crimson rose rested against his cheek, and his gray-blue eyes, so like her own, glistened through a veil of tears.

Theodor breathed a sigh of relief as he drove past the front of the gallery and turned into the back parking area. Göring had not yet arrived, and that gave him the advantage. He could think of only one way to prevent young Brant's execution, though there was no guarantee that Göring wouldn't go back on his word. A gentlemen's agreement was only as binding as the honor of the agreeing gentlemen — and Göring was no gentleman.

He squashed the pesky temptation that threatened to suck out his own honor. Hendrik was an old fool. Alison would never set foot on American soil again. If all went as planned, she would arrive at the Scheidemann chalet in a day or two. Her watercolors now graced the walls, and her mother's portrait rested on an easel in an upper room that contained a wealth of paints, brushes, tools, and special equipment. Everything she needed to restore the portrait. She could wish for nothing more.

Tugging at the hem of his jacket, he took quick strides to the gallery's back door and twisted the handle. To his surprise, the door opened and a three-note bell tinkled. Hesitating in the partially open door, he drew his sidearm. When several seconds passed without him hearing any noises, he quietly made his way to the kitchen.

Hendrik's chauffeur sat near the stove, feeding paper into the open stove door. When Theodor entered, Brant glanced up, nodding a hello as if the count were an expected guest instead of an intruder with a drawn gun, and never pausing in his systematic feeding of the fire.

Let the papers burn. Nothing could stop Theodor's plan now. Smug satisfaction buoyed his spirits. Events were turning out better than he hoped. Alison would have eventually told him what he wanted to know to save Brant the younger; of that he had no doubt. But so would Brant the elder.

"Your son is under arrest."

"So I've heard."

"He will no doubt be executed. After he is tortured."

A grimace crossed Brant's face and disappeared, leaving his jaw solid, his expression impassive. "Why are you here?"

"Reichsmarschall Göring is on his way. He believes that your son's traitorous activities are headquartered here. You understand these implications?"

"Let him come."

"Alison has agreed to come with me."

Brant stared at Theodor, his hands finally stilled.

"You are surprised? Yet she is so willing." Theodor pulled a chair from the table and sat down, enjoying Brant's puny efforts to hide his anger. "Not even Reichsmarschall Göring will find it easy to execute my wife's father. Or to make sport with my gallery."

"And Will? What about my son?"

"Göring requires a scapegoat. Justice demands one." Theodor examined his buffed nails, patiently waiting for Brant to make the next move, confident of what it would be. He was not disappointed.

"You will trade my life for Will's?" Brant's expression was both shrewd and wary. "You can arrange this with Göring?"

"If you confess to masterminding the operation, yes. But you must name names. Everyone except Pieter Schuyler."

Brant slowly nodded.

"There is one more condition."

He waited for Brant to meet his gaze and relished the utter defeat in the other man's eyes. "I have researched the Van Schuyler Gallery's inventory and records. When Reichsmarschall Göring acquired the gallery contents a couple of years ago, a certain Vermeer should have been included in the shipment. The Reichsmarshall has quite a fondness for Vermeer."

"You want the painting?" Brant asked in disbelief.

"I want all the hidden paintings." Theodor stood and hovered over the chauffeur. He placed the barrel of the revolver on Brant's neck. "Tell me, and only me, where the paintings are hidden. I will ensure that Göring gets the Vermeer. In exchange for such a generous gift, he *may* let you die in your son's place."

Struggling to his feet, Brant knocked the revolver from his neck and let the papers fan across the floor. Overcoming his surprise, Theodor regained control of the gun and stuck the barrel into Brant's side. Brant grabbed Theodor's tie, yanking until their noses were within inches of each other. Theodor choked, gagging on the stale tobacco on the older man's breath.

"I'll tell you where the paintings are," Brant hissed. "But not until you save Will."

All he had to do was pull the trigger, but Theodor's finger refused to move. His eyes, entranced by the smoldering hate in Brant's face, refused to look away, refused to even blink. Fear squeezed his jaw and his chest. The noose tightened around his neck as Brant twisted his tie, choking his throat.

"Do we have a deal, Count?"

"Ye-es." Theodor gripped Brant's forearm, surprised by the hard muscle he felt beneath his grasping fingers.

Another twist. "Upon your honor? Say it."

"Upon my honor," Theodor said, choking on each syllable.

He coughed as the tie went slack. His watery eyes finally blinked, wouldn't stop blinking, and his hand shook so hard that it took all his effort not to drop his revolver.

Brant sank to the floor, amid the paper debris, his legs splayed out before him. Standing over Brant, Theodor loosened his tie as he tried to stir up anger for what the chauffeur had done to him. But instead of fiery embers, he only succeeded in poking the unfamiliar ashes of cowardice.

"She's going with you?" Brant spoke so softly that Theodor strained to hear him. "Miss Alison?"

"She is."

"Don't you dare hurt her." Tears welled up in the chauffeur's eyes. "Don't you dare."

Still breathing deeply, Theodor holstered his revolver and fixed his tie. "On your feet," he ordered, tugging at his jacket hem.

"I can't."

"Stand up, I said."

Heavy pounding sounded at the front door, followed by a single gunshot and the cracking of wood.

Brant smirked. "Your friends have arrived."

"Back here," Theodor called. Several Nazi soldiers entered the kitchen, rifles at the ready. Theodor gestured toward Brant. "Arrest him."

Two soldiers, one on each side, grabbed Brant by the arms and dragged him from the room. The chauffeur's legs, seemingly helpless, trailed behind.

Theodor watched him disappear through the kitchen door, a weak and broken man.

Somehow the victory left a sour taste in his mouth. He turned to the sink and vomited.

CHAPTER THIRTY-THREE

Alison crossed her arms, hugging the mish-mash of sorrow and fear that threatened to explode — afraid that if it did, she'd never find the pieces of herself again. "I promised Will."

"I promised your father." Monsieur Duret stared ahead, maneuvering the Bentley away from the hospital.

"I may never see Papa again. Or Will." Her voice trembled. "Please, let me do this one last thing. Then we can leave."

"You will find no more excuses?"

"None."

"Which is the way? Back streets, if you please."

Alison directed Duret to the street where the de Graaf family lived. Outside the narrow house, two Nazi soldiers waited by the curb.

"Get down before they see you," Duret demanded.

Alison knelt on the floorboard while he drove past the soldiers, his eyes never veering from the street. "We have to go back."

"Absolutely not." Duret's voice brooked no argument.

"What if they arrest Hannah? What will happen to the children?"

"There is nothing we can do."

Alison crawled onto the seat and looked out the rear window. "Can't we at least watch a minute? See what happens?"

"No."

She slumped back in the seat, arms hugging her chest again. The sky darkened as heavy clouds covered the sun. "It's going to rain."

"I hope so. It might help our chances of getting you away."

"What about Hannah's chances?"

"I will return later and see what can be done for her. Does that ease your mind?"

"You'll be too late." She bit her lip and stared at the traffic ahead of them, biding her time.

Duret braked for an intersection, and she clasped the door handle. "Forgive me, Monsieur." Before he could stop her, Alison opened the door and slipped out. She quickly walked back toward the de Graaf home, careful not to let the Nazi soldiers see her. Before slipping to the rear of a neighboring house, she turned around and waved to Duret, then crept to the back of the de Graaf house. She listened at the back door and, hearing nothing, cracked it open. An elderly woman, whom she recognized as Danny's mother, sat at the kitchen table humming to herself. A lacy cap covered her silver hair and a crocheted shawl enveloped her frail shoulders. She peered at Alison through rheumy eyes.

"Shh." Alison placed her finger on her lips. The poor woman, already in poor health, had rapidly declined since Danny's death. She smiled and hummed her tune. No wonder Hannah was reluctant to leave her.

Hearing voices from the living room, Alison listened at the door to Hannah's desperate pleas. "I know nothing. My husband never told me of his plans. Herr Brant was *his* friend, not mine."

"The saboteur Brant was seen coming and going from this house," said a dispassionate male voice. "Do you deny it?"

"He only came to see if I needed anything. We've known each other since we were children."

"He is your lover, perhaps? Is that why he came to see you?"

"Of course not. Only as a friend. My husband's friend."

"Nevertheless, you will come with us. If what you say is true, we will return you to your home. If not . . ." He let the sentence hang.

"My children . . . I can't leave them."

"I give you the time it takes me to smoke my cigarette to make your arrangements."

A momentary silence ended when the kitchen door opened. Alison sprang back as Hannah entered, eyes wide in fright. Catching her breath, she pointed to the pantry and pushed Alison into it. "Did you hear?" she whispered frantically, clasping Alison's hands.

"Hannah, I'm so sorry."

"Is it true what he said? Will was arrested?"

Alison nodded, her mind racing to come up with a plan. "We need to leave right now. I'm going to England, and you can come with me."

"To England? Now?" Hannah smiled and her face brightened. "I prayed for a deliverer, and you came."

"Hurry, Hannah. We can go out the back."

"No, Alison. I will go with the German. You will take the children." Hannah placed her hand against Alison's mouth to stop her protest. "Please, there is no time to argue. Take the children with you. To England. Will you?"

Both women froze as the kitchen door opened. Alison pressed her back against the pantry's rear shelf. Though she couldn't see who spoke, she recognized the German's harsh voice. "No more delay."

Hannah held Alison's gaze, her question in her eyes. Alison nodded, and Hannah squeezed her fingers, then grabbed a jar of peaches from the pantry shelf. She slipped through the door, leaving Alison alone in the shadows.

"Mama de Graaf, here are peaches for your supper." Hannah's voice sounded calm and soothing. "Take them next door to Beppie. She will take care of you now. And tell her the children are napping. Can you do that?"

Alison heard the scrape of chair legs on the floor and the humming changed to muttering. Shutting her eyes, scarcely daring to breathe, she pictured Hannah helping her mother-in-law to her feet and leading her to the door.

"I'm ready now." Only the slightest tremor betrayed Hannah's fear.

Alison forced herself to count to one hundred once, then again, before she ventured from the pantry. Taking care not to make any noise, she peeked into the living room and breathed a sigh of relief at finding it empty. She rushed up the stairs and into the children's bedroom. The window, covered with a heavy blackout curtain, let in no light. Alison turned the switch and glanced around the room. The twins napped in a narrow bed, Aaron's arm carelessly slung over Anna's shoulder.

Alison carefully moved aside the curtain and peered out. Rain splattered against the windowpane in thick drops. The Germans, Hannah with them, were gone. Alison started to turn away, then did a double take as a dark Bentley drove slowly up the street and parked several houses down. Monsieur Duret, coming back for her.

As quickly as she could, Alison rummaged through drawers and the wardrobe, gathering a change of clothes and supplies for each child into a bag. She found their jackets and nudged Aaron awake. As she helped him into the jacket, footsteps sounded from downstairs.

"Alison?" Monsieur Duret called quietly.

She went to the top of the stairs. "Up here."

By the time he entered the room, both children were wearing caps and jackets, rubbing their eyes and asking for their mama.

"They took her," Alison said, glancing at the children.

"I saw them leave." Monsieur Duret clasped his hands behind his back. "You are taking the children?"

"All the way to England."

"Come, then. We've already delayed too long."

They managed to get the twins downstairs with little fuss. Alison looked out the front door, where the rain, now a downpour, created a gray screen between them and the Bentley. Duret sniffed, then bent his head and hurried toward the car. In a few moments, he pulled in front of the house. Alison settled the children in the backseat, talking quietly to them while Duret concentrated on navigating the rain-soaked streets.

Alison's dress, totally drenched, clung to her legs, and her wet hair stuck to the back of her neck. She rubbed her chilled arms and silently prayed for Papa and Will, Opa and Hannah. She couldn't bear to think about Will and Hannah in Gestapo interrogation rooms, or that her grandfather might never leave the colorless hospital ward. That she might never see any of them again.

Papa might have been arrested too. Or perhaps he was hiding somewhere in Amsterdam. Had he really thought he could get close enough to Göring to kill him? Or had that been Will's role in the failed attempt? So many secrets. Despite all the trips she had made, escorting children to the safe houses and foster homes, they had never trusted her with their sabotage plans.

But their secretiveness had not been enough to protect her. Hannah was taken from her home simply because Will had visited her. The Germans would have even more reason to suspect Alison than they did Hannah. If not for her grandfather's heart attack and Theodor's warning, she might be in an interrogation room herself.

She shivered again.

At least Ian was safe at Colditz.

CHAPTER THIRTY-FOUR

Ian drove the truck for several hours, stopping only for Libby's needs. He avoided towns as much as possible and used the descending sun as his guide for keeping to his southwesterly tack. When night fell, he drove cautiously without headlights until he dozed off, jerking awake when the truck bounced into a rut. He leaned out the window, peering into the darkness, until he found a cutoff in a stand of trees. Parking the truck as far off the road as possible, he slept fitfully until sunrise.

He guessed they were about fifty kilometers, as the crow flies, from the Swiss border when the truck's engine sputtered and died, the result of another in a long line of calculated decisions he had been forced to make since his escape from Colditz. He couldn't get fuel without going into a town or village, and he didn't want to risk arousing anyone's suspicions. Especially now that he had Libby with him. Besides, he might need the little bit of money he had to get across the border.

In studying the silk map, he also guessed he was farther west than his original destination, an outcropping along the border known as the Ransom Salient. A returned escapee, who had been caught in Italy, had given Ian detailed instructions on how to cross the border at that point. But Ian's primary concern now was to get out of Germany as quickly as possible. He'd have to trust God to lead him to a safe crossing point. At least he had managed to put some distance between him and Gretchen's farm. For that, he was thankful.

He folded the map, consolidating the contents of the truck into two bags, then used the blankets to fashion a type of backpack. With frequent checks of his compass, he and Libby walked through the quiet countryside. Eager to please, Libby seldom complained, but their pace was slow and their stops frequent. As the day drew to a close, Ian's patience thinned. He hid his frustration, knowing she was doing the best she could to keep up. The closer they came to the border, though, the more anxious he became.

Though reluctant to stop, he scouted

around for a suitable campsite when the sun touched the horizon. If he'd been alone, he'd still be walking, at least a couple more hours. But Libby had stumbled twice in just the past ten or fifteen minutes. Both times, as he brushed the dirt from her knees, her little lip had quivered, but she had refused to cry.

He took a deep breath and smiled at the girl with more warmth than he felt. "I don't think I can take another step. How about you?"

"I can walk all night long, Papi," she said in a singsong voice. Giving lie to her words, she sat on a fallen log near a broad-bottomed evergreen and rested her cheek on the cloth doll she clutched tightly against her chest.

"Look, Libby," he said with false enthusiasm. "You found our shelter." The ground beneath the evergreen, about a meter and a half below the tree's lowest branches, was packed dirt with a smattering of dried pine needles. A perfect place to spread their blankets.

"I did?" Her brown eyes, half-closed with weariness, grew round.

"Supper first, then bedtime." Ian shrugged off his makeshift backpack and sat on the ground, adjusting the Walther at his hip as he rested his back against the log. Libby slid down beside him, and they shared a cold supper of cheese and apples.

When they finished, Ian crawled beneath the branches and stashed their bags next to the evergreen's trunk. Another source of irritation: Before Libby joined him, he traveled light. Now he carried food and supplies, the Hebrew Tanak, the Steinberg family photograph, and blankets. Sometimes he carried Libby.

He arranged the blankets, and Libby crawled in after him. Lying beneath the evergreen, his forearm behind his head, he peered through the fringe of the branches at the dusky sky. One by one, pinpoints of starlight appeared, brightening in intensity as darkness settled across the land. Libby, curled up next to him, hugged her doll and quietly sang her lullaby.

Twisting his head, he found the North Star and remembered boyhood camping trips with his brother and with Mark. How they stretched out just like this, pointing to and naming the constellations. Libby snuggled closer and he patted her slender arm. A gentle peace stilled his lingering tension and he breathed deeply of the pine and dirt and long-ago summers. The smells of freedom.

■ ■ ■ ■

Ian slept soundly, his first good night's sleep since escaping Colditz. But he woke with a sense of dread, an out-of-sorts absence that pushed him fully awake when he opened his eyes.

Libby was gone.

He crawled out from the branches and looked around. They were on the edge of a rolling meadow, dotted with evergreens and wildflowers. Hearing a giggle from beyond a rise, he pulled the Walther from its holster and raced that way.

Libby's back was to him as she waded in a narrow creek, the water barely above her ankles. A woman waded beside her. A woman wearing a nun's habit, the long black skirt hiked to her knees.

She must have heard his approach, because she looked up as he neared. A snowy-white wimple framed her oval face.

Libby turned too and waved. "Hi, Papi. I found a lady."

A wide smile further brightened the nun's lightly sunburned cheeks. She reached for Libby's hand and led the child from the creek to a gravelly sandbar where they'd left their shoes. Ian joined them, holding the pistol at his side.

"We played, Papi." Libby wiggled her toes, wrinkled from cold water. "I'm wet."

"That's fine, sweetheart." Ian stepped next to her and rested his hand on her shoulder.

"I didn't mean to frighten you." The nun looked pointedly at the gun. "You were sleeping so soundly, it seemed a shame to wake you."

"Too soundly, apparently."

"Don't be so hard on yourself. I often walk here early in the mornings." Her gray eyes twinkled. "Though it's not every day I find a pixie washing her hands in the bubbling brook."

"I'm a pixie." Libby giggled and tugged at Ian's sleeve. "Isn't she pretty, Papi?"

The nun's musical laugh infected Libby with another case of the giggles.

"Very pretty," Ian agreed. "Does the pretty nun have a name?"

"I'm Sister Regina. And my convent is beyond that hill." She pointed southeast. "You are welcome to come. For a hot meal. Some needed rest."

"May we, Papi? Please?"

"Shh, Libby." Ian holstered the Walther. "I appreciate the offer, Sister, but we'll continue on our way."

"It would be wise to reconsider. German

358

patrols pass through here frequently. They are suspicious of strangers." She spoke with a casual indifference, but her pale eyes focused with an unspoken intensity on Ian. "We are not far from the border, you know."

"How far?"

"Two days on foot." Sister Regina smiled at Libby. "Longer with a child."

The frustration that had gnawed at him yesterday attacked again, eating at his stomach. With Libby tagging along, it might take four days, a week even, to reach the border.

"We are a small order, but we do what we can for the lost, the hungry." She paused. "The foreigner."

"Please, Papi?" Libby hopped up and down beside him.

"Let's get your shoes on, shall we?" Ian knelt down and helped Libby scrunch her toes into the worn leather boots. An idea niggled at the back of his mind. Perhaps Sister Regina was the answer to a prayer he didn't realize he'd prayed. Convents often ran orphanages, especially during war. Libby would have shelter, food. And he'd be in Switzerland in two days.

"You are not the first travelers to need our refuge," said Sister Regina, her good-natured expression undisturbed by Ian's scrutiny. "Nor will you be the last. I suppose the convent will shelter those in need until the world ends."

"Do you think that's what it will take to end this war? The end of the world?"

"Perhaps not. But war will follow peace as surely as night follows day."

"That seems a pessimistic point of view for someone of your vocation."

"Only a realistic one."

Ian found his distrust fading beneath her confident serenity. "German patrols, huh?"

"I fear so."

"I need to get our gear."

"I'll help."

Ian crawled under the tree to retrieve the bags while Sister Regina and Libby laughingly shook out the blankets and folded them. Following the creek bed toward the convent, Ian and Sister Regina walked together while Libby alternately ran ahead and lagged behind them.

The nun, her hands hidden within the folds of the blankets she carried, smiled up at Ian, her eyes sparkling. "May I tell you something?"

"Please do."

She leaned closer, lowering her voice. "I think you are not Libby's father."

Ian looked at Libby, a few meters ahead

of them, dragging her doll as she followed the hops of a brown toad along the shallow bank. "She believes I am. I haven't the courage to tell her otherwise."

"Where are her parents?"

"I don't know what happened to her father." He hesitated, feeling again the weight of Gretchen's body in his arms, hearing the distant disturbance of the water when he lowered her into the well.

"What about her mother?"

Ian shifted the weight of the bag he carried on his shoulder. "Dead. Libby doesn't know."

Sister Regina stopped walking, and Ian turned to face her. "Are you responsible for her death?" Her grave eyes searched his face.

"I tried to protect her." He lowered his eyes. "I failed."

"Protect her from what?"

"A thug dressed up as an officer."

"A German officer?"

Ian looked at her and, jutting out his chin, nodded once.

"What was his fate?"

He didn't answer, and she tilted her head, her eyes never wavering from his, as if she could see into his soul. "You did what had to be done. That's the end of it."

"Are you giving me absolution?"

"Only God can do that." She walked away, but Ian hesitated, his troubled spirit anxious to find solace wherever it might be found.

But he didn't expect to find forgiveness from Sister Regina or at the convent. Not when he planned to compound his sins by breaking a promise he'd made to a dying woman.

CHAPTER THIRTY-FIVE

Duret stopped the Bentley across from a warehouse near the Amsterdam docks and blinked the headlights. Through the drenching downpour, a yellow light twinkled on and off in a short, rhythmic pattern. Duret blinked his headlights again, then drove through the opening doors of the building. He switched off the ignition and, shifting in his seat, looked at Alison. "It's best the children stay in the car until it's time to go."

"What about me?"

"Do you need my permission to leave the car?" he asked with a wink.

Alison lifted her shoulders in an appropriately repentant shrug. "I guess not."

"Come on, then."

Lifting Anna across her lap, Alison set the child next to Aaron. "Stay here, okay?"

"I want Mama," Aaron said. Anna pulled her thumb from her mouth only long enough to echo Aaron.

"I know," Alison said soothingly. Their little faces tugged at her heart. She quickly exited the car and joined Duret at the boot, where he and two other men talked in quiet voices.

"You know this gentleman, I believe," said Duret.

"Conductor," she said in surprise. After giving Alison his train schedule, marked with the tiny fish, the conductor had passed Will's scrutiny. She had traveled with several children under his watchful eye since then, taking them from Rotterdam to safe houses throughout northern Holland.

"I am honored to conduct you and your young charges on this final trip." He drew the sign of the fish on the car's wet boot. "May our God watch over you."

"Thank you for helping us."

"This is my son." The conductor gestured toward the younger man, who barely nodded. He wore a boating cap so low over his eyes that Alison found it difficult to make out his features in the dim lighting. "You can call him Skipper. He's taking you to England."

Suddenly overwhelmed by the gravity of the situation, she bit her lip and turned away. Monsieur Duret patted her shoulder, then opened the boot and pulled out a small drawstring bag. "Your father packed this for you weeks ago," he said, handing it to Alison and pointing to a door. "You can change in there."

Alison carried the bag into a cramped office, lit by a single overhead bulb. Closing the door behind her, she set the bundle on a scratched desk that dominated the room. As the finality of what was happening settled upon her, she squeezed the top of the bag so hard that her knuckles turned white. Tears stung her eyes, but she didn't dare cry. If even one tear fell, she might never stop. She needed to be brave. For the twins' sake, if not her own.

Hannah's words whispered inside her. *"I prayed for a deliverer, and you came."*

"I'm not a deliverer, Father," Alison whispered. "How can I leave when those I love need me to stay?"

"Strength and honour." The phrase from Proverbs 31 rose from her heart. If she ever needed to be strong, it was now.

" 'Strength and honour are her clothing,' " she recited, her voice barely a whisper. " 'She shall rejoice in time to come.' "

A promise she had held on to when her father left her in Belgium. A promise she had clung to when she left Ian in the lobby of the Wellington Hotel the day they first

365

met, thinking she would never see him again.

Fingers trembling, she pulled apart the drawstrings and removed a man's shirt and pants, heavy socks and workman's boots, a knit cap. As she changed into the dry clothes, the Scripture resonated within her, as if she were literally clothing herself with the verse. She tied the boots with resolve, finally certain that God was using her to answer Hannah's prayer and determined to save these two children.

A rap sounded against the door. "Hurry, *cherie.*"

"Coming." Alison opened the door, tucking her hair beneath the cap as she joined the men. The conductor lifted Anna from the car and handed her to his son. Then he picked up Aaron, and they carried the children to the rear of the warehouse.

Without saying a word, Duret enveloped Alison in a long embrace. He kissed both her cheeks and embraced her again. Tears welled within her eyes and slipped silently down her face. "Be brave, *ma cherie,*" Duret said, his voice husky. "Let us know when you are safe."

She nodded, unable to speak.

"Go now. Godspeed."

Wiping her eyes on her sleeve, Alison

walked away, glancing back only once. Monsieur Duret stood in front of the Bentley, a darker image against dark shadows. The contrast struck her like a slap — how she had left her grandfather in shades of white, how she was leaving Duret in shades of black. Two men who had taught her everything they knew of color and light.

Her fingers tingled with their desire for a pencil as a vision slammed into her head — a cataclysmic, colorless vision of loss and surrender. In the distance, a crimson spot swirled, an opening rosebud, a promise of hope.

It would be unlike anything she had ever painted before.

After a day such as this, she was no longer the same artist.

She lifted her hand, a farewell wave to the shadow standing by the Bentley, and Monsieur Duret raised his hand in return.

" 'Strength and honour,' " she breathed, then followed the conductor out of the warehouse into the rain-soaked night.

CHAPTER THIRTY-SIX

Ian patted his clean-shaven face with a rough towel and examined his reflection in a mottled mirror. The toll of two years' imprisonment marked the corners of his eyes, his gaunt cheeks, and the protruding of his ribs. But walking in the sun the past few days had added color to his skin. Or maybe it was the healing air of freedom.

A wimple-encircled face appeared in the mirror. Sister Regina carried his shirt, laundered while he had bathed and slept. "You clean up handsomely," she said.

"Thank you," he mumbled, his face reddening as he took the shirt, stiff from drying in the sun, and thrust his arms into the sleeves. Its warm, fresh scent reminded him of summer days at the seashore, when he'd put on his sun-soaked clothes after a swim.

"Don't be embarrassed." Sister Regina's melodic laugh echoed against the stone walls of the cell-like room. "I grew up with six brothers."

"Large family."

"You've yet to tell me your name."

"Perhaps it's best you don't know."

"I thought so at first. But I wish to pray for you. And though God will know whom I mean when I ask Him to bless Libby's protector, I prefer to call you by name."

"Ian Devlin."

"You are a British soldier, no?"

"Lieutenant."

"How long have you enjoyed our German hospitality, Lieutenant Devlin?"

"Only for the past few hours," he said with a grin. "But I've been a prisoner since Dunkirk."

"One of my brothers died at Dunkirk." Her pale eyes momentarily darkened before she blinked and her smile returned. "Supper will be served soon. Will you stay?"

He shook his head. "The sooner I cross that border the better."

"Your guide is ready to leave whenever you are."

"I can trust him?"

She tilted her head, the expression clearly telling him that he had asked a silly question.

He grinned and put up his hands in mock surrender. "Just wanted to be sure."

"Shall we go, then?"

"First, I need to ask a favor." He retrieved the Hebrew Tanak and Steinberg family photograph from a bag beneath the cot. "These belong to Libby. She'll have nothing else to remind her of her parents. Will you keep them for her?"

Sister Regina accepted the treasured items and studied the photograph. "What were their names?"

"Hans and Gretchen Steinberg."

"It looks like you have similar coloring. No wonder Libby is confused."

"I should have told her from the beginning that I wasn't her papi. But at the time —" he shrugged — "I had more immediate concerns."

"The thug."

"Yeah." He rubbed his shoulder, not wanting to revisit the memory of his confrontation with Hauptmann Huber. "Where is she?"

"Bathed, fed, and helping Sister Agnes in the kitchen garden."

"She needs new shoes."

"I will do my best to find her a decent pair."

"If I make it home, I'll send her new ones. And a coat for winter."

"She'll be glad of your gifts, that you are

remembering her."

"What can I send to you?"

Her eyes widened, settling on him with an expression that left him feeling vulnerable. "You are thoughtful to ask. But sending me a gift will not alleviate your guilt."

"Nothing will do that."

"All I ask is that you seek God's guidance for your journey. And for that I will pray."

Ian nodded his gratitude and shouldered the pack he'd prepared. The bag contained the pistol and ammunition, the remaining apples, and a small canteen Sister Regina had found for him.

He followed the nun along the corridor past similar cell-like rooms, then outside to a cloistered walk. Laughter drew his attention to several youngsters playing a game of tag in a nearby orchard, darting here and there among the trees. Another group of children circled a nun who held a large book on her lap.

"Are they all orphans?"

"Most," Sister Regina answered cryptically.

Ian studied a few of the children as they walked toward the kitchen wing. The Jewish heritage of one or two showed in their thin faces. Libby would not be alone here. He took a deep breath, dreading what he had to do. Only a coward would leave without saying good-bye to the little girl, but the temptation to do just that tugged at his elbow.

A tall hedge marked the boundaries of the kitchen gardens, broken here and there by a metal gate. Ian followed Sister Regina through the nearest one and along a dirt path past rows of beans and mounds of potatoes. Libby squatted beside a row of greens, her doll at her feet. Sister Agnes, kneeling beside her like a cheery-faced garden gnome, showed Libby how to select the greens to add to their basket.

When Libby saw Ian, she jumped to her feet. "Papi, come see. I'm helping."

Ian stood beside her, his hand resting on her head, smoothing her dark hair as she leaned against his leg. "You're such a good girl, Libby."

"I picked radishes, too." She plucked one from the basket and handed it to him, her brown eyes shining with pride.

"Thanks, sweetheart." He brushed most of the dirt off the radish and bit into it. "Best radish I've ever tasted."

Libby giggled. Lowering himself to the ground, Ian pulled her onto his lap. Sister Regina gestured to Sister Agnes and the two nuns silently glided away.

Ian picked up the soiled doll and handed her to Libby. "There's something I need to tell you," he said. "Something important."

"What is it, Papi?" So much trust and love filled her eyes as she gazed at him that Ian's heart beat against his chest, a hammer ruthlessly pounding stone as he faced the dreaded task.

"I'm not your papi, Libby. I don't know where he is or what happened to him. Maybe he'll come back someday." The words tasted bitter in his mouth and he despised himself for giving her false hope. But what else could he do? There was no easy way to tell her the truth.

Libby bent over her doll, twisting its leg, her voice a murmuring whisper. "We can play you're my papi. That's a good idea."

"I have to go, Libby." Her back stiffened against his arm. "You get to stay here with Sister Regina and Sister Agnes. They're going to take care of you."

"Until you come back?"

The easy lie rose to his lips, but he couldn't tell it. Maybe someday he would come for her. But right now, he couldn't even be sure of getting himself across the border. He refused to make what his mother called a pie-crust promise — easily made and easily broken.

"I don't know," he said, his voice cracking on the words.

Libby twisted and flung her arms around his neck. "Don't leave me, Papi." Her plea turned to a heart-wrenching sob. "Please don't leave me."

He hugged her as tight as he could, reminding himself that leaving her at the convent was the responsible thing — the best thing — to do. Here she would be safe, taken care of, even loved.

Kissing her tear-dampened cheek, he stood and tried to loosen her grip around his neck. She held on even tighter as sobs wracked her thin body, and Ian feared she might break a rib. He motioned for the sisters.

"Libby, honey, please. I need to go."

"No!" she screamed. "No, Papi, no."

With the nuns' help, Ian extricated himself from Libby's grasp. He tried holding her hands as Sister Agnes held her around the waist. Libby kicked and thrashed to get away from the nuns and back into Ian's arms. Sister Regina's voice, soothing and calm, was lost beneath Libby's pleading cries.

"Go," said Sister Agnes. "She'll be all right. She just needs time."

Doubt assaulted him. "Maybe —"

Sister Regina stepped between him and Libby. "Sister Agnes is right," she said softly. "Prolonging this will only make it worse." She took his arm. "Come, Lieutenant."

"Good-bye, Libby," he said as Sister Regina pulled him toward the kitchen. "I'll never forget you."

Libby kicked and scratched at Sister Agnes. "Papi, no. Don't leave me."

"Keep walking." Sister Regina's voice trembled. "Don't turn around."

They entered a utility room with dried herbs and flowers hung from the ceiling. The thick door shut out Libby's screams, but Ian could still hear her, knew he would hear the echoes of her cries for a long time to come.

Sister Regina touched his arm. "You made the only choice you could."

"I promised her mother."

"You found her a safe place where no one will harm her. Surely that was her mother's wish."

"I suppose."

"Do not doubt it," she said, then led Ian through another door into the large kitchen with its black stoves and long tables. An older man with a fringe of gray hair ringing his head sat at one of the tables. He wiped an already-pristine plate with a crust of bread and stuffed it in his mouth.

"This is our handyman, Schultz. He will guide you to the border."

Ian held out his hand. "I'm —"

"Don't need to know your name." Schultz handed Ian a parcel. "Sister Agnes made this up for you. A bit of something for your stomach."

Ian mumbled his thanks and stuck the parcel in his bag.

"We might as well go. While there's plenty of light."

"I'm as ready as I'll ever be."

Schultz grabbed a flashlight and led Ian and Sister Regina down a flight of stairs into a maze of underground corridors that extended beyond the outer walls of the convent. Ian lost track of the twists and turns, but both Schultz and Sister Regina seemed familiar with their route. After several minutes, they arrived at an iron door.

"We don't often come this way." Sister Regina produced a key from within the wide sleeves of her habit. "If it's ever necessary, this is where we will hide the children."

"Hide the children?"

"Not all of them have the required documents. Rather than raise questions about their parentage, we'll bring them here."

"You would hide Libby here?"

"If necessary."

She unlocked the door, and Schultz shouldered it open. They entered an old burial chamber with stone ledges holding skeletal remains partially covered in decomposing cloth. Metal coffins rested on wooden platforms in the center of the chamber. The musty air of the cellar gave way to a chilly dampness.

"Do you believe in ghosts?" Sister Regina asked.

"I never did. You?"

"Only when I'm down here."

They followed the beam of Schultz's light through the chamber and a coffin-lined passageway to a second metal door. Sister Regina unlocked it, and Schultz pulled it open. Sister Regina pulled back the tapestry that hung in front of the door, and they entered the back room of a chapel partially built into a hillside.

The tiny sanctuary held five rows of pews separated by a center aisle. The late-morning sun slanted through stained glass windows on its eastern side, casting prisms of color across the interior.

"This chapel is only used on rare occasions. The funerals of our elderly sisters, mostly. Few outside our circle even know of its existence."

An almost tangible serenity infused the centuries-old sanctuary, as if the presence of all the prayers, worship, and praise ever uttered there lingered within the stone walls. Ian recalled the verse from Psalms that Mitch, his POW buddy at Laufen and Colditz, had prayed over him before his escape: *"Thou art my hiding place; thou shalt preserve me from trouble; thou shalt compass me about with songs of deliverance."* In this holy place, Ian believed God's hand was upon him, to preserve him and deliver him. This war wasn't over for him yet.

"I'll go out first," said Schultz, clicking off his flashlight and giving it to Sister Regina. "Listen for my whistle."

They watched him through a narrow window beside the arched double doors. He sauntered along an overgrown path toward the nearby woods.

"Thank you. For everything." Ian swallowed past the lump in his throat. "For Libby."

"My prayers go with you, Ian Devlin."

He gave her a halfhearted grin. "My friends call me Dev."

She smiled, her pale eyes hard to read in the sanctuary's dim light. "Fare thee well, Dev. May God be with you."

CHAPTER THIRTY-SEVEN

Ian lagged behind the others walking along the hedgerow, the Walther stuck in his waistband, and searched the distant evening shadows for any movement. His unease thickened with each step as he sensed an indefinable menace in the air.

He and Schultz had walked several hours before they stumbled upon a small band of refugees. Schultz knew their guide, a hard-eyed, wiry Swiss who declined to give his name. Ian didn't want to join the refugees, but Schultz gave him no choice. "Good luck to you," he had said with a clumsy salute before hightailing it back the way they had come.

Ian's value to the Swiss guide appeared to be his obvious military background. The other refugees — a young couple with a baby, a woman and two men in their thirties and forties — appeared exhausted. Whether they were related to each other, or even knew each other, Ian didn't know. But clearly, none of the men were trained soldiers.

After the Swiss guide said he was taking them to an abandoned shed where they could spend the night, Ian considered his options. He figured he might as well go to the barn with the others. But he planned to slip away before daylight and find his own path out of Germany.

The sun descended below the horizon, trailing the last vestiges of daylight. At an inward curve in the hedgerow where the brush was especially thick, the Swiss waited with the others for Ian, bringing up the rear, to catch up. "From here on, there's a road on the other side of this hedge. We'll follow it for about ten more minutes, then head across the field to the shed. Watch your feet."

The baby whimpered and its mother swayed, whispering softly.

"Keep that baby quiet," ordered the guide, turning on his heel and leading the way. The others followed while the mother looked helplessly at her husband. He put his arm around her and stroked the baby's head.

They had only taken a few steps when shots rang out ahead of them, followed by shouts. Ian grabbed the father's arm and herded the young family back to the curve in the hedge where the brush was heaviest. "Get as far in as you can," Ian whispered urgently.

The baby fussed as the parents shoved their way into the brush. The others stumbled back to them, and Ian directed them to crawl beneath the branches. They snapped at each other in angry whispers as each sought a hiding place.

With no more room, the Swiss guide took up a position near the curve, rifle at the ready. Ian ran a few meters back and lay flat on his stomach against the hedge, gun drawn.

Because of the descending darkness, he couldn't see the curve or the guide. Hopefully, whoever was shooting wouldn't be able to see them either. Another gunshot boomed, followed by an eerie quiet that was broken by the baby's cry. Its whimper ended as abruptly as it began.

Ian heard running footsteps, a guttural shout, an anguished cry. The flash of gunfire sparked the night, instantly followed by sharp reports. His eyes adjusted to the night, but he could barely make out the shapes moving far out in the field.

The minutes passed; the shapes moved farther away; the guns didn't sound quite so near. But the distant hum of an engine grew louder. Not just one, but several. Trucks, cars, even motorcycles rounded the bend on the other side of the hedge.

Ian controlled his breathing, ignoring the ache in his cramping legs and the chill of the ground that dampened his shirt. And he gave thanks for the moonless night that prevented the enemy from finding the little band of refugees.

Long after the last engine died away and the final report of a rifle echoed through the night, Ian and the refugees stayed hidden. Adrenaline and the need to guard the others kept him awake. Through the long hours, he focused his eyes on various points of the field, alert to any danger. But his mind wandered as he gazed upward to the North Star. Had Libby seen it before she went to sleep? Did it shine on Alison in her gallery studio?

What would Alison think of him for leaving Libby at the convent?

Remembering the little girl's cries troubled his heart and stung his eyes. He blinked and focused on that part of the field where he thought the shed was located. He suspected others had hidden there for the night. Had hidden there and been found.

He no longer resented their slow pace

when they were walking to the same shelter. That delay had no doubt saved them from an ambush.

Eventually the night faded, pink and yellow streaks lightening the sky in the east. When it was light enough for him to be sure no Germans lurked nearby, he sat up and rubbed his legs to get the blood circulating. The Swiss guard met his gaze across the distance and nodded an all clear. Ian returned the nod, then headed toward the curve.

One by one, the refugees emerged, scratched and bleeding, faces covered with dirt that had turned to mud with their tears. The baby's father crawled out, then reached beneath the brush and pulled out a small, stiff bundle. His wife followed, her eyes vacant and cold.

"It wouldn't stop crying," the father said. "They would have found us."

Ian's stomach lurched, and he shut his eyes against the horrid truth before him. Sour bile rose, and he turned away to spit.

"They may be back," said the guide. "We need to hurry."

"The baby," said the father, his voice unnaturally high. "We can't leave the baby."

"Then stay behind." The guide pointed to the south. "Whoever wants to get across the border needs to get moving."

Ian glared at the guide. The other man's cold eyes glared back.

"You want to take them across, be my guest. But you don't know how, do you?" He narrowed his eyes. "Wonder what the Krauts would pay to know your whereabouts. Eh, Brit?"

"There'll be a special place in hell for people like you."

"Look around you. We're already in hell." The Swiss gestured at the others. "Let's go."

"We can't stay," the father said to his wife. Her unresponsive eyes stared ahead.

"Go with the others." Ian patted his shoulder. "I'll take care of the baby."

The father drew back, then seemed to reconsider. "You'll do the right thing?"

"God be with you. Be safe."

The young man's jaw twitched, and he brushed his lips against the tiny forehead before gingerly placing the baby in Ian's arms.

"Go," Ian urged.

The man took his wife by the hand, and together they followed the guide and the little band.

Choking back hot tears, Ian covered the baby's face with the blanket and headed north. This might not be hell, but it was a bleak world when parents shipped their children to foreign countries to keep them safe. When parents killed . . . He couldn't finish the thought.

It was too late to protect this little one he carried. But there was a girl who needed him. And come what may, he was taking her home.

CHAPTER THIRTY-EIGHT

Alison blinked against the sudden glare from a lantern when the false wall slid open. She held up her hand while her eyes adjusted to the light.

"You can come out now," said the skipper. "We're in open water."

"Are you sure it's safe?"

"As sure as I can be. How are the children?"

"Sleeping." Her muscles aching, Alison crawled out of the cramped cupboard into the boat's cabin. Skipper swung the lantern into the enclosed space. The twins, thumbs in their mouths, curled beside each other in the cubbyhole. Alison reached back inside and pulled the blanket more tightly around them.

"They will sleep for a while. We'll leave the door open."

"It's still raining." She could hear the

pounding of the downpour outside the cabin.

"Hasn't stopped. Makes it a good night for a crossing." He hooked the lantern from the ceiling and poured her a hot cup of ersatz coffee from a thermos. She sat on a cushioned bench and wrapped her chilled hands around the cup. The cabin windows were covered with blackout cloths.

"Where are we?"

"About five kilometers from port."

"Have you done this often?"

"A few times." His voice sounded eerie, coming from a face hidden in shadows. "Usually for the *Engelandvaarders*, though. Not women and children."

Alison caught the faint resentment in his tone but chose to ignore it. "The 'England farers.' I don't think I've heard that term before."

"Dutch Underground fighters who join Queen Wilhelmina in her exile. They go to England to fight for the Allies."

"I see." If only Will and Pieter had chosen that patriotic route instead of engaging in sabotage. She sipped the coffee and made a face at its bitter taste.

"Drink it." Skipper chuckled, apparently able to see her better than she could see him. "It will keep you warm."

"If it doesn't kill me."

He chuckled again, then moved to the door. "Try to sleep. It will be a long night." He opened the door only wide enough to slip through, but a gust of wind whipped rain through the cabin before he got it shut again.

Alison shivered against the sudden onslaught and forced herself to take another sip of the bitter drink. What she wouldn't give for a cup of steaming coffee made with freshly ground beans. Or a big mug of Gerta Brant's hot cocoa with a dollop of fresh whipped cream melting on the surface.

She checked on the twins, ensuring that they were as warm as possible. And still breathing. She had been horrified when Skipper showed her the small space where he expected the three of them to hide. But he assured her that the air holes would provide enough oxygen for them. "If Nazis board us," he had warned, "you'll be glad of this place." He had also given bottles of milk laced with a mild sedative to the twins, to keep them quiet, he'd said.

Wrapping herself in a blanket, Alison returned to the bench, knowing sleep would be elusive. Skipper had offered her a sedative too, but she refused, wanting to be alert in case there was trouble. She forced herself to gulp the cooled coffee and yawned. Her thoughts became fuzzy and she lay on her side. Perhaps she could close her eyes for just a minute or two.

Ian fell to his knees before the altar in the ancient stone chapel, head bowed in weary reverence, and laid his cherished burden at its base. He rubbed his hands over his face, wiping away sweat and grime, and pressed his palms against his thighs. The arduous trek had dulled his mind and numbed his heart. He closed his eyes and breathed a wordless prayer, seeking respite in the solace of this holy place.

The flutter of wings drew his gaze to the rafters. A brown wren, barely visible in the shadows, flitted beneath the eaves above the stained glass windows. A tinted beam of light shimmered through the delicate blue of Mary's veil, the royal purple of the Christ child's blanket, their amber halos.

Ian studied the classic design, then followed the beam through the dim interior to the foot of the altar, where it held the tiny bundle in a cradle of light. He exhaled, releasing his burden into hands more powerful than his. The beam weakened and the light faded, but the sanctity of that moment lingered, a healing balm for his troubled soul.

Ian followed the high wall surrounding the convent to the front gate and pulled on the bell rope. A white-clad novice soon appeared.

He gripped the iron bars of the gate. "Let me in. I must see Sister Regina."

"I will find her for you." The girl, hands tucked in her sleeves, walked away from him with slow, measured steps.

"Quickly," he said, with more force than he intended. The girl ran.

A few moments later, Sister Regina appeared and unclasped the gate. "I prayed for your return."

"Where is she?"

"In the garden. With Sister Agnes." Sister Regina paused to catch her breath and her eyes glistened. "She hasn't said a word since you left. Not one word."

Ian rubbed his shoulder. "I should never have left her."

"Come. I'll take you to her."

"Wait." He grasped her arm. "There's something I have to tell you."

She looked at him expectantly, but the words didn't come easily.

"What is it, Dev?"

"I brought back a baby."

"A baby?" Her eyes darted past the gate. "Where is it?"

"At the old chapel." He grimaced. "The baby's dead."

Sister Regina gasped.

"Schultz left me with these others." Ian worked his jaw, tamping his rising anger.

"Yes, I know. He told me."

"Tell him from me to stay out of my sight."

"What happened?"

"We had to hide. I'm not sure what was going on, but there was gunfire. The baby cried and . . ." He squeezed his eyes shut, unable to put the tragic deed into words.

"Oh no." Sister Regina touched his arm, and he reached for her hand, needing to feel living warmth.

"Will you take care of the baby?" he asked quietly.

"Yes," she said. "Right after I take you to Libby. She needs you. But I wonder if you don't need her more."

"I'm taking her with me."

"Of course you are." She tugged on his arm. "Follow me."

Ian saw Libby as soon as he entered through the kitchen garden gate. She sat on the ground, her back against a stone birdbath, and poked at the dirt with a stick. Her cloth doll was sprawled across her lap.

His heart picked up a beat. "Libby!"

She looked up, startled. Seeing him, she jumped to her feet and ran to him, leaving her doll in the dirt. He scooped her up and hugged her tight.

As if she feared he would disappear, she placed her hands on his cheeks and stared into his eyes. "Papi!"

He hesitated, but the need in her soft brown eyes trumped brutal honesty. "Yes, Libby. It's me."

She wrapped her arms around his neck and placed her head on his shoulder. "Keep me, Papi."

"Always, Libby. Always."

"You drugged me." Alison stood on deck as the fishing boat bounced across the rough seas. The white-capped waves glinted in the weak sunshine, but dark clouds loomed overhead.

"You wouldn't have slept otherwise." Skipper guided the wheel, idly watching the horizon. "How do you feel?"

Taken aback by the question, she shrugged. "Fine."

"Then why are you complaining?"

"Just don't do that again."

"Won't have to."

Irritated by his lack of remorse, Alison

returned to the cabin. She tidied up by folding her blanket and rolling up the blackout curtains. Squares of sunlight entered the cabin. The twins awoke, wet and hungry. After a meager breakfast, she entertained them with stories she remembered from her childhood. A wave of homesickness for those long-ago days flooded over her.

Rain fell again, though not nearly as hard as the night before. The sun briefly appeared, and Alison played with the twins on the deck until a cloudburst sent them scurrying back into the cabin. When a ship appeared on the horizon, Skipper shut them inside the dark cubbyhole with a warning to keep the twins quiet. He needn't have worried. They cuddled close to Alison, clutching her clothes with their little fingers, eyes wide with fright. By the time Skipper opened the door, both were asleep.

"Land ahoy," he said, with a wink. He reached for Aaron, leaving Alison to emerge with Anna.

"We're here?"

"Almost. Come up on deck and see."

She followed him from the cabin, eager to see land. Shading her eyes against the slanting sun, she looked to the west, where a long shore beckoned. On a southern point, she could barely make out the outlines of buildings and ships. "Where are we?"

"That's Harwich." Skipper pointed to the harbor town.

"England?" She needed to hear him say it, to make it real. To bring this part of her nightmare to an end.

"Unless she moved during the night." He set Aaron in a seat and steered the boat one-handed so that they motored north, parallel to the coastline and away from the port.

"Where are we going?"

"Out of sight." He checked the instrument panel. "After the sun goes down a little more, we'll go ashore."

Alison stared at the receding town, unsure whether her cheeks were damp from the spray or from tears. Placing Anna in the seat with her brother, she stood beside them and wondered how long it would take the sun to go down. The North Sea crossing hadn't made her seasick, but she longed to step on dry land. Yet she didn't want to lose her last connection with home.

"How long will you stay?"

"Only a few hours." He shut off the motor, allowing the boat to drift, and tapped Alison's arm. "Stay here with the children. I'll be right back."

He returned from the cabin with an oilskin pouch and handed it to Alison.

"Monsieur Duret said to give you this when we arrived."

"What's in it?"

"I didn't look."

She opened the pouch and examined the contents. Money, lots of it, in British pounds. Her passport and birth certificate. A few British birth certificates, blank except for the official signatures. Perfect forgeries, created by Pieter just in case. All she had to do was fill in the twins' names and an appropriate birth date. Biting her lip, she closed the pouch and stuck it in her pants pocket.

Another day was drawing to a close. What had it held for Hannah? For her father and Will? She didn't dare dwell on such thoughts. Instead she let her mind drift, like the boat, toward England. The last time she was here, only two years ago, she had sketched a boy and his champion at Waterloo Station, eaten cherry scones at Minivers, and reluctantly given away her heart.

Looking back, her anguish over saving Ian from the family fate seemed hopelessly naive. She had thought her heart would break when she told him good-bye. But that heartache, though real, couldn't compare to the grief she had endured since.

She had left England, in the summer of

1940, as the pampered granddaughter of a prominent Dutch businessman. Now she returned with nothing, her home destroyed, those she loved most either sick or missing, in prison or dead.

Knowing what she knew now, she wished she could go back to that day in Waterloo Station. Their days together might have been few before Ian left to fight the Germans in France. But she understood now, as she never quite had before, the senselessness of trying to outwit fate. She fingered Tante Meg's locket and prayed that God would give her and Ian a second chance.

She stared westward, at the bands of pale color above the distant land, backlit by the setting sun. The day was ending, and with it her life as she knew it.

CHAPTER THIRTY-NINE

Stretching his long legs in front of him, Ian leaned back on a stone bench built into a monument to some obscure saint. From his vantage point, he could see the cloistered walk leading to the cell-like rooms where he and Libby were staying another night. Probably more than one until he could come up with a plan for getting across the border. He pulled out his button-sized compass and peered at the needle, difficult to see in the twilight. Getting his bearings, he stared northwest. Toward home. But not the direction he needed to travel if he hoped to get there.

"Is she asleep?" Sister Regina's silken voice slipped into his reverie.

Ian grunted as he stood. "I couldn't be out here if she weren't."

"I heard she wouldn't let you out of her sight." Sister Regina laughed softly. "Please, sit."

"Only if you'll join me." Ian gestured toward the bench, and she accepted his invitation with a smile. He sat beside her, thankful that Sister Agnes had preoccupied Libby long enough for him to clean up. "We looked for you at supper. Where have you been?"

"At the old chapel."

"That's what I thought. I should have gone with you."

"There was no need. Sister Matilda and I took care of the babe."

"The parents didn't tell me a name. I think they were too shocked."

"God knows who he is, Dev. And He knows what happened out there."

"So he was a boy."

"A perfect, beautiful, precious boy." Her voice broke, and she turned her face away.

Ian shifted uncomfortably, regretting that she lived in a time and place that forced such abhorrent tasks upon her, wishing he could put his arm around her and dry her tears. He didn't even have a handkerchief to offer her.

"I'm sorry," she said, hands clutched in her lap.

"You have a tender heart. Never apologize for that."

She smiled up at him, her pale eyes glistening. "You made a big impression on Sister Matilda."

"Have I met Sister Matilda?"

"You will. She may have a plan for getting you and Libby into southern France."

Ian raised an eyebrow.

"It is a daring plan. You may think it too dangerous."

"What is it?"

"If she can work out the details, you will know in the morning. But tonight, I need to cut your hair."

"Why?" he asked suspiciously.

"So you look less like what you are and more like who we want you to be." Her lips curled upward in a teasing smile. "You do trust me, don't you, Dev?"

"With my life."

The normalcy. It was so surreal, Alison decided as she combed Anna's hair. People, ordinary people, taking the train from Harwich to London. Getting off and getting on at the various stations along the way. Worry bothered their eyes and their worn shoes carried a sense of making do during hard times. But they tended to the business of their daily affairs totally oblivious to the escapees from Nazi terror in their midst. They didn't fear the Allied soldiers, their fellow passengers. They didn't fear arrest or torture. None of the conductors or train officials would demand to see their papers.

Alison's destination, Waterloo Station, was next. As they neared the stop, she tied the yellow ribbons of a new white bonnet beneath Anna's chin and spit-bathed a bit of grime from Aaron's cheek. Their hosts in Harwich, friends of the skipper's, had found appropriate clothing for the twins and a brown dress for Alison. Not the kind of thing she usually wore, but who could be choosy in these circumstances?

The twins passed her scrutiny, and she smiled at them.

"Are we going home now?" Aaron asked.

"I'm afraid not," Alison said soothingly. "We're going to visit someone. It will be fun; you'll see."

Aaron looked doubtful, and Alison didn't blame him. She wasn't expecting fun either. She only hoped for a cordial welcome, and then only if Trish Devlin Manning had received the cryptic telegram Alison had sent before they left Harwich: *Arriving Waterloo Station 3:15 pm today. A.S.*

It might be irrational, but she felt safer not signing her name to the message. The fear of discovery, of Theodor or his cronies tracking her down, still held her in its grip.

Now he could only hurt her by hurting her family. Which was why she should never have come to England. Why she needed to find a way to go back.

When they reached the station, Alison balanced Anna and a travel bag in one hand and held tightly to Aaron's hand with the other. "Don't let go," she said, clumsily stepping off the train. "We'll get a taxi. Won't it be fun to ride in a taxi?"

Maneuvering through the crowd with her charges, she refused to remember Josef and his patriotic rendition of "Rule, Britannia!" or to envision Ian standing beside the frail boy. The memories were too painful.

"Alison!" A female voice broke through the noise of the crowd.

She froze, unsure whether to heed the voice or run.

"Alison, is that you?"

She turned as a woman she didn't know, fashionably dressed in a pale-blue summer suit and matching hat, came toward her. Her hazel eyes sparkled with glints of gold.

"Trish?"

"I knew it was you." Trish looked at the children, her generous smile broadening even more. "Who do you have with you?"

"This is Anna and Aaron."

Trish reached out her arms, and Anna

readily went to her. "I want to go home," the little girl whimpered.

"I'm sure you do," Trish soothed. "But will you come to my house for a bit first? We'll have little cakes. Wouldn't you like that?"

"Yes!" piped up Aaron.

"Then you shall have some." Trish laughed, then glanced at Alison, unspoken questions in her eyes.

Alison barely shook her head. "I didn't expect you to come to the station. How did you know me?"

"Because I know my brother." Trish's mischievous grin looked so much like Ian's that Alison's heart ached. "And because I was hiding nearby when you left two years ago. I saw Ian waving good-bye to you."

Alison flushed, and Trish touched her arm. "Come. Let's get you home."

Ian stepped off the train, almost tripping over the long hem of the cassock he was wearing, and looked up at the station platform sign. *Lorbonne, France.* He shook his head. "I can't believe it worked," he whispered to Sister Regina.

"Shh. You're not supposed to talk," she whispered back, then pointed to a bell tower rising above the roofs of the nearby town.

"There's the church."

Ian pressed his fingers against the white bandage encircling his neck above the stiff clerical collar. The story Sister Regina had told the Nazi guards at the last station before crossing the border had been a pitiable one. Poor Father Andrew, she told them, pointing at Ian, had courageously and at risk to his own life stopped a young Polish thug from slicing a brave member of the *Hitler-Jugend* with a switchblade. Father Andrew suffered a life-threatening cut that impaired his vocal cords. What a world they lived in when a subhuman cretin attempted to kill one of Germany's young boys, who only wanted to uphold the ideals of the Führer, and maimed such a hero as Father Andrew.

She smiled her pretty smile and laughed her melodic laugh, casting her own sweet spell over the station guards who, Ian imagined, would have believed her if she had told them he was the pope. They scarcely glanced at his papers, the property of the real Father Andrew, who just happened to be Sister Matilda's brother.

Neither were they interested in Libby's papers, which belonged to an orphan at the convent. However, they listened spellbound as Sister Regina told them how she and

Father Andrew were escorting the unfortunate child to her mother's family in France after both her parents, loyal Germans to the end, perished when their house was mysteriously set on fire by misguided neighbors who did not believe in the Führer's vision. Such a shame for the little girl, Sister Regina sighed, her eyes brimming with tears. Ian had turned away so the guards wouldn't catch him snickering at her melodramatic performance.

Through it all, Libby behaved admirably, not saying a word. Their papers stamped, they were given clearance to cross the border. Now they were in unoccupied France. By this time next week, he and Libby might be home.

"Come, child," Sister Regina said authoritatively for the benefit of those around them. "We mustn't dawdle."

They followed the road into the village and made their way to an old church, sixteenth- or seventeenth-century from the architecture. A priest hailed them from the cemetery, and they met him at the gate.

"Father," said Sister Regina, bending her head respectfully, "I have a message from Father Didymus."

"Father Didymus, eh? Then we should go inside."

Ian picked up Libby, carrying her as they followed the priest to the rear entrance of the church and into his study. He gestured for them to sit while he turned on the lamps. "How is Father Didymus?"

"He is well, thank you," Sister Regina replied. "And sends his highest regards."

"What does he request of me?"

"The delivery of two packages."

The priest cast his eyes over Ian and Libby, then nodded. "How far?"

"To the king."

"Ah." The priest pursed his lips. "I thought as much. POW?"

Sister Regina glanced at Ian and nodded.

"Since Dunkirk," Ian said.

"What prison?"

"First at Laufen. Then at Colditz."

"You escaped from Colditz?" The priest's face lit up and he sat back in his chair. "Well done, *mon ami.*"

"You can help us, then?" Sister Regina asked eagerly.

"It would be easier if the child stayed behind."

Libby, sitting on Ian's lap, quickly looked up at him. He held her closer. "That's not an option," Ian said. "She's coming with me."

"For what your countrymen did for mine

at Dunkirk, I now do this for you. Yes, we will send you home. Both you and the petite mademoiselle."

"Thank you, Father."

"What about you, Sister?"

"I need a way back to the convent. Preferably not by train."

At the priest's questioning glance, Ian chuckled. "She has admirers at the German station."

"Sister," the priest said, his tone mildly admonishing, "it's not seemly for a nun to use her feminine wiles to distract the soldiers from their duty. However, in such perilous times, we must all use those talents God has given us for His greater good."

"I also lied, Father."

"And apparently quite well. Else you would not be sitting here with me now." He suddenly stood. "You will be my guests until arrangements can be made. Follow the path behind the cemetery to my house and tell my housekeeper Father Didymus sent you. She will take good care of you. I'll be there soon."

Once they were outside, Ian turned to Sister Regina. "Exactly who is Father Didymus?"

She laughed. "He doesn't exist. Father Andrew — the real Father Andrew — told me what to say."

"*Didymus* means 'twin,' doesn't it?"

"Yes. The apostle Thomas was sometimes called Didymus. It seems especially appropriate as a code right now since we have two Father Andrews. But I don't think it really means any specific person."

"More of a recognition signal, then."

"I suppose."

"It all seemed too easy."

"You've already walked through fire, Dev. Maybe you're due for 'too easy.' "

"Maybe." The promise from Psalms came back to him. *Thou art my hiding place; thou shalt preserve me from trouble; thou shalt compass me about with songs of deliverance.* He looked toward heaven and silently prayed that he and Libby would remain hidden from the evil that surrounded them. *Deliver us, O God. Deliver us soon.*

CHAPTER FORTY

Trish served refreshments in her garden, a rectangle of colorful flower beds and variegated roses separated by stone paths. They gathered around a wicker table in the shade of a gnarled oak and feasted on a selection of sweets. Anna clapped her hands in delight at the tiny white cakes iced with pink frosting while Aaron's cheeks bulged with chocolate cream biscuits.

"I doubt they've ever eaten anything like this before," Alison said, apologetically.

"Poor little dears. I wish I had enough sugar coupons to create such treats for them every day. At least I can get honey from the estate." Trish placed another biscuit on Aaron's plate. "Eat up, children. Then I have a surprise for you."

"What surprise?" Aaron asked despite his full mouth.

"Let's swallow our food before we talk," Alison gently corrected, patting his arm.

Trish just laughed. "You'll see soon enough. Now drink your lemonade."

Alison gazed around at the garden, breathing in the sweet fragrance of the purple lilacs that graced the nearby corner of the brick wall. A caressing breeze rustled the broad leaves of a nearby maple, and the flower beds along the paths enchanted her. For the first time since leaving Holland, she relaxed. Within the walls of Trish's garden, surely she and the children were safe.

"This is a lovely place," she said, allowing her weary body to sink into the chair cushions.

"It's been in Mark's family for at least a hundred years. We've lived here since we married. A little over five years ago."

"Where is Mark?" In her letters, Trish had written that her husband had been promoted to major since his return from Dunkirk, but little about his current duties.

"He's involved with training exercises somewhere." Trish gave a halfhearted shrug. "I don't know where he is."

"Don't you hear from him?"

"His letters come from a central office here in London. At least he's no longer in France."

"That's good." Alison smiled, but her heart wasn't in it. She glanced at the children, absorbed with their treats. "Can you tell me, do you know what happened at Dunkirk?" Her real question remained unspoken: *How did Ian get left behind?*

"I don't know much. Mark was so badly wounded that he was barely conscious. Ian helped him to the boats, then went back for another soldier. That's when he was captured." Trish's voice caught on the last word, and she looked away as tears welled in her eyes. "The Red Cross could tell us nothing else."

Alison's heart went out to her.

"I done." Anna brushed her sticky hands on her dress before Alison could stop her. "Where's surprise?"

Trish chuckled and stood. "Let's wash your hands first."

When Alison started to rise, Trish raised a hand to stop her. "I can see to them. You relax." She herded the children toward the house and returned a few minutes later with a squirming ball of chestnut-and-white fur.

"My surprise." She handed the spaniel puppy to Alison, who immediately got a face lick.

"Where are the twins?"

"With the best of all housekeepers, Mrs. Crewe. She'll bring them out in a few moments."

Alison stroked the spaniel's soft fur and wrinkled her nose at his sweet puppy breath. "Thank you for meeting us at the station. For all of this," she said. "I didn't know where else to go."

Trish placed a comforting hand on Alison's arm. "I've been hoping you would come. Can you tell me what happened?"

Alison closed her eyes, determined not to cry. "My grandfather had a heart attack. My father may have been arrested." She bit her lip, unable to say any more about the horrors that had forced her across the North Sea.

"The children. Are they related to you?"

"No. I went to school with their mother." Alison took a deep breath, gathering her thoughts. "Her husband died a few weeks ago. Then Hannah was taken away. I tried to convince her to come with me, but she couldn't leave her mother-in-law. I'm afraid I'm not telling this very well."

"The only thing that matters is that you're here."

"I know it's an imposition, but may we stay a few days? Just until I figure out something more permanent?"

"Mrs. Crewe already has rooms prepared for both you and the children." Trish's eyes misted. "You'll stay with me, all three of you, as long as you need a home."

"I can't expect you to —"

"I insist. Besides, it's lonely here. It'll be nice to have children around."

"You do have a way with them."

"I always wanted a houseful. Unfortunately, God hasn't seen fit to bless us with our own."

"I pray that He will."

"Me too. But for now, it looks like He's blessed us with Anna and Aaron."

As if they'd been summoned, the twins appeared with freshly scrubbed hands and faces. They scampered along the path from the house as quickly as their little legs would carry them. A sternly dressed woman with crinkly blue eyes watched them from the terrace, then disappeared into the house.

The spaniel's ears perked up and he wriggled from Alison's grasp. The twins squealed as he nipped their heels in an impromptu game of tag. Anna fell and tore her dress, but Trish jumped up and dried the little girl's tears.

"I need to go shopping for them," Alison said when Trish returned to her seat. "There just wasn't time before."

"Not to worry. Mrs. Crewe just left to pick up a few things for them."

"She didn't!"

"I couldn't have stopped her if I tried. Which I didn't." Trish's eyes twinkled, then grew serious. "Let me take care of the twins, Alison. At least for a while. You have enough to worry about."

To have someone else share her responsibilities eased Alison's heart. Except for the drugged sleep during the night on the boat, she had slept restlessly, disturbed by visions too horrific to recall when she awoke.

"Thank you, Trish. I can't begin to tell you how much this means to me."

"I hope you'll think of me as more than a friend. That someday we'll be sisters."

Alison averted her eyes, not sure whether she could share that hope. "Have you heard from Ian lately?"

"I got a letter a week ago. It was dated sometime in May."

"My last letter was dated in April."

Trish's eyes clouded over. "There's something I have to tell you."

Alison's mind reeled, and her stomach clenched as she braced herself. "Tell me quickly."

"Ian escaped from Colditz."

"Escaped?"

"The Red Cross contacted my parents two days ago."

"Where is he?"

Trish lifted her shoulders. "We don't know."

Alison pressed her fingers against her temples. All this time, she had thought he was safe in the prison, had gripped that certainty as a lifeline. No matter what else went wrong, at least she had known he was alive, could pinpoint where he was on a map.

Now nothing was certain. The yipping puppy and the giggling children grew faint as anxiety numbed her senses. The branches of the gnarled oak swayed above her, spinning her head. She shut her eyes to end the dizziness and felt herself slipping into unconscious darkness, where nothing mattered.

CHAPTER FORTY-ONE

The priest said grace over their breakfast and leaned back in his chair. "God must be watching over you, Father Andrew," he said in German. "Your timing is impeccable."

"Why do you say that?"

"London is sending a supply plane tonight. Usually they attach parachutes to the cargo containers and drop them. But when they heard about you, they decided to actually land. You'll be home by this time tomorrow morning."

Relief swept over Ian, lightening his spirits. By tomorrow morning. It hardly seemed possible. "That's great news."

"Oh, Dev. Our prayers have been answered," Sister Regina said.

"One of the local farmers will drive you to the rendezvous point. He'll be here in about an hour."

Ian smiled at Libby. "Did you hear that? We're going to fly."

"Is it scary?"

"Nah. It's an adventure."

"My housekeeper's son is about your size," said the priest. "She's getting clothes from him so you don't have to travel in that cassock."

"I appreciate that. I'm not sure how God feels about priestly impersonators."

The priest and Sister Regina chuckled good-naturedly. He'd miss them, especially Sister Regina. It didn't feel chivalrous to leave her here, especially knowing she planned to return to the convent. Only God knew what might happen to her there.

After breakfast, Ian once again changed into borrowed clothes, transforming into a common workman. Tomorrow, he promised himself. Tomorrow he would be back in uniform. Ready to serve the Allied cause and defeat the Nazis. Perhaps then he could plan a future with Alison.

He folded the cassock and carried it to the kitchen.

"Papi, look at me." Libby stood on a chair dressed in a boy's pants and shirt. The housekeeper circled her, pinning the hem of the pants.

"Who is this young fellow?" Ian teased. "What did you do with my Libby?"

She giggled. "It's really me, Papi. See?"

She pulled the cap off her head, releasing her long dark hair.

"Well, so it is."

"I hope you don't mind, monsieur," the housekeeper said. "I thought these clothes would be warmer for the petite mademoiselle. It will be cold in the sky, no?"

"*Merci,* madame. For all your help."

She waved away his gratitude, her attention focused on the needed alterations.

"I have to return this to Sister Regina. Do you know where she is?"

With pins now clenched between her teeth, the housekeeper gestured toward the back door.

Ian found Sister Regina kneeling beside a grave in the cemetery, idly clearing it of weeds. He plopped on the ground beside her and read the tombstone. The lad, just a few days shy of his nineteenth birthday, had died on June 1, 1940.

"Another casualty of Dunkirk," Sister Regina said. "So young."

"And you are so old?"

She barely smiled at his teasing.

"Come with us. You'll be safer in England than here."

"With 'us'?"

"With Libby and me."

"My life is here." She gave a little sniff.

"Not *here*. At the convent."

"You have a choice. Right now, you can choose to live a different life."

"You aren't married, are you, Dev?"

"No."

"But there is a woman."

"How did you know?"

"I see it in your eyes."

He grinned. "Her name is Alison."

"You love her very much."

"Yes."

"Does she feel the same for you?"

"She's hasn't said so. But yes, I believe she does."

"Is she in England?"

"Holland," he said, grimly. "Rotterdam, actually. Her home was destroyed in the invasion."

"I'm so very sorry."

"It wasn't your fault."

"But it is the fault of my countrymen." She pulled at a stubborn root. "All the killing, the destruction. To what purpose?"

Greed. Power. Lunacy. He could have given her a dozen answers. But none that would ease the guilt she felt because of Germany's crimes. The sound of tires caught his attention, and a truck drove around to the rear of the church. The local farmer, he surmised.

He held out the folded cassock. "Father Andrew's papers are in the pocket. Please give him my thanks. And Sister Matilda, too."

She barely nodded, eyes focused on the weed.

"Father Andrew!"

Ian looked toward the shout. The priest waved his arm.

"Be right there," he shouted back, then leaned toward Sister Regina. "Will you come?"

"This is God's plan for me. To atone for the trouble caused by the Nazis."

He stood and extended his hand to Sister Regina. "Libby will want to say good-bye."

She hesitated, then brushed the dirt from her fingers before accepting his hand and rising gracefully to her feet.

"I want you to know something, Dev," she said without looking at him. "My brothers. They are honorable men. If you met them, say at one of your English pubs, or at one of our German *biergartens,* you would like them. And they would like you."

"I'm sure of it."

She looked up at him then, each of her pale eyes a beautiful misty pool. "I will pray for you, Dev. For you and Alison. That you'll be together soon."

He had little hope of God answering that prayer. But if it hadn't been for Sister Regina, there would have been no hope at all. Touched by her compassion and bravery, he ran his finger along her cheek. "Forgive me, Sister."

"For what?"

"For this." He slid his fingers to her neck and lightly kissed her cheek.

Chapter Forty-Two

Ian and Libby hid in the barn with the rest of the Resistance members, waiting for the signal from the Allied plane. A middle-aged Frenchman, smoking a hand-rolled cigarette, had given Ian strict instructions. No talking. No asking questions. As soon as the plane's cargo was unloaded, he and Libby were to board. Quickly.

The tension inside the barn was palpable, the only sound an occasional murmur and the intermittent crackle of the radio. Libby sat on Ian's lap, her head against his chest, her cloth doll clutched tightly. The priest's housekeeper had laundered the doll, with Libby's help, but the stain of German dirt clung fast.

When the signal came, the men sprang into action. They lit lanterns to form a makeshift runway and, seconds later, the plane bounced to a landing. While the engine hummed, the Frenchmen unloaded the cargo. Ian ran with Libby to the cargo door and waited, sweat trickling down his neck, till the leader gave the all clear. He lifted Libby into the hold, then braced his hands on the platform to jump in. Someone grabbed his jacket, pulling him inside. "Hurry up, Dev," said a familiar voice. "We don't have all night."

"Mark?" Ian stood and stared at his brother-in-law, then found himself wrapped in a giant bear hug. "What are you doing here?"

"No children," someone shouted from the cockpit. "I'm not cleared to take children."

"Too bad," Ian retorted, releasing Mark and grabbing Libby. He squinted as his eyes adjusted to the dark interior that smelled of sweat and gun residue. "She's not staying behind."

"Shut the doors," Mark ordered. "Get us out of here."

"If you say so, Major."

"Major?" Ian grinned. "What happened to Captain?"

"Since you weren't around, the brass promoted me," Mark teased. He handed Ian a couple of heavy jackets. "Here. Put these on and get strapped in. It might get bumpy."

"Thanks." Ian buttoned one around Libby, not even bothering to put her arms in the adult-size sleeves, then slipped the other one on himself.

The doors closed, the engine whined, and the plane taxied between the lanterns before rising into the sky.

"Are we safe, Papi?" Libby asked as Ian strapped her between him and Mark.

"Safest we've been in a long time, honey." He held her close and grinned at his brother-in-law, reassured by his presence. This wasn't a dream. They'd soon be home.

"Papi?" Mark mouthed over Libby's head.

"It's a long story."

"We have a long trip."

"Later." Ian nodded at Libby. "I can't believe you're here. I can't believe *we're* here."

"We've all missed you, Dev. How're you doing?"

"Good." Ian took a couple of deep breaths. "Tired, but good. You certainly look better than the last time I saw you."

Mark rubbed the spot on his chest where he'd been wounded. "Feel better too."

"How's my family?"

"Worried about you. The Red Cross told them just a few days ago that you'd escaped."

"Do they know I'm coming home?"

"We didn't know for sure who we were

picking up. I pulled strings to tag along just in case it really was you."

"Glad you did."

"Me too." Mark playfully slapped Ian's leg with his hat. "Sleep if you can, Dev. We'll have plenty of time for catching up when we get home."

Home. Ian closed his eyes and let the word soak into his spirit. A boring weekend at Kenniston Hall — he looked forward to it.

Alison awakened to the cool touch of a hand on her forehead. "Tante Meg," she murmured and blinked open her eyes. But instead of her bedroom, she was in a place she didn't recognize. Blue-and-yellow fabric decorated each corner of a large four-poster bed. Matching drapes hung at the windows. The delicate mahogany furniture, polished to a high sheen, appealed to her sense of balance and proportion.

"Alison," whispered a nearby voice.

"Tante Meg." Feeling groggy, she turned her head.

"It's me, Trish."

Trish. Ian's sister. She closed her eyes as the memories flooded over her, threatening to drown her in grief.

"This is our family physician," Trish said softly. "Dr. Richard Ericson."

Alison opened her eyes as the doctor held her wrist. His trim mustache gave him a distinguished appearance, but she doubted he was a day over thirty. "Hello, Miss Schuyler."

"What's wrong with me?"

"Based on my extensive years as a medical diagnostician, I am confident that you, Trish's mysterious friend, are utterly and completely —" he paused dramatically — "worn out. But never fear. I have written you the perfect prescription."

"Medicine." She grimaced.

"How about fresh air, good food, and most important of all, a long night's sleep?" He snapped shut his medical bag. "I'm leaving sleeping powders for you. The directions are on the packet. Mix some up before you go to bed tonight."

"I will. Thank you."

"Rest now. I'll be around tomorrow." He pecked Trish on the cheek. "No need to see me out. I know the way."

"Good-bye, Richard. Thank you for coming."

He left, closing the door behind him.

Alison slowly pushed herself to a sitting position. "I don't want to be any trouble."

"You're not to worry about that," Trish said. "Or anything else."

"The twins?"

"Bathed and napping." She chuckled. "With the puppy. They are so adorable."

"You really don't mind us moving in on you like this?"

"Not at all. Perhaps in a few days, when you're feeling better, we can take the train to Kenniston Hall. My parents would love to meet you and the twins."

A vague memory drifted into Alison's consciousness. Ian, hesitating when she had asked if he would take Josef home with him. *"I'm not sure,"* he had said. Better that she find out now just how welcome the twins would be at Kenniston Hall.

"Trish," she said, taking a deep breath, "you do know the twins are Jewish, don't you?"

"I know."

"Will your parents accept them?"

"Before the war started, my father might not have," Trish admitted, flushing scarlet. "But that was before Ian was captured, before we heard the rumors. It's true, isn't it, that even in Holland the Jewish people are being persecuted?"

"Since the Nazis invaded Holland, I have hidden dozens of Jewish children with Christian families to keep them out of the camps. We hear such horrible stories that I don't know how they could be true. But they're so gruesome, who could make them up?"

"I don't know." Trish shook her head. "I can assure you, though, that my parents will welcome the twins with open arms. You too."

"How can you be so sure?"

"Because Ian loves you. That's all that matters to them."

Alison lowered her gaze. *How will they feel about me if I break their son's heart?* She didn't want to, God knew she didn't. Some days, she was determined to leave her future in His hands; on others, she could see no hope for a life with Ian.

Now she might not have a choice. Why couldn't he have stayed at Colditz?

CHAPTER FORTY-THREE

"Are you sure we shouldn't have called Trish and let her know we were coming?" Ian asked as the staff car pulled up in front of the Mannings' brownstone.

"And miss the look on her face when she sees you?" Mark turned off the ignition. "Not a chance."

"I guess I should be grateful you let me call my parents."

"I'm a considerate son-in-law." Mark chuckled. "Just a cad of a husband."

"I tried to tell Trish that before she married you. But she wouldn't listen." Ian glanced at his brother-in-law. "What's your plan, Major?"

"Ring the doorbell and see what happens."

Ian shifted around and looked at Libby, primly sitting in the backseat wearing a red dress with a white pinafore, ruffled white anklets, and black patent leather shoes. "Are you ready to meet your Aunt Trish?" he asked in German.

"Are you meeting her too?"

"I sure am." Ian stepped out of the car and opened the back door for Libby. His freshly pressed uniform felt good against his skin, and he straightened his posture as he took Libby's hand. He was a soldier again. Not an escapee, and definitely not a POW.

Mark led the way to the house and winked at Libby as he unlocked the door. Stepping into the foyer, he called, "Honey, I'm home."

A door opened and closed on the second floor, and Mark motioned Ian and Libby out of sight in the sitting room. Within seconds, Trish appeared at the top of the stairs. "Mark," she cried.

Ian heard her scurrying down the stairs, and he covered Libby's ears when he heard kissing.

"I'm so glad you're home," Trish said. "I have such news."

"I've got news too." Mark led her into the sitting room. "Look who I ran into."

"Hi, Trish."

"Ian." She flew into his arms, tears streaming down her cheeks. "It's you; it's really you."

"It's me," he laughed, swinging her around.

"Let me look at you." She stepped back from him and saw Libby. "Who's this?"

"This is Leiba Steinberg. But I call her Libby." He knelt beside the little girl and spoke in German. "This is my sister, your aunt Trish."

" 'Aunt Trish'?" She glanced at Mark.

"It's a long story," he said coyly.

"Ian?"

"Later."

Trish eyed both men before bending toward Libby, her hands on her knees. "Welcome, Libby," she said in German. "I'm so very glad to meet you."

"You're Papi's sister?" Libby asked shyly.

Trish raised her eyebrows at Ian. *"Later,"* he mouthed.

"Yes, I'm *Papi's* sister."

She straightened and hooked her arm through Ian's. "I have a big surprise for Papi."

"What's that?" asked Ian.

She escorted him to the French doors that led to the garden. "Out there."

Ian opened the door but hesitated when Trish didn't follow him. "Aren't you coming?"

"You go ahead. We'll be out later."

"Papi?" Libby ran to him and grabbed his leg. He smoothed her hair.

Trish knelt beside her. "He's not going to leave you, sweetheart," she said in German. "Would you like to see my puppy?"

Libby looked up at Ian, who said, "It's okay, honey. I promise I won't leave you."

Mark poked Trish. "You got a puppy?"

She laughed. "I've got a lot more than that." Holding out her hand to Libby, she switched to German again. "Come on, he's upstairs in the playroom."

"We have a playroom?" Mark gave Trish a puzzled look.

"Why do I have to go to the garden?" Ian asked.

"You —" Trish pointed at Ian — "get out there. And you —" pointing at Mark — "come with me."

Ian looked at Mark and shrugged. "Go see the puppy, sweetheart," he said to Libby. "I'll be up in a minute."

He watched Trish take both Libby and Mark by the hand and lead them toward the stairs; then he stepped into the garden. Following the brick path, he headed toward the ancient oak in the far corner. As he neared the wicker furniture, his breath caught in his throat. He stood still, not believing his eyes.

On the settee, a sketch pad in her lap and the tip of a pencil pressed against her lower lip, Alison concentrated on the oak.

His heart began to beat again, and he gave thanks for Sister Regina's promised prayer. He'd never expected it to be answered so quickly. Staring at the woman he loved, his thoughts turned to their parting at the Rotterdam station. He'd bared his soul to her, but she hadn't done the same. Despite their letters, she remained trapped in her family's superstition. Would she even be glad to see him? Maybe he should go back to the house, leave her in peace.

But still his feet refused to move.

Alison tapped the end of her pencil against her chin as she studied the intriguing nooks and crannies at the base of the gnarled oak tree. She could imagine a family of gnomes seeking refuge within the massive trunk. But what — or who — threatened gnomes so they had to hide? No matter how hard she tried to focus on the tree's knots and limbs, her thoughts turned to home and the danger she had left behind.

Dr. Ericson's sleeping powder had worked its magic — she had slept even better last night than she had when Skipper drugged her coffee.

She outlined two tiny gnomes on her drawing of the oak, then felt a presence behind her. She shifted in her seat to greet Trish.

Except it wasn't Trish who stared back at her.

She blinked, refusing to believe her eyes. "Ian."

He didn't move. Despite his scrubbed and starched appearance, the rigors of the past two years marked his face. In the creases near his eyes, across his forehead, she detected hardship, privation, and unspeakable sorrow.

"How did you . . . ?" Ian began, then swallowed hard. "What are you doing here?"

"I didn't know where you were." She stood, then suddenly feeling lightheaded, sat down again. He hurried to her side and hesitantly reached for her hand. His fingers brushed the hair from her temple, traced the fading scar as if it provided proof that she wasn't a mirage. "Trish said you escaped from Colditz."

"I did." His familiar grin flipped her heart. "And now I'm home."

Tears welled up in her eyes, and she touched his cheek. "I've been so worried."

"How long have you been here?"

"Since yesterday. So many awful things have happened."

"All that matters is that you're safe."

"No." She traced his face with her fingers, memorizing the contours and lines. "All that matters is that *you're* safe."

They both laughed nervously. Then Ian drew her close, finding her mouth. She wrapped her arms around his neck, inhaling his warmth, and returned his kiss, hungry for the taste of him. Never wanting to let him go.

"I love you, Alison Schuyler," he whispered between kisses. "Always be mine."

Her heart pounded against her chest. Did she hold on to the family fate? Or trust God with her future?

She leaned back and gazed into his hazel eyes, finding in their depths a love that could only come from heaven. Swallowing hard, she took a deep breath. "I love you, Ian Devlin. I'll always be yours."

CHAPTER FORTY-FOUR

AUGUST 1942

Sunpennies glinted like an abundance of diamonds upon the gentle waves in the Bristol Channel off the shores near the Devlin estate. Alison shaded her eyes and looked out at the boulder protruding above the blue water.

"I see why it's called the giant's hand," she said. "You can actually swim that far?"

"Used to," Ian said.

Alison didn't think he even realized he rubbed his shoulder when he spoke, the gesture was so unconscious. But she knew the injury bothered him and that he ached for the strength that two years in a POW camp had stolen from him. Not that he ever complained. Others had lost limbs, their sight, their lives. Those were the ones who deserved sympathy, he had told Alison, not him.

"You ready?" He held out his hand to help

her into the skiff. When their hands touched, Alison smiled at the tingle that quickened her pulse, knowing he felt it too. She hoped it never went away.

Two months had passed since their reunion beside the gnarled oak. Ian's new assignment, teaching escape and evasion techniques to Allied airmen and setting up safe routes through occupied Germany, had earned him a promotion to captain. He and sweet little Libby had settled into a brownstone within easy walking distance from the Mannings, where Trish mothered the twins and Alison. And Alison mothered Libby while Ian worked.

Though Alison had met Ian's parents when they came to London after Ian's return, this was her first visit to Kenniston Hall. The squat manor was much as she had imagined it, and she relished the feeling of stepping back into the past when Ian had taken her on a tour of the older section.

"Do you know what today is?" Ian sank the paddle's end into the channel, keeping the skiff on course to the giant's hand.

"Monday," she said mischievously, knowing that wasn't the answer he wanted.

"The date."

"August 24."

"Three years ago today, we met at Waterloo Station."

"And had Miniver scones."

"You told me you'd never see me again."

She trailed her hand in the water, then flicked the drops at him. "You've been persistent."

"Because I love you."

Smiling, she captured his face in her heart. How ruggedly handsome he was with his strong chin and Anglo-Saxon features. The haunted expression in his gold-flecked eyes had disappeared, replaced by an intensity that softened whenever he looked at her. The gauntness was gone too, but not all the creases beside his eyes. The hard months had aged him, but she cherished each line, knowing its cost.

"I love you too," she said and delighted in Ian's affectionate smile. How easy she found it now to say the simple words. And she meant them. From the bottom of her heart, she meant them. The family fate no longer controlled her destiny. Only God could do that. Come what may, she treasured that belief deep within her soul.

Ian steered the boat onto a slender shelf, and they climbed the pathway across the top of the giant's palm and settled upon the wind-carved bench.

"That's Wales," he said, pointing to the

northwest.

"Such a beautiful view," Alison exclaimed.

"It's always been one of my favorite places."

"I can see why." Gazing across the blue waters, Alison remembered her trip to the Welsh quarry. Great Britain hadn't found it as necessary to hide her cultural treasures as had Holland and France. Not that those countries' efforts had done much good. Stories of looting circulated throughout the art world. Galerie nationale du Jeu de Paume in Paris was rumored to be a collecting point for treasures being shipped to secret caches throughout Germany.

To think, because of her trip to Wales she had been in Waterloo Station three years ago to be captivated by a boy violinist and his soldier-hero.

She smiled at Ian. "I wish I had my sketch pad."

"No sketching today. I've got something else in mind."

"What's that?"

"This." He dug a jeweler's box from his pocket and opened it. Brilliant diamonds flanked a square sapphire, their prisms of color sparkling in the sun.

Alison gasped as her heart pounded. Joyful tears clouded her vision.

"The blue reminds me of your lovely eyes, and how you see beauty in what most people ignore. The diamonds are for your strength and your courage." He took the ring from the box and, kneeling awkwardly on the narrow path, cleared his throat. "Alison Schuyler, will you do me the honor of becoming my wife?"

She tried to say yes, but the small syllable caught in her throat. Laughing, she nodded eagerly. He slipped the ring on her finger, a perfect fit. She admired the way it looked on her hand, then threw her arms around his neck. "Yes," she said, finally able to speak. "With all my heart, yes."

She said yes! Ian smiled toward the heavens. The sky looked bluer, the wisps of clouds even whiter as he and Alison walked hand in hand across the lower garden. Trish, Mark, and the elder Devlins relaxed within the shade of the arched gazebo, enjoying the seaside view, while Libby and the twins played with the spaniel puppy. All three children had gained weight in the past two months, and their squeals and giggles added to the joy of the day.

Ian watched as Libby tried, without much success, to boss the twins into playing some game only she understood. Her brown eyes expressed frustration with her playmates, but no hint of fear or grief. She no longer clutched the cloth doll, now propped on her bed in the newly refurbished nursery — Lady Devlin's special project before the arrival of the children.

Earlier that day, Alison had braided Libby's dark hair with ribbons that matched the little girl's purple dotted swiss dress. She looked so different from the tiny vagabond that had traveled with him from Germany. His own sweet princess.

The unbidden thought stopped him in his tracks. Caught off guard, Alison turned. "What is it?"

"Libby."

Her eyes darted to Libby and back at him. "She's fine."

"I want to adopt her."

"So do I."

"You agree?"

She chuckled and kissed the corner of his mouth. "Did you have to ask?"

"No, I guess I didn't." He grinned as he drew her close. "I want to adopt her soon."

"Then I guess we'd better get married soon."

He mimicked an evil laugh. "The sooner the better."

"Papi! Alison!"

They interrupted their kiss to see Libby racing toward them. As he often did, Ian bent down and caught her in his arms, then swung her around. Holding her with one arm, he drew Alison close with the other. "My girls," he whispered, kissing first one then the other. "My family."

CHAPTER FORTY-FIVE

OCTOBER 1943

Theodor read the message twice, absorbing the cryptic news he had waited so long to receive. *Pieter Schuyler arrested. Gestapo headquarters, Amsterdam.*

He penned an immediate reply with clear instructions to safeguard the prisoner until his arrival, then poured himself a double scotch and toasted his good fortune.

More than a year had passed since Alison's disappearance. Theodor guessed she was in England, having heard that several hundred Dutch had somehow managed to elude the mines that littered the North Sea and reached those shores. Probably with that Brit she couldn't stop thinking about. His chest tightened and he downed the scotch, welcoming its burn.

He had trusted her, and she had slipped through his fingers. Given the opportunity, he'd return to that dismal day and change what happened. If only she understood how much he loved her, the plans he had made for their future. The risks he had taken for her.

The chauffeur Brant, to his credit, had kept his part of their bargain. He confessed to planning the assassination attempt on Göring's life without implicating Alison's father. And he told Theodor where to find the hidden art cache, a fortune in paintings and sculptures that were now hidden in a cave not far from the Scheidemanns' Bavarian chalet.

Despite the danger to his own life, Theodor had kept his word to Brant and arranged for Will's successful escape. That may have been his mistake, he mused, speculating for the millionth time whether Will and Alison had left Holland together. All he knew for sure was that the Dutch saboteur hadn't been seen since. He never should have let the criminal go, but he'd given his word. On his honor, he'd given his word.

When he had returned to the hospital to claim his prize, Alison and Hendrik were gone. Even Duret, that simpering French minion, had disappeared. Theodor posted guards at the hospital, the gallery, and even the destroyed canal house, but to no avail.

Despite an interrogation so severe that it twisted Theodor's stomach, Brant refused to give any helpful information. The next morning, he was found dead in his cell.

It was as if the entire Van Schuyler family had vanished into thin air.

But now Pieter was within his grasp. And if Theodor calculated his moves with enough cunning and finesse, Alison soon would be too.

"Are you certain? Completely certain?" Alison sat on the edge of the chair in Dr. Ericson's snug office.

The doctor chuckled. "One hundred percent."

"When?"

"Mid-May. Give or take."

Alison blew out a breath of air and leaned back in the chair. "I thought so. But I didn't dare hope."

"Allow me to be the first to congratulate you. And tell Ian that when the blessed event occurs, I want the finest cigar he can round up. Nothing cheap."

She smiled, her heart so filled with excitement she thought it would burst. "I'll tell him. He'll be home in three or four days."

"Off on another secret mission?"

"Only he knows for sure." That wasn't

444

quite the truth, but she didn't dare say more. Ian's position with the escape-and-evasion office, known simply as Room 900, required him to meet with returning Allied airmen for debriefings. Two Americans who had been shot down over Belgium had managed to connect with the Comet Line resistance group and were being flown from Spain to an undisclosed location in southwestern England.

"I must fetch Libby." Alison stood and gathered her things. "She's taking piano lessons now."

"Any progress on her adoption?"

"Not yet. We have no proof that she is an orphan. For all we know, her father is still alive."

"Even if he is, how would you ever find him?" Richard walked with her to the door. "Surely the court understands how impossible that would be."

"At least we have legal custody." Josef's uncle, Abraham Talbert, had gladly assisted them with that hurdle. "The rest is in God's hand."

"I'll pray for His providence."

"Please do." Alison smiled brightly, struck anew by the miracle happening within her. A baby. She shivered with joy. "And thanks for such wonderful news."

"Thank me by taking good care of yourself. And don't forget about that cigar."

"I won't; I promise." She glanced at her watch. "I really need to run. Thanks again."

She practically waltzed out of the office, her thoughts filled with visions of baby layettes and nursery schemes. Primary colors or pastels? Pink or blue? Humming the lullaby that Libby had taught her when they first met, Alison hurried to hug the little girl who would be a big sister in the spring.

"Pieter Schuyler. At last we meet." Theodor paced around the broken man strapped into a wooden chair in the middle of the interrogation cell. Both of Pieter's eyes were black-and-blue, the left swollen shut. His fractured nose seemed held in place by the swelling beneath his eyes and above his lips. The horribly distorted face sickened Theodor's stomach. But his blood boiled at the unnatural angles of the fingers on Pieter's right hand. Only a moronic Neanderthal could have done such a thing to an artist. So much destruction was making animals of them all. What had happened to the Aryan dream?

"I don't know you," Pieter said through bloodied lips.

"I am an art collector. An admirer of your work."

"Impossible."

"Why do you say that?"

"My work only —" he struggled to speak — "in the United States."

"But that's not true. Your works are all over Holland. Forged identification cards. Forged ration cards and birth certificates. If I'm not mistaken — and I'm certain I am not — even forged paintings. You have a great talent, Herr Schuyler. However, you have chosen to use it quite unwisely."

Pieter didn't attempt to answer.

"We are not your enemy, Herr Schuyler. We came to protect you and your countrymen."

Still no response.

Theodor sighed heavily, as if exasperated. He turned to the guard, standing quietly in the corner. "Bring water for the prisoner."

"Major?"

"You heard me. Go."

The instant the door closed behind the guard, Theodor stepped behind Pieter. "I know who you are. And I know your daughter. We are friends. At least we were, before this dastardly war."

Pieter's head jerked upward. "No."

"It's true. I also arranged Will Brant's

447

escape. Surely he told you."

Pieter slowly nodded.

"Reichsmarschall Göring does not yet know of your arrest, but he will soon. And when he does, he will demand your execution. There is nothing I can do to stop that. But if you will allow me, I will write to Alison on your behalf."

"My father didn't trust you."

"There are things about me your father didn't know." Theodor gripped Pieter's shoulder. "The war is going badly for Germany. Hitler knows this. Göring knows this. When the war ends, there will be trials. While your father sees me as Göring's friend, I am instead his enemy. His crimes are many, and I have the proof."

"Why should I believe you?"

"I risk my own neck telling you these things." He walked toward the door and stood with his back against it. "The guard will return soon. What may I tell your daughter?"

"There is nothing." Pieter's words were strained. "She knows I love her."

"At least she is safe."

"Yes."

Theodor frowned in frustration. He had only one more card to play. He took a deep breath. "I have your paintings, including *The*

Girl in the Garden."

Pieter's head shot up. Theodor refused to waver, though the distortions of his prisoner's features made him ill.

"I wish for Alison to have her mother's portrait. Your masterpiece. As Germany is taking your life, allow me to make this small amends."

Pieter stared at Theodor with one eye, now filmy with unshed tears. "You could get the painting to her?"

"I have connections with art dealers in both Sweden and Switzerland. It could be arranged." He willed himself to be patient, to allow Pieter's deep attachment to the painting to cloud his judgment.

"She's married now."

Theodor's jaw stiffened and his breathing slowed. But it didn't matter. He couldn't let her marriage change his plans. What he told Pieter was true. The Aryan vision was crumbling amid cruel debauchery. He needed Alison more than ever to restore the Nazi dream.

"To Ian?" he asked casually.

"Ian Devlin. London." Pieter gasped for breath. "That's all I know."

"It is enough."

CHAPTER FORTY-SIX

Alison wiped chocolate icing from around Libby's mouth, then lovingly tapped her button nose. They were enjoying a treat at Minivers after the piano lesson, part of their weekly routine. As Alison wiped the pastry crumbs from her daughter's fingers, she thought of the earlier conversation with Dr. Ericson and the secret about Libby he could never know

The day Ian and Libby arrived at the Mannings', after the little girl and the twins were tucked in bed for the night, the adults had gathered in the sitting room. With halting words and raw emotion that tore at Alison's heart, Ian had told them about Gretchen and the German captain, the pitchfork and his promise.

The four of them, Ian and Alison, Mark and Trish, had agreed that only they would know the truth. Everyone else, including the elder Devlins, would be told a slightly

450

skewed version — that Ian found shelter at the farm of a dying woman who begged him to care for her daughter. Her husband's whereabouts were unknown.

"May we feed the birds now?" Libby asked.

"Of course."

As if on cue, the Minivers hostess appeared with a small paper bag of stale pastry crumbs. In their frequent visits to the cozy tea shop over the past few months, Libby's good manners and German-mangled English had endeared her to the woman.

Alison paid the bill while Libby told the hostess about her morning's lesson, demonstrating a finger pattern on the table.

At the park, the same one where Ian had taken Alison after their first visit to Minivers, Libby skipped along the path with the bag of crumbs clutched tightly in her little hand. Alison followed, smiling contentedly and wishing Ian would come home soon so she could share the precious news. Here, in front of the granite fountain.

She sat on the bench while Libby scattered her crumbs along the path and in front of the fountain. Pigeons quickly gathered, snatching up the bits of pastry and cooing for more. Libby laughed at them and danced around the fountain.

"Miss Schuyler?"

Startled, Alison looked up at the slender man who towered over her, his hat in his hand.

"Forgive me; I didn't mean to frighten you," the man said with a distinct Swedish accent. "May I speak to you a moment?"

Alison stood and glanced at Libby, busily occupied in picking up colorful leaves scattered beneath the autumn-kissed trees. "Do I know you?" she asked, turning back to the stranger.

"My name is Isak Edstrom. I've done business in the past with your grandfather."

"I don't remember you."

"It's been many years. My customers became less enchanted with the Old Masters after the Great War. But before then, I made several trips to the Van Schuyler Fine Arts Gallery."

"What can I do for you, Mr. Edstrom?"

"I bring you sad news, Miss Schuyler. About your father."

Alison meant to correct him, to tell him she was Mrs. Devlin now, but his last sentence drove that thought away. Her pulse quickened. "What about my father?"

"The Gestapo finally found him. He is in prison and will be executed in a matter of days."

Blood drained from her head, leaving her dizzy. Alison grabbed for the side of the bench and lowered herself to the seat. *No, her brain screamed. This can't be happening. Not on this perfect day.* The joy that had buoyed her spirit dissipated, replaced by a stone of fear.

"How do you know this?" she said weakly.

"Though Sweden is officially neutral, there are those of us who assist the Dutch Underground. We received the news of Pieter's arrest. May I?" At her nod, he sat next to her on the bench. "Your father was a very brave man. His forgeries saved many people from the Germans. This is how you must remember him."

Stunned by the news, Alison sat speechless, while a corner of her brain realized she wasn't crying. Had she no tears to shed for her father? It couldn't be true — that's why she didn't cry. It just couldn't be true.

"Miss Schuyler, I have a favor to ask of you."

She stared at the man, taking in his crystal-blue eyes, pale skin, and Nordic features. "I am Mrs. Devlin now. Mrs. Ian Devlin."

"My apologies, yes. I know of your marriage. But your grandfather spoke of you as his little treasure, did he not?"

Alison nodded, remembering Hendrik's thready voice as he lay in the hospital bed. *"Mijn schatje."*

"It's hard for me to think of you as a married woman."

"What is your favor, Mr. Edstrom?"

"It is a difficult one, a dangerous one. I wish I did not have to ask, but other lives may be at stake."

Her curiosity aroused, she stretched her tensed fingers and folded her hands in her lap. "What could I possibly do?"

"Your father has information vital to the Underground. We believe that the Gestapo chief will allow a visit from his daughter. You could get this information from Pieter." He leaned slightly forward. "You would also be able to tell your father good-bye."

Alison straightened as an array of emotions swirled within her. Shock followed by confusion followed by a yearning to see her papa one last time. She looked toward Libby, who smiled and waved her collection of leaves. Alison automatically returned the smile. "Once I'm in Holland . . . how would I ever get out again?"

"We will do our utmost to ensure your safety. You will be gone from your family only two days. Three at the most."

"What is your plan?" Her words sounded

as lifeless as she felt, as if all warmth had drained from her. To see Papa before he died — could anything else matter?

"My plane leaves for Stockholm in an hour. We fly from there to Amsterdam. You see your father, get the information we need, and we bring you home again."

"You make it sound so simple."

"The only danger is in Amsterdam. But the Gestapo chief has been bribed before." Edstrom looked at her appraisingly and Alison shrank back. "Forgive me. But I will say that the chief is not immune to a lovely woman's tears. The plan will work."

"In an hour?"

"Yes. I have a car waiting. We can go there immediately."

"I have to go home first."

"May I drive you there?"

Alison glanced at her watch. So much to do and so little time to think, to plan. She searched the Swede's eyes again but found no answers.

"I am sorry about Pieter," he said, his gaze steady under her scrutiny. "He will always be remembered as a hero."

"Yes, he will." *And a hero's daughter must also have courage.* "Libby," she called, standing and holding out her hand. "It's time to go."

The Swede also rose. "You will come with me, then?"

Alsion straightened her shoulders and looked down at the little girl she thought of as her own daughter. "I will come."

Forgive me, Ian.

CHAPTER FORTY-SEVEN

Inside the brownstone, Alison left Libby in the parlor with a storybook and headed for the kitchen, where their day-woman, Mrs. Beall, was rolling out pie crust. "Good, you're here," Alison said, pausing to catch her breath. "I need to go away, just overnight. Please take Miss Libby to the Mannings and tell them . . . never mind. I'll write Trish a note."

"I beg your pardon, Mrs. Devlin, but I am not a nursemaid. Cooking and housekeeping, that's my service."

Alison forced herself to stay calm and vowed that next time she would take care of hiring their household staff instead of leaving it to Ian. She felt just as sorry for the woman as he did, knowing Mrs. Beall was alone since her only son had joined the Army. But Alison found her annoying and often plotted on how she could kidnap the Mannings' marvelous Mrs. Crewe.

"I understand you are not a nursemaid, Mrs. Beall. And believe me, if I had the time I would take Miss Libby myself. But I must leave immediately, and Miss Libby must be taken to the Mannings."

"This is highly irregular," Mrs. Beall said, pursing thin lips. "Highly irregular."

"Yes, it most certainly is. Please, may I count on you?"

"Very well. Though don't blame me if the supper is ruined."

"No one will be here for supper, Mrs. Beall. And your services won't be needed tomorrow, either."

"Not needed?"

Alison sighed. "Don't worry. Your pay will be the same. In fact, more. For the inconvenience."

"Why, thank you very much, Mrs. Devlin. I'm glad to be of help any way I can during these troublesome times; yes, I am."

"Good. Then you can pack Libby's bag. And don't forget her doll."

Without waiting for a response, Alison rushed upstairs. She changed into a pair of trousers and layered a jumper over a long-sleeved blouse, remembering Ian talking about how cold it was in the plane that brought him and Libby to England. After lacing up and tying her hiking boots, she packed a small bag.

Returning to the parlor, she wrote a brief note to Trish, asking her to care for Libby and promising to be home within a day or two. As she folded the paper and slipped it in an envelope, she breathed a prayer of thanks that Ian was gone. Never would he have allowed her to return to Holland. Whenever she talked about her guilt over leaving her family behind, he had held her tight and reassured her that neither Hendrik nor Pieter would want her to risk her life for them.

But the guilt had never gone away, not completely. Somehow it felt wrong that she was so blessed when so many around them suffered. Her beloved husband, though gone occasionally, was home most nights for supper. They had Libby. And now she had her own precious secret.

At least, if Mr. Edstrom could be believed, she'd be home before Ian's return. A definite case of asking forgiveness instead of permission. When she returned, she'd explain that this had been her only chance to see her papa this side of heaven. Ian would just have to understand.

She glanced out the door to where the Swede leaned against his car, smoking a cigarette. He saw her and pointed at his watch.

Taking a deep breath, she drew Libby onto her lap. "How would you like to spend a few days with Anna and Aaron?"

"And the puppy?"

"And the puppy, of course."

"And you, Mama?"

"Mama has to go on a trip. Just for a couple of days." Alison squeezed her tight. "But I'll come back soon. I promise."

"Can I go with you?"

"Not this time." She closed her eyes against a sudden sting of tears. "But when I get home, and when Papi comes home, maybe we can go a trip together. Would you like that?"

"Is Papi coming home?" Her tiny voice chipped at Alison's heart.

"He's coming home, sweetheart. You know he has work to do. But he'll be back in just a few days." Alison lifted Libby's chin and looked into her dark eyes. "And I'll be home before he is. I promise." *God, please don't let me break this promise.* "Okay?"

Libby nodded doubtfully, biting her bottom lip.

"Come on, then. Mrs. Beall is going to take you to Aunt Trish. And I'll see you very soon."

"I miss you, Mama."

"I'll miss you, too, Libby. I love you so much."

"Bigger than the world?"

"Bigger than the world."

Mrs. Beall entered the parlor, pulling on her gloves. "I have a bag for Miss Libby. Shall we go now?"

Alison nodded and handed her the note for Trish. "I'll be back. Tomorrow, the day after at the latest." She put on Ian's brown hunting jacket, gave Libby a last hug and kiss, then walked out the door. Quickly, before she could change her mind.

As Mr. Edstrom pulled away from the curb, she looked out the window. Libby stood on the stoop of the brownstone, clutching her doll, tears running down her face. As Alison smiled weakly and waved, her fingers ached for a pencil. How else to ease the ache in her heart?

Alison and Isak Edstrom were the only passengers in the small cargo plane that flew from a tiny airport outside of London to Stockholm. The Swede busied himself with a briefcase full of documents and newspapers while Alison stared out the window at the misty clouds. He encouraged her to sleep, but the closer they got to Stockholm, the more adrenaline pumped through her veins. Despite the warmth of Ian's jacket, she shivered, praying the plan would work, that the Gestapo chief would permit her to see her father. And she prayed for a miracle that would allow her to take him back to England.

Her stomach lurched as the plane descended and taxied along the rough Swedish runway. She braced herself as the brakes squealed and the plane hopped to a screeching halt.

"We can go inside the terminal while the plane refuels," Edstrom said, smiling. "It won't be long until you're back in Holland, Miss Schuyler."

"I prefer to be called Mrs. Devlin," Alison said coldly.

"My client prefers that you not." His strange chuckle sent a shiver up her spine.

"Who's your client?"

"He's waiting for you. Inside."

The Swede preceded Alison down the steps of the plane, then escorted her to the terminal. He opened the door and smiled as he gestured for her to go inside.

Doubt tingled at the base of her skull as she stepped into the building. Two German soldiers rose as she entered. One was a stranger, the other all too familiar.

"Hello, Theodor," she said, proud her voice didn't shake.

"My dear Alison."

"Has my father really been arrested? Or is this all a trick?"

"Your father is in prison and scheduled for execution in the morning. I am sorry."

"Will I get to see him?"

Theodor stepped forward, compassion in his eyes. "My apologies for the deception. I feared if you knew it was I who engineered this plan, you wouldn't come."

"I only want to see my father." She gazed at him, hoping that he could see her gratitude and not her unease. "And then I wish to go home. To London."

He lifted her left hand and gazed at her rings, the sapphire offset by diamonds and the gold wedding band. "The Brit has good taste."

"My *husband* has excellent taste."

"A point that cannot be argued," he said smoothly, lifting her fingers to his lips. "After all, he chose you."

She pulled her hand away, wiping her fingers on her trousers.

He seemed amused by the childish gesture. "Would you like some refreshment?"

"No, thank you."

"At least have some coffee. It's not too

bad, and it will warm you."

Even though she didn't answer, Theodor motioned toward the other German. The soldier immediately disappeared down a short corridor and returned moments later with two hot mugs of coffee.

Alison wrapped her hands around the steaming mug and sniffed it, wondering if it was drugged.

"I managed to acquire your painting from Reichsmarschall Göring," Theodor said. "I promised your father I would return it to you."

In her surprise, Alison almost spilled her coffee. "*The Girl in the Garden?*"

"Yes." Theodor's proud smile reminded her of Alice's Cheshire Cat.

"Where is it?"

"Safe. With your watercolors."

"You have them, too?"

Theodor leaned close, speaking in a soft, confidential tone. "You know as well as I do that Göring is no artist, has no true appreciation. You should see his estate, Carinhall. Paintings, sculptures, enough to furnish a fine museum. But he displays them with no eye toward composition. It's disgraceful. I couldn't bear to think of your delicate watercolors in his clumsy hands."

Alison tried to reconcile this Theodor,

who showed such care for her artistry, with the man whose political ambitions thrust him into the same circles as brutes like Hitler and Göring. Even at the hospital all those months ago, he had risked Göring's wrath by offering his protection to her and her family. If only she could have loved him . . . how different things might have been. Her family and her gallery would be safe.

"Do you know what happened to my grandfather?"

"Don't you?" he asked in genuine surprise.

She shook her head. "I've not had a word from him. From anyone."

Theodor shifted uneasily in his chair. "I couldn't get back to the hospital until the next day. Hendrik was gone. His doctor couldn't, or wouldn't, give me any information."

"You went to the gallery. Did you talk to our man Brant?"

"Do you really not know, Alison?"

The compassion in his voice frightened her, and she merely shook her head.

"Göring's soldiers arrived while I was there. They took him away. He . . . he died."

"They killed him?"

"They broke him. But I believe he died by

his own hand. I'm not sure how."

She lifted the mug to her lips, purposely burning her mouth with the hot coffee to lessen the pain in her chest.

"Perhaps it will comfort you to know his son escaped. With my help."

She raised her eyes to his. "You mean Will? You helped Will escape?"

"I promised Brant I would. Just as I promised your father I would reunite you with *The Girl in the Garden.* Whatever you may think of me, I am a man of honor. I keep my word."

Before she could respond, the terminal door opened and a gust of wind whooshed through the room. The tall Swede ducked inside. "The plane is ready, Count Scheidemann."

Theodor took the mug from her hands. "Come, Alison. You'll soon be home."

Something about the lighting was wrong. Alison shoved up the long sleeve of Ian's jacket and checked the time. They'd been flying at least half an hour, she calculated, as she stared back out the window. Beyond the misty clouds, the sun descended toward earth.

She faced Theodor, strapped in the seat beside her, and pointed out the window.

"That's west. Practically due west."

He glanced out the window. "Does that concern you?"

"I don't know. It just seems we should be turning more to the west. If we keep going south, we'll be in —" Horror churned her stomach, and she held her mouth closed to stop the sudden urge to vomit.

"Germany?" He half-smiled. "More precisely, Bavaria."

"You promised to take me to my father."

Theodor gazed at her, his blue eyes steady. "Your father's last wish was for you to be reunited with *The Girl in the Garden.* I'm fulfilling that promise by taking you to the painting."

"What about your promise to me? That I could see my father?"

"I made no such promise."

Alison stared at him, open-mouthed.

He shifted in his seat so he faced her more directly. "Your father did not want you to see him."

"I don't believe you."

"I went to Amsterdam as soon as I heard of his arrest. But it was too late. They had already . . . His hands . . ." Closing his eyes, he shook his head, and fear gripped Alison's heart as she imagined what he so obviously wanted to forget. "Barbarians," he muttered.

A sob broke from Alison's throat, and Theodor clasped her hand. "I gave him as much medical care as I dared. He wanted you to know how much he loves you."

She leaned her forehead against her window, too aware that the crisp autumn sun descended behind them, its rays trailing their eastward path. Each minute taking her farther from Papa. Farther from Ian and Libby. Barely aware that Theodor still clasped her left hand, she pressed her right one against her still-flat stomach while tears streamed freely down her cheeks.

CHAPTER FORTY-EIGHT

The plane, flying from an undisclosed location in southwest England, touched down at the military airbase outside of London. Ian stretched his legs and stood, eager to get home and hug his girls. The two Allied airmen, physically weak from their trek across the Pyrenees to Gibraltar but otherwise unharmed, were still recuperating in a Plymouth Sound hospital. Both had given Ian updated intelligence on the resistance groups operating in France and Spain that he could use in his escape-and-evasion training.

He stepped from the plane, scrutinizing the jeep headed toward him, then smiled as he recognized his brother-in-law at the wheel. "Hey, Major," he said, throwing his duffle in the back and climbing in the passenger seat. "I thought you were in Scotland."

"I was." Mark clipped the words.

Ian glanced over, his nerves tingling. Dark sunglasses hid Mark's eyes, but his lips were a grim line. "Something wrong?"

Mark steered the jeep away from the plane and parked in the farthest space from the hangar door. He turned off the ignition, removed the sunglasses, and rubbed his hand over his eyes.

"What's going on?"

"There's no easy way to tell you this, Dev. But I wanted it to come from me."

"Is it my dad?"

Mark barely shook his head.

"Trish?"

"Trish is fine. Your parents are fine." Mark bit his lip.

A thousand nightmare scenarios collided in Ian's brain, throwing painful shards against his temples. "Not Libby? Please, God, no, not Libby."

"It's Alison, Dev. She's gone."

Ian opened his mouth, but no words came out. His muscles tensed, on full alert. "What do you mean *gone*? Where is she?"

"There was an accident and she . . . she died."

The words slammed into Ian's stomach, and he gripped the door handle. "No," he groaned. "You're wrong."

"I wish I was."

"I don't believe you."

"Do you think I would lie to you about something like this?"

Alison gone? She couldn't be. Ian's eyes burned as a sob caught in his throat. "How?"

"It's the craziest thing, Dev. She was on this boat —"

"What boat?"

"A small steamer out of Sweden. It exploded off the Aberdeen coast. Her name was on the passenger manifest. *Alison Schuyler Devlin*. I saw it myself."

"No!" Ian smacked the dashboard with his fist. "She's home. With Libby. She wouldn't leave Libby."

"But she did." Mark pulled an envelope from his pocket. "Here's the note she left for Trish."

Ian's hand trembled as he took the opened envelope from Mark. Trish's name was written in Alison's familiar handwriting on the outside. He tried to remove the letter, but his fingers fumbled and he creased the envelope. He pressed it against his leg, wanting to remove the crease he'd made, wanting it to be as pristine as when Alison last touched it. "Just tell me," he managed to mumble.

"It says her father was arrested, but that

Swedish resistance had arranged for her to see him before his execution. She asked us to take care of Libby and said she'd be back the next day."

"The Swedish resistance?" Ian shook his head in a vain attempt to free his thoughts from the gripping throb of his headache. "That doesn't make any sense."

"I talked to your housekeeper, Mrs. Beall. She said Alison came rushing in, changed into men's clothes, and left with some chap who was waiting outside for her."

Ian squeezed his eyes shut, hearing Mark's voice, trying to make sense of what he was saying. But none of it made sense. "What chap?"

"Tall, blond, and Scandinavian, according to Mrs. Beall. Which fits with the Swedish connection."

Ian's thoughts swirled. What an incredible story, yet Alison had believed it. She had left him on the vain hope that she could see her father.

"I don't believe it. She couldn't have been on that boat."

"The steamer wasn't that far offshore when it exploded. I helped oversee the rescue and recovery." He took a deep breath and exhaled slowly. "You remember Sergeant Gregg — freckles, always sunburned?"

"Yeah, he got you on the boat at Dunkirk."

"He was in the communications room when the manifest came in. Happened to see the name and brought me a copy." He gripped Ian's forearm, and his voice cracked. "It's her, Dev."

Ian leaned back in the seat and shaded his closed eyes with his hand. *Alison.* His lovely Alison, who had stolen his heart with a single glance. Visions of her danced before him. Alison at Waterloo Station, at Minivers, at the little park that Libby now loved so much. Alison at the canal house with the white bandage against her temple. The delicate white scar he so often kissed. Alison sketching the ancient oak. Wearing her painter's smock, dabs of blue and yellow on her face.

This isn't how it was supposed to be. The Van Schuyler family fate dictated his death, not hers. Just a superstition, that's what he had told Alison. That's what he believed.

"Oh, God, help me," he moaned. *Thou art my hiding place. Don't let me slip from You.*

Libby clutched Ian's hand throughout the mercifully brief memorial service, held in their neighborhood church the Saturday after his return. The little girl's sad eyes pierced Ian's broken heart, and he wished for an end to all the formalities. As soon as the last of the well-wishers said good-bye, he planned to take her to Kenniston Hall. Perhaps there, in the gardens and near the sea, he could find the comfort that eluded him in town.

Yesterday he had wandered alone through their brownstone, remembering Alison's joy in transforming it into a home. Pausing before the fireplace, he had gazed at her oil painting of him and Libby beneath the oak tree in Trish's garden. How proud she had been of that portrait. Even he could see the influence of her father's masterpiece in how she brought light into the foreground. Painting it had eased the heavy grief she carried in her own heart, providing a blessed healing that caused her beautiful gray-blue eyes to sparkle.

But the dream had come to an end. Everything in the brownstone, except for the portrait and a few other keepsakes, would be sold or stored away. He intended to never set foot in the house again.

Dr. Richard Ericson touched Ian's arm, forcing him to return his attention to the church foyer. Looking for Libby, he saw her with Trish, talking to the piano teacher.

"I'm so sorry, Ian," said Richard. "To think how quickly . . . Just last week, she

474

was glowing, and then for this to happen."

"Thank you," Ian said dully, the same meaningless words he'd spoken too many times the last few days.

"If you need anything, you'll let me know."

"Of course." The practiced smile barely curved Ian's lips. He was so weary of the same sympathetic condolences. *"I'm so sorry. Is there anything I can do? Just last week, she was glowing. . . ."* "You saw Alison last week?"

Richard flushed. "She came to see me." He hesitated and his jaw twitched. "I should have realized . . . She didn't tell you."

"Tell me what?"

"This isn't the place, Ian. Come by later. Or I'll stop in to see you."

"Was she sick?"

"No, not at all."

Ian raised his voice. "Then what?"

Richard drew Ian away from the curious stares. "She . . . you . . . She was pregnant."

"Pregnant?"

Looking miserable, the doctor slowly nodded. "I am so sorry, Ian. You shouldn't have found out like this."

"When?" Ian blinked and chewed on his lip. "When would she have had the baby?"

"Middle of May." Richard clasped Ian's shoulder. "I really am sorry."

Unable to speak, Ian bowed his head. *God, wasn't it enough to take my wife? Why did there have to be a child, only for it to die too?* The unfairness of it all gnawed his gut and filled his chest. Drawing back his fist, he punched Richard's jaw.

The doctor staggered backward, his hand pressed against his bruised face. Immediate guilt slammed Ian's gut, and he reached out to steady the doctor.

"I don't know why I did that," he said. His skinned knuckles ached, but somehow the pain soothed the raw cut in his heart. "Are you all right?"

"I think I'll live." Richard rubbed his jaw. "Feel better?"

"A little." Ian half-shrugged. "I am sorry."

"Don't ever do that again."

"I won't." Ian looked straight in Richard's eyes. "Alison was happy? About the baby?"

"Ecstatic."

Of course she had been. And when she had come home, they would have celebrated. If only she had come home.

CHAPTER FORTY-NINE

APRIL 1944

Ian swiveled back and forth in his office chair as he stared at Alison's photograph. He had taken the picture himself in the gazebo, after they announced their engagement to his family. Her hair, ruffled by the summer breeze off the sea, framed her pale cheeks and dazzling smile. Her eyes sparkled as she gazed straight at him.

In his dreams, she still lived, her body heavy and round — and more beautiful than ever — as their baby's birth drew near. Brushing the glass covering the photo with his finger, he tried to imagine his hand on her taut belly, feeling kicks and flutters beneath her silky-smooth skin.

"Why did you leave me?" he whispered.

At least his ragged grief wasn't as razor-sharp as it had been six months ago. Needing to be strong for Libby, he had found strength deep within himself. His faith had seen him through the darkest nights, and his little girl had brightened his days. He missed her, now that he couldn't see her as often as he wanted.

Ian and Libby had lived with the Mannings until about four months ago. Then the Army brass transferred Mark to Italy and Ian to SHAEF, the Supreme Headquarters Allied Expeditionary Force, headed by US Army general Dwight Eisenhower. With Mark gone and Ian often traveling with Ike, Trish had taken all three children to Kenniston Hall.

A knock sounded at the door, and Ian swiveled to face his desk. "Enter," he said, then stood and saluted as Colonel Roger Davies entered.

The American officer, an intelligence expert, returned the salute. "At ease, Captain. Please sit."

"Thank you, Colonel."

"May I?" asked Davies, reaching for the photograph.

Ian handed it to him, then settled in his chair.

"I've read your file, Captain. I'm sorry for your loss." The colonel looked at the photo, then gave it back to Ian. "She's lovely."

"Thank you, sir."

"I've asked around about you, Captain.

You're not dating anyone, are you?"

Taken aback by the question, Ian furrowed his brow. "No, sir. I couldn't."

"Because you still love your wife?"

"Colonel, with all due respect —"

"Captain, have you heard of Double Cross?"

Ian shrugged, confused by the sudden change of subject. "Rumors."

The colonel chuckled. "That's the way they like it. Basically, the Double Cross Committee is the puppeteer manipulating our intelligence strings. Agents, double agents. And to some extent, Operation Overlord."

Ian leaned forward with interest, recognizing the code name for the upcoming Allied invasion.

"The operation requires too much preparation to keep it a secret," Colonel Davies said. "But we're doing our best to keep the Germans from finding out when and where it's going to take place."

"With misinformation?"

"That's right. Double Cross believes you're the perfect candidate for a special mission."

"Me, sir?"

The colonel nodded. "You have two necessary qualifications. First, you've impressed

General Eisenhower and earned his trust. Just as important —" he paused and pointed to Alison's photo — "is her."

"I don't understand."

"This mission requires an officer with access to Ike to become romantically involved with a Double Cross agent."

Ian held up both hands, palms out. "Impossible."

"Which is why you're perfect. We need an officer who can protect our agent's cover without falling in love with her."

Ian grunted. "Who is she? Bathsheba?"

"See for yourself." The colonel slid a folder across the desk.

Leaning back in his chair, Ian opened the folder and stared at an eight-by-ten professional headshot of one of the most beautiful women he had ever seen. Black lashes fringed her doelike eyes with their slight come-hither look, and dark, glossy hair accentuated her classic cheekbones. Her kissable lips curled into a perfect smile.

"Her name is Marie Wyatt."

"French?"

"On her mother's side. But she's an American. Came here with the USO and was recruited by the Twenty for courier work."

The Twenty, another name for the mysterious Double Cross because of their XX symbol.

"What's her cover?"

"That's the beauty of this mission. She's her own cover. And so are you."

"I'm an officer with access to Eisenhower."

"And Marie is an American actress. We've already arranged for her to appear in an upcoming theatrical production of *A Midsummer Night's Dream.*"

"How does this confuse the Germans?"

"Marie's assignment is to attract the attention of a certain Spanish embassy official. If all goes as planned, she will provide him with falsified documents she 'steals' from you."

"And he'll give them to the Germans."

"That's the plan."

Ian studied the photo again. This time he noticed something fragile beneath the beauty, an innocent vulnerability. "What you really mean is that she will seduce this Spanish chap."

"She'll string him along." The colonel shrugged, clearly indicating that how Marie handled the Spaniard wasn't his concern. "But whatever she does, we can't have our officer losing his head over the situation and threatening the mission. Too many lives are at stake."

"What do I do?"

"Take her out for dinner, dancing. Be seen around town together. Have a good time." Colonel Davies glanced at his watch. "Other than that, continue your regular duties with the general. I'll provide you with the false documents."

The mission seemed harmless enough. Yet Ian felt uneasy. He gazed at Alison's photo, her pale loveliness tugging at his heart.

"You're not being unfaithful, Captain. Whatever the world thinks about you and Miss Wyatt, Double Cross expects you to keep it platonic."

"You won't have to worry about that, Colonel."

"Marie is a very attractive woman."

"Not compared to my wife."

The colonel chuckled. "Then I can tell the committee that you've accepted the assignment?"

"I'm willing to do anything I can to support Operation Overlord."

"Good." Colonel Davies provided additional details of the mission, then stood. "Good luck, Captain. To both of you."

"Thank you, sir," Ian said as they shook hands.

The colonel hesitated at the door. "One

more thing. No one can know of your mission."

"No one will, sir."

"That includes your brother-in-law, Major Manning, and your family. They must believe, along with everyone else, that you are very much in love with Miss Wyatt."

"Understood, sir."

Holding Marie's photo, Ian swiveled his chair away from his desk as the sudden thought of a future grandchild popped in his head.

"What did you do in the war, Grandpa?"

"Why, I duped the entire German army."

"How did you do that, Grandpa?"

"I dated an American actress."

He grinned at the absurdity, then straightened his tie and put on his jacket. It was time to see if the girl was as lovely in person as she was in her picture.

Before he left, he took off his wedding band and stuck it in his pocket. Glancing at Alison's photo, he frowned. "Colonel's orders. But you know you're the only girl for me. Always."

CHAPTER FIFTY

MAY 1944

Alison stood on the chalet balcony outside her bedroom, watching the swans floating serenely beyond the tall reeds of the crystal-blue lake. How graceful they were. How free. While she was trapped, a pampered bird in a gilded cage.

Through the long winter, she had grown accustomed to the boundaries that barred her escape. The snow-blanketed mountain slopes, the ice-encrusted lake, the bone-chilling cold. Nature itself conspired against her.

Hearing a motor, she looked toward the winding drive that snaked between stands of firs. A flash of metal appeared as the vehicle maneuvered up the long road. Theodor was returning to the chalet, just as he promised.

Her nerves tingled with unease, and she caressed her rounded stomach as another contraction seized her. The baby wasn't due for another two weeks and the pain, squeezing her abdominal muscles with a fierce compulsion, frightened her. When it ceased, she returned to her room. Sinking into an upholstered chair, she lifted her swollen feet onto the matching stool.

If only she were home, in the brownstone with Ian and Libby. She envisioned them reading together after dinner and Ian tucking Libby into bed at night. At the end of June, Libby would celebrate her seventh birthday. She must be getting taller, losing her baby teeth, speaking better English. And Alison was missing all of it.

A few weeks after her arrival, Theodor had given her the London newspaper announcing her tragic death. "The Brit believes you're dead," Theodor had said, unwilling ever to refer to Ian either by name or as her husband. "He will mourn you, and then he will meet someone new. But I will always be here for you, Alison. We will be together, as we were always meant to be."

She had railed, threatened, even kicked and thrown things in those first days while Theodor stood calmly by, waiting for the storm to end. Eventually, they settled into a routine. He provided Alison everything she needed to restore *The Girl in the Garden* and now it proudly hung in the chalet's main parlor, lit by gold sconces specially placed to highlight the painting's playful subject and the vibrant colors of the flowers at her feet.

The studio he made for her was an artist's dream and, after covering dozens of canvases with dark oils and angry shapes, she had returned to painting the light, bright watercolors she loved. Even in the midst of winter, she had sometimes bundled up and sat on her balcony with her easel and paints, delighting in the breathtaking scenery that surrounded her.

As the tides of war turned against Germany, Theodor's absences had grown more frequent. Though she couldn't pinpoint when it happened, she eventually realized she missed him when he was gone — and hated herself for it.

Another contraction squeezed her, and her heart seemed to beat in rhythm with the labor. She took deep breaths to ease the intensifying pain, refusing to cry out her distress. A strange kind of pop released a warm oozing against her legs.

Leaning forward, she tried and failed to push herself from the chair. Catching her breath, she tried again and took one cautious step after another to the bell pull. She yanked it, hard as she could, then sank to the floor as the most intense contraction she had yet experienced gripped her body. An anguished cry escaped her lips as the seconds slowed and she prayed for the pain to cease.

When the agony receded, her ragged breathing returned to normal, but another contraction followed close behind, a giant hand gripping her abdomen. The rhythm continued until, as she prepared for another onslaught of pain, her door opened. She moaned and footsteps hurried toward her.

"Alison!" Theodor knelt beside her and brushed her sweat-dampened hair from her face.

"The baby."

"Go for the midwife," he ordered the housekeeper who hovered behind him. She hurried out as he lifted Alison and carried her to her bed.

"Everything will be fine," he said, but Alison heard the worry in his voice. The room shimmered in front of her eyes, a dizzying assault that threatened her with its mirage-like appearance.

"Ian," she said, her breath expelling in a final burst before she closed her eyes to pain and sadness.

CHAPTER FIFTY-ONE

Ian shoved the chairs that usually flanked his fireplace against the hearth. "Your stage." He gestured with a flourish toward the bare space in the center of the room.

"Perfect." Marie Wyatt, as beautiful as her photograph, handed him a copy of the script for *A Midsummer Night's Dream.* "I appreciate this so much."

"Glad to do it. So far, this has been one of the easiest assignments I've ever had."

"Me too. So far." She grimaced, and Ian knew what she was thinking. Only a week before, he had escorted her to a benefit ball where she had attracted the Spanish official's attention, then coyly inflamed his interest by refusing to dance with him a second time. The Spaniard had sent her a dozen pink roses the next morning. Ian hoped she could slip into the part of mercenary ingénue as skillfully as she did Shakespeare's Titania. For the vital role of temptress, she would have no rehearsals.

They had gone through several pages when a knock sounded at the door. Marie dropped her fairy queen persona and glanced at Ian, sitting at a small table near the flat's window. "Should I get it?"

"No, you take a break."

"Mind if I get some juice?" she asked, heading for the kitchen alcove.

"Help yourself." He crossed to the door and opened it. Trish stood in the hallway, a forced smile on her face. Surprised that she had come to town without letting him know her plans, Ian felt his heart skip a fearful beat. "Is something wrong?" He looked past her. "Where's Libby?"

"Nothing's wrong, and Libby is at the estate. I just came up to see how you are." She entered the flat and looked curiously at the pushed-back furniture. "What are you doing?"

"Rehearsal." Ian glanced at Marie, her dark curls clasped at her slender neck, as lovely as ever. He had hoped to make it through this assignment without lying to Trish. With a deep breath, he held his hand out to Marie. "I want you to meet someone. This is Marie Wyatt. My sister, Trish Manning."

Marie smiled warmly. "Ian has told me so

many stories about the two of you. I feel like I know you already."

Trish pressed her lips in a tight smile. "I wish I could say the same. Apparently my brother decided to keep you a secret."

"Not a secret," Ian said, trying to sound sheepish. "Just waiting for the right time." He exchanged a quick glance with Marie.

"I should go," she said, retrieving her purse and jacket from the coat tree. "Give you two a chance to catch up."

"Will I see you later?" Ian asked.

"If you're free." She smiled at Trish. "It was nice meeting you."

"You too."

Under Trish's glare, Ian gave Marie an awkward peck on the cheek. "I'll call you," he said as she left the flat.

Once in the hallway, Marie turned to him and mouthed, *"I'm sorry."* He gave a slight shrug before closing the door and turning to Trish.

"You weren't very polite."

"I'm astounded, that's all." She pulled at her gloves. "What about Alison?"

Her words strangled his heart, and he scraped the wooden floor as he moved a chair to its proper place.

"Would you watch what you're doing?" Trish grabbed the chair and shifted it slightly, causing another scratch.

"And would you leave Alison out of this?" He clutched the back of the other chair, intending to move it, too. But instead he simply stood behind it, fighting the waves of emotion that threatened to drown him.

"It just seems so soon," she said softly.

"We're not getting married, Trish. We're just spending time together." At least that wasn't a lie.

"A wartime romance?"

"Maybe." He moved away from her and plopped into the chair. "War affects everything."

"It won't last forever."

"It already has." That wasn't a lie either. Peace could come tomorrow, but a treaty wouldn't bring Alison back.

"I'm sorry, Ian. It's just hard seeing you with someone else. You'd feel the same if something happened to Mark and I showed up with a new man."

"Probably," he admitted. "But I wouldn't want you to grieve forever. Or to never laugh again. You don't know what it's like to walk around with a heart that keeps beating because it doesn't know it's dead."

Trish bent her head, and Ian stared into the empty fireplace. The mantel clock ticked off the seconds that stretched into eternity before he could speak past the lump in his throat. "Marie gives me life, Trish."

"Do you love her?"

"I care about her. Very much." And he wasn't lying.

CHAPTER FIFTY-TWO

Waves of light and muted voices accompanied Alison's return to consciousness. Dreamlike visions floated before her, vague memories of piercing screams, a calm voice urging her to relax, to breathe. Her parched throat scratched and her abdomen ached, but the agonizing contractions no longer gripped her. Burning with fever, she kicked at the sheets imprisoning her legs.

"Now, dearie," said a soft voice with a heavy German accent. "Don't want to catch a chill, do we?"

Alison forced her eyes open and saw Frau Mueller, her housekeeper, cook, and jailer.

"You want water, yes?" She offered Alison a glass and helped her sip the cool liquid, easing the dryness in her mouth and throat.

"Where's my baby?" Alison asked, her voice weak and hesitant.

"I am sorry," Frau Mueller whispered.

"I want to see my baby."

Shaking her head, the housekeeper walked out of the room, shutting the door firmly behind her.

The click of the latch sounded ominous in the silent room. Alison strained her ears, listening for an infant's mewling cry. But she heard only the sound of the wind rustling through the alpine trees, the distant honk of a flock of geese.

Then the murmur of voices in the hallway.

With herculean effort, she freed her legs from the covers and eased her feet to the floor. Her entire body protested, and she braced herself against the headboard, willing the weakness to go away.

The door opened, and Theodor entered. The blood seemed to drain from his face, and he quickly reached her side and grasped her arms. "You mustn't get up, Alison. It's too soon."

She flinched from his touch. "Where's my baby?"

"Please. Get back in bed."

"Not until you give me my baby."

"Alison," he said softly, gently. "There were complications. The baby . . . we couldn't save him."

The pain in her abdomen paled as Theodor's words wrenched her heart. Her eyes pooled with hot tears. "Him?"

"Yes."

Her son. She swiped at her eyes, her spirit turning to stone as she faced this latest sorrow. Was it not enough that her entire family had been taken from her? That her own husband believed she was dead?

Could she not have been given this one gift, the joy of holding her infant to her breast, to examine tiny fingers and toes, to love as she had never loved before?

"Where is he?" She tried to move past Theodor, but he held her arms. "I want to see him."

"It's too late. The midwife took him away."

"If you had left me alone, taken me back to London . . ." She pushed against him, hitting his chest, wanting to hurt him. "I hate you. I'll always hate you."

"Alison, please. You'll injure yourself," he whispered, absorbing her anger until her heaving sobs caused her to collapse against him. He lifted her and laid her on the bed. Turning away from him, she curled up within herself.

He touched her shoulder, and she swiped at his hand. "Leave me alone," she said between sobs. "Let me grieve for my son in peace."

"Sleep, Alison."

She barely noticed the muffled sound of

his boots on the thick carpet as he left the room, closing the door behind him. Finally alone with her sorrow, her cries turned to an anguished prayer. Didn't God know that she had renounced the Van Schuyler fate, banishing it as a superstition and trusting her future to Him? Was this the price she had to pay for loving Ian? For marrying him?

Not only had she been taken from her husband, but now her baby had been taken from her. Before she could even hold him in her arms, gaze upon his tiny face.

The cruelty was more than she could bear.

As hot tears swarmed down her cheeks and another sob tore from her throat, she pounded the mattress with her fist.

No more, God, her heart cried. *No more.*

Chapter Fifty-Three

JULY 1944

Theodor bounded up the veranda steps, but Frau Mueller had the front door open before he reached it. "Where is she?" he asked, handing the housekeeper his hat and gloves.

"On the west balcony, sir."

"Has she been eating?"

"Like a bird. I was about to serve the tea."

"Give me a few minutes first."

"Very good, sir." She disappeared into the rear of the house.

Theodor entered the main sitting room and stared out the French doors leading to the balcony. From his vantage point, he could see Alison half-reclining on a chaise longue, her forearm over her eyes to keep out the afternoon sun. She wore a turquoise satin robe and a lightweight afghan covered her feet. Her blonde hair fell in ratty tangles below her shoulders.

This wasn't how it was supposed to be. She needed time to grieve, to get over the loss of the baby, but he hadn't expected this kind of decline. For a moment, he was tempted to tell her the truth, but he waved the thought away. The baby was part of another life, her life with that British cretin who had stolen her away.

If only this war would end. The Allied invasion of Normandy last month had caught Hitler and his cronies by surprise. Heads had rolled, and Theodor enjoyed a stronger position than ever within the Nazi leadership.

Time. He just needed to be patient. Germany's victory would come. And Alison would willingly join him at the top of the elite ruling class. Especially after he showed her the London newspaper he carried under his arm. A smart move on his part to have the dailies monitored for any mention of Captain Ian Devlin, the heir to Kenniston Hall. As if that lordship could begin to compare to Theodor's own vast holdings. What was Alison thinking?

Hearing a rattling behind him, he turned. Frau Mueller, pushing the tea cart, hesitated.

"Bring it." Theodor motioned, then opened the French doors and pasted a smile on his face.

Alison peered at him from beneath her forearm and slowly sat up.

"How are you?" he asked. "I hear you haven't been eating."

"I'm not hungry," she said coldly.

"Frau Mueller is bringing the tea." He turned as the housekeeper pushed the cart onto the balcony. "Come, Alison. Let's sit at the table. I have something for you."

She kicked away the afghan, and he noticed her feet were bare. He pulled out a chair for her and she plopped into it without looking at him. It was as if a troll had snuck in during his absence and replaced his lovely, well-mannered Alison with a common peasant.

Sitting across from her, he followed her gaze to the panoramic view. The breeze kicked up gentle whitecaps, and the graceful swans floated near the shore. He almost envied them their freedom from such cares as love and war.

After Frau Mueller poured the tea and disappeared into the chalet, he laid the precisely folded newspaper beside Alison's dessert plate. "News from London," he said, watching her eyes flicker with interest before she turned away.

"About the invasion?" The superior tone

in her voice grated on his nerves, but he chose to ignore it. Let her have her moment. It would be brief.

"This edition came out before the invasion. *Times of London.* Saturday, May 20, 1944."

She picked up the paper and read the headline. " 'American Actress to Debut as Titania.' What does this have to do with me?"

"I thought you might be interested in her photograph," he said carelessly, adding blackberry preserves to a freshly baked roll. He endured Alison's irritated sigh and watched her unfold the paper, revealing the photograph of her husband with his arm around the beautiful, vivacious actress. Alison covered her mouth as she stared, seemingly unable to take her eyes from the picture.

"He was never good enough for you. This proves it." Theodor reached for the paper, taking it from her shaking hand. "You're upset. Let me read the caption for you."

Glancing at the photo, he cleared his throat. " 'Miss Marie Wyatt, American actress, escorted by British Army captain Ian Devlin, starred at last night's Moonlight Serenade Ball. The lovely actress and her handsome officer danced the entire evening together. We predict wedding bells will ring soon.' "

Alison folded her arms across her chest as if to shelter her troubled heart. Her lower lip trembled.

"You aren't angry?"

"It's been nine months," she said, struggling to control her voice. "I can't expect him to grieve for me the rest of his life."

Her sadness tore at his heart, but he couldn't let up now. Not if he wanted to break her ties with that Anglo-Saxon usurper.

"I believe a year is the customary mourning period." He shrugged. "She has clearly enchanted your husband with her charms."

"If he knew I was still alive, he'd have nothing to do with her."

Gratified by the spark of anger heating her voice, Theodor thrust his blade into the Brit's marital coffin. "Perhaps. But he may marry her."

"That would be bigamy."

"He doesn't know that."

"When I get home, he'll know it."

Theodor found her determination adorable, though misplaced. "And then he will have to choose." He twisted the knife, wishing the blade was deep within the Brit's flesh. "The wife he has mourned or the wife who now shares his bed. A difficult choice for any man."

She stared at him, the light gone from her eyes. "Who would you choose?"

"Fräulein Wyatt is a most beautiful and talented woman. It's not surprising your husband is smitten with her." He hesitated, a dramatic pause. "But I would always choose you."

"If they do get married, will you tell me?"

Theodor leaned forward, putting on his most compassionate gaze. "You know that I will." A promise he would keep. Though that wasn't the primary reason for monitoring the London dailies. He could only learn of Captain Ian Devlin's demise through the obituaries. So many men died in wartime. He just hoped the Brit would be one of them.

Alone in her bedroom and unable to sleep, Alison stared at the newspaper photograph. Ian's face was slightly tilted toward the woman, as if the camera had interrupted an intimate moment between them. His familiar smile tugged at her heart. The woman — she refused to even think her name — radiated youth and vivacity. The grainy photograph couldn't dim the sparkle in her lovely eyes. With her beauty, she could have any man she wanted. Why did she have to choose Ian?

Not that she wanted him to grieve forever. But it broke her heart that he had found someone new to love.

Somehow, she had to find a way to get home. Before Ian married this woman. Ironic, wasn't it? Her husband briefed Allied airmen on how to find escape routes out of occupied Europe, but she didn't have the slightest idea how to get away from Theodor.

Climbing out of bed, she turned on a light and sat at her vanity. For a long moment, she stared at her reflection, then grabbed a brush and worked on the ratted tangles in her long hair. As she did, a familiar phrase floated into her consciousness, the rhythm of the words matching the strokes of the brush. *"Strength and honour are her clothing; and she shall rejoice in time to come."*

By the time she laid down her brush and returned to bed, the promise had warmed her heart. She didn't know how or when, but someday she was going home. For the first time since she'd lost her baby, nightmares didn't disturb her sleep.

CHAPTER FIFTY-FOUR

SEPTEMBER 1944

"Good-bye, Marie." Ian mouthed the words and waved as she peered out of the small window. She lifted her hand in farewell as the plane taxied away, but he couldn't see through the thick glass well enough to know if she smiled or if she had given in to the tears that had threatened to fall when she hugged him one last time. *"God be with you."*

He watched the plane's ascent as it banked left and headed northwest on the long journey, first to Iceland and then to New York. American soldiers were going home, some wounded and others whose long tour of duty had finally ended. Marie was the only civilian among them, but Ian had pulled the necessary strings to get her on board. Her heart's desire, a German soldier who had worked as an agent for the Allies, was now in a POW camp near Jacksonville, Florida.

As a liaison with Eisenhower, it hadn't been hard for Ian to find out the agent's true identity or his whereabouts. He just hoped he had done the right thing by giving the information to Marie. The German's loyalties had never been entirely clear as he walked a fine tightrope between patriot and traitor. But Marie loved the chap. And Ian was an expert in the pain of being without one's true love.

It had been almost a year now, yet he still ached for Alison. Working with Marie had been a welcome diversion. As long as he focused on their mission, on protecting her from harm, he could blunt his grief. But now Marie was gone, and there was nothing more he could do for her.

"Major Devlin." Colonel Davies joined Ian on the tarmac. "It's been a long time."

Ian snapped to attention, surprised by the officer's sudden appearance.

"No need for that, Major. Not out here. Congratulations on the promotion, by the way."

"Thank you, sir." Both men watched the plane, no more than a bright speck in the western sky, the sun reflecting on the tail wing, as it disappeared into the clouds.

"I wasn't sure you'd let her go."

"Sir?"

"Your assignment ended on D-Day. But you and Miss Wyatt continued seeing each other." He clapped Ian on the shoulder. "You weren't supposed to fall in love with her, Major."

"True. But I never said I wouldn't love her, Colonel. And there is a difference."

"Maybe she'll come back."

"Maybe," Ian agreed. But he hoped not. Marie deserved the happiness waiting for her at that POW camp.

As he walked back to the hangar with the colonel, he reflected on the three ladies who had waltzed into his heart in the past five years. His beloved Alison. Little Libby, whose serious eyes still hinted at past horrors. And Marie, who'd started out as an assignment, but had healed his heart as no one else could have.

Only his precious Libby remained. He intended to never let her go.

CHAPTER FIFTY-FIVE

MARCH 1945

Theodor stood on the west balcony of the chalet, barely aware of the chilling breeze as he gripped Hitler's order in his gloved hand. Anger tightening his chest, he stared beyond the tranquility of the mountain scenery. Out there, on the other side of the Alps, squalor and carnage and destruction made mockery of the Third Reich's superior ideals. The regime was failing. He held the final proof of its slow demise in his hand.

"I thought I heard you arrive," Alison said as she joined him, shivering despite the heavy sweater she had wrapped around her. "Why are you out here?"

"This," he said, waving the order. He smiled down at her, the anger dissipating at the sight of her pale loveliness. Her blonde hair, braided and coiled, formed a coronet on her head. The cold breeze painted roses on her delicate cheeks. His plan had worked.

After seeing the photograph of her husband with the other woman, Alison had emerged from her sullen depression. Had become friendlier, more interested in his affairs.

"What is it?"

"Let's go inside." He clasped her elbow and gently guided her through the French doors. "I don't want you catching a cold."

"I'm fine," she protested, though not too hard.

Settling in the corner of the sofa nearest the blazing fireplace, Alison read the order. Theodor removed his gloves as he paced around the room, his anger rising again.

"He can't mean this," she said, eyes wide in horror.

"He absolutely does."

"He's a madman."

"Don't say that too loudly, my dear," Theodor warned, putting his finger to his lips. "But I agree with you."

"To destroy priceless art, just to keep it from the Allies . . . it's barbaric." She looked up at him, eyes wide with concern. "You won't allow this, will you? You can't possibly."

He stopped pacing and sat on the edge of the sofa, his elbows on his knees. She needed to know the truth. It might be the only way for the two of them to escape this madness. Taking a deep breath, he leaned close to her, keeping his voice low. "I have a cache of art hidden in a cavern about a mile around the mountain from here. Most of it is for Hitler's *Führermuseum.* Some was looted by Göring. The rest is mine."

"That's the art referred to in the order?"

"Yes. I can't prevent the demolition expert from setting the explosives. But I will not allow anyone to blow up that cavern." He looked around the room. "An explosion like that might even destroy all this."

"Can't we hide the art somewhere else?"

"Perhaps. Some of it, anyway." He stared into her eyes, needing to trust her, wanting her to trust him. "There's a secret passageway in the cellar, skillfully hidden, that leads to the cavern. Would you like to see?"

Her eyes lit up. "Yes."

"First you must promise not to attempt an escape. You'd only get lost."

Her eyes darkened and she hesitated. He knew her so well that he could read her thoughts. Escape hadn't occurred to her. Only the art mattered.

"Will you promise?" he asked gently.

"Yes." She gave a slight nod. "I promise."

"Excellent. Go change into something warmer. And boots. I'll send Frau Mueller on an errand to the village. That will give us some time."

He watched Alison leave the room, then picked up the order and tossed it in the fire. A discussion he'd once had with other students at an art symposium came to mind — what a professor had called "the *Mona Lisa* question." He'd had no doubts then and he had no doubts now. The *Mona Lisa* was worth any sacrifice. And so was the art in his cavern.

At Colonel Davies's recommendation, Ian joined the briefing on protecting Europe's cultural treasures at SHAEF headquarters. An agent from OSS, the Office of Strategic Services, outlined his efforts to trace the smuggling of stolen art to the German embassy in Spain.

"We found an actual catalog listing about two hundred paintings," he said, shaking his head in disbelief. "We know for a fact that several of them came from the Goudstikker collection."

"Goudstikker?" asked an American major.

"A Dutch Jewish family," explained the OSS agent. "Göring, that German goat, stole almost all of their art."

The major turned to Ian. "I understand your wife's family owned a Dutch art gallery, Major Devlin."

"They did." Ian nodded. "My wife and her grandfather hid some Old Masters, but Göring looted their gallery. He also had her father executed."

"I'm sorry to hear that," said the major. "And for the loss of your wife. Colonel Davies thought you might be interested in finishing her work."

"How could I do that?"

"We want you to join our Monuments, Fine Arts, and Archives unit in Germany." The major paused to light a cigarette. "They're short-staffed and could use the assistance of someone with access to General Eisenhower."

The OSS agent pointed to a map of northern Europe. "The Germans used the Jeu de Paume museum in Paris as a collecting point. From there, Hitler and Göring shipped trainloads of art to hidden caches throughout Germany. We've heard reports that Göring has a huge collection of stolen art at his estate, Carinhall. Then there's Major Theodor Scheidemann. A Prussian count."

"Did you say Scheidemann?" Ian interrupted.

"That's right. Do you know him?"

"I never met him. But Alison, my wife, she knew him. He brought Göring to her grandfather's gallery back in '39."

"According to our reports, he's 'acquired' quite a collection of his own. Most of it, along with other looted art, is stashed in a cavern near his Bavarian chalet." The agent frowned. "Not only that, but he may be working with the SS and *Die Spinne.*"

"Die Spinne?" asked Ian.

"The Spider," said the agent. "A secret group setting up escape routes to get high-ranking officers out of Germany."

Ian took a deep breath and exhaled slowly, taking in everything the OSS agent had told them. He'd like to get Göring in his sights, but he wanted Scheidemann even more. True, Göring had shot Alison. But Scheidemann had let him get away with it. Besides, he didn't like having a rival for Alison's affections. Not even now.

"How about it, Major?" The OSS agent interrupted Ian's thoughts. "Do you want to go on a treasure hunt?"

"There's nothing I'd like better." *Especially if the count is guarding the loot.* "How soon can I leave?"

The entrance to the cellar was in an alcove next to a huge kitchen hearth that probably hadn't been used in a century. In the year and a half Alison had been at the chalet, she'd never been in this part of the house. Not surprising, since Frau Mueller grumbled if she ventured anywhere near what the housekeeper considered her private domain.

Theodor pressed one of the chimney stones and a panel in the alcove slid open. Alison followed him down stone steps into a narrow passageway. At the bottom of the stairs, he flicked on a flashlight, revealing water-streaked walls carved into the mountain. Hearing the skitter of tiny feet, she squealed, and Theodor took her hand. "Stay close," he said.

"Don't worry." Her earlier promise not to escape grated on her heart. Not that she had made it, but that escaping hadn't been foremost in her thoughts. When Theodor confessed to stockpiling stolen art, she only wanted to see its hiding place. Even now, protecting the art was more important than her freedom.

They followed the passageway as it snaked through the mountain and joined the underground tunnels and caves chiseled by nature. Their path ran beside, and sometimes through, a stream of black water that fed into an ancient pond, filling all but a slender ledge of the cavern floor. When they stopped at the angle where their path joined the ledge, Theodor shone the flashlight beam against the wall, spotlighting an electrical switch. He flipped it, and a string of bare bulbs flickered on the wall around the perimeter of the oval pond. The flutter of wings drew Alison's gaze upward, but the roof, several stories above them, was hidden in shadows.

"Are those bats?" she asked, gripping Theodor's arm.

He shone the beam upward, and dark shapes swooped and soared. "Those are bats." Turning off the flashlight, he stuck it in his pocket. "See that door over there? The lighted one?"

Alison looked across the narrow end of the oval to the broader ledge on the far side of the pool. Stalagmites, glowing eerily golden in the dim light, rose from the cavern floor. A few rose high enough to form columns with the limestone stalactites hanging from the high ceiling. She peered past them to a lighted passageway, its door framed by wooden planks. "I see it."

"That's the one we want. Stay close to the wall until we get over there."

Thankful for the lights, Alison cautiously followed Theodor. "Who did all this?"

"I don't know. Before the lights, the cavern was lit with torches. You can see the sconces next to the bulbs."

"You really don't know the history?"

"They say every great fortune was built on thievery. I suppose my family is no exception."

Alison smiled to herself, remembering how Ian had told her that the Devlin wealth may have come from piracy and smuggling. At least she could hold her head high, secure in the knowledge that *her* family legacy was built on respectable hard work. Perhaps a bit of overzealous wheeling and dealing through the centuries, but nothing illegal. At least, nothing that could be proven.

When they reached the place where the ledge broadened, Theodor turned. "Are you all right?"

"Fine." She looked back the way they had come. The ledge seemed even narrower from this perspective. "Do we have to go back that way?"

"Afraid so." He smiled, revealing his dimple. "Come on, we're almost there."

They entered the lit passageway, which seemed to dead end after only a few meters, an optical illusion caused by the placement of the bulbs and the shadows of an outcropping of rock. Theodor switched on the flashlight again, and Alison followed him through a sharp zigzag into another passage. At its end, Theodor unlocked a wooden door braced with steel and switched on a light.

Alison stepped through the door into a large cave and gaped at the number of crates stacked inside, the marble statues tucked here and there, the antique furnishings. She recognized the soft whir of an air-quality mechanism similar to the one Brant had designed for the air raid shelter back in Holland.

"That door leads to a smaller cave that opens to the outdoors." Theodor pointed to a wide steel door set in tracks so it could be raised and lowered. "A forest trail leads to the main road."

"Where did all this come from?"

"Different places."

"And if the Allies get too close, Hitler just wants to blow it all up."

"Him and his fanatics." Theodor's eyes took on a faraway look. "It's over, Alison. The Allies have already won. But Hitler won't surrender his spoils."

"This isn't spoils, Theodor. These are priceless, irreplaceable pieces. They belong in museums, in galleries." She stepped closer to him, stared into his eyes, and almost felt sorry for him. What could he have been if not for this wicked war? No doubt an art connoisseur. An overprivileged Prussian snob. But what would have been so wrong with that?

"They need to be returned," she said softly, pleadingly. "You know this."

He nodded. "Perhaps arrangements can be made. But not yet. All of it must be here when the demolition team arrives. They will set their explosives, and someone will be left behind to blow the charge should the Allies come too close."

"What can we do?"

"For now, we play along. But before the Allies come, we disable the explosives and start moving all this out of here."

"Move it where?"

He shook his head. "I've only told you this much because I know you feel the same responsibility, the same passion, that I do. This must be our secret, Alison."

"Who would I tell?"

He half-smiled, his eyes suddenly weary. "We need to get back. I have to leave in the morning."

Reluctantly, Alison followed him from the cave. Her fingers itched to explore the riches hidden here. After locking the wooden door, he handed her the key. "If anything happens to me, it will be up to you to protect the art."

The brass key warmed her palm, and a shiver raced up her spine. "I will," she said solemnly. "With my life."

CHAPTER FIFTY-SIX

APRIL 1945

Ian spread the map across the bonnet of the jeep, holding the corners down with concrete chunks from a bombed-out building. "Where exactly are we, Cowboy?" he asked the lanky American corporal, born and raised beneath the big skies of Montana, who served as mechanic and forager.

"Here, sir." The corporal stuck one grimy finger on the map and another a few inches away. "And here's where we need to go."

"How much longer?"

"Two or three hours. Depends on what lies between here and there."

Ian blew out a deep breath as he folded the map. The detours and delays had become more frequent the deeper they drove into Germany. The bomb-cratered roads were clogged with refugees — little more than rag-covered bones shuffling to the displaced-person camps — German soldiers

519

eager to surrender, and indescribable destruction. A world so easily destroyed. How long would it take to rebuild?

As Cowboy maneuvered the jeep along the rough road, each kilometer bringing them closer to Scheidemann's chalet, Ian's gut tightened with nervous anticipation. Not that he expected to find the count at home, just waiting around for Ian to show up and arrest him. But he liked to dream that could happen.

Mostly, though, he hoped to find art that had been stolen from Holland. If he could return even one Old Master on Alison's behalf, then the grueling journey across France and Germany would have been worth every sleepless night and tasteless meal.

He pulled the last letter he had received from Libby out of his pocket. She had drawn him a picture of her and the twins in front of the gazebo, labeling each of them by name. Hard to believe she would be eight years old in just a few more months. No matter what happened at the chalet, he planned to be home for the biggest birthday party she'd ever had. And to become the dad the war, and his grief, hadn't allowed him to be.

■ ■ ■ ■

The demolition team rigged the cave with explosives under the personal supervision of a surprise visitor — Reichsmarschall Göring. Alison didn't protest when Theodor suggested she stay in her room after Göring coerced an invitation to dinner and a night's lodging.

The next morning, she watched from her studio window as Göring and his adjutant drove down the mountain. Going downstairs, she joined Theodor in the sitting room where a small fire crackled in the fireplace, more for its ambiance than its heat. He sat on the cocoa-brown sofa, still as the Grecian statue in the corner except for the nervous tapping of his fingers.

Unsure of his mood, she sat in a nearby chair without saying a word.

"He's a monster." Theodor spat the words.

"I know," she said quietly, her fingers unconsciously rubbing her scar.

"He demands I move all these paintings to the cave." He waved his hand about the room.

Alison glanced at the painting above the mantel, the place of honor. "He remembered *The Girl in the Garden?*"

"He remembered, all right. Sat at *my* table, ate *my* food, then pardoned me for my transgressions."

"What transgressions?"

"Stealing *his* painting." Theodor rose and walked toward the hearth. "Apparently I should be grateful I'm not being court-martialed."

Alison bit her tongue to keep any of the hundred retorts in her head from coming out of her mouth. She had seen Theodor angry, but never like this.

"He ordered me — *ordered* me — to take all my paintings to the cave."

Her heart stilled. "Why?"

"To protect them from the Americans. 'The Americans will not appreciate their value. The Americans are degenerate scum.' This from that Nazi nincompoop who can't even spot a forged Vermeer."

She smiled slightly, remembering Theodor's humorous anecdote of how the Reichshmarschall spent a small fortune on a supposed Vermeer that so obviously wasn't. They had both laughed at Göring's foolishness. But the pretentious toad wasn't so funny now.

"How could the paintings be safer in an explosive-rigged cave than here?"

"He shot at your father's painting, Alison.

He doesn't care if they're destroyed."

"But he can't make you move them."

"He gave me a direct order. And a veiled threat."

Alison gazed up at the restored portrait, studying her mother's playful smile. Theodor had brought the painting here for her, and now Göring held it like a sword over his neck. He had no choice but to comply. "Can I help?"

"Göring is sending the guards from the cave to 'help.' "

"Is he coming back?"

"Not today."

She stood up and gave him a determined look. "The guards aren't touching my father's painting. Or my watercolors."

Theodor smiled for the first time; then he walked toward her and brushed her loose hair away from her scar. "I promise you, Alison. I will not let them blow up that cave."

"I know," she said softly.

"I guess we'd better get started." He looked up at *The Girl.* "She'll have to come out of the frame."

"I think there are packaging tubes in my studio. I'll go get one."

"Change your shoes if you want to go to the cave."

She did a quick about-face. "I can go?"

"If you'd like. Just hurry."

By the time Alison returned from her studio, dressed in trousers and hiking boots, Frau Mueller was dragging crates into the dining room for the collection of watercolor landscapes that hung on its walls. Theodor stood on a ladder in front of the fireplace, maneuvering *The Girl* from its fastenings.

The guards arrived with more packaging materials. Within a few hours, the walls of the main rooms were bare, the art packed and loaded in the guards' truck. The smaller sculptures and figurines were placed in Theodor's car. "We'll follow you," he told the guards, sending them on ahead.

After they left, he beckoned Alison to follow him into his study. He opened the bottom drawer of his desk and pulled out a small pistol. "I want you to take this."

She stared at the gun, unsure what to say or do. "I've never fired one before."

"Hopefully you won't have to now. But at least you'll have it. Just in case."

"What are you planning?"

"I'm not sure." He stared at her, a strange light in his eyes. "Will you do me a favor?"

"If I can."

"Don't use that pistol on me."

■ ■ ■ ■

Cowboy parked the jeep outside the village tavern near several other Allied vehicles, including two American tanks. Ian found the Army unit's captain guzzling a mug of beer and introduced himself.

"Jeremy Taggart," replied the captain, raising his mug in salute. "Friends call me Tag."

"Have you heard of Count Theodor Scheidemann? He has a chalet somewhere around here."

"Hey, innkeeper," shouted Tag. "Do you know a — what was the name again?"

Ian turned to the grizzled man behind the bar. "Count Theodor Scheidemann."

"Ja." The innkeeper nodded, wiping his hands on his grimy apron. "His family here long, long time."

"How do I get to his chalet?"

"My grandson can show you. He's a good boy."

"Where is he?"

"I get him for you."

As the innkeeper disappeared through a swinging door, Tag nudged Ian. "What unit are you with?"

"Monuments, Fine Arts, and Archives."

"No kidding? What are you doing out here?"

"Recovery and protection of cultural treasures."

Tag whistled. "Treasure, huh? Mind if I come along?'

Ian hesitated, sizing up the American captain as he considered the offer. Light brown hair in need of a trim, scraggly chin in need of a shave. "Where are you from?"

"Small place you never heard of. Prairie Pines, Illinois. Near Chicago."

Ian's jaw twitched. If he could ever visit any American city, that one would be it. The city where Alison had lived as a child.

"You may not think it to look at me, Major, but I know a Rembrandt when I see one," Tag said. "At least twice a year, my mom dragged me to the big city for a little culture."

Ian didn't anticipate any trouble at the chalet, but another gun might come in handy. And he'd need the extra muscle if they recovered any looted art. "Do you have any buddies who might be interested? Dependable chaps?"

"My entire unit came ashore at Normandy, Major. We're all dependable."

"I'd say you are," he said, clasping the captain's shoulder. "Choose two or three of your men and meet me out front in fifteen minutes."

"We'll be there, sir." Tag downed the rest of his beer in one huge gulp and hurried out the door as the innkeeper reappeared with his grandson, a spare-shouldered boy in his mid-teens.

"Major Ian Devlin." Ian extended a hand and the boy took it, his grip surprisingly strong.

"I am Kurt," he said, his accent passable.

"Your grandfather said you could guide me to the Scheidemann chalet. You know where it is?"

"I have been there." The boy tilted his head toward his grandfather. "We make deliveries sometimes."

"Do you know when the count was last there?"

"He came yesterday. With other officers. One very important, with flags on his car."

"Yesterday?" Ian stared at the boy. "Is he still there?"

The boy shrugged. "The important officer left today. But I don't know about the count."

Adrenaline pumped through Ian's veins, speeding his pulse and putting every muscle on full alert. "Come on," he said. "I want to see if Count Scheidemann is still at home."

Chapter Fifty-Seven

Theodor shut the passenger door after Alison climbed into the Mercedes, then walked around to the driver's side. Before opening his door, he gazed up at the chalet, postcard perfect against its alpine backdrop. He pressed his lips together, experiencing an unfamiliar sense of loss. Generations of Scheidemann nobles had found refuge within its rustic walls, but he sensed that when he drove away this time, he would never return, even if circumstances allowed it. Göring's vile presence had sullied its serenity, defiled its beauty.

For now, he had two concerns: to protect the art in the caves and to escape the Allies with Alison. As he slid into the driver's seat and started the ignition, he glanced at her. Her blonde hair hung in a single braid down her back, and she held a man's hunting jacket on her lap, the same one she had worn when her plane landed in Stockholm.

"Do you have the pistol?"

"In my pocket." She patted the jacket.

"What about the key?"

"I have it, too."

"As soon as you can, unlock the door. Just don't let the guards see you. Can you do that?"

"Yes." She stared at him. "Is that how we're getting away?"

"If necessary."

"And then what?"

He guided the Mercedes around a deep rut caused by winter's bitter ice. "One thing at a time, Alison."

Out of the corner of his eye, he saw her bite her lip and turn toward the window. With a noiseless sigh, he tried to focus on steering the heavy car down the long slope. But his heart wouldn't let him. Memories of the long-ago Vermeer exhibit, where they'd first met, interrupted his concentration. She'd delighted him with her spontaneous gaiety and depth of artistic insight. He knew then that he wanted her for his wife, no matter how long he might have to wait.

She didn't know of the many arguments he'd had with his father because he refused to consider any other prospects. Not one of his father's chosen beauties, heiresses with impeccable lineages, could seduce his heart from Alison.

It had never occurred to him that she didn't feel the same for him, that she would marry someone else. If only his father hadn't forbidden him to see her during those first years, hadn't stopped him from writing to her, perhaps he wouldn't have lost her. He had obeyed his father, ever the dutiful son, biding his time until the old man's death.

Still he waited, his heart praying for her to give up her romantic illusions and give herself to him. All he needed was more time. He sensed it in her recent watercolors. The ethereal spark he'd seen in her painting of the London fountain no longer appeared. Instead, an exquisite wistfulness graced her latest works. He had given her that. Someday she would realize it.

Ian leaned forward, staring up at the picturesque chalet as Cowboy braked in front of the broad veranda. Tag and his two buddies, following behind, parked beside them. Climbing out of the jeep, Ian unsnapped his holster and assessed his surroundings. No other vehicles, no moving curtains. All was quiet.

Too quiet.

"Stay in the jeep, Kurt," he said softly. "Captain, you and your men have guard duty."

Tag nodded and motioned for his men to take up sentry positions.

"Cowboy, you come with me." As Ian headed for the porch, Cowboy grabbed his rifle and joined him.

"You want me to kick in the door, Major?"

"Let's try knocking first."

"Beggin' the major's pardon, but that's not as much fun."

Ian rang the bell and pounded on the door. "Anyone home?"

A few moments later, the door cracked open. A gray-haired woman wearing a black dress and white apron peered at him with frightened eyes.

"Good afternoon," Ian said in German. "Is Count Scheidemann at home?"

She shook her head and started to close the door, but Ian stuck his boot in the jamb. "Do you know where he is?"

"I can tell you nothing." She backed away as Ian forced open the door.

He stepped inside, followed by Cowboy, and looked around the foyer, sensing a strange vacancy before realizing that the walls were bare. The woman cowered against a far wall as Ian entered a handsomely

531

furnished parlor. A ladder stood in front of the massive fireplace and, here again, the empty walls lent a desolate air to the room. He frowned and returned to the foyer. A rapid stream of colloquial German poured forth from the woman.

Ian turned to Cowboy. "Did you understand any of that?"

"She's upset, sir."

"No kidding." He tilted his head toward the door. "Bring Kurt in here."

While he waited for the boy, Ian decided to take a different approach. "I'm Major Ian Devlin, British Army. We aren't here to hurt you, only to find Count Scheidemann."

"The count isn't home."

"Please, your name?"

"Frau Mueller."

"Is there anyone else in the house?"

"I'm alone." She started as Kurt came through the door.

"Do you know her?" Ian asked the boy in English.

"She is from the village."

"Persuade her to tell us where we can find the count. And tell her we want to know where he hid the stolen art."

Ian listened, understanding most of the conversation, as Kurt explained that the soldiers knew the count had been there the day before, and she nodded vigorously. He arrived with no notice, and she had prepared dinner for him and his guests. Kurt appropriately sympathized.

Tamping down his irritation, Ian stood at the entrance to the parlor and studied the fireplace. "Why the ladder?" he interrupted Frau Mueller. She stared at him, and he asked again, "Why is the ladder in front of the fireplace? Speak slowly."

"To remove the garden picture." She waved around the room. "They take all the pictures."

"Who did?"

"The count. His lady. The soldiers."

"His lady?" Ian stiffened as a flash of light exploded in his brain. He rubbed his temple against the impossible thought. "Who is she?" he demanded.

"The lady who stays here. The artist." She pointed toward the ceiling. "Upstairs."

"What's her name?"

"He doesn't tell me her name. He doesn't allow me to speak to her."

"Is she here now? Upstairs?"

"She went with the count. About an hour ago."

Ian grabbed Kurt's shoulder. "Find out where they've gone." Then he raced up the stairs, looking into each room. The third one he entered, decorated in tranquil blues and greens, seemed to beckon him inside. A hairbrush and cosmetics neatly adorned a rosewood vanity, but a woman's dress and heels littered the floor. He was bending to pick up the dress when he noticed a sketch pad on top of the dresser.

Heart pounding relentlessly against his ribs, he lifted the cover of the sketch pad. His own face stared back at him.

Stumbling backward, Ian knocked against the vanity and its chair toppled over with a crash. He gasped for air and bumped a lamp, sending it tumbling to the floor as he staggered to the bed with the pad clutched to his chest.

He sat on the edge of the mattress and swiped his eyes as he flipped the pages. Sketches of Libby, of the twins, the ancient oak and the gazebo. Of the lake he had seen outside the chalet. Of graceful swans and towering pines. Tears burned his cheeks and red-hot anger flared throughout his body as the drawings changed to grotesque monsters and misshapen faces.

"Major?" Cowboy stood in the doorway, concern etched on his young face. "You okay?"

Ian rubbed his eyes against his sleeve and slowly stood. "Did Kurt find out where they went?" he asked as he closed the pad.

"To a cave. Just around the mountain a ways."

"Can he find it?"

"He thinks so."

"I want to make one thing perfectly clear. To you and to your buddies out there."

Cowboy's eyes shifted nervously. "What's that, sir?"

"When we catch up to Scheidemann, he's mine." Ian's voice, strong and determined, sounded strange in his ears. He pulled out his pistol and checked that it was loaded. "Understood?"

"Okay," Cowboy said hesitantly. "If you don't mind my asking, sir, just what are you going to do with him?"

"I'm going to kill him."

The corporal's eyes darted around the room. "I'm guessing you know the lady."

Ian holstered the Walther and strode from the room. "She's my wife."

CHAPTER FIFTY-EIGHT

Alison wandered through the cave while the guards unloaded the truck. Lines of wiring snaked among the crates and display racks, connecting bundles of dynamite. She wished Theodor had given her a knife instead of the pistol.

Reaching the wooden door, she glanced over her shoulder. A wall of crates blocked her view of the entrance. She unlocked the door and turned the handle, tensing as the hinges creaked. For a brief moment, she considered dashing through it. But even if she reached the chalet — and without a flashlight she'd never make it through the tunnel — she would still be trapped.

As she returned to the entrance, Theodor came toward her, the packaging tube containing her mother's portrait slung over his shoulder. At his questioning look, she nodded slightly. He held out his hand, and she gave him the key.

Wishing she knew his plans, Alison browsed through the display racks until a still life stopped her cold. The last time she had seen this particular Caravaggio was when she had photographed it at the air raid shelter. One of Hendrik's colleagues had entrusted it to them for safekeeping.

She stared at Theodor, who was preoccupied with telling the guards where to put the fragile items they were bringing in from the Mercedes. Taking the still life from the rack, she carried it to him and thrust it in front of his face. "Where did you get this?"

He slightly reddened, then looked aggravated. "In a trade."

"A trade for what?"

"I don't have time for this now, Alison."

"Who told you about the air raid shelter?" she demanded. Her mind flicked through the handful of people who were in on the secret, unable to believe any of them capable of such betrayal. Behind Theodor's back, the guards exchanged amused looks. They loitered inside the open steel door, apparently not wanting to miss any drama. Their nosiness increased her anger.

"Who?" she shouted.

He snatched the painting from her, scraping the skin from her fingers. "Did you honestly believe I risked my neck to help your chauffeur's son escape without exacting a price?"

His dismissive tone rankled, but she was even more disturbed by his insinuation. "Will told you?"

"Guess again." His mouth curled into a smirk.

She bent her head as the sad truth became clear. Brant had told their secret to save his son's life. And sacrificed his own. Her anger lessened, overcome by an abiding sorrow.

"I'll put it back," she said quietly, reaching for the painting, but spun toward the entrance as a spray of gunfire spit up dust near the German guards.

"*Amerikaner!*" shouted one of them as he fired his gun.

A responding shot immediately echoed through the cave, and the guard staggered backward with a scream, grabbing his wounded arm. The other guard raised his hands as uniformed men, guns drawn, came deeper into the cave.

"Nobody move," drawled an American accent.

Surprised by the Allies' sudden appearance, Alison took half a step forward before Theodor dropped the Caravaggio and grabbed her. She struggled, but he slipped his arm around her waist, pulling her against his chest like a shield.

"Let her go," said a commanding voice in a familiar British accent.

Alison stopped struggling, unable to take her eyes from the officer who emerged from the shadows.

"Ian," she breathed as his gold-flecked hazel eyes met hers.

"Ian?" Theodor tightened his grip, causing Alison to gasp. "At last we meet."

"I'm not telling you again." Ian's eyes grew cold with controlled anger. "Let her go."

"I don't give up that easily," said Theodor, maneuvering backward. A click sounded as he held up a lighter, the flame flickering near Alison's cheek as he pinned her now with both his arms. "Look around you, Brit. See the dynamite? This cave is rigged to explode."

The American whistled. "Say your prayers, boys."

"He'll never do it," Alison managed to say despite Theodor's crushing hold around her ribs. "He won't destroy the art."

"I would to kill you," Theodor said, gesturing toward Ian with the lighter. "To free Alison of you once and for all."

Alison held her breath, fearful Theodor

just might light the fuse. Until now she would never have believed he could destroy such valuable works. But his hatred of Ian consumed him.

"She'll always be mine," Ian said softly, his gaze shifting to Alison. "No matter what happens here."

"Always yours." Alison smiled, willing him to know how glad she was to see him, even if it was for the last time.

"Don't follow us, Brit. Not if you value her life."

Behind Ian, Alison saw the sudden flare of a match. In a deft motion, one of the Germans lit a nearby fuse before his American guard could stop him.

"Ian," she shouted, struggling against Theodor. "The dynamite."

Ian pivoted as a shot echoed in the cavern, and the German who lit the dynamite staggered backward before crumpling to the ground. Alison shouted Ian's name again as Theodor yanked her behind the wall of crates, then propelled her through the wooden door, closing and locking it. She heard muffled shouting and struggled to get around him.

"Come on." He grabbed her wrist, dragging her through the zigzag in the short passageway and toward the ledge surrounding the pool. An explosion sounded from the cave, its deafening boom pounding against Alison's ears. She fell, breaking Theodor's grip and gashing her palms and knees against the rough ledge. The pistol bounced against her hip, and she yanked it from her pocket. With both hands wrapped around the handle, she pointed the wavering barrel at Theodor. He stared down at her, uncertainty in his eyes.

"Just go." Her aching ears blurred her voice. "I don't want to hurt you."

"Not without you."

She glanced behind her, closing her eyes against the vision of broken limbs beneath exploded rubble that assaulted her imagination. Breathing a prayer, she faced Theodor. "I'm going back for Ian."

His brilliant-blue eyes darkened, and he slid the packaging tube from his shoulder.

"Are you sure you won't change your mind?" He swung the tube holding her father's masterpiece over the dark pool, the strap loosely clasped between his fingers. "You know what's in here."

"You wouldn't."

"Unless you come with me, I swear I will."

Lowering the pistol, she slowly rose to her feet, mesmerized by the swaying tube. She needed to save the painting, to save Ian.

Hendrik's voice whispered: *"The* Mona Lisa *or the child?"* Her finger curled on the trigger and she raised the barrel skyward, determined to save both.

She pressed against the metal prong with all her strength, firing into the overhead stalactites. As mineral deposits rained upon them, she rushed forward, and Theodor stepped backward, ducking his head. Lunging for the tube, Alison slipped on the damp ledge and tumbled into the pool. She screamed as the dark water splashed upward and choked as it enclosed her in its murky depths. With a kick, she propelled herself to the surface, taking a quick breath before descending again, weighted by her clothes. She struggled to remove the heavy jacket, tangling her arms in the sleeves as her world darkened.

So this was the end. Wanting it all, she was left with nothing. Not even her life.

CHAPTER FIFTY-NINE

Time seemed to slow as Ian pivoted toward the bleeding German, then back to Alison as she disappeared behind the crates.

"Get down," Cowboy shouted.

The explosion whooshed hot air and debris across Ian's back as he hit the floor, hands over his head. When the rumbling ceased, he raised up, shaking his head to clear his senses. Crates near the entrance had blown inward, littering the cave floor with bits and pieces of wood, canvas, and packing materials. Tag knelt beside the wounded German. Cowboy, knife in hand, scurried toward a length of glowing fuse and cut it before more dynamite exploded.

Ian stood, a little unsteady on his feet. "Did you shoot that Jerry, Tag?"

"That'd be me, sir," Cowboy said. "Just not soon enough."

Ian half-grinned. "Secure the others. I'll be back." He sprinted toward the still-standing wall of crates, grimacing when he accidentally stepped on a twisted canvas, and Cowboy followed him.

"Not without me, Major."

"This is my fight."

"Mine too."

Ian didn't bother to protest. Behind the crates, he grabbed the handle of the thick wooden door. Locked. Aiming his gun at the latch, he pulled the trigger. The wood splintered, and he kicked open the door, then zagged through the passageway. Where it opened into a cavern nearly filled by a pool of water, he hesitated and peered around the corner. Alison stood, her back to him, while Scheidemann faced her, holding a packaging tube over the dark pool in one hand and the revolver in his other.

Before Ian could make a move, Alison fired a pistol into the ceiling and grabbed for the tube. Scheidemann pulled back and she slipped. Ian's boots seemed stuck, his legs dismembered as he watched Alison tumble into the pool.

Not again, God. The helplessness that had dazed him when his brother drowned threatened to paralyze him.

Alison's scream slapped him from his stupor. He fired into the cavern, and Scheidemann staggered behind a stalagmite column. "Cover me," Ian ordered Cowboy, and he dove into the pool to the sound of ricocheting bullets.

His boots weighted him, dragging him downward, but his strong kicks propelled him to where he sensed Alison should be. He willed his eyes to focus, searching the murky shadows, unable to give up hope despite the pressure building in his air-starved lungs.

Whether it was a trick of the sparse light lining the cavern's perimeter or an answer to prayer, Ian could never be sure. A glint of gold — Tante Meg's locket that Alison always wore — caught his eye. He snared her waist and kicked upward, adrenaline powering his legs and arms.

They broke the surface near the edge of the pool. Holding tightly to Alison, Ian gulped air and shook the water from his eyes. Tag, his rifle trained across the pool, crouched near Cowboy, who grabbed Alison, pulling her from the pool and rolling her onto her side.

She coughed, spitting up water as Ian heaved himself from the pool. He drew her into his lap, brushing her clammy hair from her pale face. Her eyes fluttered and he kissed her forehead.

"Ian." She said his name with the gentleness of a breath, and her slight smile sent a warm current into his heart.

"I'm here." He freed her arms from the twisted jacket, then pulled her shivering body close to his chest. She opened her gray-blue eyes, enchanting him with their light, and touched his damp cheek with her cold fingers.

"Brit!" The shout echoed around the cavern. Scheidemann stood near a passageway, staring at them as he gripped the packaging tube. He held his revolver at his side, the barrel pointed downward. "Will she be all right?"

Ian resented the worry he heard in Scheidemann's voice, and fury clenched his stomach. Tightening his hold on his wife, he glared at the Nazi officer. His lungs still ached, but he found the strength to bellow, "She's not your concern. Not now. Not ever."

"Just give me the word, Major." Cowboy picked up his rifle and aimed it across the pool.

"It's not too late, Alison. You can have your father's painting." Scheidemann held up the tube. "Only come with me."

Ian's blood boiled at the man's arrogance. He held out his hand to Cowboy. "Give me your gun."

"No, Ian," Alison said softly. "You're not a killer."

He hefted Cowboy's revolver, gritting his teeth to control the anger that had driven him to slash Gretchen's murderer with a hoe, to bash the German's head against a bloodied rock. He had killed for a woman he didn't know. What tortures could he inflict on the man who had stolen his wife?

"Remember the psalm?" Alison pressed her hand against his jaw so his eyes met hers. "The one that brought you home from Colditz?"

Thou art my hiding place; thou shalt preserve me from trouble." Ian held on to his anger even as the familiar words played in his mind. *"Thou shalt compass me about with songs of deliverance."* He glared at Scheidemann over Alison's shoulder, certain he deserved to die.

"Ian, he's not worth it. But you, you're worth everything." Alison unexpectedly stood, bracing herself against him. He quickly stood too, positioning himself to partially shield her from Scheidemann's stare. She hugged his arm and leaned her head against his biceps. Seconds ticked by, and with them, his desire for revenge.

The Nazi held out the tube. "Here it is, Alison. It's yours."

"I don't want it." Her voice rang out clear and strong. "I only want Ian."

"Have him, then." Even across the distance, the coldness in Scheidemann's eyes was evident. "You've lost more than you know."

He fired across the pool and Ian pulled Alison to the ground. Cowboy returned fire, but Scheidemann was gone.

"Do you know where that tunnel leads?" asked Tag.

"To the chalet, but I don't think he'll go there," Alison answered. "There are other tunnels."

"Too bad he got away with that painting," said Cowboy.

"I'm sorry about that too." Ian gazed at Alison, her unkempt hair plastered to her head and her pale face streaked with grime. Never had she looked more beautiful.

"He'll keep it safe," she said, smiling up at him. "I can count on him for that."

"Did I catch it right, Mrs. Major? He took your father's painting?"

Her smile disappeared as she turned her head, staring across the pool as she slowly nodded. "His masterpiece."

"I'd have liked to take a look at that."

"I wish I could show it to you."

"Cowboy," Ian said in exasperation.

"You're dismissed."

"Dismissed to where, Major?"

"Come on, Corporal." Tag shouldered his rifle. "Let's follow that tunnel a ways."

"Good idea, Captain," said Cowboy. "I think I might have winged him." He tipped his hat to Alison. "Nice to meet you, Mrs. Major."

The two Americans walked single-file along the narrow edge to the opposite tunnel.

"Alone at last," Ian said, cupping her face in his hands. His voice grew husky. "You're alive."

She smiled up at him, her gentle fingers tracing his whiskered jaw. "Because you saved me."

CHAPTER SIXTY

Alison followed Ian through the remnants of the wooden door into the cave and cringed as her foot landed on pieces of canvas. Blown-up crates and paintings littered the cave floor. The loss pained her, as if her skin had been pierced by the jagged fragments. She rubbed her arms, seeking both warmth and comfort.

"We didn't have time to stop it," Ian said, gesturing toward the debris. "But Cowboy cut the fuse to save the rest."

She nodded, numbed by the exploded treasures, now irreparably lost to future generations. "I can't believe he did this. Not Theodor."

"Nothing Scheidemann did would surprise me."

"But this was art. It can't be replaced."

"And neither can you." Ian gently pushed her damp hair from her neck. "You need to change out of those wet clothes."

"You too."

"Duty before comfort." He looked toward the cave entrance, and she followed his gaze. The two Germans, hands bound with lengths of fuse, sat on the ground in front of the Americans.

"That soldier — Cowboy. He called you Major." Alison touched the insignia on Ian's collar. "I'm sorry I missed your promotion."

"I'm sorry too."

"Libby must have changed so much since I left. Do you think she'll remember me?"

"She keeps a photo of the three of us beside her bed."

"Taken at the gazebo?"

"That's the one."

"I can't wait to see her again."

"Here, take a look at this." Ian pulled a soggy piece of paper from his pocket and laid it on a crate. He carefully unfolded it, revealing a smeared drawing, and laughed. "I'm afraid she'll never pass for a Van Schuyler."

Alison examined the childish picture, her professional eye blurred by motherly love. "She uses color in an interesting way," she said defensively. Her fingertips brushed the labeled figures, pausing over the one of Libby. Priceless art surrounded her, but her daughter's drawing was the most valuable of them all.

"Scheidemann disappeared," Cowboy announced as he strolled into the cave. He tipped his hat at Alison, and she smiled at his unsophisticated gallantry. "He's wounded, but not bad enough to leave much of a trail."

Ian muttered something under his breath, and Alison bent her head. Theodor had gotten away. Both surprised and ashamed by the relief that flooded through her, she focused on flipping through the inventory lists she had found while they were waiting for Cowboy and Tag to return from the tunnels. There'd be no arrest. There'd be no trial.

Most importantly, there'd be no more confrontations. She shuddered, remembering the hard glint in Ian's eyes when he had glared at Theodor. That same glint may have been in her father's eyes when he confronted her mother's cruel uncle. Life had scarred Pieter, slowly consuming him with heartache and guilt. She couldn't bear the same thing happening to Ian. He had already killed once, a justified death that had given him nightmares. How could they survive if he gave in to his desire for vengeance now?

All she wanted was to return to England.

To be a family again. Unless Ian . . . Jealousy stabbed her heart as she remembered the newspaper photo of him with the American actress.

She lifted her eyes, watching Ian as he and the Americans talked quietly. They obviously respected his leadership and judgment. Pride surged through her, and she closed the inventory folder. He was a man worth fighting for, but what could she do if he loved someone else?

Ian and the Americans, eager to return to the chalet, gave her little time to dwell on such thoughts. When they arrived, they discovered that Frau Mueller had disappeared. Tag, as the commanding American officer, claimed the chalet as Allied headquarters for his jurisdiction before he and Cowboy searched the chalet's end of the tunnel for any signs of Theodor. They found nothing.

While Alison freshened up and changed clothes, the other two Americans transported their German prisoners to the village. Kurt rode along, returning with more Allied soldiers and his grandmother, who donned an apron and claimed command of the kitchen.

After a hearty supper, Alison and Ian stole away from the boisterous dining room. The slanting rays of the evening sun cast long shadows on them as they lingered in the chalet's rose garden. The well-tended blossoms filled the summer air with their distinctive aroma. Butterflies flitted in Alison's stomach. It had been a long nineteen months. How could they ever make up for that absence?

Taking a switchblade from his pocket, Ian cut the stem of a pink rose and handed the large bloom to Alison. "Careful of the thorns," he said as she inhaled the lovely scent.

"It's so fragrant. Smell." She lifted the rose to Ian, and he flinched. Blushing with uncertainty, she fingered the silky texture of the petals.

"Roses." Ian waved his hand at the beds. "There were so many at your . . . They made me ill."

"My funeral." She bent her head over the flower. How hard that must have been for him.

"I should have known you were still alive." Passion and anger intermingled in his voice. "Somehow I should have known."

"How could you? Theodor set it up so completely." So completely that Ian could never have guessed she was actually a prisoner. Or that he shouldn't be dating beautiful actresses.

Ian interrupted her thoughts. "What did he mean, about losing more than you know?"

"I'm not sure." Alison twirled the stem, wishing Ian hadn't brought that up. With all her heart, she was certain that Theodor's last words were meant for Ian, not for her. Tears sprang to her eyes and she hugged herself, the rose wavering in the light breeze. "There's something I have to tell you."

His eyes darkened and his voice shook when he spoke. "You can tell me anything."

"When I left London . . ." She paused, then blurted, "I was pregnant."

He wrapped his arms around her. "I know."

"How could you?"

"Richard told me."

"Something went wrong." She leaned her head against his chest, avoiding his gaze. "It was like a bad dream. I think the midwife gave me something to make me sleep."

"It's okay, Alison. Just tell me what happened."

"The baby . . . he died."

"A boy?" Ian's voice cracked and Alison's heart melted at the tears welling up in his eyes. "My son."

"I'm sorry. I'm so sorry."

"It's not your fault; it's Scheidemann's." Thirst for revenge shimmered in his gold-flecked eyes.

"I blamed him too, for a while." The memory of the dark days after her baby's birth coiled around her heart. But she had believed God's promise of future rejoicing, and now it was coming true. Unless Ian had fallen in love with someone else.

"Then Theodor showed me a newspaper photograph. Of you and an American actress." She watched Ian carefully, hating the jealousy that raked her stomach when his eyes widened. In surprise? Or guilt? "It made me realize how much I had to live for, how hating Theodor was hurting me more than him. And somehow I knew I'd get home. It was as if God whispered to me that I would. I just hope it's not too late."

"Why too late?"

"She's very beautiful." Alison took a deep breath and forced a smile. "And you obviously like her."

"Yes, I like her." His eyes softened. "I think you'd like her too."

"Perhaps."

"We teamed up for a mission, Alison. That's all it was."

"It must have been a very special mission."

"I pretended to love her so that she could pretend to steal classified information from me."

"And now? Is she waiting for you?"

"She's in America. Waiting for the man she loves to get out of a POW camp."

"A POW camp in the United States?"

"It's a long story." He took both her hands in his and kissed each one. "I thought I had lost you, Alison. I can't tell you how much that hurt. And then I was assigned to this mission with Marie and we . . . we cared for each other. But only as friends."

"Friends?"

He grinned, then pulled something from his pocket. "You left this at home. I guess that's why you didn't write," he teased.

She took the gold Montblanc pen, examining his initials as tears moistened her lashes.

He lifted her chin and, between soft kisses, murmured, "I've always been, and still am, heads-over-heels, every beat of my heart, in love with you."

CHAPTER SIXTY-ONE

JUNE 1945

As the train from Dover neared Waterloo Station, Alison stared out the window at the people on the platform, absorbing the details as she searched for Trish and Libby.

"Do you see them?" Ian asked, peering over her shoulder.

"No." She squeezed her fingers to keep them still. "Are you sure they'll be here?"

He covered her hands with his. "They wouldn't miss it."

"What if she doesn't remember me?"

"She remembers."

Alison hoped he was right, but her own experience of missing her father had taught her that a long absence was a lifetime for a child. She still found it hard to believe that only a few weeks ago she had been a prisoner in Theodor's chalet. It had taken that long for Ian to work out the transportation for them to return to England.

Meanwhile, she had worked tirelessly, sorting through the treasures in the cave and identifying the contents of the blown-up crates. The paintings that belonged to the chalet were returned by the Army unit Ian rounded up to help her. She had packed and labeled crates with the art that had been stolen from the air raid shelter. Other crates were addressed to museum curators in Amsterdam and Paris. Her own watercolors were in the train's baggage car.

Ian arranged with Tag for Cowboy to oversee the guarding of the cave until the crates could be shipped. The selected soldiers, tired of fighting and tired of Germany, welcomed an assignment that gave them the freedom to explore the network of tunnels and caves when they weren't on duty.

Alison took Ian's hand as they left the train, nervously searching the crowd.

"Papi!"

A gangly girl, all arms and legs, raced toward them. Her hat flew off her dark head, but she didn't stop. Just left it for Trish to pick up.

Ian held out his arms, swinging Libby around as she hugged him.

"Papi, you're home."

"Happy birthday, sweetheart." He kissed both her cheeks, causing her to giggle, before standing her beside him.

"Hello, Libby. Remember me?" Alison took a deep breath as the girl stared up at her. "You've grown so much."

"Mama. You came home," she said shyly, her English impeccable.

Alison knelt in front of her. "I didn't mean to stay away so long. Please forgive me."

"Don't cry, Mama." Libby brushed a tear from Alison's cheek. "God answered my prayers."

"Your prayers?"

"I prayed for you every night."

"You did?"

Libby nodded. "When you didn't come home, I thought maybe you got lost. And had to walk a long way like Papi and I did. So I asked God to help you find your way. And He did, didn't He, Mama?"

"Yes, Libby," she said, hugging her little girl. "He did."

Looking upward, Alison caught Trish's eye. *"Thank you,"* she mouthed.

"Welcome home, Alison," Trish said softly, slipping her arm around Ian's waist. "Come on, you two. Libby and I aren't the only ones here to greet you. Come and see."

They entered the station, and Trish gestured toward a seating area behind one of the columns. Alison gasped as Will limped toward her.

"You silly goose," he said, holding her tight. "Don't ever do anything like that again."

"Never." She laughed and then noticed Hannah, painfully thin and wearing long sleeves despite the summer heat. Alison embraced her gently, then turned to Ian. "This is Will. And Hannah. The twins' mother." She faltered on the last word and glanced at Trish in time to see the hurt in her eyes before she blinked it away.

"I can never thank you enough for saving my babies," Hannah said in her gentle voice. "When I came for them, they did not know me. I scared them." Her shoulders dropped slightly, and Will put his arm around her.

"Hannah is living with us for now," Trish said. "Until she and Will get married."

"You're getting married?"

Will grinned. "We've just been waiting for you to get home." He looked at Ian. "Your parents have been kind enough to offer us a cottage at the Kenniston Hall estate."

"So you see," Trish said brightly, "Mark and I will be able to see the twins whenever we want."

Alison ran her fingers through Libby's dark hair, needing to feel her daughter's presence. What would she do if Libby's father suddenly appeared? She shivered against the thought. Her heart ached for both Trish and Hannah, two women bound by love and loss. Breathing a prayer for both of them, she immediately sensed God's assurance that the twins had been doubly blessed.

"Am I the last to be greeted?"

Afraid to believe her ears, Alison pivoted toward the booming voice.

"Come here, *mijn schatje.*" Hendrik, sitting in a wheelchair steered by Monsieur Duret, held out his arms.

"Opa." She gently embraced his fragile shoulders, then clasped and kissed both his hands. "I've been so afraid for you."

"And I for you."

"Where have you been?"

"Hiding." His gray-blue eyes, so like her own, grew momentarily vacant before flickering with warmth. "But those are stories for another day. This day, we celebrate."

"Where are Mark and the twins?" Ian asked Trish as Alison greeted Monsieur Duret.

"They're home, with Mum and Pops. Overseeing the preparations for your homecoming party."

"Oh, Mama, Papi, guess what?" Libby reached for her parents' hands. "We're having specially baked Miniver scones."

"Miniver scones?" Ian teased. "I fell in love with a girl once over Miniver scones."

"And I fell in love with a soldier," Alison said, laughing.

"Wisest thing you ever did." His heart-flipping grin lit the gold in his eyes.

"I agree." She sighed with contentment as Libby and Trish, Hendrik and Duret, Will and Hannah readied to leave. "This all seems too perfect."

"You've walked through fire, Alison." Ian held her gaze, but for a moment he seemed lost to another time and place. "Maybe you're due for 'too perfect.' "

Walking toward the station's exit with those she loved, Alison realized she had come full circle — all the way back to the place where the notes of a violin beckoned her to a hazel-eyed soldier. The intervening years had brought grievous heartache and pain, but God's mysterious purpose, not a superstitious family fate, had brought her home again. She smiled, confident that no matter what the future held, she could rejoice in the days to come.

Epilogue

MAY 1950

Pieter Schuyler's lost masterpiece hangs in a remote Argentinian villa near a town populated by Germans living under assumed names. It's rumored that Göring himself once shot at the painting, but onlookers search in vain for the damage. Some whisper that the artist's daughter handled the restoration while a guest at the owner's European home. When they question that noble gentleman, however, he only smiles mysteriously, refusing to deny or give credence to their suppositions.

The gentleman's son understands none of this. He only knows that the woman in the painting beckons him with her playful expression. The portrait affects him unlike any other in his father's fine collection. He's too young to put the feeling into words, but it tingles his fingers and evokes a strange longing deep inside him.

He taps the end of a paintbrush against his chin, gazing up at the girl and her garden with his gray-blue eyes. Childishly pleased with his watercolor version, he prints his name in the lower left corner with careful strokes.

Schuyler.

WHERE TREASURE HIDES
DISCUSSION QUESTIONS

1. Ian's sister says if it is God's will, Ian will see Alison Schuyler again. Do you ever struggle to leave things up to God?

2. While trying to escape Germany, Ian wonders if God is deaf to his prayers. Can you think of a time when your prayers seemed to go unanswered? How does this affect your relationship with God?

3. After her great-aunt dies, Allison struggles to understand why God saved her instead. Do you ever question God's choices?

4. While Ian prays for guidance after Libby's mother dies, he believes he does not need to wait for God's voice before taking action. Have you ever felt called to a decision? Did you follow through? Why or why not?

5. Ian often relies on the verse "vengeance is mine; I will repay, saith the Lord" (Romans 12:19). Do you find it difficult to leave judgment to God?

6. Allison's trust in God wavers because of her struggle with her family's superstition. What do you think gives her the strength to finally believe and entrust her fate into God's hands?

7. In your opinion, why does Ian return for Libby?

8. In chapter three, Ian believes that "though he hadn't prayed, he knew the idea to have Josef play the violin had been divinely inspired." Describe a time where you clearly saw God's hand at work within your life.

9. Ian worries that God may not listen to his prayers because of the crimes he has committed and the men he has killed during the war. Do you ever feel beyond God's love and forgiveness? How do you think God would respond to this sentiment?

10. Ian describes Sister Regina as "the

answer to a prayer he didn't realize he'd prayed." Can you think of a time when someone came into your life and brought you exactly what you hadn't realized you were missing?

ABOUT THE AUTHOR

Johnnie Alexander writes inspiring stories that are heartwarming and memorable. *Where Treasure Hides,* her debut novel, won the ACFW Genesis Contest (2011) and Golden Leaf Award (2014). A graduate of Rollins College (Orlando) with a Master of Liberal Studies degree, Johnnie treasures family memories, classic movies, road trips, and stacks of books. She lives in the Memphis area, where her morning chores include feeding dogs, cats, chickens, and a small herd of alpacas. Visit Johnnie online at www.johnnie-alexander.com.

The employees of Thorndike Press hope you have enjoyed this Large Print book. All our Thorndike, Wheeler, and Kennebec Large Print titles are designed for easy reading, and all our books are made to last. Other Thorndike Press Large Print books are available at your library, through selected bookstores, or directly from us.

For information about titles, please call:
(800) 223-1244

or visit our website at:
gale.com/thorndike

To share your comments, please write:
Publisher
Thorndike Press
10 Water St., Suite 310
Waterville, ME 04901